Be whisked

and en

Passionate Knights

The Knight, the Knave and the Lady
by Juliet Landon

North Yorkshire, 1350s
Lord Alain of Thorsgeld had no scruples about
compromising innocent Marietta into marriage.
Then Marietta began to find pleasure in married
life – *and* her husband – until memories of his
late wife led Marietta into danger…

My Enemy, My Love
by Julia Byrne

England, 1141
Kept hostage during a royal feud, Isabel de Tracy
held fast to the memory of tough, yet tender,
knight Guy fitzAlan. Reunited years later,
Guy was convinced Isabel had betrayed him.
Could Isabel prove her innocence to her
one true love?

Juliet Landon's keen interest in art and history, both of which she used to teach, combined with a fertile imagination, make writing historical novels a favourite occupation. She is particularly interested in researching the early medieval period and the problems encountered by women in a man's world. Her heart's home is in her native North Yorkshire, but now she lives happily in a Hampshire village close to her family.

Julia Byrne lives in Australia with her husband, daughter and a cat who thinks he's a person. She started her working career as a secretary, taught ballroom dancing after several successful years as a competitor, and, while working in the History Department of a Melbourne university, decided to try her hand at writing historical romance. She enjoys a game of cards or Mah Jong, usually has several cross-stitch projects on the go, and is a keen preserver of family history.

Passionate Knights

JULIET LANDON
JULIA BYRNE

MILLS & BOON®

*First published in Great Britain 2005
Harlequin Mills & Boon Limited,
Eton House, 18-24 Paradise Road, Richmond, Surrey, TW9 1SR*

PASSIONATE KNIGHTS © Harlequin Enterprises II B.V., 2005

The Knight, the Knave and the Lady and *My Enemy, My Love*
were first published in Great Britain by
Harlequin Mills & Boon Limited in separate, single volumes.

The Knight, the Knave and the Lady © Juliet Landon 1996
My Enemy, My Love © Julia Byrne 1993

ISBN 0 263 84945 7

118-0905

*Printed and bound in Spain
by Litografia Rosés S.A., Barcelona*

THE KNIGHT, THE KNAVE AND THE LADY

by

Juliet Landon

Chapter One

The richly embroidered curtains across the back of the travelling carriage parted just wide enough to allow the passage of a small brown and white terrier, wriggling frantically against the grip around its middle, its short legs scrabbling helplessly in the air way above the dusty track. Already, a hot stream of liquid had begun to leak down the arms of the maid who held it, causing a hint of irritation to colour her plea to the rider beyond.

"Here, Master Bruno, please...quickly...grab it!"

Bruno leaned forward over the stallion's neck.

"Here, catch its rope."

But it was too late. The yapping creature had already half leapt from the restraining hands and Bruno, not wishing to be wetted like the maid, had released it before being able to snatch at the cord dangling from its jewelled collar. He watched in exasperation as it disappeared like a white rat between the horses' hooves, across the track and on up the bank into the field beyond, scattering sheep and lambs, yapping frantically, pausing to lift a leg tantalisingly out of reach and then on again as it discovered an irresistible trail.

"Oh, Master Bruno...please, don't lose it!" The maid's

voice was a wailing whisper. She turned to peep into the carriage and then at him again. "My mistress! She'll…"

"I'll get it! Damn stupid animal! C'mon, you lot!" He turned to the young grooms and pages who rode behind. "Give me a hand," and pulled away in front of them, not looking to check their response.

His command had not included his sister, but after riding soberly along the highway since dawn, she longed for a few moments of excitement and saw no reason to be excluded from the chase. Without waiting for her ladies, Marietta followed, digging her leather-clad heels into Dulzelina's dapple-grey flanks, taking the high bank in two easy strides, ignoring the shouts of alarm behind her.

From the corner of her eye she saw her father in the distance at the head of the cavalcade, still unaware of the diversion, too far away to hear. Well out of range, her stepmother's huge carriage rocked and jolted its occupants over the pot-holed track, the maid's face a mere pink blob of anxiety like a button on the curtain's opening.

The mare's legs stretched across the field in an easy rhythm, her snorts and swishing tail signalling that this escape was long overdue; as the riders sped to overtake the terrier's tiny white form, Marietta smiled in anticipation of her parents' reaction. Her father would, she was sure, try hard to hide the twinkle in his eyes behind a stern expression and a slowly shaking head, as much to convince Lady Alice of his disapproval as herself.

Her stepmother would see Marietta's behaviour as just one more reason to support her argument that the girl was unmanageable, unladylike, un-everything, and that she should have been married years ago. Why Sir Henry had allowed his daughter to turn down so many good offers she would never understand.

As though to exacerbate the forthcoming disapproval,

Marietta pulled her gold circlet from her brow and slid it over her wrist, then pushed the white linen wimple down into folds around her neck, allowing her long thick braids to stream behind her like coils of brown rope. How could one be truly free, even if only for a few moments, she thought, unless her hair was free too?

She shook her head and laughed at the merry grins of the grooms, but her laugh turned to a puzzled frown at their shouts of alarm, their sudden check as they wheeled away. The terrier was still ahead, rooting into a rabbit hole, its white rump and wagging tail waving like a mast above the ground.

Her brother, dismounting and ready to throw himself upon the terrier, turned at her arrival and shouted a warning, pointing to something behind her and making a grab at her bridle. But, for the second time, his efforts came too late; the mare's head jerked away, not from him but from two large wolfhounds that bounded between them, startling the horse by their silent and explosive approach.

Had Marietta not been a good horsewoman she would undoubtedly have been thrown off to one side. Instead, she clung to the rearing mare, riding out its terrified plunging and doing her best to calm it by the sound of her voice. But the two unruly hounds would not let well alone. Having seen the effect of their presence on the mare, they leapt alongside, clearly enjoying the event, then, as they spotted the white terrier once more in flight, gave chase as cats after a mouse, their jaws dripping with saliva.

For Dulzelina, however, that was not the end of the episode—she was convinced that the yapping beasts were still at her heels and, taking the bit hard between her teeth, she set off across the open field as though all the demons of hell were after her. Even the heavy thud of hooves behind them made as little check on the mare's speed as her rider's hands, for she refused to respond to any sound, and Marietta's efforts to turn her away from the coppice ahead went unheeded.

Thinking that the pursuing horse was a servant's, Marietta yelled at him to stay aside as she saw a fallen tree across her path at the entrance to the shadowy coppice and, knowing that her mare could not feel the pull on the reins and dreading the ache in her arms as a sign that she couldn't hold on much longer, she wondered whether the jump over the tree would be a parting for them both.

With a feeling of mixed irritation and fear, Marietta realised that the pursuing rider had not understood her warning to give her a clear run and, as they approached the barrier, she let out a final yelp to keep away. It was all she remembered before the ground and the trees unexpectedly changed places and the grass came crashing down on top of her.

It was by no means the first time she'd ever dismounted so rudely and her fingers were well disciplined to hold onto the reins and prevent the escape of her mount when she needed it most. But at one point beyond her vision, something wrenched persistently at her shoulders and a voice was growling through a haze of whirling images. Briefly, for an instant, she wondered if the trees were talking to her.

"Let go, lass! Open your fingers. Let go!"

"Bruno!" She struggled to get up. "I told you to…"

"Open your fingers, woman! God's wounds, Will, cut the reins, will you?" The voice turned to one side, obviously exasperated.

"No! Don't you dare!" Marietta yelled, pushing at the hand enclosing her wrist. "Bruno!"

"It's not Bruno. Open your eyes, lass. Come on, open them and look at me. That's it. Now, let go the reins, or we'll all be trampled to death."

"Who're you?"

"Let go, damn it!" he shouted at her.

Bruno would not have yelled at her like that. She unclenched her fingers and heard the exclamation of relief, her senses doing somersaults as she frowned at the unfamiliar face peering down into hers. "Who *are* you?" she repeated.

"Never mind."

Two strong hands slipped beneath her armpits and heaved her backwards to lean against the log. The sky and trees came to rest and a head moved about in front of her, a dark head, older than her brother's. This was no mere lad of sixteen summers, but a man more like thirty, his voice authoritative, his shoulders even wider than her father's. What's more, no one had ever spoken to her in that tone before, nor had anyone ever felt at her shoulders and arms in such an intimate and probing manner.

"No broken bones here, anyway…" His words came to an abrupt halt as Marietta's arm swung back and made a lightning arc through the air towards his head. But it was caught well before it made contact with his ear and held out of the way while a hand gripped her chin, the strong fingers turning her head this way and that under the gaze of two laughing dark eyes. "Nothing wrong with the arms, either. Now, any bruises? Uh-huh! A few grazes on the cheek and forehead. Scratched nose. Not too serious, I think, eh, Will?"

She snatched her face out of his hand and saw Bruno running. "Go away!" She sucked in her breath at the effort. "My brother's here. He'll attend me. Let me *go*!"

The man turned, released her wrist and stood to face Bruno. Even from this angle, she could see the difference in their height and width, though her brother, at sixteen, was no weakling. The man waved a hand over to the distance. "Get those hounds off that white thing, will you?

And hold them. Will, give the mare a quick check over…her legs.''

Bruno bent over his sister. ''Is she all right, sir?''

''Yes, lad. She's all right. You're her brother, are you?''

''Yes, sir. Bruno Wardle.'' He pointed to the track where the cavalcade still wound its way down towards the village in the distance. ''We're on our way to Monksgrange just down the hill yonder. We were after my mother's terrier, but…'' He swung round to survey the bloodied heap now lying lifeless in the grass some distance away.

The man looked Bruno up and down, noting the well-bred appearance and noble bearing in spite of the dusty clothes. The lad was well built and honest looking, dark-haired, like his sister and father. ''So, you're Sir Henry's lad, are you?''

''Yes, sir. I'm to be squire to Lord Alain of Thorsgeld Castle from tomorrow.'' He could not contain the unsolicited information; he was proud of the new connection and this man would surely be impressed, though he realised that this was hardly the time or the place for such a display of vanity.

''Well, well! And here's your father… Sir Henry.''

Marietta saw the figure of her father canter towards them across the field and struggled to rise, but before Bruno could come to her aid, the man bent swiftly towards her and swung her easily up into his arms, ignoring her protests and moving her head away from her brother so that she could not see him. ''Put me down!'' she yelled. ''Put me…'' A pain shot through her head.

''Ah, Sir Henry,'' he called.

''My lord! Is she…?''

Bruno ran to hold his father's bridle. ''Yes, Father, she's shaken but not badly hurt.''

In spite of her protests, she was pinioned helplessly

against the man's chest, furious that he was taking charge of her, not even asking how she felt but taking it upon himself to find out as though she was a horse. "Father, Father, get someone to attend the mare, please." She winced at the pain.

"Yes, lass. What happened to bring you off like that?"

"Two great hounds and a fallen tree. But tell this oaf to put me down! Tell him!"

"It was my fault, I'm afraid, Sir Henry. My hounds saw the terrier, and your daughter's mare took exception and bolted…"

"It did *not*, Father. I was in control. If this fool.."

"I managed to catch her just in time…"

"…had not chased after me…"

"…and she came off with quite a thump…"

"…I'd have stayed on and brought the mare…"

"…perhaps she needs a few lessons, sir." He smiled down at her infuriatingly.

"…back to the track! Let me *go*!"

Sir Henry Wardle looked sideways at the man as they turned to walk back. "Lessons, my lord? It's taken me eighteen years to get this far…" he nodded to Marietta's struggling form "…and still some way to go."

"Then a change of hand is what's needed, sir." The two men exchanged grins, noting the two half-undone plaits hanging over his shoulder and arm, the loosened wimple and torn gown.

Marietta's angry face was still beautiful, despite the red and soiled graze on her cheek, her large dark eyes still sparkling with embarrassment at this unwarranted handling of her by a stranger. But his tight grip told her quite plainly that she was not to be released, and his long easy stride at the side of her father and brother seemed not to affect his conversation in the slightest. Obviously, he felt her to be no weight at all, rejecting both Sir Henry's and Bruno's offers to take turns at carrying her.

"Did you say 'my lord,' Father?" Bruno asked, incredulous. "It's not Lord Alain, is it?" The thought that their neighbour could be here at this time suddenly seemed to be quite a possibility. The town of Thorsgeld was, after all, only across the valley from Monksgrange.

"Yes, lad," said Sir Henry, "you've run into your future master sooner than you expected. I was to have brought my son to you tomorrow, my lord."

"Then I shall spare you the journey, Sir Henry. I fear I owe someone a new terrier. Was it Lady Alice's?" He glanced across at the limp form in the arms of one of the grooms, its jewelled collar and bloodstained cord hanging from its ripped neck and badly mauled body.

"Holy saints, man!" Sir Henry barked at the unsuspecting servant. "Don't let Lady Alice see it like that or she'll pass out before we get there. Take that collar off and bury the body under those bushes before we get to the carriage. Hurry!"

So, this was Lord Alain, the man with whom Bruno would be living for the next five years, the man he'd talked about incessantly since his return from Sir Robert Finch's household where he had been a page since he was seven. Marietta peeped through her lashes, knowing that Lord Alain would certainly be aware of an open stare, his cheek being only a few inches away from her nose.

The soft green velvet under her cheek now took on a new significance and, even while retaining her anger at being held so closely against the rich stuff, its clean newness and well-tailored cut told her what she might have noticed earlier, that this man with the commanding manner was someone of importance. Through half-closed eyes, she allowed herself to note the comfortable folds of the fur-edged hood around his wide shoulders and the row of tiny gold buttons on the sleeves from elbow to wrist, the strong lean fingers around her knees.

His jaw was square and strong, clean-shaven; thick swathes of dark hair fell in layers over his head, jutting out over his forehead after the exertions of the afternoon. Marietta thought his mouth firm, too firm for kindness, though she could make out a dimple at one corner as he smiled at her father's remark. Well, she wished her young brother joy of his new master. She doubted if he'd find any softness there, but perhaps that was something her brother would regard as a good thing. A challenge. At least *she* wouldn't have to see any more of the arrogant brute.

"Put me down, sir!" she growled again, squirming.

Lord Alain looked down at his new squire's sister, still fuming, as they drew level with the track once more where carts were still moving. A group of ladies and grooms awaited them, clearly relieved to see that there was no cause for alarm.

"Ready to find your feet, demoiselle?" he asked.

"I could have walked, my lord, if I'd been allowed," she snapped, suddenly even more aware of how close their faces were to each other. She squirmed again, straining away from him, seeing the grins on the faces of those who waited and suspecting that he held her deliberately longer than need be, just to thwart her attempts. "Let me down," she hissed.

"Certainly, demoiselle."

Had she timed her demand more accurately or even made it sound more like a request, she might have spared herself an undignified gallop into the bottom of the ditch and a scramble up the other side onto the track. Though willing hands were there to aid her, her bruised limbs and torn gown became the source of humiliation before the gaze of so many, especially that of Lord Alain, who stood above her in the field, quietly laughing at the sight of her struggles.

She heard his chuckles but refused to look, shrugging off the hands, clambering up the lowered tailboard of her stepmother's carriage and disappearing inside with a sigh of relief. Now she must bear the petulant and scolding tongue of Lady Alice, who had wanted to be among the first to arrive at the manor, not the last. But even this well-rehearsed tirade was preferable to being manhandled by that man, lord or no.

"A fine way to begin, I must say," Lady Alice grumbled, removing the tangled wimple from around Marietta's neck and handing it to a maid. Her own cauled and braided hair was still immaculate, even at the end of the rough journey, her plump pretty face contrasting sharply with the grimed and fierce beauty of her stepdaughter. She pursed her lips, as Marietta knew she would. "Just when we wanted to make a good impression."

"Well, I don't have to make an impression, Mother," she replied. "You can still do that without me, thank goodness. You've got until we return home after harvest. That should be long enough for anybody."

"I only hope you're right, Marietta. It's just as well your father met Lord Alain before this...at least he knows what *we*'re like. And you've lost the gold circlet your father gave you." She dabbed gently at Marietta's grazed face.

"No, I haven't. Bruno's got it safe."

"Did he catch Sugar?"

"Er...yes." Not a time to tell the whole truth, she thought, coming so soon after this. "They've got him back there, somewhere. They're keeping him safely out of the way."

Fortunately, Lady Alice accepted the explanation as being perfectly reasonable, for there'd be enough to do as soon as they reached the manor after a day's journey of almost twenty-five miles.

They made the move to one of their four manors several times a year to keep them tended and in good repair, to see to the needs of their tenants and villeins, to hold manor courts, to check on accounts and sales, workers and lands. They were all quite used to it, though it was always easier to travel down the dale than to return to Upperfell in September for the winter.

Such moves took days to organise and sometimes a week to prepare for, food to pack, bedding, furnishings, hangings and arms, everything from the kitchen, the offices and the chapel. The staff and members of the closer household numbered over one hundred, including Sir Henry's knights and esquires, yeomen, men and personal officers as well as those who served Lady Alice.

Some of them, mostly kitchen and household servants, had come down a few days in advance with Sir Nicholas Bannon, Lady Alice's younger brother, to make the place habitable. But even so, it would be far into the night before everything was unloaded from the wagons and installed once more into its rightful place.

"Nearly there!" The youngest maid turned back into the carriage; her bright face reflected their relief.

Lady Alice rolled her eyes heavenwards at the news; even in a sumptuous carriage like this, lined with tapestried covers and feather-filled cushions to ease the jolts, even so, they were glad that the village was now in sight. She had been pleased when Sir Henry had announced that they would spend the summer months at their newest manor, for Monksgrange had only recently been purchased from nearby Bolton Priory. Reluctantly, the Augustinians had let it go in a lean year after the pestilence and the drought of more recent times.

It had hit everyone hard, it seemed, though the monks had escaped the worst effects, thank God. But the landscape already showed signs of change. Now fields were enclosed by stone walls and full of sheep instead of crops, small hamlets were emptied of villeins, woodland was less tended and harbouring larger bands of outlaws and thieves.

It was most convenient, Lady Alice thought, standing up to peep through one of the flaps in the sides, that they could bring Bruno to begin his new life at nearby Thorsgeld Castle, something they'd not thought possible two years ago when all that had been arranged. Then, Lord Alain had been married. But his young wife had died of the pestilence and Lady Alice was eager to discover whether he was looking for a suitable replacement.

If he was, she had two fair and pretty daughters, at least one of whom would gladden any man's marriage-bed. She looked sideways at Marietta's grazed cheek and angry frown. A far cry, this one, from her own gentle two, for they would never have gone tearing across fields like that or been brought back torn and bruised under the stares of half the household. She tightened her lips again: the eldest she may be, but no nearer finding a husband at eighteen than she'd been at three, when Alice herself had been a bride of fifteen marrying the widowed Sir Henry.

It had been difficult, taking on a wilful babe of three and the newly born Bruno, especially when her own two had followed on so soon, but Sir Henry had been a good catch and had made her life as comfortable as any woman had a right to. Except for Marietta, who'd always needed a firmer hold than her father was willing to exert, in spite of a steady stream of offers to take her off his hands.

She sighed as the heavy carriage rumbled to a standstill.

"Wait there, Marietta. I'll get Sir Nicholas to carry you in."

"Oh, no, thank you, Mother, I'll walk." And she disappeared over the tailboard before Lady Alice could insist, determined to deprive her uncle of that joy, above all else.

The courtyard was already crammed with wagons, carriages, horses and people, shouting orders, waving arms, laughing and exclaiming at their first-ever glimpse of the newly acquired manor house. The smell of new woodwork lingered in the cool passageways and the sounds of the carpenters' hammers echoed off the stone walls where doors were still being hung. Maids, grooms and officers of the household swarmed from the wagons, dusting down long gowns and helping the older ones to stagger, stiff-legged, indoors.

Hereward, her father's household steward, greeted the family. It was his responsibility to allocate and prepare their rooms, an onerous job, for Monksgrange was far larger than some of the other properties they lived in, and here they could have rooms with more privacy than anywhere else. "Come, mistresses—" he bowed to Marietta and her maids "—I've saved the sunniest room for you." He had a soft spot for Sir Henry's eldest daughter and she for him, for he was rather like an indulgent grandfather.

"We want to know what he's like," whispered Anne, the elder of the two maids, giggling as they followed Hereward along the upper balcony around the hall.

"Who?" Marietta said, innocently, though she knew who was meant.

"Lord Alain," the maid replied, round-eyed. "He carried you, didn't he? What's he like? He looks so strong, so courteous…"

"Courteous, my foot!" snarled Marietta, under her breath. "It was his hounds that caused the mare to bolt.

And as if that wasn't enough, he had to come chasing after us to make matters worse. The fool should have left me be. I'd have managed better without him.'' She limped up the stairs.

They were shown into a fair-sized and pleasantly sunny room at the back of the house that overlooked the kitchen-gardens, a view that Hereward knew would please the young mistress. The windows had recently been glazed with new green glass, which let in a fair amount of light though not quite clear enough to see through.

The large bed was already being assembled by a group of carpenters and assistants and the bed-hangings lay in neat piles ready to be fixed. In through the open door chests and panniers were being carried, rugs lay in rolls near one wall, tapestries drooped in narrow tubes over a trunk, while tables, stools and the prie-dieu stood in one corner.

"This is your private solar, Mistress Marietta,'' said Hereward, beaming, "and look here, your own private garde-robe.''

He opened a tiny door to a closet where a wooden seat was fixed to the wall and where hooks were ready to receive her furs. "And here…'' he opened another door off the main room "…here is a small room for your maids.''

This was luxury, indeed, for not only had she always shared a room with her maids but with her half-sisters and their maids, too. Now, she could be quite alone whenever she wished, a rare treat indoors, for privacy was a rare commodity unless one could go out alone, a risk she'd been warned over and over not to take. Naturally, she defied the warning, for to be alone was one of Marietta's addictions; her frequent escapes were a release from the imposition of too many people in too small a space.

As if to take instant advantage of their seclusion, Anne and Ellie tended their mistress's grazed face, her bruised thigh and shoulder. The mare had caught her with its hooves and dragged her hard along the fallen log, scraping the skin off her elbows and leaving semi-circular imprints on her leg. The numbness had now begun to wear off, leaving a painful ache as the stiffness set in.

Her face felt hot and tender, in spite of their applications of witch-hazel, and the dull ache in her head pounded across her eyes, leaving her light-headed and nauseous. She was never ill and had little patience with those who were, so fought against it, clenching her teeth against the throbbing pains and brushing away her maids' suggestions that she should rest. There was exploring to be done first.

Sounds of high-pitched voices floated along the passageway towards them and two younger girls stood in the doorway, their eyes round and pale blue like forget-me-nots, their hair in long flaxen plaits.

Emeline, at almost fifteen summers, was so well developed that her eighteen months' lead over her sister Iveta looked more like twice that. She was exceedingly pretty, an indication of how Lady Alice must have appeared to Sir Henry at the time of their marriage, quiet, grave, and yet with a certain vague recognition of the impact her looks were having on the men of the household, the delicious feeling of power when heads turned for her, as they always did for Marietta.

Iveta, at well past thirteen, was set to become just as pretty, though her expression was kinder. She was more aware of others than of her effect on them, more animated, less self-centred, and found it easier to talk to Marietta than Emeline did, for Emeline saw her elder half-sister as a rival, which Iveta did not.

"You've got a pretty room, Marietta," Iveta piped, clearly pleased for her. "Ours isn't as large as this, is it,

Emmie?'' The question was quite without guile, but it received a stony stare from the other forget-me-not eyes.

''No, we have to cram four of us into our room.''

Marietta ignored the pettish remark and took Iveta's outstretched hand. ''Come and look out here. We can see the garden, and look, there are two gardeners already digging it over. See…the beeward's already at the hives.''

''Where?''

''Over there. Shall we go down?''

Together, they turned and saw that Sir Nicholas stood in the doorway directly behind Emeline, his hand gently resting on her shoulder, his forefinger slowly moving up and down her bare neck, a seemingly innocent gesture. But Emeline had flushed bright scarlet and was powerless to move away.

His finger dropped as Marietta glared at him, both of them fully understanding that the caress had the double effect of wielding a power over Emeline while sending a clear message to Marietta of his desire for her. He was as aware as the rest of the family of Marietta's dislike of him and, from time to time, their antagonism flared before reverting to polite atonements on his part, for the double game he played was finely balanced.

''Shall we all go down?'' he asked, bending his head to Emeline, ''or shall I show you my room first?''

''Where is it, Uncle Nicholas?'' Iveta asked.

''Next door to this one.'' He cast a sideways look at Marietta. ''Isn't that convenient?'' He laughed and led the two girls out.

It was obvious why Emeline adored him, for he was handsome in a brown and blond way which set his grey-blue eyes and white teeth glinting like pearls in sand. Like his sister, Lady Alice, he had come to live in Sir Henry's household when she married, and at twenty-five years old he was still landless and desperate for property.

With no household of his own, he was in no position to marry, despite his attractive appearance and his knighthood, and though he was given a certain amount of responsibility and duties by his brother-in-law in return for his keep, he looked forward to the time when his plans for the future would materialise.

"Is there a lock on this door?" Marietta whispered to her youngest maid Evie, who was already bustling about the new room. "Just check, will you?"

"Bolts, mistress. Top and bottom."

"Good. We'll have them drawn into place every night. Will you all remember? To prevent intrusions."

The maids understood without the need for further explanations; they had been with Marietta for upwards of six years and knew her ways well. Anne took a look at her mistress's pale face and frowned. "I think you should lie down for a while, love. Your bruises are getting to you, aren't they?"

Marietta nodded. Yes, they were. "But where…?" She spread her hands helplessly; the pages still carried panniers in and the carpenters had not finished with the bed.

"Stay there," the maid said, "I'll be back in a moment." She returned in the blink of an eye to lead Marietta slowly into a large solar two doors away, where the workmen had finished erecting the large curtained bed and where now all was quiet and orderly. Marietta hardly noticed. She felt dizzy and the ache was beginning to spread from her buttock down to her knee. Knowing almost nothing of how she got there, she allowed Anne to help her onto her parents' bed and to tuck her underneath the soft furs, then to draw the curtains to keep the painful glare of sunlight at bay, easing her into sleep.

* * *

It was the sound of quiet sobbing that woke her, and for some moments she lay in the warm cocoon of the furs, attempting to marshal her senses into order. Then her father's voice added a second layer of sound and she understood where she was, though the light was now fading.

"It didn't stand a chance, love, against those hounds. It wouldn't have felt a thing. Don't be upset, lass. There…there…"

More sobs followed, mixed with incoherent words.

"Yes, of course, he said he'd find you a replacement. He's to come over tomorrow and take Bruno back with him at the same time. Saves me the ride, though I might go over some time." He turned away so that the rest of his words were lost.

"Tomorrow? He's coming here?"

"Yes, I told you."

"Henry, why on earth didn't you say before?"

"Why, love…?"

"Well…" Marietta could almost see her stepmother splaying her hands in an attempt to make her point, a common enough gesture she used to indicate that an explanation would only be required by a half-wit. "Well, you know I want him to see the girls…no, not Marietta…I can't see that *that* matters, but especially Emeline."

"Marietta's the eldest, dear, you know…"

"Yes, dear, but she's obviously not interested…never has been…look how many offers…already turned down…"

At the distinct "Sshh…" Marietta turned onto her back, knowing how such a sound was invariably followed by a revelation of importance.

Lady Alice continued, "It's just that he's already seen her and he'll think they're all as…as wayward—" Marietta smiled at her stepmother's search for the kindest word

"—as difficult as *she* is, and I want him to see how well behaved and pretty Emeline can be. You know how *you* fell for me when I was that age." And in the silence that followed, Marietta could imagine how Lady Alice was wheedling her husband with pretty sidelong glances. A low chuckle confirmed his reaction.

Looking up at the canopy of the large bed, Marietta felt the loud thud of her heart, not so much for being an eavesdropper, but at the thought of *him* being here, tomorrow. Lord Alain, here, at Monksgrange. Well, she could think of no reason why she need be anywhere in evidence at that time; she could say her farewells to Bruno beforehand and keep well out of the way until they'd gone, for it was quite obvious that Lady Alice wanted him to see the younger girls, not her.

Lord Alain himself would certainly not miss her after shouting at her so rudely and taking the force of her own discourtesy, and she was quite sure she'd be happier somewhere in the garden, anywhere, than near such a person as that. He had not even apologised for allowing his hounds to unsettle Dulzelina and for causing her fall.

She feigned sleep as a shadow approached the curtains of the bed and made a convincing return to consciousness as her father roused her gently. It was time for supper, he told her. Did she feel easier now that she'd rested? Would she come down to the hall to eat on their first night at Monksgrange? Or would she prefer a tray in her room?

Stiffly, she sidled down the stone staircase to the great hall, feeling that it would be a pity not to do justice to the feast which had been specially prepared. Earlier, in the privacy of her own solar, she had twisted round to see her bruises, finally getting Evie to hold a mirror to one side so that she could see the full extent. Sure enough, her thigh was slowly turning purple from hip to knee and was now so painful that she was obliged to sit lop-sided on the hard bench at the high table.

Later, back in her own chamber, she sat with her father for a few precious moments, discussing what would have to be done on the estate in the days and weeks ahead, how she would need to begin checking the stores and ordering more stocks from the local markets and from York. These were things Lady Alice preferred to leave to Marietta, aware of how she enjoyed the management of the household affairs, the tending of the garden and the beehives, the making of salves and potions for her medicine cupboard and the ordering and buying of supplies.

It was true that Hereward was highly efficient, but he had taught Marietta far more about housekeeping than Lady Alice had and appreciated her attention to detail. It would be no hardship to be fully occupied tomorrow, or any other day.

They wandered slowly around the room. Marietta pointed out where the tapestries would be hung on the morrow, identified a chest that was in the wrong room, showed him where she would place her possessions and her bowls of flowers from the garden.

Later still, as she wriggled into the dark warmth of her feather bed, listening to the strange sounds outside, of servants calling to each other and the distant crash of a last piece of furniture being brought in, her hands crept spontaneously over her bruises, retracing the path of that man's fingers over her shoulders and arms, recalling the memory of his grip beneath her knees, his glinting eyes close to her face. Too close.

He had refused to allow Bruno or her father to carry her

but that, she was sure, was because he was amused by her anger and wished to infuriate her more. Yes, he'd much prefer pretty Emeline, one he could intimidate without a murmur on her part. And then she slept, disturbed by aches, no matter how she turned.

Chapter Two

The silk cote-hardies and brocade surcoats lay on the bed in a pile so high that they were in imminent danger of falling off. Iveta sat to one side, sulkily fingering the fur edgings and embroidered borders, watching from beneath lowered lids the maids who fussed around her sister. Lady Alice Wardle directed the transformation from a stool by the window. Emeline was getting the full treatment early in the day, for none of them knew at what hour Lord Alain of Thorsgeld would come to collect young Bruno. Even if Emeline had to sit still all day, she would be ready for that event.

Indeed, as the long golden hair was combed out around her pale blue neckline, she was a model of patience, gazing with empty acceptance at the pretty surcoat edged with marten-fur over the silk cote-hardie. The narrow front panel was deeply cut away at each side and sat so low on her hips that the dainty gold girdle was quite exposed, though Lady Alice would allow only her gold circlet as jewellery.

"Your turn in a moment, dear." Lady Alice smiled at the younger beauty. "We'll have you dressed in no time."

That was not exactly what Iveta wanted to hear; she would have liked as much time lavished on her as her sister had, but it was no use pretending that she'd look like that, even so. She gazed somewhat enviously at her sister's profile, allowing her eyes to rove furtively downwards to the swell of the breasts under the silk. Could they not see the clear outline of her nipples? Did it not matter that they showed? Was that the idea? She examined her own flat chest; no matter what gown she wore, she would never look as interesting as Emeline or as lovely as Marietta, she mused.

At a mere thirteen summers, Iveta was not to know that it was not only an interesting silhouette which decided the amount of approval but an animated expression and liveliness, which she had in plenty. The simple cream surcoat she was given to wear echoed the colour of her hair, and the compliments of her mother and maids were gratifying, though Uncle Nicholas's stares made her blush.

"Heavens, Nicholas! How long have you been standing there?" Lady Alice turned sharply, noting Iveta's reddened cheeks.

Sir Nicholas lounged inside the doorway, his slow perusal well under way long before his sister had noticed her daughter's blushes.

"Long enough. I have a message for you, sister dear. Your guest has arrived. Sir Henry wants you to greet him in the great solar, if you please."

The excitement was almost tangible. "He's arrived? So soon? Emeline dear, come. Iveta, you too."

"Wait," Sir Nicholas said, pushing himself away from the door. "You take Iveta in. I'll bring Emeline." He stared at his sister's hesitation. "Go on, I'll bring her in, in a moment."

Iveta frowned. "Why can't she come with us, Mother?"

"Hush, child." Lady Alice took her hand firmly and drew her to the door. "Come now, don't forget…your best courtesy," and with a last smile at Emeline, she left the room, bustling the maids out ahead of her and ignoring their glances of disapproval.

Sir Nicholas sauntered across to where Emeline stood, biting her lip and burning with confusion. "You're not going to get far with the old goat if you stand there and bite your lip, you silly wench," he said, softly, touching her neck with his fingertips. "Are you?"

Emeline looked away, her blushes spreading down her neck and over her shoulders. She wished her mother had not left her here alone with Uncle Nicholas. "He's not old, is he?" she whispered.

"How do I know, lass?" Sir Nicholas drew his fingers around her neckline, pulling it a little wider over her shoulders. "I've never clapped eyes on him. Anyway, it doesn't matter a toss whether he is or not. He's a widower, and you know what *they* look for, don't you?" He slipped his hands under the fur edges of her front panel and pulled her a step nearer.

For a moment, she was puzzled and resisted his pull, but his pale eyes held hers and eventually she moved forward, flustered and surprised by the closeness of his hands.

He leaned his face to hers. "Listen to me, Emeline," he whispered, "this is important. The first impression has *got* to work. He's got to want you...do you understand me, lass?"

Her big blue eyes stared into his. She understood his words and yet she had no way of knowing what she was supposed to do. Then she felt his hands move down the fur as though he caressed its softness, allowing his fingertips purposely to brush past the peaks of her breasts as he did so in a flagrant gesture of intimacy that took her breath away.

"Stop!" she whispered, grabbing at his wrists.

"Let go. Let go of my wrists," he commanded, softly.

With not a streak of rebellion, she obeyed, watching his narrowed eyes and quivering under the movement of his hands which slid up and down the fur over the silk cote-hardie. "Uncle Nicholas…!" she gasped.

"Understand me, wench. When you get what *you* want, I get what I want. So look lively, as though you know what you're about. Wet your lips with your tongue…go on, do it! And part your lips. Now, let's have a look at you." He held her back and looked intently at her heavy lids over the darkened eyes, her flushed cheeks and then, more directly, at the place where his hands had lingered. "That's better. Perfect. Now, are you ready?"

She nodded, quite speechless. And on trembling legs she was led into the great solar as though in a trance.

Marietta's quick peep in the polished steel mirror verified the presence of a red-streaked graze over one cheek, on her forehead and on the tip of her nose. All the other more painful signs of her mishap were hidden beneath the comfortable loose-fitting kirtle and green bliaud, tied around the waist with an old plaited leather girdle. Rejecting any attempts to dress her hair, she had insisted there was no time if she wanted to find Bruno where she could speak to him in private. Instead, the glossy brown curls had been bound up on top of her head with braids. It would have to do.

Certain that the rest of the family were occupied with their guest, Marietta slipped through the busy hall, still teeming with servants putting the place in order, carrying in the last of the household goods from the wagons, hanging the tapestries and hauling up the great wooden candle-brackets towards the beamed roof.

Sneaking through the stone-flagged screens-passage and out through the heavy door at the back of the house, she flattened herself against the stone wall as a page passed close by, his arms laden with clanking shields, swords and belts, heading towards the armoury. He caught her wary expression, her defensive posture, and grinned cheekily, then skirted round her very slowly in an exaggerated arc, looking over his shoulder as she relaxed.

He was as old as Marietta. "Feelin' better, mistress?" She laughed at his overreaction. "Thank you, Ben. I'm well enough. Where's Master Bruno?"

"Gettin' ready to go, mistress. Upstairs."

"When you've taken that, tell him I'm in the garden, if you please."

The lad nodded politely and went about his business, though he took time to watch Marietta disappear into the cobbled courtyard.

Through the arched gateway at the side of the stables, Marietta passed into a more peaceful world of greenery and lush spring growth where two men pushing wheelbarrows moved silently along straw-covered pathways. From this large kitchen-garden, she could see across a deep valley to the hillside beyond, where patches of light and shadow rippled across the woodland.

Set high up above the trees, she saw the great stone Thorsgeld Castle, looking for all the world like an outcrop of sculptured limestone grown up from the forest floor. She would be able to see Bruno, if he hung a red banner from one of the battlements. The idea made her smile. She would miss her brother again.

At the side of one of the high white-washed walls, an arbour was lightly covered with new leaves and, over in one sunny corner, the lids of cold-frames yawned like open mouths, waiting to receive new supplies of cucumber, specially brought down from Upperfell Manor by her father, who loved it. He had bought her a plant in London some years ago and insisted on it being grown in all his manors.

She looked around her, nodding in satisfaction; the monks who had lived here previously had been gardeners, too, for new shoots of spinach were showing and fruit trees had been trained along one wall. It looked as though she'd have to do something about the herb-plot, though, for many gaps showed that they'd taken those precious plants away with them.

Arching her back and wincing at the pain in her shoulder and legs, she heard Bruno approach. He pointed to her green bliaud. "Had a job to see you in that," he grinned. "If it had not been for the white kirtle, I might have mistaken you for a tree and gone without you."

Marietta laughed. "Silly. Are you ready to go, now?"

"Yes, love. I was told to go and get cracking, so we'll be off as soon as they've said their farewells. Lord Alain's in Mother's good books now; he's brought her a pup like the one his hounds ate."

"Oh, Bruno! Don't say that. They didn't really eat it, did they?"

"As good as. They'll eat anything that yaps and pees all over the place like that one did. Serves it right. Doesn't it hurt you to laugh?"

"Yes, you dolt! It does!" she gasped, holding her ribs. "I shall miss you, dear one." She linked her arm into his and lowered her voice. "I wish Emeline was going instead of you."

"Well, by the way she's trying just now, it won't be too long." He jerked his head towards the house. "You should just see..."

"I'm glad I can't. Is she trying hard?"

"Hard? Lord Alain will have to be blind not to see what she's offering. I'm glad he knows we're only half-related."

"My bruises were a good excuse to stay out of the way. Lady Alice didn't want me to appear, anyway. Not after yesterday." She placed a hand over her cheek and looked away, mentally trying to evade the picture of Emeline simpering before two dark eyes.

"He asked about you."

"Who did?" There was an instant thud in her breast.

"Lord Alain. He asked where you were."

Marietta turned to her brother, her heart now leaping. "And they told him…?"

"That you were in bed, quite poorly. I went to your chamber to look for you, but Ben told me you were here."

Noting her expression, her pained frown, he put his arms around her and bent his head to draw her eyes upwards from their study of the pathway. "What is it, love?"

"Oh, Bruno, they didn't need to make such an elaborate excuse. Really, they must have known I'd be perfectly happy to stay out of the way. I don't mind Emmie getting wed. The sooner the better. I wouldn't do anything to make it difficult for her. And anyway…just look at me."

Bruno knew she meant her scratched face, but he saw only his beautiful beloved sister, her dark eyes bordered with thick lashes, the perfectly boned features and lovely mouth. Her coils of dark hair spilled in wayward strands around her ears and neck and he knew, even in his youthful innocence, that Marietta would need none of Emeline's tricks to snatch a man's heart away.

"I don't think of myself as competition, even at the best of times…" she tried to laugh, brushing away a tear with the back of her hand "… but, love, you must be going. You don't want to keep your lord waiting today, of all days. Say farewell now. Shall we see you before we return to Upperfell in the autumn, do you think?"

"Yes, love. Sure to. But it should be you they're trying

to find a husband for, Marrie. You're the eldest, and the nicest, by far.''

''Oh, love, if you can find me one like Father, let me know and I'll show some interest.'' They hugged, carefully avoiding Marietta's bruises, then Bruno stepped back, kissed her knuckles and both cheeks.

''God speed, love. Be an obedient squire and make us all proud of you.''

Without another word, he trotted away up the path, pausing at the gateway to wave, then turned and rebounded into the figure of Lord Alain.

With a noiseless wail of ''Oh, no!'', Marietta whirled away into the opening of the arbour. Through the new leaves, she watched the two men pause to speak, saw Bruno point to where he'd left her, then bow and leave Lord Alain to find his way down the path. Silently, she moved away to the far end, expecting to find a way out, but last year's tendrils of honeysuckle had not been pruned back or retrained and she was obliged to face her unwanted guest with their tangle at her back.

Though her green bliaud gave her some concealment, his slow and purposeful approach signalled quite clearly that she had been spotted. For the first time, she had a chance to see him entirely, to complete her fragmented image of him from the previous day. She saw the almost black hair again, the square jaw and high cheekbones, the powerful neck and shoulders.

This much she had already glimpsed but now she noted the clothes, too, the calf-length bliaud of deep blue figured-velvet, split up the front and back for riding, every edge decorated with an embroidered band of silver and red. Over his slim hips a garnet-studded belt was slung; his sword-belt, resting below it, glinted with silver buckles, finely chased. Deep red sleeves with silver buttons came almost to his knuckles and Marietta saw that his hands were strong and brown, the fingers splayed over his hips as he stood at the entrance to the arbour, eyeing in some amusement her attempt to disappear backwards into the sparse green foliage.

He walked slowly towards her, like a cat. "Bolting again, demoiselle?"

Marietta glared. There was no reply to that.

"I was told that you were ill. Is this what your mother meant?" He looked up and around him at the green structure.

"No, my lord. It is not. And the Lady Alice is my step-mother." She held a hand flat against the graze on her cheek. "She thought I would stay in bed, but I..."

"But you had other ideas?" He laughed, a deep throaty chuckle. "Yes, I can imagine you would. You seem to have a flair for escape, do you not?"

Irritated by his quick perception, she attempted to turn the direction of her enforced conversation away from herself to him. "Have you come to apologise, my lord?"

His eyes widened in surprise at that, then creased into laughter. "Apologise? Do I owe you an apology, then?"

"You must know that you do. It was your hounds that unsettled my mare." She was careful not to use the word bolt. "Surely that deserves an apology?"

He kept his hands on his hips, filling up the width of the arbour. "Very well. You first."

Marietta frowned and searched his eyes for a meaning. "Me first what?"

"Your apology first. Ladies first."

"My apology for what, pray? It was I who received the bruises."

"For your incivility. You don't remember?" He was laughing at her, she was sure, provoking her again.

"No, my lord, I do not. I remember being extremely civil, in the circumstances."

"As you are being now."

"Yes," she snapped, turning away.

"Then it's time you had a husband to teach you better manners."

Marietta was forced to react to that with a look of undisguised contempt. "I have no wish for a husband, my lord."

"I thought that's what every woman wanted. Marriage. Bairns."

Her irritation surfaced again. So typical of a man's thinking. So predictable. "You are mistaken. It is what every man *thinks* that every woman wants. But I am not every woman and I allow no man to make my decisions. I have a mind of my own!"

He flicked one eyebrow, but stood his ground, enjoying her fencing. "I see. And the other part?"

"What other part?"

"Babies."

Since he was intent on asking personal questions, she would give him the truth. "My mother died giving birth to Bruno when I was two years old. She was just my age. I'm not going the same way, my lord. I intend to live longer than eighteen years."

"And you've staved off marriage for that reason?"

"That's as good a reason anyone could ever come up with," she retorted. "The ninety-nine other reasons I have for not wanting a husband are quite niggling by comparison."

"Such as…?"

"My affairs cannot possibly be of interest to you, my lord."

"On the contrary, they are of great interest to me. I intend to change your mind."

"Oh!" She threw back her head to let him see the full effect of her grazed face. "You have someone in mind for me, do you? Forget it, my lord. Find someone else for your favourite retainer."

"It was not one of my retainers I was thinking of, demoiselle, it was myself."

Now she knew he was jesting. That remark could never be taken seriously. "It pleases you to jest, my lord. Kindly leave me now. I am supposed to be in bed, and you were supposed to…"

Yes, my girl, he thought. That's exactly where you should be. "Yes? What was it I was supposed to be doing?"

Marietta was silent, realising that she'd allowed him to goad her towards indiscretion. Was it possible to redirect the words?

But Lord Alain had already caught the drift. "I was supposed to do what, demoiselle? Show some interest in your half-sister, was that it? Well, well." He threw back his head and laughed with a rich bellow of sound, showing his white teeth. "Thank you for the warning. I had already begun to suspect, though, I must admit."

"No…no…you mustn't think…" The argument and her pain were beginning to make her feel dizzy and slightly sickened. "Emmie is a lovely girl, and—"

"And you?" he interrupted, taking her shoulders in his hands. "Why were you not with them in the solar? Why are you not dressed up to the eyebrows, but out here in working clothes? Is this how they treat you?"

She winced at the pain of her bruises under his fingers, hardly able to think coherently. "No, my lord, on the contrary. I dress as I please, but I did not wish to…I had other things to do.'' She floundered further into the mire. No matter what she said, it was going to sound unmannerly. "Let me go, my lord.'' She pushed his hand off her shoulder.

"Yes? You did not wish to meet me? You decided to be somewhere else," he answered for her. "And next time I come you'll have bolted again, will you?"

Marietta turned away, desperate to escape and furious at his exact summary of the situation. "Yes," she whispered, "yes, I will."

But he caught her back by a hand beneath her arm and swung her painfully towards him, holding her immobile. "Then I am forewarned, demoiselle." Before she could make any response, and before her fuddled mind could understand what was happening, she was being wedged against his shoulder and her lips were being sought by his without any consideration for her battered state.

She knew what he was saying, that if she chose to hide away, he would find her and show her no mercy until she'd learned not to. He was relentless and she was in no condition to fight him as she would surely have done at any other time. She merely hung on like a drowning woman, too weak to cry for mercy.

He held her in the crook of his arm, too close for her eyes to focus. "Bolt as far as you wish, but I shall find you and bring you back until you tire of the game. And now, you are forewarned, too."

For an instant, she surfaced enough to rebel. "I suppose that is your apology, is it, my lord?" Her lips tingled with the shock of his kiss.

"No, wench. It's yours."

She did not see him pass through the swirl of greens and the distorting tears, nor did she hear his receding footsteps over the sound of her first uncontrollable sobs. Hanging onto the trellis-work of the arbour, she shook at it in a spasm of fright, anger and helplessness, endeavouring to shake away the pain of his hands on her bruises and the humiliation of being held captive in his embrace.

Gasping to keep back her tears of rage and to still the waves of pain, she felt again the merciless kiss and the hard pressure of his hand behind her head. Her legs buckled, threatening to give way. If he'd known how ill she felt, would he have tormented her so?

He was for Emeline, not her, and judging by his remarks, he'd seen how amenable her sister could be. Surely, if he was so keen on obedience to his wishes, he would prefer Emeline's certain co-operation to her own prickly manner, so why would he derive any satisfaction from teasing her like that? Unless he enjoyed the idea of playing people off against each other. Did it boost his ego, perhaps? Had he also teased Emeline like that and then tried it on her, to see the difference?

She shook the trellis again and let the sobs gush out, relishing the ache in her limbs as a distraction from her confusion. Her father's heavy tread gave her warning of his approach and his hands on her shoulders came as no surprise to a body throbbing with the imprint of strong fingers. Marietta turned gratefully into the comfort of his arms and moaned with anguish.

"Hush, little one, hush, it's all right. We'll go in now. Enough, hush."

"No, Father, I can't...can't go in like this."

"Yes, you can...like this...put your arms around my neck." He bent and picked her up in his arms, cradling her against him. "Turn your face into my chest, lass, and close your eyes. They all know you're not too well. It's no cause for remark." And he carried her along the pathway, through the courtyard of servants and into the house.

They must both have known that they'd not get far before the sound of Lady Alice's voice assailed them. As it was, they were fortunate to reach the solar stairway in the corner of the great hall. "Sir Henry, take Marietta to my solar, if you please. I need to speak to her," she called.

To Marietta's amazement, her father stopped on the lowest step, swung round from his greater height and replied with withering coldness. "Mind who you speak to in that tone, m'lady. I'm taking Marietta to her chamber because she is unwell after her fall yesterday. And you will leave her in peace and tend her with all heed to her comfort. You have your new lap-dog and this lass still has her bruises. Look you sharp and tend her."

He continued to the top of the stairs and waited until Lady Alice had passed him and opened Marietta's door. "And send that hussy to our solar. *I* need to speak to *her!*" He glared at Emeline, who stood behind her mother, her face a picture of apprehension and alarm.

"Now, lass—" he placed Marietta carefully on the bed as her mother hustled the maids into action "—you're going to get back into bed and stay there. Understood?"

"Yes, Father."

"Good. I'll come to see you later on and we'll see how you feel then." He smiled and touched her sore nose with one finger, then stood to face his wife who hovered at the end of the bed, wringing her hands in uncertainty. "She's tired, and overwrought, and in some pain. A little more attention in this direction and a little less in *that*…" he pointed to Emeline "…and I'd be better pleased. See to it!" He closed the door quietly behind him.

Lady Alice turned to her stepdaughter. "Marietta, dear," she said.

For the rest of the day Marietta was tended as carefully as any father could have wished, bathed and salved again, warmed and banked up with soft pillows, fed with soothing draughts of feverfew and honey and left to rest in peace between visits from her stepmother, the maids and her father. Compresses of witch-hazel had been placed over her sore face and as soon as one dried, another one took its place. The coolness and the fragrant smell calmed her spirits and helped to remove the vexations of the morning, and when Emeline finally appeared along with the trays of food at suppertime, Marietta was almost relieved to see her.

Nothing had been said about Lord Alain's visit, no information offered and no questions asked, though the new pup had been brought in to see her and had caused the usual hilarity associated with baby creatures, puddling in the rushes and chewing at everything it could get between its tiny jaws. They had decided to call it Comfit.

Now Emeline sat with her sister and they ate together, quietly, though both were a little subdued, Marietta half-expecting to be told of Lord Alain's reaction that morning and yet not wanting to broach the subject in the light of Emeline's obvious disfavour with their father. Had something gone seriously wrong? she wondered, glancing at her sister's reddened eyes. She decided to ask.

"What did you think of Lord Alain, Emmie?"

Emeline looked up quickly and lowered her eyes again, playing with a piece of soft cheese while she thought of the best words to use. "He's very charming," she said.

"Does Mother think so, too?"

"Oh yes, Mother thinks so. She's thrilled with the pup."

"But what, Emmie?"

"Oh, nothing." She popped the cheese into her mouth at last. "Father seems to think I overdid it, but I don't know what I was supposed to do different. Trouble is, it's a bit difficult to know when he's being serious."

"Who? Father?"

"No, not Father, Lord Alain. He says serious things with a twinkle in his eyes, and then he says funny things seriously, and I don't know how to tell one from the other. So I suppose I got a bit muddled and Father thought I was being silly. But he didn't seem to mind."

"So you think he'll make an offer for you?" She made the question sound casual as she looked firmly into her goblet of watered mead.

"Mother's sure he will. She seemed pleased by the way things went, but I don't know what Father thinks about it. He says he's going to check what I wear next time he comes."

"He didn't like what you wore?"

"Father? No, not much. He says it was immodest. Do you think it's immodest, Marrie?"

"No, love. I think you look wonderful." She had no time to weigh up the implications of her reply, but even as it formed she knew that it was not what a loving sister ought to have said who was totally impartial to the outcome of the proceedings.

This would have been the perfect moment to be helpful, to say that the kirtle beneath the brief surcoat was too sheer, too clinging, too revealing, and that *that*, together with her muddled responses to Lord Alain's remarks, would have been enough to give the impression that she was trying too hard, which her father had deplored.

How strange, she thought, that Emeline and her mother thought it necessary to try at all, in view of Emeline's fair, fashionable prettiness. And how strange, too, that her father should think Emmie had tried too hard and that she, Marietta, had never tried hard enough. Indeed, why should either of them have to try? Were they not acceptable just as they were, without this silly charade?

"Yes, well, I thought it looked wonderful too."

"And did he say he'd visit again?"

"No, but I expect…oh, wait a moment, yes, he did. He said he'd come back when you were better and see how your bruises did. But Mother says he spoke to you in the garden just before they went off. Did he ask you about them?"

"Yes, that's all he wanted to know. Just that."

"Mother's been dying to know all day but Father said not to ask you."

"Well, there's no mystery about it. He'd never have known I was there, if Ben hadn't told him where Bruno was and he came to look for him." She didn't regret the lie. It would not help Emeline to know what he'd said. She had also discovered that he said serious things strangely, and she supposed that when he'd said it was himself he was thinking of as a husband for her, he was jesting. Yes, of course, he was jesting.

Before sleep came and after the events of the day had been turned over in her mind for the hundredth time, Marietta had to admit that she was no nearer understanding Lord Alain's attitude towards her than she was to understanding her own towards him. Emeline had found him charming; she had found him arrogant and domineering. His manner to Emeline had been courteous; to her it had been discourteous in the extreme.

And yet, she could not help but wonder. Why had he gone to such lengths to tell her that he would search for her, and find her, and bring her back if she continued her avoidance of him? Well, they would see about that. There must be plenty of places where one could keep out of the way of another, here at Monksgrange, and perhaps she'd discover a few of them in the next few weeks. After all, Lady Alice and Emeline had decided he was for them, and it would be a shrewd man who managed to deprive them of what they sought.

For one night's reflections, that should have been an end to the matter, but in her memory, his face pressed close against hers and his lips moved incessantly to torment her through the darkest hours, and the doves in the dovecote had begun their monotonous cooing long before she sank into sleep. And though her father had peeped into the room twice before she awoke, she was still sure she had not slept.

From his distant view, Sir Henry was able to understand the cause of her distress better than most. He had observed her ways with men who would like to have come close to her and knew that it was less to do with mere perverseness than a real fear of being dominated. None of the young swains had been her match either in intelligence, in courage or in self-will and it was for this reason that he had let the matter of her marriage lie, sure that there would come a time and a place.

Meanwhile, he refused to offer her up to someone for whom she had no respect—there was no need for her to succumb to any but the ablest. And when the time was right, he, her father, would leave her in no doubt.

Now, he had met such a man, and while he had no way of knowing what had passed between him and Marietta, he had seen the effect of their second encounter when the man had obviously asserted his authority. The uncomfortable truth, however, was that Lady Alice had earmarked this man for her Emeline, or so she would have it, and as things had progressed this far in her schemes, he felt duty-bound to foster her cause. But what a waste. What a waste. Perhaps he should leave it to Lord Alain to sort it out for himself.

* * *

Lady Alice crossed herself, raised herself from her knees and closed her book of prayers, delaying as long as possible her exit from the little chapel, knowing that her brother Nicholas was waiting for a word. She did not want to face his inquisition today any more than she had yesterday. There was already more than enough expected of her without him, too.

He took her elbow and walked along the balcony and down the stairs to the hall, accepting her excuse not to go into her solar. She was far too busy to take time off for idle conversation, she said.

"It's not an idle conversation I want, Alice," said Sir Nicholas under his breath, drawing her away from others who waited to speak with her. "I simply want to know why Emeline was crying."

"Perhaps you should ask Emeline herself." She looked away and caught sight of her pantler waving his fingers for her attention. But her brother took her arm beneath the loose sleeve of her gown and gripped it painfully tightly. Alice gave a gasp of pain and turned to him, her mouth open in protest.

"I *have* asked her, Alice. You know bloody well that I have, and that she won't tell me because Henry told her not to. Now *you* tell me, or you'll find that new pet of yours in the duckpond. And then you'll have some explaining to do."

"Nicholas! You wouldn't do that!" Her face registered horror.

"Yes, I would, dear sister. Yes, I would. Now, tell me!"

"Let go of my arm, please. I'll tell you, but let go." She pulled it away from his grasp and held it, massaging the pain with her free hand and turning her back on those in the hall. "Henry scolded her about the gown, for one thing," she whispered, angrily.

"The gown? What was wrong with it? I saw her beforehand and thought she looked good."

"Well, he didn't think so. When she came into the solar with you, Henry said she looked so fuddled she could hardly speak a word of sense. And he said the gown was too revealing for a maid."

"Revealing? She was covered up. What are you talking about?"

Alice lowered her head and looked sideways at him. "Nicholas, does she…has she…?"

"Has she what?"

"Has she got…you know…a lover?"

"Hah! Well, if she has, she hadn't been with him then, if that's what you mean. Why? Did Henry object to her showing that she fancied Lord Alain so soon?"

"Sssh! Yes, I expect he thought it was too obvious. He's not what we expected, is he? Lord Alain, I mean. He's younger than me, not the old man I thought he'd be. Anyway, Henry told her to behave more modestly in future."

"Well, if I were you I wouldn't care what she does in future as long as she gets married first, old, young, fat, thin, anybody! If that old couple die before then, Henry'll put somebody else into Beckington Manor and that'll be the end of my plans to live there."

"No he won't." Alice didn't sound too convinced. "It's mine, you know."

"I know it is, sister dear, but Henry seems to have more say in who lives there than you do."

"Well, only until I pass it on…"

"…To the first daughter to get married. Yes, I know all that," he snapped, "but if Emeline hangs about much longer, my plans will go for nothing. It's clear the other one's never going to make it, is she? Prickly little bitch! If I wasn't her uncle, I'd…"

"Nicholas! Stop it, this moment! Marietta is my step-daughter—"

"Yes, and you don't know how to handle her do you? Well, I do!"

"Nicholas, for goodness sake…we're being looked at…"

"It's all right, woman, I won't. But be quick and get Emmie into bed with that mighty lord, will you? Because *I* want Beckington. And I want it soon, otherwise I'll be too old to sire any brats, too."

"Please…!" Alice pushed herself away and turned into the company who waited patiently to speak with her. "Now, let's see, I must speak with the pantler…about to-day's bread."

Sir Nicholas sat down hard on the stairway, watching the throng of people around his sister—knights, ladies, yeomen, grooms of the chamber and household servants waiting for instructions, greetings, directions for the day ahead—and thought with a resentment that deepened almost daily of how he should be the owner of such a place as this.

Five manors Sir Henry had, while he had none, being the youngest and landless son of a large family. Alice had married well, for her only dower had been the manor of Beckington, a large estate not far from Monksgrange, which had always been handed down, since it was built in the twelfth century, from mother to daughter, whichever daughter married first.

In spite of Alice's pleas, Sir Henry had always steadfastly refused to allow her to turn out the elderly couple who managed it and allow Nicholas to live there. Now his only chance of overriding Sir Henry's interference in his wife's property was to remove it once more down the female line to pliant Emeline, who had been well schooled to do his bidding. But it would not be hers until she married, and it was time she was settled.

He sighed and watched the new pup flop unsteadily down over the edge of each enormous step as it came past him to its mistress, and with one hand he scooped it up and lowered it to the floor. He felt a toe between his shoulder-blades.

"If you're not otherwise engaged, Nicholas...and if you have the time...Emeline will need an escort as soon as she's ready. Only until noon. And then, I have a job for you."

Sir Nicholas stood. "Not Marietta?"

"No, not Marietta. She'll be with me," said Sir Henry.

Not surprising, he thought. I'm the last one she'd want to be with.

Chapter Three

From the front, Monksgrange stood foursquare and solid, as though grown from the hillside, rooted for ever in the limestone crags which had given it birth. Even the sloping rooftops were stone-flagged and encrusted with lichens, mosses and houseleeks. But it was not until two days after their arrival that Marietta was at last able to take a good look at the place her father had purchased less than a year ago; not until she had been carried from the house, still too stiff to walk, placed in a horse-litter thickly padded with cushions and taken on a tour of the buildings and village.

Until recently, Monksgrange had belonged to the Augustinian priory of Bolton and was one of a dozen or so satellite sheep farms dotted about over a considerable acreage, supervised by the cellarer and run by lay brothers, reeves and a bailiff. It had been the largest of their granges; not only did it farm more land than the others but served also as a retreat and convalescent house for monks who were old, recovering from illness, or in need of spiritual solitude.

It had more rooms, its own chapel, extensive gardens and a pleasantly sheltered aspect on a hillside, lying on the edge of the village of Ings. From Monksgrange, they could see across the valley of the River Wain to the wooded scars that formed the great plateau where Thorsgeld Castle watched over the valley on one side with the town of Thorsgeld tucked in behind.

Bad times had forced the canons of Bolton Priory to let Monksgrange go; repeated raids by the marauding Scots, two catastrophic summers and bad crop-yields, followed by the predictable sheep and cattle diseases that had cut their flocks and herds to below half, made it impossible for the monks to eke out an existence. Their tenants could not pay their tithes nor could the wool-clip be sold a year in advance when so many sheep had been lost.

The monks' loss had been Sir Henry's gain. With enough reserves to tide him over the lean years, he had been less convinced than the monks that the Lord would provide and had preferred to provide for himself. With careful husbandry and protection from the Scots' raids up in the highest fells, he had weathered the storm, held onto his assets and expanded.

With Marietta in the litter and a retinue that included the bailiff, reeve and steward among household knights and scribes, Sir Henry went over the wooden bridge through the village to meet the parish priest, the new tenants and the miller, whose mill on the beck ground the corn of the villagers. As they surveyed the fields, many of them now enclosed by stone walls, Marietta pointed to black patches high up on the fell behind them. "Father, stop a moment, please. Those…what are those up there?"

The bailiff answered for Sir Henry. "Caves, mistress. There's quite a cluster of 'em round theer. Demon's caves. Nobody goes up theer."

"Demons?" Marietta scoffed, gently. "Wild animals, more like."

"Nay, mistress, there's no way o' knowing. No road.

Nothing. Village folk always keep away.'' His voice took on a dark tone.

Lady Alice might well have swallowed such nonsense with ease, but Marietta and her father were less gullible, neither of them subscribing to such superstitions. It hardly mattered—while Marietta was with her father, she was well out of range of any danger, superstitious or otherwise, and the risk of being discovered again by Lord Alain had all but disappeared.

For the next few days, her expeditions with Sir Henry became a treat, as treasured for her new mode of transport as for the comforting knowledge that, under her father's wing, she could not be provoked by this large and daunting man. Her father allowed her to walk in the mornings, attend to the garden and direct the new planting, then to take a small part in the ordering of stores, checking the malt for brewing and the fish-ponds for the kitchen.

During these days, her bruises moved through a startling spectrum of colours; by the end of the week, most of them had faded to pale green and yellow except for two crescent-shaped imprints on her buttocks which stayed violet for a while longer. On her face, the soreness vanished quickly and eventually the litter was abandoned and she was able to travel further afield and thus make the possibility of meeting Lord Alain even less likely.

Emeline had never been interested in the running of the demesne, preferring to leave such matters to Marietta, so it was hardly surprising that she was easier to find at home on the occasions when Lord Alain came. She was preparing to go hawking one morning when he appeared unexpect-edly, a week after his first call. Bruno and another squire accompanied him, showed him round the mews, and together the party went into the hills with the falcons, returning with several wildfowl for the kitchen.

Marietta was secretly delighted to have missed him, for she had been with her father and his bailiff at the new mill on that day, talking about setting eel-traps in the beck. The nearest she came to being seen was well into the second week when Lord Alain rode into the courtyard from the front as she rode away out of the back. Aware of Lady Alice's intention of asking him to share a meal with them on his next visit, there was an unmistakeable smile on Marietta's face as she rode out, knowing that she could arrange to stay out of the way until well after noon, when he would be gone.

It was obvious that Emeline was certain of a conquest; never had she been so gay, so brimful of excitement and chatter, planning for the future and even turning a new-found charm on her sisters. Lady Alice could scarce contain herself and even Sir Nicholas had begun to mellow.

Their uncle caught up with Marietta as she came in at suppertime, breathless and glowing from a ride with her father to see the new stone wall which should last, he'd told her, for a few hundred years. "Marietta!" Sir Nicholas called.

"Uncle?" She wished he would not think that she enjoyed his sudden attentions. He was no more welcome to her than he'd been before.

"If you need an escort when your father's not available one day, I'd be honoured to accompany you."

"Where to?"

He was taken aback by her abrupt response. "Where to? Anywhere."

"Anywhere?" Her smile was cynical. "Is your nose being pushed a little out of joint, Uncle? Now that Emeline's attentions are engaged?"

"Not at all. Is yours, Marietta?"

"No. That's why I'm co-operating with Emeline. But I've seen the kind of help you offer and I wouldn't like any of it, thank you. Now, would you excuse me, please?"

Sir Nicholas stood back to let her pass. "Well, then," he said, "watch them carefully at supper, and if you change your mind…"

"Them? Watch who?" She had an uncomfortable feeling that she knew the answer to that already. Was *he* still here?

"Her new suitor, of course. Did you not know?"

"No, I didn't! I thought…" She looked away angrily, but it was too late to conceal what her uncle construed as jealousy of Emeline's happiness. It was not jealousy, she thought, as much as a desire to avoid Lord Alain, for he would want to know why and how she'd managed to thrust Emeline at him, in spite of his warnings. But then, perhaps he'd changed his mind since then, after being in her company so often.

"What did you think, Marietta? That he was staying only for midday dinner? Too bad. But you'll want to see Emmie perform, surely? No?" His eyes held a mockery that she would dearly love to have wiped away with a resounding smack.

But common sense came to her rescue and in the instant before she let go of her temper, a better idea occurred to her. Make use of him.

"No, Uncle Nicholas. I'm more interested in my food than in watching Emeline. Make a place for me at your side. I'll go in with you." Before she could fully appreciate the expression of astonishment on his face, she'd swept her gown away and stalked off.

Too bemused to be angered by her imperious tone, Nicholas watched her ascend the wooden stairs, half-aware that he was being made use of, but having no idea that the alliance was meant to deceive Lord Alain rather than Emeline and the others in the hall. Still, he would go along with it. Even that was better than a total rejection.

Lord Alain's retinue, together with the large household of Sir Henry, made for a merry enough meal during which it was not too difficult for Marietta to put on a convincing show of indifference. Outwardly, she talked and laughed with the guests, even with Uncle Nicholas, avoiding Lord Alain's eyes like the plague and allowing Emeline and Lady Alice to dance around him, leaving no one in doubt that they were honoured by his presence.

Even when they assembled in the great solar before the meal, he could do no more than greet her with a solemn and studied bow before being hauled away by Lady Alice as though any lingering contact with Marietta would be precious time away from Emeline.

Inwardly, Marietta's emotions were by no means as under control as she made it seem, sensing a desperation in her stepmother's and Emeline's manipulation of events that hurt her, even while she went along with it. Disturbed by Lord Alain's manner towards her, she was sure she wanted no more of it, so why did she find it so difficult to put him from her mind? Why did her eyes fail to register any detail of the food before her, and why did she not hear when Uncle Nicholas spoke?

The guests at the high table were entertaining, but her ears strained only to catch the sound of Lord Alain's voice, her eyes glancing sideways at his fingers on the goblet of wine. And when the goblet she shared with Uncle Nicholas was filled, time after time, was it he who drank it all, or her? Was the laughter, indeed, growing louder, the musicians noisier, the room growing hotter by the minute? Was it her exasperation at Emeline's high-pitched giggles that made her want to leave and seek the cool air of the evening?

Her father leaned back from his bench and touched her arm. "You all right, love?" he mouthed, behind the backs of three people.

Marietta's cheeks were flushed and her eyes sparkled, but whether from laughter or tears not even she could have said. "Think so...Father...may I...leave?" she mumbled, almost falling backwards off the bench.

Sir Nicholas's arm caught her around the waist and pulled her to him in a gesture part-rescue, part-embrace. He laughed. "I'll take her, Henry."

That was not what Sir Henry wanted, but from that distance he could not argue. "Bring her straight back," he said.

Sir Nicholas nodded, his expression one of bland innocence.

There was nothing strange about leaving a hall during a meal of such duration but, even so, Sir Henry watched with more than a hint of concern at the sight of his brother-in-law's arm around Marietta's waist as they left through the opening of the carved screen that led into the passage.

Away from the heat and noise and cooled by the draught of air along the passage, Marietta became aware of Sir Nicholas's hand on her ribs as he led her towards the courtyard door. She pushed at the hand, vaguely irritated by its warmth on her, but before he could respond, three pages approached from the kitchen outside, bearing a huge platter between them loaded with sweetmeats and glazed fruits, nuts and tiny pastries to round off the meal.

Nicholas pulled her close up to the wall and pressed himself against her as they passed, needlessly placing his hands over her hips as though to protect her from danger.

"Uncle...Nicholas...!" Marietta twisted away, smelling

the hot reek of wine on his breath. "I can manage…alone," she said, forcing the words out in the right order. It was difficult, for while the inside of her head seemed to be in perfect working order, her arms, legs and words were disobeying her commands in a most alarming manner.

"It's all right, Marietta," Nicholas said. "Come on outside. You need some air. I need some air, too. We'll go together, eh?" His head fell towards her, too close.

"No, Uncle…I'm perfectly lone all right…let you go…now." She could hear the silly words wilfully confusing her, pretending that they'd said what she meant them to say. What *had* she said?

"Yes, all right, come on then. We'll go now." He turned her again to face the door.

There was one word she knew could not be misconstrued. "No!" she yelled.

The voice that replied was much deeper than Sir Nicholas's. "Sir Nicholas, your brother-in-law requires your presence at the table, I believe. Immediately. I will relieve you of your duty."

There was no arguing with that tone, even after so much wine. Without another word, Sir Nicholas relaxed his grip on Marietta's arm, clenched his teeth on an oath and left her to face Lord Alain's well-timed interference. If he had heard the suppressed oath, Lord Alain would have laughed.

Marietta would not. Relieved beyond words from a danger she herself had done something to precipitate, this particular form of deliverance from her uncle's company was embarrassing in a different way, one which, in her present state, she had no idea how to handle.

She discovered immediately that she was not required to. Lord Alain took her hand and led her, unprotesting, across the almost deserted courtyard and round the corner into the garden where he had encountered her in the arbour. Slowly and without speaking, they entered the same shelter where the carpenter had constructed a turf seat along one side, facing the herb-patch. At the far end, where the foliage gave them some privacy, he took her by the shoulders and sat her down, seating himself by her side.

The conflicts which had beset Marietta since their first meeting surged forward into an accumulation of futile longings and denials made so much more potent by his nearness. Hardly caring whether he scolded again, or teased, or even said nothing at all, she relished his presence by her side with few of the former inhibitions she had nurtured in defence.

Lord Alain appeared to sense this. "Does it take four goblets of wine to stop you bolting then, demoiselle? Do I have to get you pie-eyed before we can talk without you snarling like a wildcat? Eh?"

"Don't," Marietta whispered.

"Don't what?" He took the long dagged tippets of her sleeves between his fingers and held them together like reins.

"Don't talk to me, my lord." That seemed to sum it up, she thought, hazily.

"Not talk to you? Why ever not? Is it forbidden?"

The truth came out so much more easily, this time. "You're supposed to be…be talking…to Emeline," she whispered, wearily laying her head back against the trellis. If she concentrated very hard, she could just get the words out before they tripped each other up. Giving all her attention to the words made it difficult to remember what her heart and her head disagreed about.

"Aye, well…I've talked to your sister Emeline for the best part of two weeks now and, in spite of what I told you, you've managed to avoid me. Where have you been?

Do I have to camp outside the gates to catch you before you make a dash for it each morning?''

"Been felping my...felping...*helping* my father," she said, focusing her eyes on his strong hands. "I have to see to stores...order food..."

"Doesn't Lady Alice do that?"

Marietta shook her head, then wished she had not, for the action seemed to leave her eyes at a standstill somewhere out of focus. "No...me...I do it. I like it. Garden, too...all this...I like it. Haven't been voiding you..."

"Don't lie to me, wench," he said, cutting off her explanation. "I know damn well you have. Why? Come on, I want to know. And why encourage that uncle of yours? Do you like him?"

"No," she glared and pulled her sleeve tippets out of his hands. "No, I do not! I just..." She stopped, unable to remember what it was she had needed Uncle Nicholas for.

"Just to show me you don't care. Was that it?"

"I don't know, my lord. Go away, please. If you came here to pick another quarrel, you choose your times very ill. First I'm bruised from a fall and then I'm...tired. Emeline says you're charming to her, but to me you're pro...provoking."

"Leave your sister out of it, if you please. It's you we're talking about."

"And last time you spoke to me alone, you were most ob...ject...able!"

"Was I, lass? So you remembered that, did you? Is that why you kept well out of reach? So's I wouldn't do it again?"

"Yes...yes, it is!" Goaded into an admission, Marietta turned on him in fury, purposely re-introducing her half-sister as a weapon to annoy him. "Why don't you torment Emeline like that? She'd like it! I don't!" She would have risen, then, and flounced away if she could have trusted her legs to stay rigid under her, but Lord Alain reached across and caught her hands in his, and she could not release them.

"Torment?" he said. He pulled her nearer to him so that her face was only a whisper away, making it impossible for her eyes to evade his. They were dark in the dappled shade of the arbour, but she saw how they roamed over her, lingering on her bare neck and low-cut bodice, taking in every detail of the gold circlet on her brow and the mass of dark-brown curls, her lips and then her eyes. "Torment?" he repeated. "You think I should torment her, do you? Like this…?"

The world of greenery tipped over her and his head took the place of the arched bower as all details merged into one sensation of being held close to him, lowered across his lap, submerged as she had wanted to be in her dreams but never was. His wide chest was above her, his shoulders blocking out the gentle golden sunset, his head of black-brown hair framing his face. She felt his breath against her skin. "Did you tell her how hard my kiss was, Marietta? Did you? Or did you keep it to yourself…a secret?"

"Don't…please don't, my lord. Please…"

"Why, Marietta?"

She could think of no coherent reason except that he'd been earmarked for Emeline and she was not supposed to be any part of that plan. And if he was fooling with her, this was a most despicable and ungallant action for a man to perform if his intentions were indeed directed elsewhere. Yet, *she* was here, not Emeline, and she would only have to scream and make a fuss to bring help, to show him that she meant what she said.

But did she mean it? Did she not secretly want this part of him, this memory to take with her beyond Emeline's marriage? A dream, a slice of reality, a few seconds of ecstasy for the length of a kiss? His head was lowering, not waiting for her deliberations.

"You're for Emeline…" was all she could think of to say.

"Aye," he whispered on her lips, "that's what you'd all have me believe, is it not? So before I make my offer tomorrow, we'll get one or two things straight, shall we?"

If she wondered what he meant by that, she was given no chance to enquire, for his arms tightened under her back and she was brought up to his mouth and held darkly in his embrace. It was not the cruel punishing kiss of their first conversation but no less positive in its message of intent, and for the second time she felt the strength of his arms and the firm mouth seeking a response from hers.

She had dreamed of kisses, but this was far beyond her dreams. She had seen village men kissing the women in the hayfields, behind the barns, in the darkest corners of the hall, and had wondered why they writhed so, and moaned, and made it look so uncomfortable.

Now, she began to realise, in the hazy recesses of her mind, how one was impelled to search for new surfaces and tastes, to give and then to relax and accept, to accede to the demands of one more experienced and sink below the warm surface of his quest and let him go, and search, and find. Gladly, she went with him, holding his head to hers and sharing every sensation.

When she realised that his hand had found a way inside her bodice and onto her breast, she let out a low cry against his mouth and, placing a hand over his, pushed at it to heighten the sensation. He responded immediately by easing both her surcoat and her cote-hardie over her shoulders, exchanging her lips for her breast and fondling with his mouth so exquisitely that, even though this was a first experience for her, she would have done anything that he'd asked.

He stopped and raised his head, looking for a reaction, but Marietta lifted her arms and drew his head to hers again, riding high on a wave of new perceptions, matching one against the other as though time was running out. Which indeed it was. For the last few moments, she took all he offered and gave all he asked.

Lord Alain held her quietly against him and looked down at her lovely face. "So, my lovely Marietta," he whispered, "you still have no wish for a husband?"

She was sure he taunted her and would have pushed her way off his lap in sudden indignation and guilt if he had not anticipated her rejection by catching her to him and preventing her escape. "Answer me!" he said.

"It pleases you to play games with me, my lord. You know as well as I that that meant nothing to either of us." She winced as he gripped her cruelly tight in his arms.

"Stop it!" he growled. "That kind of talk does you no credit, lass. Don't try to tell me that that was a game. Even if you *are* inexperienced and tipsy, you can't have pretended that. Tell me truthfully, if you please. Do you still want me to offer for your sister?"

He had asked for the truth, but it was not hers to give. Still utterly confused, still conditioned to put Emeline first in the marriage line, still angry at her own passionate response and fearful of this man who could wield such power over her body, she was in no position to capitulate. Struggling against his hold, she replied with all the anger built up since their first eventful collision.

"Yes! Offer for her! Why should I care what you do? She's willing enough to have a husband…she'll be compliant…let me go!…and do your bidding…like a pet lamb!

Offer for her…you won't have to ask twice…let me *go*, my lord!''

Thinking that he might reciprocate in kind, which she could not have borne, she rolled away and sprang to her feet with unexpected agility, pulling at her surcoat and cote-hardie to straighten them. But Lord Alain was not injured by her outburst; on the contrary, he appeared to be somewhat amused and, keeping hold of her around the waist, eased her back onto the seat by his side.

''All right, my girl…all right…calm down. I can see your feathers are ruffled. I should have known. We both have much to learn about each other. Come, make yourself straight and composed, we must walk back into the hall as though we've been to take the air. No more. Say nothing of this…I give you my word I shall say nothing, either.''

He stood and settled her circlet straight on her head and pushed her hair tidily over her shoulders. ''There, are you ready to go in, now?''

Marietta nodded, absorbing some of his composure.

''Smile?'' he whispered, lifting her chin.

She did not smile. ''My lord, pray do not tease me any more.'' Her heart still pounded. This must not be repeated, ever; for her and Emeline's sakes, he must tease her no more.

''The only time I have ever knowingly teased you, my lovely Marietta, was at our first meeting when I insisted on feeling for your bruises to rouse you, to bring you back to consciousness. And I insisted on carrying you because you could not have walked, even though you would have tried, stubborn lass. That was the only time. Since then, everything I have said, or done, has been said in all seriousness.''

''Oh. Then you will make your offer tomorrow, my lord?'' She dreaded the reply but had to know so that she could be well out of the way.

"Yes, I shall speak to your father on the morrow. But I do not want anyone to know of this, Marietta. It must remain our secret. Will you give me your word on that?"

A woman's word. Was it worth anything, then? "Yes. my lord, I shall not…not speak of it."

"Come then. There must be no sign of tears when we return. We don't want to give Lady Alice the wrong idea, do we?" He held out his hand.

As if to add to the interminable discomforts of the night, Marietta struggled wearily into the new day with a pain in her head worse than any she could remember. Stoicism was one thing, but this was blinding. Her maids knew what to do; Sir Henry was the same after too much red wine. "Here," Ellie said to Anne, "lay the cloth out on here and hold it while I spread this over it. We'll soon have her bound up."

"This' was a mixture of chopped rue and vinegar, one of a variety of remedies which they chose according to the time of the year. Ivy berries were not available yet and plantain roots must be dug up before dawn. The red cloth, soaked with its sour-smelling mixture, was wrapped around Marietta's head and pinned in place while the two bustled about quietly and efficiently to prepare an infusion of vervain and honey for her to sip. It was not like their mistress to drink too much. Had it been Sir Nicholas's fault, perhaps?

They had noticed, for little escaped them, how her uncle had returned alone after escorting Marietta out of the hall, how his expression had betrayed only too clearly that he'd been sent packing by Lord Alain, who had followed them with purposeful steps.

Much more they'd noticed, too, enough to fix a sulk on Emeline's face for the rest of the evening and for Lady

Alice to harangue her in ear-shattering spasms until Sir Henry had gone to calm things down. She would not treat Marietta to such a tirade, that was for sure, not if she wanted to come off best. The two maids nudged each other and grinned, having worked out their own version of what the problem might be. Their mistress's sleepless night helped to confirm it.

With the dreadful pain in her head now more under control, Marietta nevertheless revised her plans to ride off to some far-flung corner of the demesne in favour of some work in the gardens. There were three which needed much attention, but the herbs were her special province and she'd be safe enough there from the comings and goings of Lord Alain and his companions.

She stayed in the shade where the bright sun could not hurt her eyes, directing the maids and the young garden lads which plots to dig, to manure and to tidy. The rosemary was already well up and covered with pale mauve flowers, the same colour as her surcoat, which she wore over an undyed linen cote-hardie.

Her hair she'd had plaited and coiled around her head, and a veil hung from its lower edges over her neck, useful, she thought, for keeping flying creatures away. And though she was unable to keep thoughts of him away as efficiently, the green foliage and the gentle industry of the gardeners gave her some peace and space in which to ponder on recent events.

It was Bruno who came to seek her, well past dinner time. He and the other young squire had demonstrated their serving graces on the guests at Sir Henry's table, but Marietta had not appeared, preferring to take a small meal of honeyed oat cakes and milk in the arbour, unable to face real food or the sight of Lord Alain with Emeline.

"I can't stay, love." He pecked her cheek in simultaneous greeting and farewell. "I have to go. My lord is waiting."

"He's still here, then?" She knew, but wanted Bruno to say.

"Yes, he and Father have been closeted up together all morning."

"And Mother…?"

"Lady Alice is in a buzz…you can imagine." He was backing away, anxious to go.

"Emeline?"

"Haven't seen anything of her." He stopped backing to think more clearly. "I think she's been told to stay out of the way until it's been announced. You'll be glad to see the back of her, won't you?" His sudden smile after the wicked question brought a gust of dry laughter from her.

"Certainly I will, love. Both of them. Now, hurry…or you'll be in trouble." She waved a hand at him.

"Yes, we've discovered how fierce he can be, Marrie. Everybody jumps when he gives an order. Bye, love. God be with you."

"And with you, dearest."

Marietta watched as he ran nimbly along the pathway towards the gate, passing the maids who approached from the house. Their faces were solemn, as she thought they might be.

"Mistress, Sir Henry asks that you attend him in the great solar."

She knew what he would have to say and that they would all gather there as an outwardly happy family, beaming with joy and relief. She would have to share it with them, pretend to be happy, congratulate Emeline and bear her empty prattle with a good grace. Rinsing her fingers in the water-butt, she shook them dry, tucked a stray lock of hair away, and went in.

Sir Henry indicated a stool by the window-seat where Lady Alice sat. "You'd better sit down, love," he said.

Marietta stood inside the large sunny chamber, bewildered by the absence of happy smiling people. Where was everyone? "No, it's all right, Father…I think I can guess the news," she assured him. "I'm so—"

"You know?"

Lady Alice looked puzzled, scanning Marietta's face, then her husband's.

"Yes, of course. It's Emeline, isn't it? Lord Alain has offered…".

"No, dear." Her father shook his head. "Look, do sit down."

Marietta sat, now even more at a loss, and glanced at her stepmother's joyless face. No excitement? He'd not been accepted, then? Perhaps the two men could not reach an agreement, after all.

"Lord Alain has asked me for your hand," he said.

The room spun slowly round, taking the words with it. She must have misunderstood. "What?" she whispered.

"He has asked me for your hand in marriage, Marietta."

Still her eyes registered nothing except the two faces in a void. Surely there was some mistake. "No, Father. That's absurd. It's Emeline he's to marry. Emeline, surely."

"No, love. He's to return tomorrow for your answer. I told him the marriage had my blessing but that you'd have to be consulted. You can have until then to think about it, but I think it would be best if we were to discuss it now rather than leave it until then. This is rather a surprise to us—"

"A surprise to *you?* You can't have understood, Father.

It's Emeline he's been paying attention to, not me. This is all wrong!'' She leapt up and strode to the door.

Lady Alice caught at her hand before she could reach it. ''Child,'' she said, unusually quietly, ''child, don't flounce out like that without trying to discuss it. We're all surprised. Think how Emeline feels.''

''You told Emeline first, then?'' Marietta's brown eyes blazed in anger.

''Yes, dear. A moment or two ago. She was expecting some news and I couldn't make her wait any longer. She needs time to get used to the idea.''

''*She* needs time? To get used to the idea of not being married? She's had nearly fifteen years to get used to that, hasn't she? And now…'' she pulled away from Lady Alice, furious at being placed second, even at a moment like this ''…now you spring this ridiculous news on me and tell me I have a mere twenty-four hours to think about it? And you tell me she needs time? God's wounds, Mother!''

''Marietta! That's enough! Don't speak to your mother so.''

She stood as stiff as a poker. ''I beg your pardon, Mother. But the whole thing is a nonsense, anyone can see that. They've been together for days, enjoying each other's company; the only times he's spoken to me he's been totally uncivil. It was no penance to keep out of his way this last few weeks, I assure you. It was a pleasure.''

''And you?'' Her father poured ale into a goblet for her. ''Have you been civil to him? Was that civility you showed him at your first meeting?''

The arrow hit the mark. Bullseye. ''It was his damn hounds that brought me off my mare. He's not apologised for any of that,'' she snapped.

Lady Alice shook her head, confused by the turn of

events. "Well, I must admit, I do find it strange, dear. They seemed to be getting on so well."

Sir Henry handed the goblet to Marietta. "Perhaps I did the wrong thing by taking you off every day. Perhaps I should not have interfered."

"It would have made no difference, Father. I would have taken myself off, with or without your help." She was shaking with anger. The man was playing a game with them, in spite of what he'd said on that first meeting in the arbour. "You've discussed settlements with him, Father?" If he'd got that far, she thought, he must be serious, for no man would tell another what he was offering in any detail unless he was in earnest.

"Yes, we've spent the morning discussing the business part of it. He brought his clerks to make notes of the transactions and they're to return tomorrow when my proposals have been looked into."

"*Your* proposals? You've got that far?" She was incredulous.

"Yes, love. He wasn't playing games. He's serious."

Tasting nothing of the ale, she pushed the goblet back onto the table. "Mother," she said, her voice shaking now as much as her legs, "Mother, I've done nothing to make this happen. Nothing! You've seen how I kept out of the way every single day. I wanted none of this. I still want none of it."

As her words fell into the quiet room, she met her father's eyes and knew that he understood the ambiguity of her dilemma, that in her most secret heart she had indeed wanted it but had not expected it, was afraid of it and, for Emeline's sake, would willingly have sacrificed it. Furthermore, she was painfully aware that, to Emeline, it would have all the hallmarks of treachery, even though Marietta had never seen herself as a rival.

Emeline was overtly ripe for marriage, and knew it. Marietta was happy to let her get on with it, for a man's dominance had never been something she craved, though Sir Henry knew better than she did herself that her capacity for loving was as great as any woman's and that her sexuality lay beneath a fine veneer of indifference, waiting to be roused.

What he had secretly wanted to happen had come to pass; obviously the man had seen her worth and made the best choice. But now, she would have to be convinced that this was in her best interests, or she would have to be forced into it. Failing that, Lord Alain himself would have to insist, and Sir Henry could hazard a guess that his stronghandedness so far had both antagonised and aroused her. He wondered how long it would take for one to fuse into the other.

Lady Alice came to sit by her, taking her hand gently in reply to Marietta's cry for help. "Would you not want to marry him, Marietta?"

"No, Mother."

"Why not, dear? He's very wealthy. You'd be mistress of a fine castle." Lady Alice was growing ambivalent about the prospect. The only problem would be to keep her brother Nicholas quiet about Beckington, but that would have to take care of itself. At least she would have a daughter married to a lord. Any daughter. Any lord. "Why not, dear?" she repeated.

"Because I'm convinced I'm not his first choice," Marietta said impatiently, revealing some of the internal conflicts her father had guessed at. "He's playing some clever game with Emmie. I can feel it. And I'm not going to be a part of it. He can think again. He can't come wooing one sister and then calmly offer for the other. It's not done. It's unfair on both of us."

"Is that the only reason?" her father asked, quietly.

Marietta looked away out of the window across the valley to Thorsgeld Castle; though nothing was clearly visible through the opaque glass, she knew it was there. His arms still pressed across her back and shoulders, the search of his mouth was still on hers, on her body, skillfully persuading. She had been light-headed with wine and he had taken advantage of her lassitude. He had sworn it was no game, that he was not teasing. What, then?

"Let me go to my solar, Father."

"No, Marrie."

She sighed, drooping her shoulders, querying him.

"You have not yet asked what your mother and I say about this. Do you think you are the only person involved? Has it not occurred to you what it will mean to us, to Bruno's future prospects, to Emeline's and Iveta's?"

"Father, surely you're not taking this offer against my will, are you? Of what use is it to ask for my thoughts on the matter and then override them with yours?"

"Marietta!" Her father spoke sternly, though he could follow her argument. He smoothed a hand down his figured velvet surcoat, feeling its soft obedience to his touch. "No one has spoken of overriding your wishes, but you must remember that discussions are between people. I've discussed it with Lord Alain and I assured him I'd discuss it with you. You are duty-bound to—"

"Then why did he not discuss it with me? Why suddenly spring it on me like this, when we all thought it was Emeline? Including her." But as she spoke the words, she knew the answer.

He had. Of course he had. She had refused to listen when he'd told her and he'd not been fool enough to argue about it but had made her take it from another source. It was her own fault.

"I've already said that perhaps I got it wrong, Marietta. I thought it would help if you were out of the way but perhaps I should have made it easier for Lord Alain to contact you. But what would you have replied to an earlier offer, lass? What have you *ever* replied to an offer for your hand?"

"No."

"Exactly! Lord Alain's nobody's fool; he's experienced. Thirty years old and a widower. He probably saw from a mile away that you'd say no at any stage in the negotiations, so his best course was to ask me and bypass you altogether. That seems reasonable to me; it's what anybody with any sense would do. He's a different kettle o' fish from all the others who've offered for you so far. I wouldn't have given you to any of them."

"And you'd give me to Lord Alain, Father?"

"Yes, lass. I would...willingly."

"Because he's a lord, and wealthy, and lives in a castle?" Purposely, she echoed her stepmother's priorities.

It was not lost on Sir Henry. "Your mother pointed that out because they are the material things every mother wants for her daughter. You would. They make life bearable—no one can deny that."

"And him? Would life be bearable with a man I don't love?"

He frowned at the irrelevance of her question. "*Love*, lass? For pity's sake, you can't have everything. That will no doubt come later. Respect is more important at this point, and you need an older man. You've always known that as much as I do. A strong man."

"I don't need any man! I don't need *him*!" she snapped, scared by this talk of strength and experience.

"Yes, you do, dear," Lady Alice said. She picked little Comfit off her feet to stop him chewing at her slippers and placed the white bundle on her lap. "All women need men. It's hard for a woman to live without them."

"I'll not be second choice, Mother! You wouldn't!"

"You are *not* second choice, for God's sake!" Sir Henry glared at her, suddenly exasperated by wave after wave of refusals. "Stop punishing yourself! He didn't mention Emeline, not once. And even if that had been the case, you still owe it to us to treat this matter seriously. Offers of this kind are not all that thick on the ground, you know, even for eldest daughters. A fair face is one thing, but land and connections carry far more weight."

"And have you offered him a good deal, Father?" she asked, scathingly.

"No, lass. I haven't. If you really want to know, I made it as hard for him as I could. If he wants my eldest daughter, he can pay dear for her."

"What?"

"I'm not discussing the details until they're finished, but it will mean that, if he accepts them, he'll have proved that he really wants you."

"Beckington goes with you too, you know," Lady Alice offered.

Sir Henry nodded in agreement. "Aye, there's Beckington. That belongs to your mother's family and goes to who-ever marries first. But we've never needed it, have we, so no great loss. Just as long as that uncle of yours doesn't get his hands on it. There'd be nothing left of it in a couple of years."

Property. Connections. Bargains. She could listen to no more. "No!" she hissed.

"What?"

"No, Father. I can't...I'm sorry."

Sir Henry turned away impatiently. "Go to your chamber, lass. It's almost time for supper. We'll talk about it some more later. Go, now.''

Marietta made her courtesies and left, noting how Lady Alice moved into Sir Henry's open arms even before the door closed, laying her head upon his chest.

Sir Nicholas was passing the door of her solar as she approached, but he back-tracked and stood with his hand upon the latch, a slight smile behind his eyes. He was quick to notice the preoccupied expression and the angry flush on her olive-skinned cheeks.

Now, he thought, he was going to have to switch loyalties from Emeline to Marietta if he wanted to retain a chance to acquire Beckington and, after his mistake last night at supper, perhaps he'd better put things on a better footing without delay. He kept his hand on the latch. ''Is that a sigh of resignation or relief, Marietta?'' he asked.

She looked at him steadily, only half-remembering what had transpired last evening. ''Resignation if you keep your hand on the latch, Uncle. Relief if you open it for me.''

He quirked an eyebrow and lifted the latch.

''Thank you.''

Chapter Four

As Marietta had expected, Emeline was alone and every bit as confused as she was herself. Overcoming her first instinct to leave her half-sister alone and to give her a chance to come to terms with the surprise, Marietta could not face the prospect of supper in an atmosphere as close to sisterly rivalry as it was possible to get. She knocked on Emeline's door and entered, having no idea what to say to ease matters. But the mixture of contempt and blatant jealousy which crossed the pretty face as Marietta entered was something never before encountered.

To say that Marietta had instantly lost a friendship in the last few hours would have been stretching the truth, for they had never truly been close friends. Their paths had diverged too much for that: their needs were too different, their characters too dissimilar. Emeline had never possessed either the energy or the rashness to pick a quarrel merely for the excitement and Marietta was far too discriminating to quarrel without the possibility of a good fight.

Now, it seemed, Emeline was indeed in a belligerent mood as never before and Marietta, while seeming to have the advantage, saw herself to be the victim of duplicity, though she had never sought the role of victim or victor, nor did she condone the events that had caused it. Whilst having every sympathy with her sister's plight, Marietta was being obliged to take on the traitor's guise, knowing that Emeline would never believe the innocence she was about to protest and feeling that she wouldn't either, if the same had happened to her.

They sat, facing each other like two farm cats waiting for the other to make first move. Emeline had been weeping; her kirtle was damp down the front and wrinkled where she'd lain on it, sobbing. Her long fair hair was damp at the ends where she'd chewed it, a baby habit of which she'd never broken herself.

"Emmie," Marietta said, "did you quarrel with him?" She waited, thinking that Emeline was going to stay silent. "Please tell me. I'm as mystified and unhappy about this as you are. Did you quarrel?"

"Have you accepted him?" Emeline gulped, petulantly.

"No, of course not. Father says I have to talk with them again after supper. But I don't want to marry him. He was to be yours, not mine."

"Then why didn't he ask for me, I'd like to know?" She buried her face in her hands as the hot tears spilled over again, sobbing bitterly.

Marietta waited, then asked again, "Did you quarrel?"

"No, not once. I told you, he was charming."

"He didn't talk of marriage?"

"No, he wouldn't, would he? Not before he'd spoken to Father." There was a silence, except for Emeline's sniffs and sobs, neither of them knowing how to alleviate the pain. Then, little by little, the sobs were replaced by angry words, spilling out at random, of how Marietta had always spoiled her plans by her wayward behaviour, how she'd never known what to do with her own suitors but taken the only one she ever wanted, while Marietta sat, dejected and hurt by the abuse.

When the noise of supper preparations sounded from the great hall, Marietta preferred to go and pretend to eat rather than stay and listen to her sister's tirade. Sir Nicholas made a point of sitting next to her again and behaving so courteously that Marietta knew instinctively that something was up. It took little reasoning to tell her that this latest bout of gallantry had something to do with her changed prospects.

Once more in her parents' solar, the cresset-lamps were lit and the scent of beeswax filled the room as darkness fell early, for the sun had set behind a thick gathering of heavy clouds, and rain threatened. Lady Alice put on a display intended to suggest that all was normal by tugging sideways at one of the long tapestries on the wall to straighten it, and sweeping her hand down the wrinkles made during transit.

"You've spoken to Emeline?" Her hands still swept.

"Yes," Marietta said, watching. "She's angry with me."

"Have you quarrelled?" Lady Alice came to the table and took a sweetmeat from the dish, pushing it across to Sir Henry.

"No, Mother. But I don't know what to say to her that she'll believe. I told her it was not my wish."

Sir Henry pushed the dish back with one finger. "Then the sooner you're betrothed the better," he said. "It's high time you were married anyway, my lass. I said as much only the other day."

"Father! Were we not to have discussed this some more?"

"I've said all I can say about it. You know my feelings, and your mother's. Those are our wishes. And now, we have to talk about times. Lord Alain wants to have the betrothal ceremony tomorrow and I've already spoken to Father Gilbert. He'll—''

"No, Father…please, no!"

"Then it will take a little while before contracts are drawn up."

"Father…!"

"Meanwhile I'll see that you have a chance to get to know Lord Alain better."

Marietta sat down hard on a stool with her back to her parents, shaking her head in disbelief. He had said they could discuss some more and here he was, telling her what he'd decided.

Down there in the hall, the subject had been carefully avoided by the closest members of the household, the chaplain, confessor, Sir Nicholas, well aware from the set faces and Emeline's absence that dark clouds had gathered above their heads. They were far too well briefed in matters of this nature to take a happy outcome for granted until it was announced. So much could go wrong.

But up here, where they could talk freely, her father had taken the reins. "Marietta, come here to me." He held out an arm, beckoning.

Reluctantly, she went to him, knowing almost word for word what he would say: that he knew better than she did what was good for her, that this was an offer too good to refuse, that it was the best she'd ever get and that, anyway, he had an inkling she was not as averse to this man as she would have them believe.

That touched a raw nerve and her eyes lifted in an instant from a study of his pointed leather-clad toes to his face, wrinkled with wisdom.

"It's true, isn't it, lass?"

She dared not admit it. "He's Emeline's," she said, looking away.

"It was a mistake we all made. He had other ideas and decided to act quickly before it went any further in the wrong direction. It's you he's asked for, Marietta. You."

"She'll never forgive me, Father."

Sir Henry ignored that possibility. "Is there someone else, Marietta?"

"No," she whispered. "No, there's no one else." God knew, there had never been anyone she'd reacted to as she'd done with this man. He had been in her thoughts every waking moment since he'd picked her up off the ground. She had felt his hands on her and needed his touch more than she needed food. And yet, she was afraid. Desperately. He was fierce and large, and she had not been able to put him down and dismiss him the way she'd done with all the others, for he had refused to be dismissed.

He was a good tactician, a soldier, and she was no match for him. She had told him that her mother died in childbirth, but that had been a lie to give some credibility to her reasons for not marrying. It sounded impressive, dramatic, but it was not the truth. The truth was that she, Marietta, was a born manager, and to hand her own reins over to a stranger was unthinkable. Madness. She would not do it.

And yet, what had she done last evening? What bliss had she felt as he had taken control? Had that been so very terrible?

"Then I shall tell Lord Alain that his offer is accepted?" Sir Henry took her silence as assent.

Marietta made one last bid to Lady Alice. "Mother, I don't want this…please…tell him."

"Hush, dear…" Lady Alice's arms were feather-light "…you are taking the only course open to you. There's nothing new in that. We've all done it. Look at me, I was fifteen, but it didn't take me long to fall in love with Sir Henry. And Emeline will have a wonderful time once she gets over the shock. Stop worrying about her and think of your own happiness.

"This is a brilliant match, Marietta. I can't deny that I thought Emeline would attract his attention first because she's more at ease with men's attentions than you are, but you have a different kind of beauty that appeals more to some men. You should be flattered, dear."

She held Marietta away from her at arm's length and looked into the troubled eyes. "He's been widowed for two years, had the pick of the north and decided on you, of all people…" she caught Sir Henry's raised eyebrows and realised how clumsily she had phrased that "… I mean, he's chosen you out of so many other rich and beautiful ladies…" She wallowed deeper and deeper into verbal quicksands before Sir Henry came to the rescue.

"You have rare qualities, love. Qualities he's been searching for and not found in others."

"He told you that?"

"Yes, he told me that. He said he admired your courage and your beauty, your pride and intelligence."

"Beauty?" She looked puzzled at that. Dark hair was not fashionable. "What was his first wife like? Did you ever see her?"

"Yes, I saw her once when I went to discuss Bruno's future, several years ago." His eyes took on a distant look as he remembered that meeting. "She was a lovely creature. Fair, petite, gay and very vivacious."

"Like Emmie?"

"Yes, very much like…" He stopped abruptly. Too abruptly. Suddenly aware of her quietly spoken prompt, he amended his mental image. "No…not really…" But by that time, it was too late. The damage was done.

Like Emeline. Now we're getting to the truth, she thought, he had been looking for someone like his first wife, the one who'd died in the pestilence. Then he'd seen Emeline and fallen in love with her but decided he could not go through with it after all. So he'd grabbed at *her* as a way of escape, suspecting that she wanted him. He'd almost made her confess as much. Not second best, but third best.

Yes, he must have searched far and wide for two such ideal targets within one family; marry her so that he could keep Emeline in his sights, to remind him of the first one.

Hurt and angered by her new discovery, she reached blindly for her father. "Father, I..." she stammered.

"Yes, love?" He turned, thinking she was about to acquiesce.

"I bid you goodnight...Mother..." She kissed them both and went to her room, too full of distress to talk to her maids, even. And as the night engulfed her in its heavy cloak, she lay in its silence, unable to surface from beneath the black pall of anger and resentment until the first rays of light stole in from the east.

The two maids cowered against the wall of Sir Henry and Lady Alice's solar, hand in hand, searching their minds for a scrap of useful information which would calm their master's rising anger.

"I don't know when, Sir Henry...we...we were asleep...an' she must've slipped out...like a mouse...we didn't hear a thing, honest!"

"God's truth! You're supposed to hear whatever sound she makes. Haven't you understood that, yet? What's she wearing? Have you noted *that?*" Sir Henry knew in his bones that he should have put a guard across Marietta's door last night; this was just the kind of thing she would do. She'd done it once before, years ago, and stayed out all night. They'd had the whole village of Upperfell looking for her. But this was unknown territory. She could be any-where.

"She was wearing her green bliaud, sir," Anne said.

"And she took her brown fur-lined mantle, too," Ellie added, "and she must have been wearing the leather chausses she uses for riding, 'cos they're gone."

Lady Alice sat up in bed, obviously concerned. "If she's not here when Lord Alain arrives, Henry, what happens then? I might have known she'd lead us a merry dance, one way or the other." She swung her legs over the side and pulled her robe off the bed. "Have you checked the stables…the kitchen…the gateman?"

"No, Lady Alice."

"Then—"

"I'll see to that, Alice," Sir Henry barked. "Get Sir Nicholas in here, you two." The maids turned and fled. "He can make himself useful, for once. This is going to look good, isn't it? After all my efforts yesterday."

"She doesn't know this area, Henry. She can't have got far, surely?"

"She knows which direction Thorsgeld lies, and she's not going to head for there, is she? And look at it…" he pointed to the window where, only yesterday, the sun's rays had filtered in to light up the room "… black as pitch! There'll be mist on the tops. I'll thrash the lass when I get her back here. Of all the times to choose…"

Even Lady Alice tightened her lips and sent a look of exasperation in the direction of Sir Henry's back, meeting her maid's raised eyebrows in a complete exchange of un-derstanding. Trust a man to think that the timing had been Marietta's choice.

If Marietta had heard the last of her father's remarks, she would undoubtedly have agreed with him as she was compelled to dismount in order to see the track through the white wet mist that enclosed her. It had been barely light when she'd ridden out through the gates of Monksgrange, unchallenged by the sleeping gateman, though it was the cloud hanging low over the hillside that made it seem more like March than May.

She had intended to gallop at a steady pace, putting as much distance between herself and Monksgrange as she could in one day, even over country not familiar to her. But past the cornmill, the track dwindled to no more than a sheep-path alongside the beck, leading steeply upwards, diverging and criss-crossing until the beck went one way and the path went the other, and by that time the white cloud had rushed towards her to draw her into its embrace.

Dulzelina snorted and shook her head, but the mist clung on. "Come on, lass." Marietta said, cheerfully, "even this is better than staying there like cooped-up chickens. At least we're free. Come on."

She led the grey mare on, watching the path, stumbling now and then as it steepened and then followed another ridge or skirted around a boulder. The eerie bleating of sheep and lambs led her on until quite suddenly the path joined the side of a stony track that ran across the hillside instead of vertically up it and where the incline was far less steep. At last, there was something they could follow.

Tucking her green woollen bliaud into her belt, Marietta re-mounted and rode at a slow walk, following the track on and upwards, relieved to see unmistakeable signs of horse dung here and there, an indication that the track was used by travellers, still.

It was a strange sensation, to have no idea of what lay behind, ahead, or to the sides, to be shut off from the rest of the world, hidden from them completely, safe from their machinations. When words had no effect, actions might

convince them. They had neither listened to her nor tried
to understand her reasons; they had decided it between
them, apparently because none of them had expected her
to consent. Not at any stage, her father had pointed out.

But consent, she knew as well as anyone, was not a vital
ingredient, only co-operation, however reluctant. And if
they had been in any doubt before, she would make them
aware now that her reluctance was something more than
maidenly coyness. She would return when she was ready
and, beating or no beating, it would be worth it, just to
show them.

The track grew steeper and hoofbeats were muffled, but
even so, Marietta could sense that they were passing
through a narrow gorge, for the mists thinned in patches
and allowed her glimpses of dark, damp, moss-covered
rocks. She could hear water, too, splashing downwards as
though over ledges. The track was wet and slippery.

Then, ahead of her, the mist grew brighter and thinner,
the air freshened into a breeze and in a few more strides,
they were out of the mist and into the hazy sunshine, high
up above the clouds. Laughing, patting the mare's neck and
whooping with joy, Marietta eased the reins over and left
the track where it curved away round the hillside, veering
up onto the highest grassy bank where the sun's rays were
brightest and warmest.

Now, looking down, she knew something of the eagle's
power when it soared high above into the clear air. Before
her were banks of white fluffy lambswool, filling the val-
ley-bottoms almost to the peaks away in the distance.

She dismounted and stood, straining her eyes to pick out
any landmark she might recognise. A white block of light
appeared on the hillside, glinting in the sun. Thorsgeld Castle. Gleaming white limestone. High up on her level, its
wall-like white ribbon stretched out sideways, watching

her, reminding her so clearly of his words. "Bolt as far as you wish, but I shall find you and bring you back until you tire of the game."

"Hah!" she yelled, throwing her arms out wide. "Hah! I'm here! Look, I'm here! Do your worst, my good lord… Oh! Saints alive…no, Dulzelina…come back! Come *back!* Oh, for pity's sake…!" Frantically, she ran to the edges of the mist, peering into its thick shroud after the startled mare, cursing and yelling at it to come back here if it didn't want to be fed to the hounds.

But Dulzelina, with not a whit of sense or loyalty, had vanished along the grassy hilltop and down into the swirling whiteness, not even her hoofbeats telling of her possible whereabouts. Her joy and fury coming so hard on each other's heels, Marietta's emotions were all set to take another turn towards fright and sheer desperation combined with vexation at herself for her own forgetfulness.

The mare had always been skittish—Sir Henry called her the stupidest mare he'd ever come across—and vanity was the only reason why Marietta favoured her above the others, for she was very pretty, dapplegrey and charcoal-muzzled, long-tailed and fine-limbed, a delicate, empty-headed, easily frightened creature. What was even worse, she carried Marietta's hastily wrapped food in the saddle-bag, her leather water-bottle and a blanket. All that Marietta needed to survive for the day.

"Damn! Damn! Stupid creature!" she yelled. "Now what am I going to do?"

The only thing she could do until the mist cleared was to sit in the sun and wait. But though time passed and the sun reached its highest point, the mist remained and eventually obscured Thorsgeld Castle as it rose higher and higher. Lonely curlews fell silent, the few remaining sheep disappeared taking their lambs with them and Marietta was on the point of making a move towards where she thought the track should be when she froze, listening into the silence for the repetition of a sound.

At first, she thought the clink of stone on iron must be from Dulzelina's hooves and she was about to jump up and run towards it when a man's shout followed, then an answering call from further down, then a neigh and a long snort.

It was them, come to look for her. It must be them! She was lost, and horseless. Should she allow herself to be caught and taken back so soon? Wavering between safety and defeat she hesitated, watching the mist thicken with every passing moment, puzzled by the apparent frequency of the calls below her, the neighing and answering snorts, far more men and horses than she would have thought necessary.

Travellers, she thought, keeping contact in the mist by calling to each other, not a search-party but travellers on the track over the hills. If she had heard women's voices, too, she would have run down to join them, gone along with them to the next town. But she heard only men, coarse and rough, not a crowd she'd want to ask for protection. They passed, and silence returned.

With the sounds went also the light and Marietta realised how, when there was nothing to see or hear, her hunger became more acute. Cursing the mare again, and threatening her with banishment, at least, she moved carefully downwards through the thickening mist towards the track. It had disappeared. Try as she might to find it, it could have been a hundred miles away instead of a few yards.

A sheer rock-face appeared before her at barely an arm's length, and a rocky floor instead of turf, and further on, where the mists parted, she found herself in the large gaping entrance to a cave, with a fresh pile of horse dung at her feet. It was then that she realised where she was: in one of the caves she'd seen from the village below when the bailiff had told them that demons lived here, that no one ever came here. Well, she thought, he was wrong on both counts. No demons, and travellers aplenty.

Here at least was shelter from the wetting mists that had already dampened her hair and mantle. Here, she would wait out the rest of the day, and the night too, and hope that she would be able to see clearly on the morrow. It would be foolhardy to venture down over the cliffs that she knew to be there.

Here also, she had time enough to think and balance the pros and cons of marrying Lord Alain of Thorsgeld, of being mistress of her own household, of forgetting the griefs and woes of Emeline and Lady Alice, of pleasing her father. She would be near Bruno too. He would love that.

It was not until sounds of approaching hoofbeats broke the utter stillness that Marietta realised how her place of safety could also be a place of no escape, for if anyone were to find her here, she would have a hard task to get out. The travellers who used this route might be glad to find a woman, alone.

She shrank against the cold stone and waited for them to pass, but to her astonishment, it was Dulzelina who appeared at the entrance to the cave and Marietta's soft cry of delight was in direct contrast to her earlier threats of the knacker's yard.

"Dulzelina...come! Oh, you've come back!" She slipped down from the shelf of rock and ran to the mare, throwing her arms around the cold damp neck and holding onto the bridle with a firm grasp. "Where's that food, girl? And my blanket..." She groped for the saddle-bag, laughing with relief.

"Looking for something, demoiselle?" a voice spoke from the entrance.

"Oh!" Marietta yelped with fright and whirled round, clasping at her chest and feeling her heart leap beneath her hand.

Lord Alain led his great bay stallion into the cave, almost blocking out the last remaining light and leaving her no room to move away. "I'll say this for you, lass, you and this mare of yours spend a lot of time bolting off together and then parting company, don't you? If I were you, I'd find a more reliable nag than this."

"You!" was all Marietta could say. Her eyes searched beyond him.

"There's nobody else here. Only me. I told you I'd find you. Didn't you believe that, either?"

With the mare's bridle in her hand, she felt almost bold again. "You were not supposed to find me, my lord. I'm not going to marry you."

She felt him smiling in the dim light as he began to unbuckle his saddle-bags and to loosen the stallion's girth. "Did you particularly want to discuss that now, or shall we leave it until we've eaten?" he said, amiably. "Loosen your mare's girths and let's get that saddle off her."

"Why take it off? Surely we can go back the way you came, can't we? It's not quite dark."

He heaved the saddle off the bay and laid it over a boulder, then took the reins and pulled them over its head. "Yes, tomorrow," he said, tying them to Dulzelina's.

Marietta placed a hand on his arm to stop him. "Tomorrow? No, now…if you please. I can't stay here all night with *you!*"

Facing her, he placed his hands on his hips, making himself appear even larger than he did already. "Where were *you* planning to stay, Marietta?"

"Here. *Alone!*" she snapped.

"Well then, demoiselle—" he touched her nose with his knuckle "—you'd better get used to spending your nights with me, because that's where you'll be in the future. Now…" he turned back to Dulzelina "… are you going to get this saddle off and give the mare a rest?"

"No."

"Very well. I take it you'll say no to food as well. Am I right?"

"No."

"Then do it, or you get not a crumb."

"I'll do it for Dulzelina's sake, not because I care…" Her about-face was cut short by his large frame nudging her out of the way, accepting her token gesture of obedience.

"Here, I'll lift it off. Now, unpack that food while I take these two out for water." He took their bridles to lead them away.

"Are you going to tether them out all night? There are travellers along this road who might take them."

His laugh was no more than a grunt. "At night? In a thick mist? Surely not?"

"Yes, in a mist. I heard them late this afternoon coming up the fell when I was on top of the hill."

Lord Alain stopped, his face serious with frowns. "You heard them? Did you see them?"

"No. I've told you. They were below me in the mist but there were a good few of them with horses. They passed along the track."

"Did they see you? These travellers with horses?"

"No, I took care not to be seen. You can tell by the droppings that plenty of them come past here. Look, there's some by your foot."

He nodded. "Yes, I noticed. Stay here, Marietta. I'll wa-

ter them and bring them back in for the night. Look in my
saddle-bags, too.''

He must have known that she'd not make a run for it,
not even bothering to remind her, but setting her to look
for food instead. It was, she thought, the most unexpected
turn of events, though whether this was better than being
found by her father's men, or worse, she was not so sure.

Certainly he was bent on making her obey him and that
was something about which he'd better be put straight, for
she obeyed only her father, and even then there were lapses.
As for his talk about spending her nights with him, perhaps
she'd better make that position clear, too. She had no intention of doing any such thing.

There were oatcakes and cheese, pieces of spiced
chicken, bread rolls and apples all hastily scavenged from
the kitchen. There was her water-bottle and, in his bag, a
huge wedge of venison in pastry and a leather bottle of ale
and one of mead. A feast. By the time he returned with the
horses, their muzzles dripping, Marietta was seated cross-
legged on a ledge of rock looking at the spread with nose
twitching and mouth watering. She was ravenous, glad that
he allowed her to eat in silence without questioning her.

It was she who asked the first question. ''How did you
find me?''

''A hunch,'' he said, briefly.

The light had almost faded now, and she could scarcely
see his eyes but knew that he watched her, for all that.

''I found your mare, so I sent my grooms back to Monksgrange to tell your father I had you safe.''

''Had me safe…? How could you possibly—?''

''Marietta, if you would stop always losing your temper
and *think*,' he barked, ''you'd work it out for yourself.''
She was silent. ''The mare had obviously not fallen. I could
see that. She's the daftest animal I've ever encountered, so

the likeliest explanation was that she shied and bolted *again!*' he emphasised. ''And with your food on board. So you were not likely to have gone far without it, were you? Particularly in this mist and on unfamiliar ground.''

''Do *you* know this land, then?''

''Course I know it. It borders on mine. It's your father's land.''

''They told us these caves had demons in, that nobody ever came near. They must have been kidding…''

''Who? Who told you that?''

''The Monksgrange bailiff. I don't know his name.''

''Village nonsense,'' Lord Alain said, dismissively. ''Take no notice.''

''I didn't. I wouldn't have been prepared to stay here, otherwise.''

''Alone.'' He handed her a piece of cheese on the point of his knife.

''Yes, my lord. Alone. Thank you. You went to Monksgrange, this morning?''

''As you knew I would.''

She looked away towards the open cave mouth. The horses stood to one side, resting contentedly together.

Lord Alain noted her glance. ''What did your father and mother say to you yesterday to make you bolt again?'' he asked in a quiet voice. He took a crunch at an apple, and she thought his question sounded more like an enquiry after her health.

''It was not so much what *they* said as what *you* said.''

''That made you run? I thought you had courage.''

''Not courage enough to spend the rest of my life with you, my lord.''

He took another bite and spoke with his mouth full. ''Nevertheless, demoiselle, that is what you will do. With or without courage.''

"No, I think not."

He continued, ignoring her retort, "I'm surprised. I thought I'd made it clear to you in the arbour the day after your fall. I could have sworn you heard."

"I *did* hear. And I was sure that you jested. I told you as much."

"I never jest about such things. I explained that to you the other night in the arbour. You should have believed me, Marietta, it would have saved you a whole day."

"You were wooing Emeline. You cannot deny that," she said sharply.

"I can and do deny it! And if she thought I was, that's because she wanted to believe it. I came to see you, but you evaded me. Now I've caught you and it's no good thinking that I'll take pity on you and let you go, because I won't. It's time somebody took you in hand, lass."

"And you're the one to do it, I suppose?"

"You've understood that, at least."

"I do not want to be taken in hand, as you put it."

"You responded to my hand very well, I seem to remember."

The man, she thought, was goading her, damn him. And how ungallant to remind her of a time when she'd had more to drink than she was used to. During the day, she'd had plenty of time to reflect on her future and had even come close to thinking there might be just a few advantages in the arrangement, but his arrogance astounded her, his nearness made her uncomfortable. She looked around her. The cave was quite large, she knew, but now, all was black except for the entrance.

"It's no good looking, lass, I know what you're thinking, but you can forget it. I shall take you home tomorrow morning and there'll be a formal betrothal ceremony, just one day later than planned."

"No!" Her voice echoed loudly inside the cave.

"Good. You can do all the shouting and yelling you like in here. Here, take a gulp of your water." He passed her the bottle.

She took a deep swig and coughed as it stung her throat. "Argh! That was mead, not water…!"

"Ah, then this must be the one…here." He took a drink and passed it to her. "Now, before it gets too dark to see what we're about…"

While she watched, sullenly, seething with resentment, he cleared away the remains of their meal, spread Marietta's blanket on the large flat shelf of rock and laid his own great cloak over it. Then he came to sit by her side, between her and the horses.

She felt his coolness, the male smell of leather, the brief warmth of his breath as he leaned his head to hers and took her hand. If only that was all there was to it, just his nearness, his arms, the warmth of him, she thought. She could bear that. But she would not be managed.

"We can talk now, Marietta. There's no one to hear or interrupt. You can tell me what it is you fear, what your objections are."

How could she voice them? "You don't realise…do you?" she faltered.

"What is it that I don't realise?"

"What a position you've put me in. I did my best to oblige my mother and Emeline, and I thought I was pleasing my father, too."

"By keeping out of my way, you mean?"

"Yes. Lady Alice had decided, long before I had a chance to—"

"To say what *you* wanted?"

"Yes," she whispered, aware of how immodest that must sound. "I heard them discussing it while they thought

I was asleep and Lady Alice said then that she wanted you to woo Emeline. So when you did—"

"I didn't. I told you."

"I can't believe that, my lord." The words slipped out, inadvertently, but Lord Alain did not take offence.

"Can you not believe, Marietta, knowing what you've been able to discover about me so far, that I am perfectly capable of making my own mind up without help from anyone?"

She could believe it, of course, but what of the reasons for his choice? What of his first wife and her likeness to Emeline? Pure coincidence? She wanted to believe it, God knew she did, but could she? She kept silent.

"Am I right in thinking, Marietta, that you are used to fighting off all suitors, whoever they are?"

That was something she could not deny. "Yes," she whispered.

"So you would have hidden, run, evaded me, even if Lady Alice had *not* planned to pass you over. That's true, isn't it?"

"Yes, I would!" The whisper was more rebellious now.

"Why? You told me you feared to die your mother's death, Marietta."

"Yes, she—"

"She died in a riding accident while she was carrying your brother, did she not? And your brother was delivered after her death, not as you told me."

"You knew!" She leapt away, angry and ashamed that her major excuse had been exposed. It had been a perfect pretext. Now she could hide behind it no longer. "Who told you? My father?"

Lord Alain kept hold of her and pulled her back to his side, placing his arms around her like a cage.

"Yes, your father. And now I begin to understand why

you're so determined not to be caught. Not because you fear childbirth or that you care so much about Emeline's chances, or that you want to please your parents by staying in the background.

"Nor is it because you think I'm one of the usual weak-kneed youths who've tried their luck in the past. It's because the more they go on about it, the more you'll show them you don't care, isn't it? The more they put you to the gate, the more you'll refuse, just to show them who's in control. That kind of courage borders on pig-headedness, Marietta, because that way you'll get hurt when you find you want to jump and your pride won't let you."

"You're talking as though I were a horse!" she said, severely.

He smiled. "When we're married, you'll discover the reason for that."

"I don't want…no…put me down! Put me *down!*"

"Yes, that's what I am doing…here…right here." He lowered her down onto the blanket and cloak and unclasped her mantle with nimble fingers before she could tell what was happening.

It was dark and impossible to do more than push at his shoulders, but they were wide and powerful and she was scooped up against his warm body, held close in his arms with her head tucked beneath his chin and there was no escape, for a wall of rock was at her back. Before she could gather a new surge of energy, his mouth was against the bridge of her nose.

"Now, demoiselle, you've already discovered how good it feels when you let *me* take control, haven't you? Eh?"

"That was unfair…I'd had too much wine."

"Not unfair…no…a good way to break the ice, but not for every time. This time, a mouthful of mead is all you get. Come," he whispered, "show me the impulsive woman I had in my arms last time. Show me again."

She felt at his face with fingers and lips because she could not see him and when she reached his mouth, her hand slid around his neck into his thick hair, drawing him to her. "Why?" she murmured. "Why couldn't you leave me be? I don't want to go back with you. I don't want to be betrothed."

"Too late…" he played with her lips "…too late. Your father and I have settled it. It's agreed. You're mine."

"Then go and marry my father!"

"It's not your father I want in my bed, but you. I want you by my side, to be mistress of my household. I want you to bear my sons. You're mine, Marietta, mine."

Punctuated by kisses, their whispered conversation was both savage and rebellious, spurring Marietta on to test his resolve and provoke him to fierce declarations of possession. His blatant determination to make her his roused her as nothing else could have done. No soft words or sweet sighs, few compliments except to say that she had fire, and beauty, and a remoteness that sent men wild.

But, he said, she'd better recognise her master now for he would have her, willing or no. And so they fought a verbal duel while surrendering to each other's arms and lips, closed in by the darkness and undisturbed by the proximity of any but the horses. Here, they could make as much noise as they liked.

No honeyed endearments passed their lips, only "my lord' and "my lady" or "lass" and "brute", for he recognised that *that* set her apart from her half-sister more clearly than the soft pleadings Emeline would no doubt have preferred. New to lovemaking she may have been, but Marietta was eager and warm, and when "my lord" pushed the bliaud over her shoulders to seek the softness of her skin, she did not complain of the cold but pulled his chainse out of his braies so that she could warm her hands on his back.

"Hell, woman, you learn fast how to keep a man awake. I've a mind to keep you awake a bit longer."

"You can tell my father you've changed your mind because the woman keeps you awake with cold hands, and I'll tell him you pester me."

"In that case, my lady, I'm going to pester you some more and make sure you get the story straight, because tomorrow *you*'re going to tell him that you're mine. Understand? Now, what's all this...?" His hand passed over the leather chausses she wore beneath her bliaud to protect her legs when she rode.

"My chausses...for riding in. And I'm not going to—"

"Take them off!"

"What?"

"Take them off. I want what's inside there."

"No, you can't...please..." She pushed his hand away. "I cannot allow it...please, don't ask me..."

"I'm not asking you. Listen to me. I know you're playing for time when you say you won't accept me, but you know that I mean to have you and that the consummation makes our betrothal legally binding."

"*Afterwards,* my lord. Not before. Afterwards."

"We'll do it the other way round, my lady. I'm not taking the risk. This is to bind you to me." The fierce words were spoken gently into her ear, caressing her cheek with his lips. "I'll be careful...I know it's new to you...we'll go slowly, I promise...don't fear me."

She *was* fearful, and excited, and curious, and she knew that, in spite of her words of rejection, she would have him and he would have her. So she allowed him to draw the leather chausses off her legs and then she helped him off with his, and one by one their garments were placed behind

her head as a warm pillow until they lay with only a cloak
to cover them.

He kept his promise to go slowly, and skilfully his hands
enticed her body to soften and bend to his touch while she
came alive with a growing fire and moaned at him to do
it, whatever it was he was bent on doing. She had expected
that it might hurt, the first time, but he was tenderly careful
and the expectation of pain was forgotten beneath his kisses
and words.

He moved upon her, claiming her at last as he'd wanted
to do since the day he had lifted her into his arms. For him,
it was victory, sweet conquest, the beginning of his new
life. For her, it was the tenderest submission and the end
of her maidenhood. The fierce words were left behind now;
this was too rare a moment to play down with ambiguities
so easily misunderstood at the moment of receiving. Such
a gift must be treasured at the first giving.

Marietta revelled in his loving words as much as in his
fierce ones, savouring the strong urges of his body, knowing that her yearnings and conflicts had met and come to
terms. She had never wanted loving from any man except
this one; her tears were of joy, not of pain.

"Tears, sweetheart? Not tears? Did I…?"

"No, Alain, no, you didn't hurt. I'm not crying…"

"It will be better next time, I promise."

She smiled and smoothed his cheek, wondering at the
size of him compared to herself, his ears, his handsome
head, the thickness of his great arms. "My tears are for
what I've gained, I think, not for what I've lost. I didn't
know I could feel such elation…but now…"

"Now? Now you think I'll expect you to change? To be
submissive? Is that it?"

"Yes." The word was no more than a breath on his
throat.

She felt his smile and the heave of his chest beneath her hand.

"It may help to stop you bolting, sweetheart, but I don't have any high hopes that you'll suddenly become meek and mild. Stay as you are, my beauty. I want you to stay just as you are. We'll fight and make love in a hundred different ways and we'll stay together and make fierce sons and wild daughters, shall we?"

That was enough to make her laugh, wondering how she would react to the idea that any daughter—or son—of hers would make love for the first time in a mist-bound cave before the day of their betrothal.

"You like that idea, do you? Good. Then sleep in my arms, woman, and rest now. You've had quite a day, even for one such as you. And I need to regain my wind, ready for the next bout." He smiled in the darkness.

Marietta lifted her head. "What next bout?"

His arm tightened about her and he pulled her hips closer in to his body, tucking the cloak around her shoulders. "I've got you to myself for the whole of the night, and I'm not going to waste it all in sleep," he said.

Chapter Five

Sounds of young men's laughter, shouts, and the neighing of a horse broke into the more restful thud and clink of gardeners' spades in the soil, causing Marietta to turn to Old Adam with a puzzled expression. He was one of the few people whose names she was sure of in this great place.

"Tiltyard, m'lady," he said, nodding towards the end of the garden and shoving his spade deep into the ground to rest on its handle. "It's young squires over in't tiltyard practising wi' their lances. Have you not been to see, yet?"

"No, Adam. Not yet." In just two days, she'd had no time to see much of Thorsgeld Castle for there'd been so many other things to claim her attention. A day seeing to the garden held the promise of some peace and a space in which to think, though this was not quite what she'd been expecting when Lord Alain had told her that there was a pleasance. It resembled a wilderness more than a lady's bower. "Has no one tended this ground in the last two years, Adam?" she asked.

"Nay, m'lady. Nobody tended it much before then, either. T'other Lady Thorsgeld warn't that interested in gardens. She 'awked and she 'unted but she didn't do much in 'ere." He carried on with his digging, heaving the sods to one side and loosening the weeds so that the two lads could pull them out.

"What about the herbs, then? Didn't she grow simples anywhere?"

Adam stood up again and shook his white head. His skin was like brown, crinkled leather, his grin punctuated by four yellow teeth.

"Nay," he said again. "She had nothing to do with all that. She let cook grow pot-herbs round by the kitchen. Come on, I'll show thee."

Deciding that it was easier to show her than to explain, Adam led Marietta up an overgrown path and through the wicket-gate that hung to the broken fence by one hinge.

She had seen the top of the dovecote already but now she saw the rest of it, piled high with droppings and old feathers in the angle of the castle wall. Ahead of them were the stew-ponds where fish were kept for the table. They were dirty and littered with last year's dead leaves and weed. All of these plots lay between the western wall of the castle and the high stone wall that she had seen from her father's land across the valley.

Through the next hedge, wild and terribly overgrown, they rounded the corner of the castle wall where, on its north side, a long narrow strip of garden was given over to culinary herbs, for along here were the kitchens. It was better tended, but here were no simples for medicines, nothing for the relief of an ache or to salve a wound.

Old Adam pointed. "Along 'ere, this is the only bit that's kept straight. An' that over there—" he pointed to the high wall that ran parallel to the castle "—that's the tiltyard where young Master Bruno is learning 'is tricks. Shall we 'ave a look?" he ventured.

A gateway led into the tiltyard from the field where the shooting butts were ranged, a large open space of dry earth where years of hooves and feet had worn tracks beneath the quintain and where a dozen or so young men practised their horsemanship by riding bareback with one hand on the reins. The horses were very large and not inclined to co-operate and one lad with blood streaming from his face was being yelled at by the mounted knight to get back on his bloody horse and be quick about it. Marietta backed away from the gateway, anxious not to interrupt, but Bruno had spotted her from one corner where he was practising with sword and shield and sidled away while the knight's back was turned.

"Marrie! Wait!" he hissed, slipping through the gate after her.

"Bruno! Don't, you'll get into trouble. Go back, love."

"It's all right. We haven't had a chance to talk since you came. Are you all right, love?"

His face was running with sweat, his tunic black-patched and sticking to his body. There was a new bruise on his cheek, but his eyes were gleaming with enjoyment. She noticed that the sword he held was almost as long as he. "Yes, I'm looking at the gardens. Adam's started to dig it over but it's in a dreadful state, like a lot of other things around here."

"It needs your hand on it, Marrie. He's been without a lady for two years now and it shows, doesn't it? Little things, eh?" Even in a male domain, the hand of a woman was appreciated. "Is he being kind to you, Marrie?"

"Oh yes…yes, he is, love. But I haven't seen much of him, except after supper. I expect he's busy at this time of the year."

She had indeed seen much of him at night, for their few hours together in the cave almost a month ago had been in total darkness and he had been as eager to see her naked as she had been to see him. He had been kind, though not perhaps in a way that many new brides would have found to their taste.

She smiled, thinking of their turbulent lovemaking when her feigned reluctance had been once more overcome by his persistence, a game in which rules were made and broken simultaneously. He *had* been kind, recognising her strong will and matching it without arousing her resentment, making his firm hand feel more like protection than tyranny. He had not allowed her to regret her capitulation. Yes, in that he had been kind.

"Well, I'm glad he's kind to somebody." Bruno laughed. "It's more than he is to us, I can tell you. He's fearsome if you step out of line."

"Have you been in trouble, love?"

"Oh not specially. Course, they all want to have a go at me, now they know you're my sister, just to see if I can take it without squealing."

The concern in her voice showed. "And can you?"

"Can I? I love it!" He laughed merrily. "I can beat the lot of 'em. The more I get chance to prove it, the more they'll respect me. I'll make you proud of me, Marrie. You'll see."

"I'll watch for you, love. Take care, do. Go now, before they come looking. Hurry…!"

With a quick grin, he blew her a kiss and was gone.

From the field where the shooting butts stood, Marietta could look up at the high walls of Thorsgeld Castle and be as impressed all over again as she had at her first sight of it. It was an immense square stone building of four towers, built around a courtyard; not a castle built primarily to defend the king's land but more of a fortified manor house on a scale large enough to withstand a raid from the Scots, or a siege. Set on the very edge of a wooded cliff, the views from the western upper rooms were superb.

Managing a place like this was going to take all the skills she'd ever learned, and then some more. For one thing, this was a far more male-dominated household than she'd been used to; apart from the dairy and laundry maids and her own personal women, all the other occupants were men and boys. Married men at the castle kept their wives at home in the town of Thorsgeld, where conditions were more suited to family life.

Since the quiet wedding two days ago, she had kept well out of the way, pretending to be too busy to go anywhere with him, holding herself back and nourishing her resentment at the coercion they'd all applied. It was sheer pigheadedness, as Lord Alain had warned her, and served only to exacerbate her feelings of isolation and strangeness.

Secretly, she longed for the night and the strength of his arms where she could find solace in this great fortress where the walls rose to five storeys above her. Secretly, she longed for his arms at any time, day or night.

The sun streamed onto that side of the castle, catching the fly-covered surface of the stew-pond and making it glisten like satin. Marietta looked again at the filthy dovecote; this place could be made so very pretty, but it would need an army. She leaned into an angle of the warm wall and closed her eyes, holding her face to the sun, absorbing its kindness, undisturbed by the sound of the rickety gate being moved aside. Old Adam with his wheelbarrow, she thought.

"Time's up!"

She opened her eyes with a start, unused to having her thoughts materialise so promptly.

Lord Alain stood before her with hands on hips, his eyes watchful and serious. "Time's up, sweetheart. Come on, now. You've been too busy to keep me company for long enough. You've made your point and I've understood. Now you can be seen with me without losing face, proud lass."

His quiet words unnerved her far more than bawling at her would have done, speaking her thoughts so accurately that she wondered if she'd voiced them out loud.

There was no need for her to deny or accept his assessment of the situation, for his arms were held out to her and she walked into them and stood quietly, feeling his hands smooth over her back from shoulder to buttock, his mouth on her forehead.

"That pride of yours is going to cause a nasty fall one of these days, my lass," he whispered. "When are you going to let it go? Is it only in bed you lose it…in the dark…where it can't find a hold? Am I going to have to knead it out of you in the daytime, too? Eh?"

Her reaction to his graphic words was immediate, coinciding exactly with his move to hold her into the wall and kiss her. She raised her arms and linked them around his neck, greedily taking his lips and the close male warmth of his skin on her face. Here, she could close her eyes to the unwanted challenge of overgrown surroundings and imagine that she was elsewhere, with only sensations and desires to attend to.

"Come on, then," he said, looking down at her. "Shall we share the rest of the day with each other?"

"Yes," she replied.

"Good. So, is there something you want to show me?"

Now was her chance. She could not let it go. Taking his offered hand she led him towards the stew-pond, a very large one on three levels in a desolate area of long grass and weeds. "Look," she said, "this could provide quantities of fish for your tables—"

"*Our* tables," he corrected her.

"Our tables. But the channels and pipes are silted up and it needs men to repair and restock it. In fact…" she pulled his hand round to turn him "…the whole place needs an army of men. It needs cutting and re-seeding, the walls whitewashed, the hedge and gate repaired and the dovecote…look at that!'' She pointed to the rotten wooden structure. ''That needs replacing. We need a stone dovecote so that the men can get at the manure, and the eggs, and the pigeons.''

''I only use them to feed the falcons,'' he said.

''Well, we should be eating them,'' she told him. ''This is a terrible waste; it could be such a lovely place. I could grow ferns round there and have water flowing in channels. I could make a paradise, like the ones they have in monasteries.''

''Queen Phillipa has a paradise in Winchester, I believe.''

''But I need men, my lord. It will take weeks of work.'' She led him through the fallen wicket-gate into what should have been a lady's private garden, a pleasance, but which now showed only the recent efforts of Old Adam and two lads. ''Look at this place, there should be herb-gardens here where I can grow my simples, and an arbour, perhaps. Do you think so?''

It was an L-shaped plot, taking in the corner of the southwest tower and now bathed in sunshine, sheltered by the high walls but with a view through the battlements out across the valley. A paradise indeed, but sadly neglected.

Lord Alain was almost glad that it was in this state for it would give her a new objective and soften the sting of her hasty removal from Monksgrange. Keeping hold of her hand, he entered fully into her enthusiasm.

''Over there—'' he pointed to the wall ''—that's where an arbour should go, so that you can sit on a raised bench inside, out of the heat, and look through the leaves and the crenels of the wall over towards Monksgrange. Do you see that tiny black spot on the fell there? Do you see it?''

"Yes," she yelped. "Yes, I can see the cave. That's it, isn't it?"

"Yes, lass..." he lowered her down, allowing his hands to linger purposely over her breasts "...that's where we spent our first night together. There, in that cave. In the mist. One month ago." He held her, laughing at her blushes. "How many times did I have you before I took you back to your father? Enough to make you change your mind?"

"That was a totally unscrupulous deed, my lord!" Marietta feigned anger and pushed at his chest, quite ineffectually.

"Hah! Unscrupulous, my foot!" he laughed. "You went into the cave, shooed your stupid horse away and waited for me. You know you did. You knew I'd come looking for you...you knew what I'd do...!"

"Oh, you ungodly oaf! How *can* you think that? I was a maiden...an innocent maiden, and you seduced me intentionally."

"Aye, that I did, wench. Rest easy...don't be angry. It was the perfect chance...I had to make sure of you." Hungrily, he sought her lips again, oblivious to Old Adam who came and went with silent tread. "Have you forgiven me for taking advantage of you?" he whispered.

Marietta prolonged the act of absolution. "It will cost you a garden, my lord, at least."

"A garden, two, three, a dozen gardens, sweetheart," he promised. "I'll set men to it tomorrow morning, as many as you need. We'll have new hedges, little fences, herbplots, an arbour, whatever you wish shall be done. And we'll have a new dovecote made and paths laid, and clean well-stocked fish-ponds. And then, you'll forgive me, will you?"

She smiled at his boyish eagerness. "Yes, my lord. Then I will forgive you."

Hand in hand, they walked on through the orchard, discussing how that, too, could be tidied and the bee-skeps attended to, then back through the gardens, seeing it all in their imaginations as a place of sanctuary, pretty with roses, honeysuckle and ivy, trim with box-hedges and lavender clumps, scented with blossom and heavy with bees and butterflies.

Marietta had seen no further than this; what lay on the rest of the southern side she had yet to discover. She had not realised that the stables on the ground floor of the castle were only for their immediate purposes, neither had she fully understood that when Bruno had told her that Lord Alain bred horses, he meant it on a scale like this.

Through heavy and high wooden gates, a huge courtyard opened up opposite the orchard, with a long stone-built stable block along one side. Storehouses, a well, water troughs and a mews ranged around the high wall and elegant heads of expensive palfreys and destriers arched over stable-doors, whinnying their greetings as Lord Alain entered. Immediately, a small wiry man came to meet them, bowing courteously.

"Greetings, Seth." Lord Alain explained, "Seth is my Horse Master, and he agrees with me that that grey mare of yours is as daft as a brush and should be used for breeding. So, if you can bear to part with her, we've found something more suitable."

Seth grinned at her. He could not be old, she thought, for his body was lean and muscles rippled over his bare arms, his face well-used looking, like a walnut, almost. "I think you'll like this'un better, my lady. Well-mannered, she is. A beauty." He called to a groom crossing the yard. "Bring the grey out, Ned."

It would have been an understatement to say that Marietta was surprised at this; it was a part of Lord Alain's business affairs of which he'd said nothing to her.

He saw her amazement. "These are only a few," he said, indicating the row of curious heads and the occasional crash of a hoof against a door. "Mostly stallions we're using. There are ten mares and foals in the paddock over there, and another ten further on…" he nodded towards a field beyond the orchard "…then some more on the other side."

"I had no idea. Do you breed *and* sell them, my lord?"

"Yes, men will always want destriers and there's nobody around these parts who breeds them, except me. Palfreys, too, for ladies. We have a stud of about twenty mares and four stallions and then we have young stallions that we train as war-horses. Ah, here's your new mare, Marietta. Come and meet her."

The young groom led the mare out, watching her legs move at his side in a quick tap-tap, the lovely dark muzzle almost touching her knees as they high-stepped towards the group. She was, as Seth had said, a beauty, larger than Dulzelina, pure white except for her amazingly luxuriant dark mane and tail that rippled in pronounced waves as though they'd been crimped.

Marietta's long "Ooh!" was as much as she could say at that moment, quite overcome by the mare's exceptional beauty and by the revelation that her new husband was not the leisured aristocrat she had thought him to be but a man of business, a breeder of war-horses, fabulously costly animals, specially trained for knights in battle. Now she understood his reputation as an expert at jousting; he must have won a fair number of stallions from his opponents.

"She's a Spanish horse," Lord Alain told her, stroking the mare's soft velvet muzzle and collecting her forelock in his hand. It came well over her dark eyes and was as silky as a woman's hair. "From Andalucia. You like her?"

"She's superb," Marietta breathed, "simply superb. Is she fast, my lord?"

"No, Spanish horses are not known for their speed but for their high showy action and their great strength and good manners. She's quite a fiery piece, but good mannered, and obedient." He glanced at her wickedly, his eyes dancing with hidden meaning. "And she has the most amazing canter. Did you ever ride a rocking horse, Marietta?"

"Yes, I had one when I was tiny, until Bruno broke it."

"Well, riding this at a canter is like that, only faster. You'll see; we'll take her out tomorrow, shall we?"

"Yes, oh yes, can we...tomorrow?" She fondled the muzzle and ran a hand over the neck and ears. "Thank you, my lord. She's the most beautiful thing. How old? What's her name?"

"Five years old. She's had one foal, a filly. And we have a stable name for her, but she's yours now, sweetheart. You can name her yourself."

Impishly, Marietta slipped a hand into his. "What about Mist?" she said, peeping up at him.

He took her hand and kissed the knuckles, sharing her mischief. "I think, m'lady, that Mist would be a perfect name, in the circumstances."

They watched the mare trot around the courtyard, lifting her knees daintily and arching her beautiful neck, the long mane and tail flowing like silken veils. In their boxes, the stallions pricked up their ears and whinnied to her, flaring their nostrils, asking for their fair share of the attention, and Marietta was introduced to them, one by one.

It was then that many of Lord Alain's previous remarks began to fall into place, his teasing about her bolting, her refusal to jump to anyone's command, her riding for a fall. As a breeder of horses, he was bound to think along those lines, she supposed, watching the way he handled the great creatures so assuredly, and she was unable to suppress a shiver of excitement at the thought of the night to come when, he'd whispered to her, she'd be able to thank him more profoundly.

Marietta's own private solar was in the southwest tower, overlooking the very garden she intended to restore. It was a large whitewashed room with a stone fireplace and high timber ceiling and windows on two sides. Tapestries lined the walls, filling the room with colourful people and galloping horses, stags, hounds, even rabbits, a scene depicting, by all accounts, the previous Lady Thorsgeld's favourite pastime, hunting. She asked Lord Alain about it after supper, but he was not eager to discuss his first wife.

"Yes," he said, drawing Marietta down beside him on the deep cushioned window-seat, "there's a deer-park that stretches northwards from here; some very good hunting country. Does Sir Henry hunt much?"

"He loves it," she replied, putting her feet up on the cushions and leaning back against his chest, "but we're not too familiar with this area yet."

"What about Beckington Manor, then, sweetheart? Your new property—it borders on my demesne between here and Monksgrange. Have you never seen it? You ought to, you know."

"No, I've never even thought about it until recently. I think Father was quite content to have the rents from it each Michaelmas and leave it at that. Apart from being determined not to let Sir Nicholas get hold of it."

"Sir Nicholas Bannon? How could he get hold of it? I thought it passed down the female line."

"It does, but Father said that, if he got hold of it, there'd be nothing left of it in two years."

"Well," he kissed her neck, "that's very interesting, but I fail to see how he could get near it, unless he married one of you. And he's too late to do that, isn't he, lass?" His arm was firmly across her ribs.

"Silly. Uncles and nieces don't marry."

"He was coming on very strong with you in the passageway that evening, though, wasn't he? Had he tried it on with you before?"

"No," Marietta turned her head to him, piling on the scorn, "of course not with *me*. It's always been Emeline he had an eye for."

"You mean, Emeline and he are…?"

"No! Heavens above, no. Not that. But she's always done whatever he told her, ever since she was a child."

"Mmm…!" The memory was still clear in his mind. He had been at Monksgrange on the morning after the Wardles' arrival, hoping to meet Marietta again as the solar door had opened. Instead of that, Sir Nicholas had escorted Emeline. Saints, how the lass had simpered! And that dress! Had Sir Nicholas had something to do with that, perhaps? Sir Henry had apparently been ill at ease and puzzled by the girl's silliness. Still, no matter, it had been this one he'd wanted to see. But how much did the manor of Beckington mean to Lady Alice's brother? he wondered.

Had he pressurised Lady Alice into pushing Emeline to fill the first Lady Thorsgeld's shoes? God forbid! "Shall we go and have a look at your property tomorrow, Marietta? Would you like that?" he whispered into her neck.

She loved the way his forelock tickled her nose. "Tomorrow," she reminded him, "you are going to organise my team of gardeners and take my new Mist out. Remember?"

"Tomorrow, I shall send for my steward and you shall tell him exactly what it is you want, draw plans for him, take him down to the plots and say what must be done. And he will obey every order, I promise. Then, sweetheart," he began to remove the veil from beneath her coils of hair, "then we shall visit your new manor on your new mare, for which you are about to thank me in great detail, are you not?" He unbraided one plait, shook out the hair over her shoulder and began on the other one. "Yes?" he said.

"Yes," she whispered.

It was wellnigh impossible for her to maintain her former ill will in the face of such opposition; even the glorious sunshine dissolved any remnants that might have lurked at the back of her mind, washed away on the memory of last night's loving in the guise of showing thanks.

It was impossible to say, she mused, who was the giver and who the receiver, for the exchange had been remarkably equal; about that, she was unable to pretend. He had introduced her to a new way of expressing herself and it was like the beginning of a new adventure with unknown excitements waiting to be revealed, with herself as participant and storyteller combined.

Her new mare was all that he'd said it would be, a far cry from Dulzelina's unpredictability and the most comfortable ride she'd ever experienced, the trot smooth and exhilarating, the canter somewhere between a prance and a rocking motion, wonderfully showy and a sure focus of everyone's attention.

But it was not only the beautiful white mare with the dark mane and tail that they watched. Marietta, eager to do justice to the occasion, had dressed with care in a yellowy-cream cote-hardie and deep gold surcoat edged with lynx fur, a full-skirted outfit that complemented the horse's col-our perfectly. Her long veil streamed behind her, attached to the back of her head beneath a double row of horizontal plaits and leaving her smooth crown adorned only by her plain gold circlet.

She was not aware that it was she who turned the men's heads more than the horse, or that her beauty alone was the cause of their undisguised stares. Trust their lord to find such a one, they commented, he had an eye for the loveliest creatures, though he'd had them all fooled for a week or two.

Well, if she'd been purposely eluding him, she'd have stood no chance against his persistence, for some of them had been waiting at Monksgrange when he brought her down from the hill that morning. There'd been no doubt about which one he was after after that.

"Where is this place, my lord?" Marietta called, keeping her mare alongside the bay stallion. "Is it far?"

"Beckington? No, midway between Monksgrange and Thorsgeld. But you don't see it from the track, it's way behind that outcrop of limestone, between my deer-park and the river. See…?" He pointed as they cantered down towards the white limestone boulders where the soil was thin. The narrow valley between crag and forest held the distinct marks of a track, and sheep and lambs scattered at the sound of their hoofbeats.

"Plenty of signs of coming and going," he remarked. "Looks as though your father's bailiff kept a close eye on things."

"Not the Upperfell bailiff," Marietta replied. "Too far for more than once a year, I know that for certain. Perhaps the new one at Monksgrange has paid them a bit more attention since my father took him on."

"Well, somebody certainly has." He pointed to the imprint of hooves in the hardened mud. "Who are the tenants?"

They slowed to a walk as the track narrowed between hillocks. "An old couple, John and Betty Fuller. They've been there since before Lady Alice married my father. I think she would rather it had passed to one of her own daughters than me."

He made no answer to that. It would have made no difference to his decision who it had passed to, though he knew Marietta still had a hard time convincing herself that flighty Emeline was not every man's desire. "Ah, here we are. Look through the trees. Can you see?"

It was well hidden against the crags in a grove of beeches and oaks, an elegant three-story house in which the undercroft was used for storage, and stone steps rose diagonally across the outer wall to the first floor. As they drew nearer, however, they noted how the moss and house-leeks on the roof barely hid broken tiles, how the place was in dire need of attention and how nobody had even noticed their approach.

Lord Alain's bailiff rode ahead of them and round the back of the building towards outhouses and a stable-yard, calling for the occupants, and while he scoured the tumbledown site for a sign of life, Marietta was lifted down and led up the steps to the battered old door.

It was not what either of them had expected, not the neat solar with table and stools and tapestried walls of most manor houses, with rushes on the floor and the welcome of homely faces, of hounds, of cooking smells. Smells there were, but of the kind to wrinkle the nose, and faces, too, but wizened, staring-eyed and mortally afraid.

Two old people cowered away from the door as far as it was possible to cringe, the old man holding his hands across his wife as though protecting her, shaking his head at the speechless group who entered his room, then frowning with uncertainty at the sight of Marietta with them.

Marietta went forward, holding out a hand in friendship. "John?" she said. "John Fuller? Betty? Is that Betty there behind you?"

The old man lowered his hands and turned briefly to look behind him, as though warning her not to move until he was sure. "Aye," he croaked. "John Fuller, m'lady."

"You won't remember me, Marietta Wardle. Sir Henry's daughter."

His eyes widened and the woman made a move, ready to emerge, but she was held back. "Wardle? Sir Henry? Are ye sure?"

It was the most absurd question, Marietta thought, but in the circumstances it had the required effect, for the smile it provoked did more than any words to assure him of their safety.

"Come," she said, laying a hand on his shaking arm. "Come and meet my husband, Lord Alain of Thorsgeld. He's a neighbour of yours, you know. Come. You, too, Betty."

Now convinced that they were in no danger, they came forward to make a bow and a courtesy; in the light from the unglazed window, the guests were able to see that they were indeed old and bent with the rheum, gnarled and hollow-eyed and only just recovering from a terrible fright. Their clothes were little more than rags and covered with old stains, and John's hair was unkempt and spidery-thin. Betty wore a wimple, but neither that nor her apron had been laundered recently. A commotion from outside caused them both to stagger across the room towards the door where a young girl was being thrust forward by the bailiff's strong hands.

"In the dairy round the back, my lord. She's a half-wit.

And they've just lost their pail o' milk 'cos she's just thrown it at me. Good job it missed,'' he finished, laconically.

"Oh, no! Not the milk…'' Old Betty ran to the stupefied girl and dragged her into the room. "Now what? Come, lass. They won't harm you. Come on.'' She drew her daughter away from the men and into the room.

The girl, pretty but very bedraggled, was probably about fourteen and clearly as afraid as her parents. Marietta could not imagine what could have caused this reaction in them; surely her father was not aware of this state of affairs.

The same thing must have been on Lord Alain's mind. "How long since the bailiff was here, old man?'' he said.

Old Betty piped up, "He was here—'' but her husband grabbed her arm to shut her up and answered with a question of his own.

"Beg pardon, m'lord, d'ye mean Sir Henry's bailiff?''

"Of course I do, man. What other bailiff would visit? When was he last here?''

"Michaelmas, m'lord. For the rents.''

"He didn't come on Lady Day?'' the bailiff asked; that would have been only twice a year, September and March, the least the man could have done.

"No, sir. Onny once.''

Lord Alain walked around the room, frowning and moving the squeaking shutters, noting the lack of food and furniture. "Then what is it that terrifies you so, John? Have you suffered from thieves?''

Again, they noted the quick glance at his wife, a quelling look before he answered, a trifle too eagerly, "Ah, yes, m'lord, yes, thieves. They took just about all our cattle. Left us hardly any food.''

"And horses? Took your horses, too, did they?''

"Ah, we didn't have no 'orses, m'lord. Me an' Betty

an' the lass have two donkeys and two oxen and a cow. But no 'orses.''

Lord Alain and his bailiff shared a significant glance. "Stay here, Marietta, if you will," Alain said, "while I go outside and take a look round. Explain to them what's happened."

The old man looked anxiously from Lord Alain to the bailiff and back again. "Nay, m'lord, there's nothing out there. Only empty sheds…"

But the bailiff steered him back into the room and followed his master outside. Marietta dusted off a rickety stool and sat.

"Come, Betty. Bring John and your daughter over here, I have some news for you."

In the dim solar that stank of refuse-soiled rushes and mice droppings, Marietta told them how the estate had now become her property and how, from now on, Lord Alain's bailiff would be keeping an eye on them. She had not been prepared for the relief by the old people who were hardly able to speak for tears, and while they struggled to contain themselves before their new mistress, the young girl looked steadfastly at Marietta without blinking.

"Are you like *'er?*" she whispered. Her tone was flat and unemotional.

"Her?" Marietta queried, gently. "Who?"

"Lady…Thorsgeld. ''

"I am Lady…ah! You mean the last one. Er, I don't know. I never saw her." Marietta glanced towards the door. "Did you know her?"

Once again, the budding conversation was cut off by John. "No, m'lady. It's first time we've seen Lord Thorsgeld. We've been neighbours long enough, but we've never met till now. 'E's a fine-lookin' chap, though, in't he,

Betty? A right grand-lookin' chap. Breeds some grand 'orses…''

"How do you know that?" Marietta asked, sharply. If he had as little to do with Lord Alain as he made out, how had he seen the horses?

"Oh… I 'eard." John clapped a hand on his bony knee. "Everybody around here's seen 'is 'orses. They all say what grand ones they are."

Marietta was convinced that this was not what John Fuller meant, but there was no pause before the girl spoke again as though she had not been interrupted. "Yes. I knew 'er, I did. I knew 'er."

Betty stood up, wincing with pain. "Shut up, Milly, do." She turned to her guest. "She didn't know her. Never seen her. It's good news that this place is yours now, m'lady. Good news. There's a lot wants doin' that we can't afford to do. Our workers all went, you know. Didn't your father tell you? Oh, aye…" she went on, taking Marietta's blank expression as a sign of ignorance "…John couldn't get them to work on the demesne so we've just had to let it go. That's why things are in such a mess."

"But why were you so afraid when we came?"

"Robbers!" John said, sharply, before his wife could answer.

"Aye, robbers," Betty repeated. "Took everything. Beat us up once."

"Do you have a garden?" Marietta enquired, desperate to get out of the stinking room. The girl's eyes had not left her face for one second.

"A small one, m'lady. Nothing grand. Nay, you don't want to see it, do you? It's only a little one. Not for a lady to see."

"I love gardens, Betty. I have one, too. Will you show me?"

Surrounded by high nettles, willow-herb and cow-parsley, the garden was only discernible by the level of its plants being lower than those of all the others, except for a few heads of cabbages which might have been mistaken for small trees. To one side, where the sunlight peeped through a gap in the trees, Marietta recognised the waving plumes of fennel and lovage, and the mauve pom-poms of chives. "Herbs," she said.

"Aye, those are pot-herbs, and my simples are over there." Betty pointed to one side. No one would have known; they ran into each other. Marietta tried to recognise them. "Feverfew, vervain, hyssop…"

"I know them…" Milly spoke quietly behind her.

"Shut up, Milly. No, she doesn't, m'lady. It's me what does the simples, not 'er She knows nothing."

"Then I think we shall have to put our heads together, Betty. I'm only just putting my plot to rights and I shall be looking for seeds and cuttings. Can I come to you for help?"

"Aye, that you can. Take anything you please. There's balm over there, look." She pointed to a pale green thriving plant.

"That's mint, Mother," Milly said in the same flat voice.

Marietta smiled. "Difficult to tell apart, aren't they? Even when they flower." She tried to be diplomatic but privately wondered how much Milly knew that her mother insisted that she didn't. Or how many times Betty had drunk the wrong infusion or administered the wrong salve if she was so easily confused.

"I'll do what I can to make life a bit easier for you, Betty," she said. "I'd no idea my father had neglected Beckington so. My mother should have made an effort to look after you, but we've lived so far away, you know.

Monksgrange is the furthest we've ever been down the dale.''

"Monks...? What...?" Betty's mouth made a hollow cavern of astonishment, for her lips had long since disappeared. "Monksgrange?" she repeated.

"Yes, did I forget to mention that? My father bought it from the priory at Bolton and he'll be there until September, at least.''

Suddenly, Betty's hand was clasped tightly across her mouth and, as she caught the sound of her husband joining them, blurted out, " John... John, Sir 'Enry's bought Monksgrange, John, just think, we'll be...!''

"Stop your shouting, woman!" he frowned at her impatiently. "She gets so worked up," he explained. "It's because we don't see anybody.''

Growing more and more perplexed by these strange people, Marietta was glad to see Lord Alain and the others come round from the back of the building to meet them. It had taken only a glance to see that the building needed much attention and that John and Betty were far too old and incapable of managing such a place alone.

She could not get away fast enough. "We *must* try to do something about it," she said, looking back barely out of their hearing. "I'd no idea it was in such a state. Could we send them some supplies, do you think?''

"Aye, lass. I think we'll have to keep an eye on them or the next puff of wind might blow them away. A good thing we went, I think.''

"What did you see at the back? Anything?''

"A lot of milk all over the floor, but no supplies to speak of. Something else interesting, though. Horse-dung.''

"Horse-dung? That's interesting?''

"For someone who says he has no horses, very.''

Chapter Six

Marietta could not help but wonder, every now and then, how Lord Alain would have managed if he *had* married Emeline, after all. There were, of course, dozens of well-trained men-servants for every department, efficient men under the sharp eye of the chamberlain, the second steward and the marshal, the butler, the cook and the constable. But, as Bruno had been quick to notice, it needed a woman's touch.

During the week that followed, Marietta was kept busy from morn till night finding out how things worked and exactly who was responsible for what. If she found it hard going, Emeline would have found it impossible.

The castle was built to be self-sufficient. Ranged around an inner courtyard were stores, granary and malting-house, bake and brew-houses, a horse-mill for grinding corn, a forge and armoury and rooms for soldiers. It took Marietta many miles of extra walking, upwards and downwards, to find her way round the four sides, for there were five levels.

The first floor held the great hall, the kitchens and guest rooms, the second floor was well above the noise and held the large chapel and the chaplain's rooms, the bailiff's chamber, retainers' hall and various solars for the lord, his lady and their servants. Spiral staircases were let into the thickness of the wall, and passageways were maddeningly deceptive, leading to garderobes or to anterooms or to somewhere Marietta didn't want to be at all. The place was trickier than a maze.

The household of men, far from resenting her interference in their domain, actually vied with each other to show her what they did, and where, and with whom. On each day, Marietta made a point of inviting one of the household officials to sit with her and to talk about himself so that she could get to know them better.

In this way, by careful observation and by listening, she discovered as much about the former Lady Thorsgeld and what she had *not* done than by asking what she had. Strangely enough, it appeared that she had taken as little interest in the management of things indoors as she had out of doors, making Marietta wonder how she had occupied her days when she had not been hunting or hawking.

With the restorations of the gardens well under way, she began to see how it would look when stocked with plants. Already the plots had been dug over and manured, paths laid with stone slabs, edges and raised areas built up, gates and walls restored and turf laid flat and lusciously green.

Old Adam now had an army of men at his command, working them from early until late while the good weather held. Marietta spent as much time as she could spare, making lists of plants she needed and talking to the cook and the steward about which fish to buy to stock the clean stewponds.

While she made headway with this venture, she was every bit as concerned to renovate Beckington Manor, too, for the pathetic plight of John and Betty Fuller was constantly on her mind, and the strange girl who seemed to want to say more than either of her parents would allow.

Marietta broached the subject the day after their visit to be told that it would be looked into, shortly. But two days later, when she asked if shortly had arrived, Lord Alain frowned with impatience.

"Hold hard, girl. You're doing the gardens at the moment, and you have your hands full with organising things in here. Enough for the time being, I think. I can't spare more men to work at Beckington."

"They could leave the garden then, couldn't they? I can't bear the thought of those three living half-scared out of their wits by thieves, and in that squalor."

"No, the garden will be done first. They've lived like that for years, sweetheart, they'll not come to any harm over another few weeks." He saw her disappointment.

"Weeks? Alain, when we visited them, you said…"

"Enough! Beckington will take its turn. Now, tell me if we're ready to invite guests to stay, m'lady, if you please."

Marietta turned away without replying. If she had her hands as full as all that, they were too full to receive guests.

He took her arm and led her towards the window where the light fell full on her face. "Marietta," he said, "guests will keep you company while I'm away."

That did the trick. Her expression changed from one of vexation to one of surprise. "You're going away? Why?"

Lord Alain smiled and laid his arms loosely across her shoulders, amused by her reaction. "Now that's an improvement, my girl. Only a month ago you'd have said good. Now you're saying why." He lured a smile into her eyes. "That's better. You care, don't you?"

"No." She tried to pull the smile back into line but it wobbled. "I don't care, my lord. But why do you go so soon?"

Laughing at her perversity, he slid a finger around her chin, lingering over its smoothness. "Business, sweetheart.

I go to York for a few days next week, that's all. Why not send an invitation to Monksgrange and have your family stay here to keep you company? Would you like that?''

"Yes, my lord, I would like that. Do you mean all of them?''

"As many of them as you like, love. There's room enough.'' It was true; the whole of Monksgrange could be swallowed up in Thorsgeld in one gulp.

"Could I not go to York with you? I've never been.''

"Another time. Will your garden be finished by the time I return? We have something to celebrate when it's complete, remember.''

She took the hand that caressed her chin and rubbed her cheek along the knuckles and, moving them under her lips, bit softly into them, drawing a huff of laughter from him. "No,'' she said. "I do not remember,'' she murmured.

His hands slipped beneath her arms like two crutches as he kissed her. "No matter,'' he whispered. "I shall take pleasure in reminding you.''

Aye, she thought, watching the heavy studded door close behind him, you could make a woman do most things if you willed it, I dare say. With her, he was not always gentle but then, neither was she with him. He was, however, intent on obedience.

Trying to push the sad spectacle of John and Betty Fuller out of her more immediate thoughts, she sent a message to Monksgrange that day, charging Bruno to return with all speed so that she could begin preparations.

He was back before dark. "Father's too busy and Lady Alice doesn't want to leave him, but Emeline and Iveta want to come. How does that suit you?'' Bruno gave his sister a hug, a familiar gesture he would not have chanced if Lord Alain had been there. He was ruddy and breathless from the ride.

"Only Emeline and Iveta? Not Father, too?"

Bruno understood her fears. "It's all right, love, she'll have got over her anger by the time she gets here. She looked excited enough by the idea, already. Surely you don't think she'll bear a grudge any longer, do you?"

"She wouldn't speak to me." Marietta swirled one finger into a mass of rosary beads lying on her prayer book, listening to their soft rattle. "That's why I didn't want to have a big celebration at the betrothal or the wedding. It would have looked like rubbing salt into her wounds, wouldn't it?"

Bruno took her hand and swung it out wide. "Marrie," he said, "you can't organise everything you do, or don't do, around what Emeline will think, you know. I should think you have your work cut out simply pleasing Lord Alain, don't you? And he's more important than family now, isn't he?"

She nodded.

"Well, then, just welcome her as though nothing had happened. Once she sees those lads out there falling over themselves to get her attention, she'll be in heaven. You'll see."

His breezy good nature lifted her introspection towards the possibility that she might indeed be doing Emeline a favour and that the absence of her father and mother might, for once, be a good thing. Bruno was right, of course; he knew how Emeline would exchange her disappointment for the adulation of so many young men all eager to impress. She would not bear a grudge.

As though to put right all the wrongs of the past weeks, imagined or real, Marietta set about making her half-sisters' visit one that would highlight the advantages of being free rather than married in a man's stronghold in the few days available to her before Lord Alain's departure for York.

She had the largest guest room cleaned and the bed re-hung with another brighter set of curtains, matching bed-cover and cushions, fresh rushes laid everywhere, sweet-scented logs for the evening fire, bowls of herbs to perfume the air and best beeswax candles in the sconces. Extra maids were briefed, for she knew how Emeline loved to be tended, and two great mirrors were brought in to stand on the floor by the windows.

"Take them hawking one day," Lord Alain suggested. "You can take any of the falcons except mine. But don't let Emeline on your new palfrey; she's nowhere near as good a horsewoman as you. Let Seth find a horse each for them." He hitched his purse-belt down over his hips and stood with fingers splayed over the leather—his most usual pose.

He was about to go, and Marietta wanted to delay him, to challenge him, anything to stop him walking away from her calmly, thinking of what was ahead instead of what he left behind. In her innocence, she said the wrong thing. "I'll be able to go to Beckington while you're away and get some plants for my garden."

It was not to be the light-hearted delay she had intended. "You will not visit Beckington without me, Marietta. Is that understood?" he answered, unsmiling. "Wait till I return."

"It is my property, my lord. Surely I'm allowed to—"

"You want me to put you under house arrest, do you?"

"No." This was particularly high-handed talk, she thought.

"Then obey me, woman. Beckington is out of bounds."

His tone riled her, adding to her annoyance that what

had been meant as a delaying tease had now become an issue in a clash of wills.

"Then why did you assure me that something would be done about it? If it's left any longer, it will be too late to salvage any of the crops. And they're half-starved already. Why am I not allowed to help them? My own tenants? Is there some reason why you want the place to fall apart from neglect?"

"Marietta! That's enough! I don't have time to argue about this…the men are waiting. You'll do as you are told. Come, bid me farewell." He held out his arms.

Bid him farewell? Like hell she would. "Yes, my lord. I'll bid you farewell, gladly." Grabbing at the window-seat cushion behind her, she spun and hurled it sideways at his chest, meaning to knock him over.

With barely a glance, he caught it in mid-air and tossed it back to the window-seat, advancing on her before she could regain her balance. She was still deciding which way to dodge when he picked her up in his arms, held her high off the floor and threw her onto the bed. She landed with a thud into the covers, totally disoriented and thoroughly angered.

"Now, my girl, if you want to make something of it, you'll have to wait until I return. And *when* I return, I'll give you a lesson in good manners."

He paused only long enough to pull the points of his sleeves back over his hands, then strode to the door and was gone. He did not hear the thud of the pillow, for by that time he was halfway down the passageway, his mind already on the journey ahead.

She had, she supposed, brought it upon herself. If she had used more wit, she would not have mentioned the place in jest, knowing his earlier thoughts. On the other hand, there had been no need for him to ride his high horse so seriously that he could ride away from their first parting without even an attempt to humour her, making her first night alone in the big bed oppressively forlorn. Emeline and Iveta's company would be a welcome diversion.

Bruno had been right, it was much better to ignore the former acrimony and to greet Emeline with a kiss and a smile of welcome. It was not as difficult as she'd feared when they had taken such care to impress, when Iveta's excited chatter, her exclamations of admiration for Mist and her joy at seeing Marietta again were so very genuine. And if Emeline's greeting was more subdued, Marietta understood that that was her way and that her smile and obvious pleasure were no less authentic.

Emeline had indeed made every effort to impress without any persuasion from her mother, for in the weeks since the family's arrival at Monksgrange, she appeared to have developed during one of nature's inexplicable surges, which abandons the slow and unobtrusive progress into adulthood in favour of the sudden and far more dramatic blossoming that takes even the closest relative by surprise. Overnight, the bud had opened. Here, at last, was the woman.

They rode, three abreast, Marietta between them.

"You're looking well, Emmie," she said, eyeing the rich jade-green velvet surcoat edged with fox-fur. This time, the wider front panel was less revealing but the curve of her breasts under the blue cote-hardie was every bit as fascinating as the more explicit version had been.

"Thank you," Emeline said in reply.

There was no reciprocal comment on her part, but then, Marietta thought, there never had been. It was not a part of Emeline's repertoire to show an interest in others, however superficial.

"Is our lady mother well? And Father?"

"Yes. They send their love and blessings to you. Would there really have been enough room for them, too, Marietta? Is Thorsgeld big enough for so many?"

Marietta laughed. It had been difficult for *her* to appreciate how many rooms there were after having shared space all her life. Now Emeline and Iveta were due for a shock. "Yes, enough and to spare. I'll show you."

"You have a new palfrey, too. It's very beautiful."

"Lord Alain breeds horses. Did you know that?"

The blue eyes opened with acquisitiveness. "Do you think he'd give me one if I asked nicely? When does he return?"

"At the end of the week." Marietta kept her tone light, though secretly she was amused at the speed of Emeline's covetousness.

Having survived the ordeal of learning her way round the vast network of rooms in the castle, Marietta enjoyed leading the two sisters through the labyrinth, peeping into the work shops and stores that surrounded the courtyard and then upwards into the living quarters. If Marietta had feared she might lose her way, she need not have feared, for the pack of admirers seemed to grow as they progressed from one part into another. She shook them off at the door of the room she had prepared for her guests, immediately above her own, laughingly shooing them away.

"Do you have them following you everywhere?" Iveta said, whirling round with a surfeit of energy. "I like the boy called Ian. He's Scottish."

"Not quite as many as that, love. Some of them came to Monksgrange with Lord Alain…" she faltered, looking for a quick way out of the reference to those times. She let it go.

Emeline made no comment, but wandered round the large room, touching, smoothing, fingering. The maids unpacked the eight panniers, as silently curious about their lady's sisters as about the contents of their baggage. "Don't stand and gawp, you two," Emeline chided them, "you haven't seen a ghost. Get on with it! I want those baskets out of here, quickly!"

Averting their eyes as they had been bidden, the maids hauled out gown after gown, stowing them into the clothes-chests and arranging Emeline's brushes and combs, her jewellery casket, her lotions and potions, her accessories, wondering how it could be that anyone could so resemble the first Lady Thorsgeld in every way, even down to her waspish command, that they'd been convinced, for a moment or two, she'd come back to haunt them. "God forbid," one of them had muttered.

"Amen to that," the other one had replied, before she was summoned to dress Emeline's hair. "I don't know what the master's going to say about this one when he gets back. He'll think he's dreaming."

"Nightmare, more like."

"How long's she staying?"

"Not long, if I've anything to do with it."

Emeline put a stop to the whispered interchange. "I'm waiting!" she snapped.

Noting the maids' glances, Marietta called to Iveta. "Come, Iveta, we'll leave Emeline in peace until later. I have something to show you."

She didn't, but Iveta was happy enough to escape, skipping and dragging Marietta forcibly until she had to skip, too.

"She's been like a bear with a sore head until Bruno came with your invitation," Iveta told her, merrily. "Are you really Lady Thorsgeld now, Marrie? Are these people all your servants? It's been so strange without you."

Neither the questions nor the observations needed answers.

Following Lord Alain's suggestion, Marietta arranged a hawking party for the next day, confident that in the company of so many attentive men Emeline would enjoy herself whether she caught anything or not. She did, but not until she had argued with Seth about which palfrey she was allowed to ride, insisting that Lord Alain would wish her to use her sister's new one, and it was not until Marietta intervened that she would accept another mount. In the circumstances, Marietta herself chose another mount to ride rather than flaunt Mist before her sister all afternoon, yet all the while cursing herself for ignoring Bruno's advice.

Marietta, with a group of Lord Alain's closest companions, was content to let Emeline show off her paces to the adulation of the younger set. She was struck, even more forcibly, how the pretty simpering blonde beauty had grown so quickly into the role of cajoling woman, flirting openly like a butterfly trying out its new wings, posing gracefully with arm upraised long after the merlin had flown from her wrist, pouting and cooing at it when it returned, glancing and laughing as she stroked its breast with one finger, knowing how they watched, entranced.

Relieved that all bitterness and rancour had now been put behind them, Marietta let Emeline revel in the sport while she and the men showed Iveta how to send her merlin up to stoop at a skylark. When it came time to go, they followed Emeline's group at a more leisurely pace, tossing coins into the cadgeman's cap to thank him for carrying the falcons.

Later, at supper, when Emeline had changed into a gown of deep madder red and had her hair dressed in a most elaborate coil of plaits around her ears, she graced the high table between the chaplain and Lord Alain's most senior member of the household, the treasurer, Sir Hugh Midgeley, two kindly and intelligent men who were firm favourites with Marietta. She had thought that this would put Emeline at her ease, but the effort misfired.

"For heaven's sake," Emeline hissed, "don't put me next to those old dotards again. I couldn't understand a word they said."

"Oh, I like them. They've both been kind to me since—"

"Yes, well, they're the kind of old men you like, Marietta. Put me next to that dark-haired man called John next time, and some of the others who laugh a lot."

"They don't sit at the high table, Emmie. There isn't room."

"Then make room. You're Lady Thorsgeld. And please don't let them hear you calling me Emmie. Mother says it's childish."

Marietta's fingers itched to box the girl's silly ears but she held her peace. This was, after all, only the first day of her visit and there was plenty of time for her to settle down. Marietta changed the subject.

"We shall leave the men in the hall while we go up to my solar, Emmie." She took Iveta by the hand. "Some of the men will join us in a little while. Shall we go?"

Emeline pouted, catching the eye of one young man who hovered, picking his teeth and watching. "No, I'll stay here. You go."

"Emmie…Emeline, you can't stay here on your own."

"I won't *be* on my own. Anyway, my maids are here, somewhere." She turned to look over her shoulder at the young man who then pushed himself off the wall and sauntered towards them, ready to escort Emeline away.

She's not yet fifteen, for heaven's sake, Marietta said to herself; either I have to stay with her down here or she has to go with me. She decided to compromise.

"Very well, we'll stay a bit longer, if you wish, and then we'll go upstairs. That way we'll both be happy, won't we?"

"You, too? I don't need you to stay, Marietta…"

Marietta had had enough. Speaking to the young man who had by now intruded upon their argument, she told him, "Be good enough to leave us alone while we talk." She watched, stony-faced as he bowed and walked off.

"You've no business to do that…!" Emeline coloured up in anger, fearing that the young swain would now abandon his vigil.

"You're quite wrong, Emeline! I *am* Lady Thorsgeld, remember? You reminded me of that yourself."

Her voice was firm, though this was the first time she'd ever had to use her authority to enforce her wishes, and the method held no appeal for her.

"Life here at the castle is not exactly the same as it is at home. We are the only women, and we do not stay in the hall for long after the meal unless Lord Alain requests us to. And since he's not here, I prefer to leave the men to have their own fun without me watching. I told you, there'll be some of the men to join us upstairs in a little while."

"Your friends, not mine!" Emeline sulked.

"Yes, my friends," Marietta agreed. "What else would you expect, enemies? And you can invite two of your friends to accompany you, since you are my guest. You, too, Iveta, you invite your friend Ian, will you? Now, we'll have another few moments in here and then we leave. And you will come too, Emeline."

It was an uncomfortable few moments. Predictably, Emeline's ill-natured chatter was directed towards Marietta like crossbow fire but, pretending not to notice, Marietta made a point of inviting Sir Hugh and the chaplain, Father Dylan, to her solar, as well as the other senior officials, as she would have done for any guest, though now she had no high hopes of Emeline remembering the duties due on her part.

As she had expected, the men could see which way the wind was blowing and were conciliatory.

"Don't be concerned, my lady," they told her, "we'll remind the lads of their courtesy to the young ladies. Wait until you've gone up, then we'll make sure they understand. They know what will happen if they put a foot wrong."

She was consoled. Still, the first evening was not a resounding success, for Emeline made her impatience known in a way far removed from the compliance she had shown while Lady Alice and Sir Henry had looked on. It was as though, freed from their constraint and suddenly aware of her new glamorous image, she was compelled by some inner urge which she could not control to try out every device, instinctive and learned, on the eager and ready-made audience.

And on the less-favoured audience, who were by no means as eager to receive her attention, she was merciless in her demands, scolding and ordering as though taking on the role of mistress of the household. Her argument with the head groom on the previous day was nothing compared to the ones that followed.

Carrying bucket after bucket of hot water up two flights of winding stairs, a team of pages was brought almost to the point of rebellion when she protested that the water was only warm, not hot, and sent it back.

Marietta intervened yet again, her heart sinking with dread at the sure knowledge of another day's wrangling.

"Emeline, you never have a bath every morning at home. Why have you decided you need so many here?"

"Because I *fancy* having a bath every morning. There are plenty of ser—"

"There are plenty or servants to do the essential work of the castle. No guest is entitled to commandeer the services of so many people, just to carry bathwater. Those lads are having to neglect their other duties for your pleasure. How *can* you be so thoughtless?"

"Don't you have a bath every morning?"

"No, I have one when I feel like it."

"Well, I feel like it every morning."

"Then you can do without, Emeline, or you can come down to my solar and have my bathwater before I use it. I'm not having the servants toil up here every day. One slipped this morning and fell on top of the one below. Two arms and a collar bone broken, just for your thoughtlessness."

Iveta followed Marietta along the dim passageway.

"Marrie, can I come and share your room? I can't stand being with her again; she's unbearable. She embarrasses me, going on so and scolding at the maids. She made one do her hair three times yesterday and the poor thing was in tears. Please don't make me share with her."

So Marietta moved Iveta's things into a small chamber at one side of her maids' room overlooking the inner courtyard where she could see all who came and went, and Marietta assigned one of her own maids to care for Iveta's needs.

Had it not been for Iveta, the week of Lord Alain's absence would have collapsed into total disaster, each day throwing up some new conflict based on nothing more serious than Emeline's imperious attempts to divert the servants' duties towards herself, to belittle Marietta's position as often and as loudly as she could and to find every means to be contrary in order, it seemed, to amuse and captivate her throng of young admirers.

The Master-at-Arms asked her at one point if she would leave the tiltyard, after sitting amongst the squires' armour and actually hiding the helmet belonging to one of her young friends. Emeline stormed round the side of the castle and into the garden where a team of gardeners were working, placing her hand on the wet white paint of the little wooden gate from the stew-pond area. The furore that followed was expected but no less uncomfortable for all that, especially so for Marietta to whom the garden was a haven, a place of peace and pleasure.

Now, at the end of her patience with Emeline's perversity, she pacified Old Adam, who had tried to defend the lad with the paintbrush against Emeline's attack on his ears, and then took the girl's arm in an iron grip and marched her back up the path to the relative seclusion of the stew-pond.

At first, Emeline was too surprised to resist, standing with a white-striped hand splayed out like a scarecrow as Marietta manoeuvred her back into the recess of the castle wall. By the time she had overcome her surprise, Marietta had launched into an attack fierce enough to keep her speechless.

"Now listen to this, you stupid child, I've had enough of you, do you hear? Enough!" She spat the words at her like pellets, stinging her into stillness.

"In four days you've turned this place upside down, and now you can either behave like the lady you claim to be or you can go back home this very morning. I can summon men like *that*…" she snapped her fingers in Emeline's face "… to escort you back to Monksgrange whether you will or no, and I can make damn sure you never *ever* get another invitation to stay here again. Do you understand *that?*''

She didn't wait for a reply. The forget-me-not blue eyes widened in total comprehension.

''You've antagonised everyone I've tried so hard to win over since I came here, and it's not been as easy for me as you seem to believe. And then you come along and undo it all with your counter-orders and your rudeness, you silly little chit. How *dare* you? And your behaviour with the squires and the young men…they're not here to amuse you, Emeline, they have duties to perform. Neither can they fulfil obligations to a guest if it conflicts with their orders. *You* should know that.

''A guest may not make demands on any servant without the permission of the host…and that's *me* until Lord Alain returns. God in heaven knows what these people think of you, screeching like a fish-wife and lashing out at the gardeners. If you'd looked what you were doing, you wouldn't have touched the gate. Any fool could have seen the lad on the other side of it.''

She glanced up the path towards the shooting butts. ''Where've you come from, anyway?''

''Up there,'' Emeline nodded. ''The tiltyard.''

''While the men were *practising?*''

''Yes.'' Emeline's lids covered the blue stare of innocence.

''God in heaven! Have you no sense, child? Are you so taken up with yourself that you try to distract them when they're in training? They're not playing games, Emeline. Was the Master-at-Arms there?''

''Yes…''

''And?''

''He asked me to leave.''

Marietta groaned and heaved a sigh of exasperation.

"For pity's sake! Another one! I'm going to have to go round the whole damn castle apologising for your behaviour. Go and pack your bags. You've done enough damage for four days. I've had as much as I can take."

She would have turned away but Emeline caught at her arm and held on.

"No, please… Marrie, don't send me back. I didn't know—"

"Didn't *know?* Didn't know what? No lady throws her weight around like you've been doing. Is that what you didn't know? Well, now you *do* know and you can go home. I don't want you disturbing the peace of my garden…this is my special place and I don't want you in it!" A warning voice told her not to tell, but it was too late. The words could not be recalled.

"Marrie, please don't send me home again. I'm sorry. Truly. If I promise to try very hard… I will do everything you want me to do without an argument." Emeline peeped up at the angry face and saw that she had Marietta's attention. "And we'll be friends again as we used to be and…you'll see…my manners will be perfect. Let me stay for a few more days, please. I'm having such fun without Mother breathing down my neck."

Marietta let out a breath in a gust of indecision. She wished that Alain was with her to take away this dilemma; he would know what to do. He would be back some time tomorrow. Let her stay till then.

"Is that what it's all about?" she said. "Lady Alice constraining you?"

"Yes, Marrie…that's it." Emeline saw her chances rising. "Mother and Uncle Nicholas between them. It's the first time I've been away alone. *He* wanted to come too, but Father would not allow it. I didn't know I wasn't supposed to go into the tiltyard… I won't do it again."

Or make a fuss in my garden. Or take my horse. Or order my servants, or dictate who sits at my table… I could go on, Marietta thought.

"If you can make an effort to behave as a lady should, Emeline, you can stay. I want to be friends, heaven knows I do, but you must see that I have to live here when you've gone home, and I won't have the place upset by your silliness."

She would like to have added that Emeline had caused enough problems before they were married, but knew how that would boost the girl's ego higher than it was already.

"You'll let me stay?"

"You can stay."

Emeline threw her arms around Marietta's shoulders impulsively, something she'd never done before.

"Thank you. Is it tomorrow that Lord Alain returns?"

Without knowing why she should lie instead of telling Emeline the truth, Marietta answered, "I'm not sure. A few days, I think."

Chapter Seven

For the time being, at least, the two sisters shared a type of peace which both of them recognised as a time of trial.

Marietta was torn between needing her husband's support more than ever she had believed she would and being unsure of his attitude towards her after their unhappy parting. Not only was that an area of unsureness, but Emeline's presence was bound to force Marietta herself into a penitent mode, for anything less than obvious joy at his return would be construed as uneasiness more to do with Emeline than with their misunderstanding about Beckington.

Marietta took her troubles to Father Dylan. To be more exact, she brought Father Dylan out to the garden on the pretext of showing him the progress so far. The golden-orange sun balanced precariously on the edge of the parapet as they sat on a rustic bench against the warm castle wall, and as it edged its way downwards and onto the opposite hillside, she told him the whole story of Emeline, herself and Lord Alain of Thorsgeld.

Father Dylan was an Augustinian monk on loan for a period of five years from Bolton Priory. He was not an old man, but wise for his years, well travelled and worldly and a considerable scholar, far from the doom and hellfire that typified many chaplains, including her father's. His face reflected his love of life and stimulating conversation but he knew how to listen, too. It was this quality, and his understanding, that made Marietta confide in him.

He heard her story in silence, occasionally nodding.

"Well, then, in a situation like this," he said, "it always helps to pull out the parts that don't allow you a choice and examine those first. The duties. And since you have a duty to your husband more than a duty towards your sister, *he* must be put first, don't you agree?"

"Yes, Father. I can't disagree with that. But I don't know how he will greet me, after his last words to me."

"Marietta…" he turned his tonsured head towards her, not knowing how his shining pate reflected the orange sun "…he's been away for the best part of a week. No man in his right senses holds onto such a mild threat of chastisement for so long away from home, especially when he has a new wife he fought so hard to bring under his roof."

He smiled at her as though enjoying their feud.

"I think…no, I'm sure you will discover that as soon as he sees you go out to meet him on the road, he will think no more about your little tiff, only about how glad he is to see you. Put on your loveliest gown and your best smile, deck the hall as though he was expected, have the gleemen ready, prepare his favourite food and do all you can to show how you welcome him. You won't even need to refer to your last words together. He'll see for himself, won't he?"

It was what she had hoped he would say.

"And at the same time," he continued, "the other question will resolve itself in the first one, because when he sees you and your loving welcome, he won't even know that your sister exists. It was you he wanted, don't forget. Not Emeline."

"According to my father, she looks something like his first wife "

"Is that so? I was not here then, so I have no way of knowing."

It was only a little less than the truth, for he *had* a way of knowing; he had heard talk, but gossip was not something he passed on.

"In any case, people change, and that was obviously not something that attracted Lord Alain a second time. So put it out of your mind, m'lady. Take your cue from him. You can't allow your marriage to be influenced by another woman, whether she exists now or did so in the past. And as for what your sister has been up to in his absence, well, he'll find out for himself soon enough. If I know anything, they'll all be at pains to tell him as soon as he gets his nose through the gates."

"And what about the ruffled feathers, Father? Should I apologise for my sister?"

"On balance I think not, m'lady. Far better if you were simply to visit the birds who have had their feathers ruffled just to show them how much you care, ask about the broken arms, discuss the horses, admire the paintwork…you know. Only the guest can apologise; you cannot do that for her. She'll not come to confession tomorrow, I suppose?"

Marietta smiled. "Father Dylan will have a couple of hours to spare, will he?" Then, realising that her peevishness still showed, asked his forgiveness.

"There's nothing to forgive, lady. A dilemma is neither good nor evil and to ask for guidance shows humility. All will be well. You'll see."

The early morning had always been Marietta's favourite time of day, so it was no hardship to be up at first light with an exciting urgency tingling through her body. But now, at the back of her mind, there lurked the dark suspicion that once Emeline became aware that Lord Alain was due home today, she would do her level best to put a fly in the ointment. And that, Marietta swore, was something she'd not let happen.

With this in mind, she dressed with infinite care in a fitted cote-hardie of rich golden apricot with a neckline that exposed much of her lovely neck and shoulders, hugged her waist neatly and flared out to wide folds at the hem, its long pocket-slits trimmed with squirrel fur. The sleeves were so long that they touched the floor unless she tied loose knots in them, the edges deeply dagged to show linings of cream silk which matched her under-tunic. She wore no surcoat.

Her hair was plaited and coiled into two gold-mesh cases which hung from her gold circlet, framing her face and sparkling in the early sunlight with pearls and topaz. Apart from her ring, it was her only jewellery.

"Oh, m'lady," Anne whispered, standing back and nudging Ellie with her elbow, "I've never seen anything so lovely in my life. Honest."

"She's right," Ellie agreed, tucking a stray lock of hair behind her ear and grinning, "and what's more, I know somebody who won't get a look in. Anyway, her maids aren't as good as us, are they, m'lady?"

"Nobody's maids are as good as you, cheeky-puss," Marietta smiled. "Now hurry up and tidy this place and then make preparations for the bath. My lord will be hot and dusty after his travels. Plenty of towels on the floor, Anne. You know what a splash he makes."

Anne pretended to scold. "Aye, well, don't let him pull you in on top of him this time, m'lady, or we'll have to dress you all over again."

A blush rose to Marietta's cheeks at the memory. He had

scooped an arm around her waist and had pulled her backwards onto his submerged lap, ignoring her cries of protest and kissing her into silence. Then he had sponged all the parts he could reach, just as she had been doing the moment before and, though it had soaked her dress, it had been a hilarious and novel experience for her. Nor had it ended there but on the floor, on a pile of towels.

After mass, she broke her fast, conferring with the household officials as she ate, checking on details. A messenger arrived to say that Lord Alain would not arrive until midafternoon; dinner would have to be delayed until suppertime.

The later-than-expected arrival, while giving them more time to prepare, also gave Emeline more time to discover what was happening, prompting Marietta to elaborate on her plans to ride out and meet him further along the highway to York, taking with her as many men as were available and leaving with such speed that Emeline would be nowhere near ready in time to join her.

The departure could not have been kept secret from Iveta whose room overlooked the courtyard, but she was as glad as anyone to leave her sister in the dark and ride off with Marietta and her new friend Ian, and it was past noon when the two young people gave a shout and pointed to a cloud of dust over in the distance.

Rounding a bend of the forest-covered hillside, the dustcloud was too large even for a team of oxen, and the occasional flash of silver indicated nobility rather than peasants. It must be them; they were sure of it.

Ahead of the others, Marietta cantered across the turf towards the lone rider who had singled himself out from the rest, unmistakably her proud lord whose arms were held out wide towards her and whose laughing face showed pride as well as astonishment. The sight of her golden figure on the creamy-white horse convinced him as nothing else could have done that her days of bolting were over.

"Come on, my lass!" he called to her, "come on, then. That's more like a greeting! Hah!" His great arms almost pulled her from the saddle as he kissed her while their mounts wheeled, head to tail. "You've come all this way…just to meet me, sweetheart? What a girl! Let me look at you…hah…tears, lass?" He laughed, pulling her chin to him. "What a welcome."

"Welcome, my lord," she said, laughing back at him between tears. "I couldn't wait when I heard you were on the way. I had to come out…to find you…to bring you back."

"You've missed me, then?"

"Yes, I've missed you. Look, here's Iveta to greet you."

"Well, well! So your sisters came?"

"Yes. Emmie wasn't up in time to leave with us."

There was something in the way she spoke that made him stifle the quick retort with a more searching look, and the way she glanced quickly up at him as they rode verified his impression that all was not as well as he'd hoped it would be. Was the silly child still sulking, then?

"Good," he said, taking her hand, "then I've got you all to myself for a bit, haven't I?"

"Almost," she said, nodding towards the retinue of at least twenty men ahead and as many behind them. "Almost."

The rich aroma of cooking from the great kitchen wafted well beyond the castle gates. Lord Alain lifted his head and breathed in deeply. "If that's not venison, I'll eat my saddle," he said.

"Hush," Marietta told him. "You must be surprised. Promise me you'll be surprised."

Twinkling, he nodded. "I'll be surprised, I swear it."

As it transpired, he had no need to swear, for the surprise that awaited him in the courtyard was more in the nature of a shock, one so tangible that Marietta could feel his reaction even at her distance from him.

Emeline, taking advantage of the extra time, and no travel to weary her, had sought her most beautiful gown of gold silk shot with mauve threads under a violet silk surcoat edged with gold braid. Her hair, like Marietta's, was in cauls of gold mesh studded with amethysts. She was busily issuing commands to pages and ushers, to grooms and porters as Lord Alain's party clattered through the echoing gatehouse, and she turned in feigned surprise at his entrance, holding his eyes.

"God's truth!" he murmured.

Marietta watched him pale, blink, and then recover himself as Emeline ran forward to make a graceful courtesy.

"Welcome, my lord—" her voice was breathless, excited "—we're all prepared. Your favourite venison, with frumenty and pepper sauce…"

"Emeline…no, don't tell him, it's to be…" Marietta waved a hand at her to stop the leak.

But Emeline ignored her, fluttering around as Lord Alain dismounted and went to Marietta's side, holding up his arms to lift her down. "And we've decked the hall so prettily, and a new troupe of jugglers, and there are gleemen, too…"

Clapping both of her palms over her husband's ears, Marietta made him look at her, showing him the fury in her eyes, shaking her head at him, almost in tears. "Don't listen, please…she's telling you all my surprises."

Immediately he understood and took her hands away,

holding them before him and bending to her ear. "I have not heard one word she's said, sweetheart. Come, let her prattle on; you shall show me everything." Plunged into the middle of sisterly rivalry and stunned by Emeline's sudden transformation into womanhood, Lord Alain greeted her courteously with a kiss to both cheeks, firmly refusing to respond to any more of her attempts to spoil Marietta's preparations.

On two counts, however, the damage had been done; one was shown by Lord Alain's look of incredulity as soon as he'd seen Emeline, his murmured exclamation, the second was that the edge had been taken off Marietta's personal welcome in which she had tried to say, without words, that she was sorry for her poor farewell. While the latter incident had been planned to cause damage to Marietta, the former was far more devastating in its effect, the reaction being unplanned, totally spontaneous. Not even Emeline could have foreseen that.

Still very new to the notion that it was she he wanted, rather than Emeline, Marietta was neither brash nor secure enough to be unmoved by his impromptu reaction there in the courtyard, and while Emeline's behaviour during Lord Alain's absence had been seriously unmannerly, this appeared to be a foretaste of real power of a kind that Marietta could do little to curtail without sending her home straight away.

That was the answer! She would send her packing as she should have done yesterday. What a fool she'd been to take her assurance of good behaviour. What a blind fool!

"Nay, lass! Don't overreact so." Lord Alain laughed at her from deep in the steaming bath. His chin rested on the surface of the water and reflected pink between the rose petals. Occasionally, he would disappear altogether, leaving only a shimmering mass of black hair like pond-weed, then come up with it streaked over his face and dripping into his eyes. He pushed it away and held up an arm for Bruno to wash.

"It's no great matter," he said. "I haven't seen anything, so it *will* be a surprise. There's no need to send her home for that, surely?"

"It's not only for that," Marietta said, handing him a towel. "You don't know the half of it."

"Well, I expect I shall soon enough. She's only a child, still. It's all innocent stuff, Marietta."

Foolishly, Bruno could not resist joining in as he reached for another bucket of hot water. "You don't know my sister, my lord," he said.

Before he could move away, a sponge heavy with water landed on the side of his head, making him lurch with the bucket and splash his tunic, and without heeding the consequences, Bruno poured the water onto his lord's head, sending much of it splashing over the sides.

With a roar of outrage, Lord Alain leapt out of the tub in a torrent of water and steam and, in spite of Bruno's quick dive to one side, grabbed him with an arm around the neck and a hand on his wrist and hustled the squirming lad towards the bath. "Here then...if you're so keen that I should be clean, you can get in now...get some of that dust off. Ready?" He thrust Bruno forward.

"No, my lord!" Bruno yelled, his lad's squawk mingling uncomfortably with his man's growl. "No...let me get my clothes off first...I beg you!" His laughter fought with his panic, for he stood no chance against Lord Alain's greater strength. "Please, let me undress first, my lord..."

Lord Alain, stark naked and glistening with water, released him. "Right...while I count to ten...one, two, three..."

Bruno had never undressed quite so fast in all his life,

falling almost headlong into the tub before the sound of ten had faded, coinciding precisely with the splash and the yelp of relief.

By this time, Marietta and her maids were both appalled by the mess the men had made on the towels and rushes, but helpless with laughter at the rough and tumble and creased up as much by Bruno's expression of jubilation as by his master's quick retaliation. Even through all that, Marietta was spellbound by the magnificent naked body, gleaming and wet, every hard muscle picked out under the shine like polished marble.

Her brother's nakedness was familiar to her, filling-out and newly firm, but her husband was tall and hardened to the temper of steel and her longing for him obliterated her niggling doubts about Emeline and his thoughts concerning her. If he'd had some kind of shock, well then, he had apparently forgotten about it in his delight to be home. Why should she insist on recalling it, spoiling her first few hours with him?

She dried him herself. "Be kind to Bruno," she whispered.

"Kind?" He glanced at the lad in the steaming bath. "How many squires get to be bathed in their lord's bath-water, I'd like to know?"

Disarmingly, Bruno smiled at them and popped a rose petal into his mouth.

Later, when they were alone at last for a few moments before supper, he pulled her into his arms. "The sooner I can kiss you without this contraption on your head, the better I shall feel."

"Don't you like it?"

"You look amazing," he murmured, "a dream. When I saw you come cantering towards me across the field, I nearly burst with pride. Golden and glowing like a ripe

peach… I want to sink my teeth into you…shall I?'' He
bent his head to her throat.

"Later, my lord. I'll take this contraption off for you.''

"Is that all?''

She giggled. "No, I'll take everything else off too, if
you wish.''

"I do wish…'' His mouth moved up and they clung
together, rapt in the touch and taste of each other's lips,
making up for lost days of wanting. Reluctantly, they pulled
apart, not wishing to keep supper waiting.

"I brought something back for you, sweetheart, to celebrate our first parting. Look…'' he presented her with a
package, linen-wrapped and tied with red ribbons. Inside
were two jewel-studded velvet and leather dog-collars, obviously for a very small dog.

Marietta looked at him with a question in her eyes.
"Dog-collars? They're exquisite, my lord, but…''

"Where is the dog? Good grief—'' he pretended concern
"—don't say it's escaped. I'm sure I wrapped it properly.''

"Stop teasing!'' she laughed. "Is there one?''

"Well, let's go down and see if anyone knows anything
of it, shall we?''

Someone did, of course; it was Bruno who held the little
white creature in his arms, a delicate greyhound pup with
great deep blue eyes. Lord Alain placed it in Marietta's
outstretched hands. "The lady of the manor always has a
lap-dog, I believe. And here's yours, sweetheart.''

"Alain…it's…it's beautiful. Thank you, thank you.
Look, Iveta…Emeline…look!''

But Emeline had turned away to talk to the young man
at her elbow and it was Iveta who came forward to nuzzle
the tiny thing and help to put its collar on. And while Marietta and the little hound came to know each other, Lord
Alain exclaimed obediently at the blossom-decked hall and

the trails of ivy on the tables, the favourite food and the welcoming minstrels who sang from the gallery throughout the meal, assuring her that it was the best homecoming he'd ever had.

Even so, as the dinner-cum-supper slowed to a halt and the tumblers came forward to entertain them, Marietta could not help but notice how her husband's eyes strayed occasionally towards Emeline when he thought neither of them was looking and how his thoughts appeared to have taken him far away once or twice when she spoke to him.

As before, all fears fled once they were together again in the haven of each other's arms, nothing existing except the soft smoothness of skin and the warmth of tender words, the touch of hands and lips, the urgency of desire. No one came between them then, nothing pushed them off course while they loved, slept, and loved again, holding the dawn away as lovers always do.

Intent on maintaining an amicable mood, despite her husband's wish that Emeline should stay, Marietta waited for an opportunity to show him the progress being made in the garden and the re-stocking of the stew-pond. She had had the two areas enclosed by new walls and white-painted fences with doors and gates and pathways leading through. He would be impressed, she was sure.

Her expectations that Emeline would stick to him like a leech were realised from the moment their business in the hall had been concluded. Taking no heed of the fact that he preferred to visit his stables with his men, Emeline tagged her arm into his, ignoring Marietta's quiet promptings that he was still on castle business. Like a father with a clinging child, Lord Alain unhooked Emeline's arm with an indulgent laugh and turned her towards Marietta.

"The stables are no place for you, young lady. Go to the

garden with your sisters.'' He looked over the top of her head to Marietta. ''I'll come to you there, sweetheart. Then you can show me.''

Emeline pouted. ''But Marietta doesn't allow me to go into her garden,'' she whined.

''What?'' He frowned, sure he had misheard.

''She said she doesn't want me to go into her garden.''

Marietta was astounded by the flagrant attempt to twist the truth.

''Wait a moment…'' she said, keeping her voice low so that the waiting men should not hear, ''you know full well why I said that.''

''It was because I put my hand on your wet paint.'' She held up her fingers to look at them, petulantly glancing up at Lord Alain and seeing his quick look of astonishment at her sister. ''She was so cross,'' she told him.

''That's not true, Em…!''

''Enough!'' Lord Alain said, gruffly, dismissing the budding argument. ''Get off to the garden, both of you, and settle your differences there. Of course you're allowed to go there, Emeline.'' His wide back put an end to the conversation.

Marietta was seething, unable to continue the dispute in the servants' hearing and now totally unwilling to accompany the little minx to her garden where she would either have to spoil its atmosphere of tranquility with a showdown or pretend an indifference she did not feel, neither of which would do.

Leaving Emeline to swish away in triumph, she signalled to Iveta, and together they took the little greyhound pup round to the shooting butts, picking up bows and arrows on the way. An hour's archery would, she thought, release some of the aggression before it became any more obvious.

Iveta, who had had little tuition with the bow, suddenly

found that she loved it, especially since her friend Ian and his young pals were also practising. Soon, she was in the midst of them being tutored from all sides, and Marietta was left to a lone contest with her hostility in which the straw butt became, once or twice, Emeline. If it *had* been, the lass would surely have been mortally wounded, for Marietta was a fair shot.

The lass in question, however, was at that moment very much alive to the effect her presence was having on the two garden lads who were doing their best to erect a wooden arbour over by the crenellated wall, as Old Adam had instructed. But while she leaned so prettily against the wall to watch them, and when they had to ease round her so carefully in order not to brush up against her or to catch her long skirt with the struts of wood the job threatened to slow to a standstill if she didn't get out of the way.

The two lads eyed her and then each other, fully aware of her game and yet not daring to take advantage.

"Mistress, would you please…?" One of them indicated a point away from the entrance. "We need to climb up there to reach…"

She looked down and then up. "Plenty of room," she said with a smile.

The younger lad blushed uncomfortably, nonplussed, then looked for help to the other one. "Could you move, please?" he whispered.

"What if I don't?" she whispered in reply.

The elder one stuck his thumbs into his belt and took a step towards her. "I'll show yer summat'll move yer, shall I?"

Recognising imminent danger, Emeline yelped, turned and fled out of the trellis entrance then stood, half laughing and flustered to see Lord Alain standing watching the dilemma, his hand still on the latch of the door in the wall.

She had no idea how long he'd been there, for by the time she had looked over her shoulder, both lads were about their business.

His expression was serious, and for an embarrassingly long time he made no move, but regarded her as though deep in thought while Emeline had time to spare for her blush to subside. He closed the door very slowly and glanced along the new-made path. "Where's Marietta?" he said.

She thought how handsome he looked in his tight-fitting chausses and short blue tunic. He had wonderful legs, but the younger boys were more fun. "I don't know," she replied, truthfully. "She wouldn't come to the garden with me. I told you, my lord, she doesn't want me here."

"Nonsense, Emeline. You know how hot-tempered she is." He led her to a bench at the end of a new plot and invited her to sit by him.

"It's not nonsense, my lord…" her eyes were downcast "…she wants me to return to Monksgrange."

"She told you that?" After what they'd said before supper, had she then disobeyed him and told the lass to leave?

"She told me before you returned yesterday, my lord." She sighed, looking away. "She said she'd make sure I'm never invited back again. And all because I wanted a bath." Her voice trembled to a whisper.

"What, Emeline? Not let you have a *bath?*" He tried hard to sound shocked.

She nodded. "Yes, she said I could have her bath water when she'd done with it and not to ask for hot water to be sent up. I think I should go, my lord. I can see it was a mistake to come."

A tear trembled on her long fair lashes and she nibbled at her lip while watching his hands. When he made no move to comfort her, as she had hoped he might, she stood as if to leave, ostensibly to begin packing.

Gently, he forestalled her. "There's no need for that, Emeline. This is a difficult time for both of you, I realise that. And I believed that you would appreciate a chance to be alone together, to patch up your differences. Of course, if you insist on going back to Monksgrange, I will do all I can to make your journey comfortable. But I would like you to stay. Will you?"

For what she deemed to be an appropriately long pause, Emeline played with her fingernails and brushed a non-existent tear from her cheek. Then she sniffed prettily and nodded. "If that's what *you* want, then I will, thank you. But do you think I could have a bath each morning as I'm used to doing at home?"

Lord Alain held back the urge to laugh at her charade. It was well done, he had to admit it, especially as he'd only just discovered that it was two of his young grooms who'd broken their arms after having been drafted in to carry Mistress Emeline's bath water every morning. And just now, he'd met Old Adam who had assured him he'd not go near Lady Marietta's garden if that sister o' hers were in theer, little troublemaker that she wor. An' had Lord Alain 'eard what she'd been up to in't tiltyard?

No, not yet, he would discover that, too, all in good time. But he'd seen for himself what she was up to here with the two young garden lads and that had been enough to assure him that he had a very appropriate role for her to play in the near future. As for making Marietta understand what it was, there was no hope of that at the present.

He knew, as he walked away towards the shooting-butts, that both he and his young wife were in for a rough ride. As for young Emeline, the time had come and gone when he didn't know what was going on under his own nose. Nowadays, he took good care to find out.

There was no sign of Marietta at the butts, only Iveta exercising her new-found skills with a team of young pages. They were behaving impeccably; no tomfoolery with weapons, they'd been told.

"Where is the Lady Marietta?" Lord Alain asked.

Young Ian pointed towards the deer-park. "She took her pup for a walk, my lord. Only a few moments ago."

He watched Iveta shoot. "Find her a shorter bow, Ian. And show her how to push. She's still pulling."

"Yes, my lord." Ian grinned, not only because his hero had remembered his name but because he'd been told to instruct. Rare praise indeed.

After the muggy heat of the day, the cool woodland was a welcome change and the general noise of castle life was replaced by the soft sighing of the beeches, ash and oaks. Standing quite still to listen, he was rewarded by the unmistakable yap from deeper in the wood and, making his way towards the sound he called, "Marietta! Marietta, where are you?"

He smiled at the lack of communication. If he had heard the pup's yap, she must have heard his voice, yet was making no reply. So, that was her game: she was angry with him, with Emeline, with everything, no doubt. And she was hiding…somewhere around…here…if only he…yes, she was wearing green, as she so often did. Then it was all over…the pup yelped again, wriggled free of her grasp and came bounding towards him, trailing its lead through the grass and twigs and indicating quite clearly where the figure in green held herself rigidly on the far side of a tree, convinced that she would not be spotted.

"Where's your mistress, then? Where is she?" he said, loud enough for her to hear while tying the lead to a fallen branch. He stalked, silently, coming at her from one side to make her run towards a fallen oak so large that no one could have cleared it without a ladder. She swerved away with a yelp, was caught around the waist and brought down backwards on top of him, angry to have been discovered so soon and so easily.

"Leave me…alone!" she growled, fighting to free herself from his grasp. "Leave me…leave me *be*!"

"Hold it, my girl! That's enough!"

"That's what you said earlier," she yelled at him, beating his chest as he pulled her into his arms. "Well, I've had enough, too! Enough of that little viper! Enough!" She hammered at him until he caught her wrists and held them.

"Hush, sweetheart, you're taking it all too seriously… Hush…you surely don't think I'm ignorant of what's going on, do you? That I can't see what's happening? Do you?"

Marietta stopped struggling at that, wondering what it was that he understood. "Well, of *course* I'm taking it seriously you great insensitive oaf!" she snapped, disconcerted to see his face break out into a laugh. "How can you laugh…?"

She twisted away, but he threw her backwards with a thud onto the softly padded forest floor and lay over her so that she could not move.

"Ouch! Let me up! You don't understand…" she howled. "She's determined to make trouble. She's done nothing but throw her weight around since she got here. I've had enough! And she told you I'd forbade her the garden because she touched the white—"

"I've seen Old Adam."

"What?"

"Ask me to kiss you, and I'll tell you, if you give me half a chance."

She paused, reading his eyes.

"Go on, ask me."

"Tell me what…?"

"No! Ask me to kiss you," he insisted.

Her reluctance was not altogether genuine. "Kiss me," she whispered.

He could have prolonged the lesson by making her say please, but there was no guarantee that she'd comply, even if she'd been lying in snow. So he kissed her into stillness, until he felt the tensions of her body soften beneath him and her arms steal around his neck, felt her fingers push into his hair and hold him, twisting her head to take in more of him.

For Marietta, this was more effective than archery, for this opponent could fight back, make her win or loss worth something, sap her energy and drain her anger, take her punishment and return it. With a surge of pent-up rage, she tore at him with her teeth, catching his bottom lip and clashing her teeth against his before he was able to pull his head away.

She tried to pull him back again, but by now he had seen her eyes, wild and dark with passion and knew that the time for kissing had passed. Silently, he untied the cords at the neckline of her green bliaud and pulled it down off her shoulders while she fought at him in a frenzy of contradictions, wanting him but determined not to give in, finally forced into immobility by his large hand gripping her chin while his mouth roamed over her breasts.

Moaning, unable to bear the torment of his nibbling lips any longer, she heaved his hand away with both of hers and pushed it aside. But he caught her wrists together and held them, taking her conflicting signals of willingly opened thighs and struggles to be free of his weight as a personal denial of her own desires, not a fight against him.

Still, without a cry for aid or mercy, nor even a word of

protest, Marietta both helped and hindered him, beating ineffectually against his great shoulders when he released her
at one end to bind her to him at the other. Only then did
she release a whispered complaint, "No, I don't want you!
Ah! I don't want…"

"Yes, my wild cat. That's it, isn't it? Eh? Isn't it?"

"Alain…Alain," she gasped.

"What, sweetheart?"

"It's not you…"

"Ssh! I know. I know what it is."

"Do you?"

"Yes. Fight me as much as you like. You won't hurt
me. Go on…take it out on me."

She would have taken up his offer if she had not already
expended her energies beforehand. Now, her antagonism
stood no chance against the physical onslaught of his loving; there was no room for them both and he was there,
above her, moving, relentless and brutally efficient as
though accepting her challenge like a knight at a joust. Too
far gone to reciprocate, Marietta wept at her own incom-
petence, at being unable to conclude what she herself had
started.

"Don't cry, sweetheart. Don't reproach yourself. Do you
want me to stop?"

"No, no, no…go on—" she pushed the tears away, angrily "—go on." Words came and went, floating past on
the hushed breath, the sigh, the moan of pleasure too great
to contain. There was no grand and glorious release for
Marietta, this time, for that had come earlier in a different
form. She had sought only the contest, not the prize, and
though vanquished, she was treasured against Alain's great
chest as though she had been his equal, which she knew
she was not.

Peaceful at last, she whispered in his ear, "Alain, where's the pup?"

"Tied up, over there. It's all right, she can't see us." He lifted his head from her shoulder and nuzzled into her neck. "Has the anger gone, now?"

"Yes, brute. Pity anyone who's drawn against you in a joust."

He chuckled. "I love it when you fight. But I don't want to make you angry, sweetheart. Shall we talk some now? I have things to tell you. Do you want to hear? Shall I let you up?"

Sitting against a branch of the fallen oak, they nestled closely like lost children, savouring the peace within themselves. Alain rescued the pup and brought it to her, laughing at the zeal of its pink tongue on his face and its flying leap onto Marietta's lap. She reminded him of his promise. "Alain, you said you'd seen Old Adam."

"I've seen Old Adam and I've also heard how two of my grooms came to have broken arms, which I am very angry about because that has a direct bearing on something else that happened last night. You didn't tell me about the accident on the stairway, sweetheart. Why not?" He thought he knew the answer to that already.

"You saw how Emeline stole my thunder as soon as you arrived home. I was furious then, but I wasn't going to plunge you into a catalogue of her doings straight away and I didn't want to spoil our reunion."

His arms pulled her even closer against him while he kissed her. "It was good, wasn't it?" he whispered. "I knew you'd be good as soon as I saw you, all those weeks ago."

"Oh, Alain, what nonsense you talk. All grazed like that, and half-dazed?"

"Yes, half-dazed you still fought me off. Passionate woman."

His soft laugh of triumph sent a wave of excitement through her, but there were more important things to discuss than that.

"Alain, what did you mean about something happening last night?"

"Another one of my horses was stolen."

"Stolen? Another one? You mean there have been others?"

Gravely, he nodded at her concerned expression. "Last night, another mare was stolen from the far field. Seth had put them there in the morning and because we were two grooms short, it was later than usual when they were brought back to the home paddock for the night. And by that time, one of them was gone. She had a foal with her, too. A colt."

"Oh, no!" The news was serious enough at the best of times, but a breeding mare and a colt were doubly valuable. "A palfrey, was she?"

"That would have been bad enough, but this was one of my breeding mares for war-horses. The colt would have been a destrier, worth thousands, eventually."

"Oh, Alain…! Have you got men out looking for them?"

"Yes, of course, but I can't help feeling that there's someone who knows what's happening here. Last time it happened was when I was over at Monksgrange and once before when I was away from home. This time, it was just as I came back, too late to be at the stables as I usually am, last thing at night."

"Someone who works here, you think?"

"Someone who's aware of my comings and goings and

who knows which horses to go for. The first one was a yearling colt. Never a filly.''

''And never a gelding?''

''Oh no, the idea is to take one that will sire others and have value as a destrier, too. They wouldn't take a mare in foal because for one thing she might have a filly and, for another, somebody would have to know how to attend a birth. That's all time-consuming and too risky. They can't get at the stallions, thank goodness, but this is getting more and more serious.''

''What are you going to do now, Alain?'' Marietta asked as they walked back across the field with their arms around each other. The pup pranced at her side, pulling at its leash to chase a butterfly.

''I'm having a horse-fair, here at Thorsgeld,'' he told her. ''While I was in York, I invited several acquaintances, mostly knights who need new stock, to stay at the castle as our guests. Some dealers, too.''

''But Alain, surely that's asking for trouble, isn't it? Getting them right here so that anybody can see what you've got and where you keep it.''

''Yes, that's what it might look like, but this is not the first time I've done this. Many of the same people were invited here every year until a couple of years ago. It's time I started again. I have a distinct feeling that one of them might be behind the thefts.''

''And you think you can discover who's responsible by having them here, under your own roof?''

''I think it's quite likely, my love, but I shall need your help. Will you help me make it a grand affair, Marietta? Feasts, hunting, hawking parties? A few of them might bring their ladies, too. Would you like that?''

The idea was audacious, and to one new to castle life quite an awesome assignment, but she would like it. Yes, she would like it very much. "Yes, my lord. Yes, that would be wonderful. When is it to be?"

"They'll start arriving on Thursday, ready for the week-end," he said, opening the gate into the stew-pond garden. "I hope *this* is going to be ready in time."

Marietta stopped, dismayed by the suddenness of the event. "Next *Thursday?* Alain, that's only a mere four days away. Why on earth didn't you tell me sooner? Four days? That's all we've got to prepare?"

He stood before her, laughing at her wifely protests of too little time. "If you, my good wife, had not forced me to go searching deep in the deer-park, and then detained me against my will, and…"

"Oh, you great fool! Who detained you against your will?"

He caught the hand that pushed at his chest and kissed the palm. "You did, little dryad in green, you lured me there and had your wicked way with me and enslaved me, and brought me back to your secret garden…"

"And you, my lord, have a fertile imagination. Are you going to tell me who it is you suspect of your thefts? You don't want me to speak of it, I assume?"

"No to both questions, sweetheart. Know nothing; say nothing. Just be the perfect wife so that I can boast of you, and look your most beautiful every day. We'll see what happens then, shall we?"

"I will do whatever you ask of me, my lord," she whispered, leaving her enquiry about Emeline to the last to savour the anticipation of his certain reply. "When shall I arrange for the return of Emeline and Iveta? Tomorrow?" She felt the coolness of the gatehouse as they walked through to the cobbled courtyard.

His answer sent an extra chill along her arms. "Oh, they can stay while we have our guests, surely? You could probably do with Iveta's help, and you wouldn't want them to miss all the fun, would you? Besides… '' he avoided looking at her unsmiling face ''…we might just find a wealthy husband for Emeline, eh?''

Marietta made no reply. She would not beg him to send Emeline home but neither would she agree that she cared two hoots about finding the girl a husband. If Emeline's last few days' behaviour were anything to go by, her conduct during the days ahead would surely change his mind.

Halting in the shadowy doorway in the corner of the court yard, he held her back against the door. ''Sweetheart, I'm home now. We're both fully aware of what a child she is, even though she looks like a grown woman. She's merely trying out her new skills, that's all. Some women have to do that—''

''I didn't!'' she snapped at his excuse for the silly creature.

''No, love. If you'd been like that, too, I would not have looked twice at you, believe me. But don't you think that you and I between us can keep her under control?''

''Lock her in the stable with your stallions, you mean?''

Placing his hands across her shoulders he heaved with laughter so much that she was compelled to join in, reluctantly.

''No, lass, no… I didn't want to go quite as far as that. We'll save that option as a last resort, I think. Don't be concerned; I have things under control. Just trust me, that's all I ask.''

Trust you, she thought. Aye, what choice do I have? Is that really the only reason you want her to stay? What was that look all about? These were questions she could not ask; she must wait and see.

"What are you going to name this little thing?" He bent to pick up the pup with one hand and place it in her arms.

"Faith," she said, running her hand over its smooth head.

"Aye, lass, that's good. Don't lose Faith, sweetheart."

Chapter Eight

With so much to be done in only four days, there was little time for Marietta to dwell on the continued irritation of Emeline's company. At the back of her mind, she supposed that Lord Alain was right; between them they should be able to keep her from causing too much havoc. But that was only the theory.

The facts were that Emeline's havoc was being directed not at the two of them but at Marietta alone, insidiously provoking on a scale so small that any reaction to it would have appeared petty. Marietta said nothing, hoping that when the extra guests appeared they would somehow keep her sister occupied in their company. Meanwhile she went about her duties, turning as much of a blind eye to Emeline's doings as she could.

There was one thing, however, that penetrated Marietta's blind eye with all the pain of a dart; Lord Alain's assurance that she must trust him to keep Emeline under control proved not to be what she'd had in mind. In the weeks since she'd known him, he had shown far less patience with her own mild perverseness than he now did with Emeline's inconvenient whims.

Where he was fierce in his demands of her, he indulged

Emeline as though making sure that she would stay for the duration of the horse-fair. Marietta would have preferred it if she had had a tantrum and gone flying off home; that would have solved all their problems. But that was now out of the question. Marietta's threat had disappeared.

"Lord Alain has asked me to stay, Marietta," she said, glancing at her reflection in the array of gold and silver dishes on the cupboard in the hall. "He's taking me hawking this afternoon. Will you be coming?"

Little cat, Marietta thought. Stick your claws in. You know full well that I'll be up to my eyebrows getting everything ready by Thursday.

"No, I'm far too busy. I can always find you a job if you prefer to stay and help," she said.

"I *will* be helping," Emeline said, "catching herons for the table."

Tight-lipped, Marietta turned away. The chamberlain and second steward were waiting for instructions.

After the mid-morning dinner, during which she watched yet again her husband's forbearance when Emeline childishly spoiled the decoration around the edge of a dish of saffron rice even before it had been set down, she walked away from the table alone, unable to conceal her vexation.

Lord Alain caught up with her in the narrow passageway from the great hall to the guest chambers. "Marietta, wait!" he called.

She did not wait. She kept on walking until she felt his hand on her elbow and was hauled to a standstill. "Let me go, my lord. I have much to do…"

"Wait, lass! What's all this? You've been like a bear with a sore arse for the last two days. What's got into you?"

His seeming ignorance piqued her every bit as much as his toleration of Emeline's scheming ways.

"How can you *ask?*" she snarled. "You asked me to trust you, too. Was *that* one of your mindless questions?" She took advantage of his astonishment to pursue her mounting anger.

"Well, ask how I like it when she flaunts herself around your home as though *she* were mistress here. If you truly wanted that, why didn't you marry her as I told you you should? I never wanted this…it was you who insisted. Was it *both* of us you wanted then…was it?" With a supreme effort, she wrenched herself away and stood out of reach, fuming with resentment.

"Marietta…listen…it's not like that, truly," he said.

"*Truly!*" she mimicked him.

"Why don't you come hawking, too? It'll do you good."

That was like a red rag to a bull. *"Now?"* she hissed. "Now? Just when you're about to set off…as an after-thought? And when you can see that I need every moment to prepare for your damn guests? I would have thought you'd be better helping me than gadding off with that stupid, scheming little…!"

"I *am* helping, sweetheart," unwittingly he echoed Emeline's words, "I am. I'm taking her out of the way. Isn't that a help?"

His last words were tossed after her as she fled along the passage. He heard the echoing slam of a heavy door, felt the shockwaves and sighed before turning back, supposing that he would have to let her win a bout, occasionally.

Marietta stood with her back to the door with the heavy bolts pushing into her, undecided whether a confrontation had been better or worse than a quick disappearance. Well, now he knew something of what she felt, though no man would ever understand why a woman found it beneath her dignity to compete for something that was already hers by right.

Cooled by the silence of the chamber, she went to sit on the bed where a pile of sheets and blankets were ready to be laid. Goose-feather pillows had been newly filled that day; the linen still had downy bits clinging to it. She picked one up and twirled it in her fingers, wondering what in God's name she was doing here.

From the half-open door into the next guest room there were sounds of maids entering, town-women brought in to help with the preparations, old biddies, but reliable and less interested in the lusty soldiers than younger lasses would have been. On the point of making her presence known, she was stopped by the slam of the far door to their chamber and their loud cackle of mirth, then a "Shh!" from one of them.

Apparently, the instruction was not one she recognised. "Did you see her?" she guffawed. "Did ye not see the little hussy?"

That, Marietta thought, must surely mean either herself or Emeline. She had to know which.

"Aye. I saw her. You'd think she were mistress here instead of the other one. What d'ye think his game is, then? Does he want both of them, d'ye think? You'd have thought he'd had enough with the last one, wouldn't you? Fancy him finding another one just like her."

There were cracking sounds of linen being shaken and words coming out in puffs as their bodies stretched and bent. "Spitting image, isn't she?" the cackling one replied. "Same snooty nose, too. You should hear what t'others are sayin' about her. They wish she'd take her bags and go home. So do I."

"Aye, well, it's not her nose that men are interested in, is it? It's t'other end." They cackled again, knowingly.

"Hey, she hasn't been busy already, has she?"

"Well, if she hasn't, it'll only be a matter o' time. Here,

pass me that pillow, will you? You know what it was like with the first one, there was only his lordship didn't know what was going on. He was so busy with his horses he'd no time to watch what she was up to.''

"Little tramp!"

"Now, the other, she's as nice as pie. I like her.''

"Aye, but they're only half-sis— Oh! Saints!'' The woman cannoned backwards into the one behind her, sending the door crashing into the tapestry on the wall.

"M'lady…I didn't know…oh—'' She clapped a reddened old hand over her mouth, struggling to remember the details of their conversation, as much distressed by the stare of the pale and silent figure on the bed as she might have been by a box around the ears for being a blabbermouth.

Curiously, Marietta felt a singular calmness, rather as though all the niggling doubts and fears of the past weeks had found a place within a much greater puzzle. Somehow, it made more sense to discover that her first impressions were, after all, correct, that he *had* been looking for a replica of his first wife, that the exclamation in the courtyard on his return had been a recognition not that Emeline had changed, but that his first wife had come back from the dead.

Why else would he be insisting that she stay? Why else would he be willing to put up with this bad behaviour except to show that, this time, he would keep her in his sights, under control, as he'd told Marietta so clearly that he could. A second chance…that's what he wanted. Two years of marriage and then her death of the pestilence; he must have been devastated, full of remorse that he'd not given her the attention she obviously craved.

Coolly, she stood and thought about the duties to be finished. "Make up the bed in here,'' she told the two astounded women, "then check to see that the truckle beds have blankets and pillows. I don't know how many servants they'll bring, but prepare three for each room. Then come upstairs to me.'' She passed them and went on in a thick mist of inner silence.

If that's what he wants, she told herself, then that's what he can have. She would not fight for her position, for she'd told him at the very beginning that marriage to him, or anyone else, was not what she wanted.

His first interest in Emeline had warned her how it was likely to be; she should have taken more heed, not been so easily persuaded by his domineering ways. Nor should she have allowed him to seduce her with barely a protest. She had been a fool. An utter fool. And now she was caught, a better housekeeper than the other one, by all accounts. But that would be no hardship.

She was in the bakehouse when the hawking party clattered into the courtyard at the end of the afternoon and, by careful determination, she contrived to appear in the hall as supper was about to commence, pretending to be unaware that Lord Alain had sent pages to look for her. Without a glance at either her husband or sister, she took a place between Iveta and Father Dylan and throughout the informal meal kept herself engrossed in their company, and those furthest away from Emeline.

Afterwards, she made a departure so furtive and hasty that Lord Alain did not see her go, and in the gentle sunshine of the evening she took tiny Faith across to the shooting-butts and leaned over one of the crenels in the high wall, sitting the pup in the space and pointing out to it the landmarks she knew so well.

Before long, Bruno joined her, padding across the grass as though on an errand. ''My lord is looking for you,'' he panted.

Marietta made no move, staring out across the beautiful green valley instead and feeling a heavy thudding in her breast at the sound of his name.

"Are you coming, love? What is it, Marrie? Tell me."

"Look," she said without turning, "there's home."

He studied her with a puzzled look. "Home? Are you homesick, love? Is that it?"

She nodded, unable to hold back the tear that plopped onto Faith's head. "Will you tell me something? Something that might help?"

"Of course, love," he whispered. "What is it?"

"Tell me what you've heard about his first wife."

"Marrie!" he rebuked her gently.

"Tell me," she insisted. "You must have heard something."

"Not much."

"What's not much? Did they like her?"

"Not the way *you* mean." His answer was reluctant and he turned to lean his back against the wall, fidgeting with the hem of his short tunic.

Marietta rolled away from the gap to face him for the first time. "Not the way I mean? What way *do* I mean?"

Bruno's cheeks tightened. "She was a bitch," he said.

She waited, expecting him to elaborate, weighing that piece of information against what she'd heard earlier. But there was no more. "Go on," she said.

"No, Marrie. I'm his squire. I may not say anything of my lord's business to anyone—"

"Not even to your sister? His wife?"

"No, not even to you. In any case, they don't discuss things like that in front of me. That's just what I've gleaned. All I know is that you are as different from her as it's possible to be. All the men say you're a lady."

"They say that?"

"Yes, they don't mind me hearing that. Come on, Marrie. He'll tear me to shreds if I don't take you back with me."

"You go, love. Tell him I'm coming. Tell him the dog is delaying me...I'll come shortly." But not until she had walked for an hour in the deer-park and lingered in her garden on the way back. And by the time she had reached her solar, Anne and Ellie were ready to pounce on her.

"M'lady, where've you been? Lord Alain is asking for you to go to his solar."

Then let him ask, she thought. And if he thinks I'm spending the evening in his company, with or without that clever little baggage, he can think again.

By the time he had put his head through the door once again, Marietta was in bed and propped up against a pile of cushions. The maids withdrew.

"Where in heaven have you been, Marietta? Did you not receive my messages?" Lord Alain sat on the bed and caught the pup as it flew to his knee.

"Yes, my lord. I've been on household business."

"What, until now? Surely everything's in hand, isn't it?"

"Yes." She stared straight ahead, refusing to meet his eye.

"And you've got extra help in from the town?"

"Yes."

"Then we're all ready for our guests?"

"Yes."

"And the garden? Will that be ready to take our guests into?"

"No, my lord. It won't."

"Not, sweetheart? Why not?"

"Because I haven't had time to attend to the planting. I was to have seen to it today, but the new plants are still in boxes and wheelbarrows.'' She had passed them an hour ago and had ordered the pages to water them, quickly, before the portcullis was dropped inside the gatehouse.

''Then you shall do it tomorrow, eh? I'll get you some extra help and we'll have it ready by evening. Perhaps you'll have time to ride with me on Mist, will you? You have not exercised her for days.''

''No, my lord, I won't. Take Emeline. She'll be glad to keep you company. Let her ride it.''

She knew her peevishness had shown as soon as she had spoken, for he sighed, recognising at once the cause of her cold formality.

''I see. So that's what it's all about. And you're tired, too. Do you want me to come to bed early, sweetheart?''

''No, my lord. I would sleep alone, if you please.''

''Oh no, my lass...'' He stood up, ready to close the argument.

''It's the time of my monthly flow, my lord. I prefer it.''

He would not deny her the right to sleep alone at such a time, though it was not what he would have wished.

''Very well, if you wish it. Sleep well, love.'' He bent to kiss her but found a cool cheek instead of a warm mouth. There could be no insisting at a time like this. To Marietta's distress, he dropped the pup down onto the coverlet and went without another word.

With knees drawn up under her chin, she sat in the great bed alone, staring out towards the deepening sunset, hardening her heart against the man she knew she had come to love. She had lied; her period had been and gone before their wedding day but he was not to have known that. With any luck, she could use this as an excuse for some time and by then, he would not care, anyway. By then, Emeline would no doubt occupy his nights as well as his days.

Perversely, no matter how she tried to steer her thoughts

away from the recent memory of his arms and their nights of loving, they swung back like a rudderless vessel into the path of the storm, more than once threatening to drown her in their sweetness. Now, however, they were coloured by bitterness, warped by her own furious manipulations and by the gossip of the two townswomen. Bruno had verified it; the woman had not only looked like Emeline but had been as mischievous, too. Perhaps more so.

Dwelling on the change in Emeline as an escape from a surfeit of pain, Marietta wondered at the swing from submissive child to spiteful coquette, remembering her uncharacteristic and virulent attack at Monksgrange after Lord Alain's offer of marriage, her subsequent prolonged refusal to respond to Marietta's attempted explanations. It had been there then, Marietta mused; *that* had been the catalyst.

And now, the sudden knowledge that she was desirable, brought about by Lord Alain's companions, perhaps, who had welcomed her visit to Thorsgeld with such enthusiasm; that, combined with her humiliation at not being the next Lady Thorsgeld, had produced another kind of Emeline here, under their roof. But was she a bitch, like the other one?

Wriggling down into the bed, Marietta stretched her hand across to where he should have been, stroking the sheets, the ache in her heart keeping her awake in spite of her tiredness. It was there every time she woke, every time her arm wheedled its way into the cool space where he was not.

At first light, when she knew that the porter at the gatehouse would be astir, she left a note for Iveta to find her and went round to the still-unfinished garden. How much easier it would be, she thought, if a door had been knocked out of her solar wall and steps laid down to the outside.

They would have led straight into it, so much quicker than going halfway round the castle to reach it.

As the team of gardeners joined her, she laboured all morning to plant her medicinal herbs in the square plots outlined by low box heges, tall elecampane, balm, feverfew and rosemary nearest the two walls, then rue, self-heal and soapwort in the middle, and periwinkle, catmint and lavender nearer the paths. Others were placed wherever there were spaces.

Her trees, elder, bay and witch-hazel, stood at the ends of white-painted fences as focal-points, not too near the ornamental pond now teeming with new golden carp. Water-lilies were planted in here and Old Adam had laid a stone fountain in the centre that bubbled and poured from a great shell. Vervain, hyssop, bugle and betony, valerian and centaury were all found a place, some round the edges of the lawns and shade-lovers on the far side of the stew-pond.

The new dovecote in the corner was a wooden tower on a stone base, its openwork top already adorned with white and buff-coloured pigeons cooing and rattling in perpetual surprise at the goings-on, their valuable droppings now falling inside the tower, rather than on the paving.

At mid-day, she sent a message to Lord Alain, asking to be excused from the meal—she would have a picnic in the garden instead—not pausing for a moment but going from garden to orchard to supervise the planting of vines and cherry-trees against the wall, to have the grass mown and the hedge trimmed.

Returning to the garden through the prettily fenced walk-way, her attention was caught by a brilliant flash of blue and red by the entrance to the stew-pond garden from the shooting-butts. Shouts and shrieks caused the garden-lads

and Old Adam to look in surprise to see who intruded,
breaking the peace of the afternoon.

Marietta, with hackles raised, strode up the path towards
the adjoining gate and pushed it open, infuriated by the
sight of two young men scooping water from the stew-pond
and flinging it in sparkling arcs towards two others who
held the shrieking Emeline. She laughed and twisted in
their arms then ran aside, trampling over a newly planted
patch of dyer's madder.

"Get out!" Marietta was in danger of losing all control,
seeing nothing but the desecration of her own sacred place,
the haven she had built up from nothing. "Get out! *Out!*"
She picked up a terracotta plant-pot and hurled it, screaming, at the group, hitting one lad fair and square on the side
of his head. Then picking up a broom that lay nearby, she
flew at Emeline, laying it about her back.

"No...Marietta, no!" Emeline shrieked, standing her
ground. "Lord Alain said I could come in here...ouch!
Stop it!"

"I don't care a tinker's cuss *who* said you could! *I* say
you can't. This is *my* garden...it's private..." Each phrase
was punctuated by a hard thwack across their shoulders as
they crouched away. "And if you dare to set foot in here
again, I'll get a cross-bow to you. Yes, you too, you whey-
faced, sly, puking...clever little bitch! Don't think you've
got the better of me...yet...you'll have to get up earlier to
outdo me...trollop!"

"Stop, please...Marietta...don't...look, he's bleeding.
Oh, poor..."

"Then go and tend him! You're a woman, aren't you?
Tend him!"

Panting with white-hot rage, she flew at Emeline like a
whirlwind, pushed hard at her back with both hands and
propelled her through the gate at an undignified gallop.

Then, keeping hold of her bliaud, she pulled the unfortunate lass round to face her, grabbing at her hair and half-veil in one fistful, her savagery now unrestrained.

"And keep your pretty unsoiled hands for those louts…Emeline *dearest,*" she snarled, "and well away from *my* property! You are *not* the mistress here…I am! Understand?"

She pushed Emeline back, step by step, towards the wall, oblivious to the audience of squires, young knights and the Master-at-Arms who could barely be expected to ignore such an example of aggression.

"*I* will decide what our guests will do. *I* will decide what *you* do, not the other way round. And if you seek to prattle to my lord, or ogle him the way you've done since he returned, *this* is what you'll get!"

And with one mighty swing and before Emeline could guess what was meant, Marietta hit her across the side of her head with all the force she could muster.

Emeline fell like a stone onto her hands and knees, placed a hand against her head and pushed herself upright, holding onto the wall for support. She made no sound but quietly moved away, aware that she must now pass the stares of the unsympathetic older men to reach the kitchen garden and thence through the well-peopled gatehouse. Her young escort had long since disappeared.

It was only then that Marietta saw how many people had witnessed her violent rage, an exhibition she had assumed was private. But only one face caught her eye among those who had lowered their bows; the Master-at-Arms was as near to a smile as he ever got, his head nodding in a clear signal of approval. Before she could turn, he had reached the gate and held it open for her, bowing respectfully as she passed through.

"Thank you," she whispered.

In all truth, she hardly knew which way to go, so dizzy was she with spent rage and distress, so shaky were her legs, her hand stinging with the force of the blow to Emeline's head. She had never before hit anyone except a young lad, once, and Bruno in half-play. Never her sisters. Nor had she ever completely lost her temper. But never had she so consistently and sorely been provoked, nor for so long.

Holding a hand to her mouth to stifle the sobs, she saw the trampled plants, the broken plant-pot, the new waterlilies half pulled out of the stew-pond and, still too upset to cry, she stood panting in loud rasping moans as her anger flared again and simmered.

Old Adam came through from the pleasance, unperturbed, and without a word directed two of the lads to re-set the plants and tidy up while Marietta went along to the new fountain to splash water on her face and hold her wrists into its coolness.

It was then that Lord Alain came into the pleasance. Marietta was quite sure that, by now, Emeline would have told him some tale of an unprovoked attack, of a personal assault on herself, of a lad's bleeding head, and she was prepared for the full force of his wrath, even a beating. Consequently, she braced herself for his first onslaught, undeceived by his quiet approach but not willing to stand meekly and take her punishment without some contest. She glared at him with undisguised animosity as he advanced.

"That's my girl," he said, quietly, "that's my beautiful wild cat. I wondered how long it would be before you stopped sulking and fought back. It took trespassers on your garden to rouse you, did it? Eh?"

Still unsure of his humour, she watched to see what his hands would do, how his eyes might narrow before he struck, but there was nothing of that, only amusement and approval and an all-encompassing glance that swept her from top to bottom, making her angry so soon after the conclusions she'd been forced to arrive at yesterday.

"If you're going to beat me," she spat, "get on with it before the gardeners get back. I don't want an audience." Her heart was racing now with a new threat and she held onto the wall of the fountain-pond, bracing herself.

"You think I'm going to beat you, lass? For doing what you should have done days…weeks ago? Nay, I can do better than that." Without any warning—and she was too confused to anticipate—he grasped her shoulders and pulled her into his arms, closing her cry of protest with his lips and holding her painfully hard onto his chest. His kiss was like strong wine.

After the exertions of the last few moments when she had released so much pent-up anger, it would have been easy for her to soften and hold onto his supporting arms and be cradled like a child. But her pride struck a course of its own and she pushed away from him, unable to forget what she knew.

"Go!" she panted, "go and tend your precious Emeline. *She* needs you, not me. And when she tells you she doesn't know why I hit her—"

"You *hit* her? God's truth!" His eyes danced. "Where?"

"Where? On her head…where d'you think?" she growled.

"I didn't see that part…wonderful…what a woman!"

A thought occurred to her that he must have seen what happened.

"You saw? Where were you? You sent her here to provoke me, did you?"

"Nay, lass. Give me *some* credit! Up there, look." He pointed to the windows of his solar high up next to hers, overlooking the garden.

"I heard their commotion as soon as they went in, and looked out to see what was happening. I saw you chase them off and hustle her round the corner, but I couldn't see the rest."

"But you heard?"

"Yes, sweetheart, I heard most of it. And I saw the approval of your audience, too. It was a treat."

"Then if you approve so much, why have you encouraged her to goad me so? Why did you not chastise her yourself instead of leaving it to me?" She pushed past him and tried to walk away but the seat was there in the corner and he would not let her pass.

"Because, my fierce woman, she is a guest here, for one thing, and I may not do that. And for another, she is *your* sister and, if anyone has to take her in hand, it has to be you. But you've been pussy-footing around her all this time as though she was made of thistledown, terrified of hurting her feelings any more. It's taken you all this time to do what you should have done ages ago."

"How can you say that...how *can* you? When I told you how she'd annoyed me, you told me we'd manage her together. You didn't say you'd give in to her every whim and that I'd be the one to bear the consequences. If you'd said *that*, I'd have insisted she went home, there and then."

"I don't want her to go home. If she asks to go home after this, I shall not co-operate. She can stay put and learn to behave herself."

"And you'll do all you can to make things comfortable for her, I suppose...and give way to her...while I do the housekeeping and...run round after you both...get off me! Take her into your bed, too, why don't you?"

She beat at him now in a frenzy of jealousy, torn between hurting herself and hurting him at the same time, all caution gone.

"Take her...I don't care if you bed her day and night...but she'll not come into my garden...get off! If she comes in here, I'll tear every plant up with my bare hands and throw them over the wall. I swear it!"

"There's no need to be jealous of her, Marietta. I've told you over and over that it's you I want...not her. Be still and hear me—"

"I won't hear you! I won't! I know more than you think I do. I'm not stupid...I have ears...it's Emeline...you can't fool me any more."

He grabbed her flailing arms and slammed her back against the wall, stopping her struggles with a grip so fierce it took her breath away.

"Then listen to me, woman, once and for all. Until I can tell you what my reasons are, you'll have to go along with it. She'll stay here while we have guests whether you like it or not, and as soon as they've gone home I'll be glad to see the back of her.

"Now, I don't know what you've heard and I haven't time to find out, but hear this, and understand me plainly, Marietta. We'll have no more of this hiding and sulking. You will be at my side at every meal...at *my* side, do you hear? And you will play the part of mistress of the house and attend me on every ride, dressed in your finest, on every hunt and at every gathering. I want no evasions!"

"My flux...I cannot hunt..."

She had seldom seen him so angry. "Don't lie, woman! Do what you like to me, but don't lie! You tell me you're not stupid, so give me the same credit, for pity's sake. It's not your monthly flow and you know it as well as I do. And let me make something else clear; you'll share my bed every night. If I'm not in yours, you'll be in mine. Then you'll know for certain where I am at night, won't you? Eh?"

"You can't make me…" She made a last attempt to flout him.

"Oh, yes, I can, my girl, I can make you do that too. You know I can."

As if to demonstrate how easy it was, he slipped a hand round to the back of her neck and drew her forward to his mouth, holding her still just long enough for her to have moved away if she had wanted to. Teasing her lips to prove his boast, and lingering with the tenderness she had longed for during the lonely night, he let his hands fall, holding her there with his mouth alone.

"Now, my lady," he whispered, "you will come inside with me and do what we should have done last night. Then you will refresh yourself, dress in your brightest gown and ride your new horse with me until supper. She's getting almost as frisky as you are. Come. I'll have your obedience now."

Silently, Marietta took his offered hand and allowed herself to be led back into the castle with all the meekness of a lamb, little Faith romping after them quite unnoticed and trailing her lead.

No nearer to making any sense of things than she'd been before, Marietta's first instinct was to obey her husband. Which was, fortunately, the pleasantest road to follow since it led her into his arms for the best part of an hour. That she had vowed never to allow that to happen again was something that lost credence somewhere along the way in a jumble of revelations and dismissals bandied about like ammunition in their earlier confrontation and which now seemed vaguely irrelevant.

Strive as she may, she could make no sense of it; it was as though he realised there was something for her to discover—at no time had he pretended otherwise—and yet felt that it was not essential she should be told. Not at this time, at least. Could she have got it all wrong? In the light of his approval of her disciplining Emeline, was it possible that he had chosen her, Marietta, because she was different? Not the same? Had she been barking up the wrong tree?

Whatever it was, she decided that, for one day, enough was enough, that she deserved some respite from the conflicts, theirs and her own. If he wanted her company enough to demand it, then her obedience could hardly be called surrender, though no one would have known the difference. And later, when she rode by his side on Mist, she adopted a mantle of serenity rather than a forced ebullience which, after her victory, might have been permissible.

She stayed near him, watching the mares and foals, observing the training of the destriers and, in the tiltyard beyond, shouted gentle encouragement to Bruno and his friends who practised with unwieldy lances against the spitefully small ring that swung in the breeze. And when the squires urged Lord Alain to show them how it should be done, she cheered with the rest when he did, and gave him the kiss that he claimed as reward.

Afterwards, she took him on a tour of every department where her skills as mistress of the household had been put to good use over the past few days, surprising him with the extent of her preparations, the detail of her planning, her forethought, her knowledge of every man in every job. At the same time, it satisfied Marietta to show him something of the work that had kept her so occupied when he had assumed that part of her absence was due to pique.

His arm stealing around her shoulders when the cook's staff, the marshal's staff, the chamberlain, the steward and the treasurer, too, all attested to her competence was a recognition that he was proud of her. She showed him the prepared guest-rooms, the supplies, the extra accommodation for servants, the lists of entertainments, the plans for outdoor food for a picnic in the garden with musicians, and several feasts.

New liveries had also been prepared for all his staff—blue badges outlined in yellow on a grey background, blue and grey parti-coloured chausses and yellow shoes—and new banners for the hall.

When they sat down to supper, they sat Iveta between them to make a fuss of her, not even asking where Emeline was. Even so, Marietta sent her a well-filled tray of food and wine and noticed that it was returned at the end of the meal, empty.

They took Iveta and Bruno to the garden after that, where all was now serene and well kept and where the lads were quietly watering the plants before sunset. The pigeons had lined up on the edges of the two ponds to take their last drink of the day, and a few late bees bumbled over the marjoram in a last raid.

Old Adam came to Marietta, ambling up the path with his hand stretched out towards her. He had known Lord Alain since he was a lad and saw no reason to stand on ceremony at this late stage.

"Look 'ere, m'lady. This is summat I were given by Lord Alain's father."

He opened his fist to reveal a mound of tiny black seeds. "He brought 'em back from t'Holy Land when he were on one o' them crusades. Seeds, they are. I've 'ad 'em all this time waitin' for't right person to gi' 'em to. Now look…" He took her hand and poured them into her palm "…thou can have 'em. They're yours."

Marietta was delighted by the honour. "Thank you, Adam. I'll plant them straight away. Do you know what they're called?"

"Nay, m'lady, I'm not sure what proper name is, but he

called 'em love-in-a-mist, 'cos they have a blue flower wi' fuzzy stuff all round, like mist.''

Lord Alain nodded wisely. ''Then we'd better find a good place to plant this love-in-a-mist, hadn't we? Do we have a place in the sun?''

''Over here,'' Iveta called. ''Look, Marrie, here's a space, next to the self-heal.''

So they sprinkled the seeds on the dampened soil and pressed them down, and Iveta tied one of her red ribbons to a stick to mark the spot and to keep away the birds.

''Winged or otherwise,'' Lord Alain murmured.

Marietta wondered why the first Lady Thorsgeld had not been the right person to give them to. Had it been because she took no interest in gardens?

Chapter Nine

The musicians, rising to a crescendo at the end of their chorus, drowned out the words of the handsome guest sitting next to Marietta, and she was obliged to lean towards him and watch his lips to catch what he was saying.

His shoulders were turned towards her and she caught a faint whiff of some perfume from his thick well-groomed hair, and before she caught his eyes, she saw that they had already lingered on her bared neck and the outline of her breasts. More than that, while meeting hers, they flickered beyond her for a split second, to where Emeline sat further along the table.

"Until I met your husband in York last week," he was saying, "I had no idea he'd re-married. Did he take you by surprise?"

Ignoring the implications of the seemingly artless question, Marietta gave him more solid information to consider. "I came to live at Monksgrange for the summer with my family in late April. It's across the valley, you know. My young brother Bruno is one of Lord Alain's squires. That's how we met."

She pointed Bruno out to him, kneeling before one of the guests further along the table and holding the bowl for finger-washing, a towel draped neatly over one shoulder. He looked solemn and very fine in his new livery.

Her companion, Sir Bastien Symme, looked puzzled. "I always thought that Monksgrange belonged to Bolton Priory," he said. "Have they let it go now?"

"Yes. Difficult times, you know. My father bought it."

"Your father...would I know him, d'ye think?"

"Sir Henry Wardle. I was Marietta Wardle."

The news appeared to distract him somewhat, for he looked up sharply at that and studied her, though Marietta thought that he saw something else.

"Sir Henry Wardle. How interesting. He owns a fair bit of land hereabouts, I suppose?"

She recognised the mildly spoken question as being more than a polite observation, for he held his head at an angle, suggesting to her that he expected a full inventory. But he was a stranger to her; such information was best kept close to one's chest. Instead of answering directly, she smiled, as though such things were taken for granted.

"Do you know him, Sir Bastien?"

"Er...not personally, no. But everyone knows of him, of course. Have the lay-brothers entirely left Monksgrange now?"

"Oh, yes."

"And when do your parents leave? After harvest? You'll be on your own then, will you?" His smile caressed her skin.

Enigmatically, she replied, "Hardly," allowing her own glance to take in the hall packed with people. Too many questions, she thought.

When he laughed, which he seemed to do readily enough, he showed remarkably even teeth and his eyes almost closed so that one could not tell whether they saw or not. He was dark, of lighter build than Lord Alain but well-proportioned, and elegantly dressed in deep mulberry and black with far more gold jewellery about his person than her husband wore.

"And your sisters?" His eyes strayed to Emeline again before returning to her. "Do they live here with you, or with your father?"

"Like you, Sir Bastien, they're guests here. And they're my half-sisters. Bruno and I have the same mother...the first Lady Wardle."

"Ah...I see. That accounts for it."

"Yes." She knew he referred to the colouring.

"I should like to meet Sir Henry Wardle. He appears to be a fine judge of women. Perhaps he could give me some advice."

"You are a horse-dealer, are you not, sir?"

He accepted the mild rebuke with another laugh.

"Yes, my lady, I buy and sell horses, not nearly so complicated as breeding them. Your husband is far more knowledgeable than any dealer about that side of things. The land up here can support beautiful mares, fine-limbed fiery creatures."

Whether it was intentional or not, he made it sound as though he was speaking of women rather than horses, for his eyes betrayed the direction of his thoughts when the smile faded from them and allowed a slow search of her face that halted fractionally on her mouth.

Fortunately, she was spared the embarrassment of making any response when Bruno placed a bowl of rose-petalled water with a graceful bow and stood back to watch them dip fingers, washing away the stickiness.

On the first floor, the great solar was a conveniently pleasant chamber in the northwest tower, overlooking the kitchen garden on one side and, on the other, the stew-pond garden with the view over the great wall across the valley.

Taking the opportunity to mingle, Marietta went to speak to the couple who looked slightly less at ease than the others, all of whom appeared to know each other.

"Master Geoffrey...Mistress Jean," she said, holding out both hands to them.

They were young and unremarkably attractive people, plainly dressed but neat and wholesome, glowing with health. They seemed pleased to be singled out for her attention; since their arrival last night there had been little time to do more than eat and sleep. These two, the de la Dales, were employed by a wealthy breeder of palfreys and workhorses over in Wensleydale, Mistress Jean almost as knowledgeable about them as her husband and an indispensable half of the partnership.

This was the first time they had been to Thorsgeld; they had not expected such a well-attended gathering, nor such a welcome, having understood that Lord Alain was a widower. His lovely wife quite won their hearts.

"Such luxury," Mistress Jean smiled. "You must have had some experience to control a place as large as this."

"Not at all. My home was the usual manor, but I was used to overseeing the housekeeping, and there are plenty of men here who know what they're doing. It's the same, only larger."

They liked her modesty.

"And horses?" Master Geoffrey de la Dale asked. He was a shrewd-looking man, his face weather-beaten and alert.

"Not my department—" she smiled in response "but I shall be there when Lord Alain shows you the stud."

She knew little enough about the other guests except what Alain had told her. Sir John and Lady Isobel de Rhenne lived in an ancient manor house near York, buying and selling war-horses for local knights. He had come pre-

pared with a list of requirements and a clerk to make notes
of his transactions. They were old friends of Lord Alain
and had known his father, in which case, Marietta thought,
Lady Isobel might be encouraged to tell her something of
the first Lady Thorsgeld. She looked approachable enough,
middle-aged and comfortable.

They were the senior couple; the others, Sir Richard and
Lady Mary Capestone, were somewhat younger, more like
herself and Alain. Enthusiastic and quite noisy, drawing
people to them like magnets, they had already begun a
good-natured ribbing of both Emeline and Iveta, aided and
abetted by Sir Bastien. Marietta wondered how long it
would be before the one bachelor in the group claimed
Emeline's company for the rest of the event.

There were plenty of other dealers who would be sleeping in the great hall with their servants, but none who expected to be entertained in the same style as these seven.

Since yesterday, they had seen very little of Emeline, and
now, though she would not meet Marietta's eye, she was
back in circulation with a much-reduced coterie, unaware
that the young men had been warned that any repeat of
yesterday's performance would see them back home in
double-quick time. No white flag had been offered, either
by herself or by Marietta, but no one would have suspected
that sparks had flown so recently.

Lord Alain's protectiveness towards Emeline was at first
taken to represent the concern of a host for a young guest.
If there were those among the onlookers who wondered
how Marietta felt about this overload of attention, they said
nothing. All the same, there was not one amongst those
who knew him well who had not made the visual connection between Emeline and his first wife.

Neither had this attention to her sister escaped Marietta's
notice. In the remaining day before the guests arrived, Lord

Alain had done much to assure her that her fears about Emeline were mistaken, not by direct reference but by his appreciation of herself, by his approval and, not least, by his tender loving.

As soon as the guests arrived, however, the accent changed, and Marietta was once again confused by this inconsistency, being still in the uncertain earliest days of marriage and desperately in need of reassurance now, of all times.

Had she not begun to love him, it would have mattered less, but her heart had opened, taking in pain as greedily as pleasure. And while she longed to screw Emeline's neck like a pigeon's, who could have blamed the lass for blushing timidly when he personally lifted her upon a gentle palfrey and whispered into her ear?

Most of the assembly who noticed this pretended otherwise and kept Marietta busy with their enquiries as they mounted horses in the bustling courtyard. But Sir Bastien was the one to take most immediate advantage. Brushing aside the young groom who held his hands for Marietta's foot, he took a stand behind her, put his hands around her waist and whispered a quick "Ready!" in her ear.

It was not until she was firmly seated in the saddle and saw who arranged the folds of her full skirt that she realised who it was. Even though a snub for such familiarity could have been all the thanks expected, Marietta did neither. It was, after all, her right to be tended by her husband and if he was otherwise engaged, he could hardly grumble at the outcome.

All the same, the man's hands on her waist had spread well across her ribs and close under her breasts, and the strength of his fingers left an imprint that tingled, even as she gathered Mist's silky mane in her hand to free it from the rein-guard.

In no particular order, the riders trooped out through the gatehouse and round the side of the castle into the stable-yard, Marietta fully aware that Sir Bastien was close by her side but saying nothing to embark on a conversation and neither returning nor avoiding his frequent looks at her. And while the destriers were brought out, one at a time, and paraded before them with glossy coats shining like satin in the sun, Marietta was drawn into the general talk, though most of the guests kept their comments for their partners.

Eventually, Marietta sidled her mount across to where Emeline sat alone, and drew her to the side with a tip of her head. Emeline must have thought she was again in the firing-line for she leaned to Marietta.

"I'm not ogling him, honest, Marietta. I've hardly said a word to him."

This was the first allusion either of them had made to their quarrel; Emeline's silence on the subject had been taken for bitterness rather than acceptance. Consequently, Marietta stared at her sister as though the denial could have been finely veiled sarcasm. But Emeline was not one to understand such sophistication. She meant what she said. "I'm doing my best, Marrie…" it was the first time she had used the pet name for many weeks "…I didn't really want to upset you, either." From Emeline, that was an admission not to be ignored.

Marietta realised what it had cost her. She moved closer.

"Come on up here, away from the ears."

They moved apart from the crowd to a space by the store-rooms.

"Emmie, I don't want to fight with you," Marietta said, keeping her voice low. "I can't believe you're happy about this state of affairs, are you?"

Emeline's pretty mouth pursed as tears gathered. "No,"

she whispered, "no, I'm not happy. I would have gone home when you…we…you know. But he said I must not. I wish he would let me go home now."

"Don't cry, Em, for heaven's sake." Marietta put a hand on her arm. "Don't…he'll think we're quarrelling again."

"He's not doing anything to help matters, is he?" She sniffed. "Is he trying to make you jealous?"

"Well, *you* were, weren't you?"

"I was, yes. Because I was still mad about the whole business. But I'm not in love with him, Marrie. He scares me a bit…he's so fierce…and he doesn't laugh like my other friends. And I'm sure that he's in love with you because I've seen how he's kissed you…"

"Where?"

"In the garden. Does he like the idea of us fighting over him. Is that it?"

Marietta sighed. Even Emeline, not-very-bright Emeline had seen that, so it must be obvious.

"It certainly looks like that. I can't for the life of me think why he should want that."

"Perhaps it's because you were so reluctant." Emeline turned to her, reining back a little as the hindquarters of the horse in front swung towards her. "You made him chase you, didn't you?"

Marietta's eyes searched him out like a homing-pigeon, alighting on his powerful black head and wide shoulders, watching as he talked, pointed, called instructions, laughed at the remarks. Proud knight. Yes, she had made him chase her. Was this a way of taking revenge for her defiance, then?

"Yes," she agreed, "but it wasn't coyness, Emmie."

"What then? He frightened you, too?"

"Yes, I suppose so." That, among other more dutiful reasons.

"Are you still frightened of him? You don't look as though you are."

"No. Angry with him but not frightened."

"Then why don't you play the same game?"

In all truth, the idea had flitted through her mind since the arrival of their guests but, short of some discussion and support, it had been dismissed as too dangerous. Now, coming from Emeline herself, it took on new dimensions.

"The same game?" She studied Emeline's pretty face.

She must have appeared puzzled, for Emeline frowned at her, leaning closer.

"Come on, Marrie. Don't be dumb. I know you're not used to flirting, but it's good fun once you stop worrying. I can't stop him hanging around me, I can't be rude to him and snub him like I can the squires. And we can both see how he's enjoying some kind of game, playing one off against the other. Surely you can fight back…like you did with me?"

"And then what…when I've flirted?"

"Well, then he'll be as mad as a hare and probably beat you and stick you to him like a leech. And then he'll leave me alone to get on with *my* flirting. None of the lads will come *near* me when he's around. Besides, I'm much more interested in…" Her eyes showed exactly where her interests lay. Sir Bastien had already edged towards them, threatening an end to their conversation. "Come on, Marrie, he's looked at both of us as though we were fillies ready for…"

"Em!" she hissed, ducking her head. "For pity's sake!"

"It's true," Emeline whispered, now laughing in anticipation. "You take him on for a bit, just for a day or so. It'll work, you'll see!"

There was no time to go into more detail before Sir Bastien drew alongside Marietta and regarded their blushing laughter with an air of faint amusement.

"Well, well. This is the first time I've seen you two speaking together. Will you escort me into the paddock to see the palfreys, or shall I escort you?"

"Neither," said Emeline without looking at him. She moved away into the crowd and left the two together.

"Good," Sir Bastien smiled at Marietta. "That's an even better proposition."

There was more room for manoeuvre in the large grassy paddock where the best palfreys were brought in to be trotted along the avenue of spectators. These were the best, the showiest mares, the most docile geldings, the prettiest riding-horses especially bred and trained for the most comfortable ride, for endurance over long distances and rough roads, for their good temper and patient disposition.

Laughingly, Sir Richard Capestone called out to Lord Alain, "What I want to see is that Andalucian your lady wife rides, Alain. You're keeping both of them uncommonly dark, you old scoundrel!"

Sir Richard was more interested in the destriers and was treating the second phase of the exhibition with rather less reverence, his wife thought, regretting the attention being drawn towards Marietta and her lovely new mount.

At that moment, Marietta was well out of earshot in the company of Sir Bastien and Sir John, discussing the merits of three of the stallions they had just watched.

Iveta called to her. "Marietta, Lord Alain wants you to go to him."

Thinking that this was no more than a request for her company, she ambled away towards him round the backs of the riders and came up behind him, waiting some moments before he realised she was there. It was Master Geoffrey de la Dale who drew his attention to her.

"Saints! There you are. Where have you been?" Lord Alain turned sharply towards her.

"Here," she replied, unhelpfully.

"Oh. Some of our guests want to see what the Andalucian can do. Let them see her paces, if you please. To the top of the paddock and back."

Marietta caught Emeline's eye. "Certainly, my lord. Mistress Jean, come, shall we exchange mounts for a while? You would like to try this one, would you not? She needs an experienced hand like yours."

Mistress Jean's face lit up with enthusiasm. "Oh, my lady, may I...really? She's such a beauty."

And before Lord Alain realised what was happening, the women had dismounted and exchanged horses. In the light of Sir Richard's remark about keeping them both dark, this was not what he wanted, for now it would look like a verification of the jibe, and though Mistress Jean was an extremely competent horsewoman, the visual effect was not half so attractive as Marietta's graceful figure dressed in cream and pale-blue.

What was more, when she backed silently away on Mistress Jean's mount, she found that Sir Bastien Symme was there to take up a position next to her, making her laugh at some innocuous remark. Already she was beginning to feel the thrill of danger.

Throughout the afternoon, she and Emeline developed their mutual plan, both of them deliberately staying aloof from the men who thought the game was of their own devising. Whenever she glanced towards her husband, there Emeline would be also; wherever she went, Sir Bastien contrived to be.

Surrounded by so many pleasant guests, Marietta began to relax and enjoy their company and when they rode into the tiltyard to see the young lads practise she stayed in the

centre of a crowd of men, talking animatedly while Lord
Alain stood aside with the ladies.

Careful not to neglect any one of them, she took the
ladies into the orchard to admire the new vines and then
into the garden. Although she had vowed that Emmie
would not be allowed in here, their conspiracy demanded
that only the two men be manipulated, not the women. To
them, they must appear as friends or run the risk of revealing the seriousness of their scheme and embarrassing
everyone else at the same time.

After supper, while the air was still warm, the men joined
them in the garden, eager to sit with them and bask in the
success of the day. Throughout the meal, Marietta had
maintained a distant attitude towards her husband, seeming
not to notice his warmth towards Emeline and discovering
how less painful that had become when she had the attentions of a handsome man to entertain her.

Knowing that Emeline was not as interested in Alain as
she had thought her to be gave Marietta free rein to laugh
merrily, her head almost touching that of Sir Bastien, coolly
ignoring her husband's glance of displeasure.

Now she sank down on the grass in the enclosure where
the arbour stood, watching the approach of Sir Bastien's
long legs and seeing, from the corner of her eye, where
Lord Alain sat with Emeline and Lady Isobel de Rhenne.
Deliberately, she waved to Lady Mary and Mistress Jean
to join her and though they signalled that they would, they
were delayed by their deep conversation.

"Scared, my lady?" Sir Bastien whispered as he sat by
her, drawing up his legs to rest his arms across. His bold
stare was impossible to misinterpret.

"You think I need protection, with my husband looking
on?" She looked away, but too late to hide the smile. The

situation would not have been half so piquant *without* her husband looking on.

Sir Bastien did not glance towards the subject of their discussion. "He's not doing a very good job of it, is he? Not as good a job as I would do if I were your husband of only a couple of weeks."

Still she would not look at him, but plucked at the short grass by her side. "Then it's as well you are not, sir," she said, softly.

"Why?"

"Because then you would not know who to flirt with most, your wife or your sister-in-law, would you?"

"Wrong, m'lady. I always know who to flirt with most. I flirt with the host's wife. She is always the most beautiful and therein lies the most danger, the most satisfaction." He gave this comprehensive answer time to sink in while Marietta remained silent.

So, the man was an accomplished rake. Presumably, Alain must know that, and yet he left her open to his advances while he had eyes only for Emeline. Again. After all his assurances. Then he deserved what was coming.

She knew he studied her face but hoped he could not recognise the conflict that stirred her, provoking feelings of revenge, pain and confusion. Rejection, above all. Rejection of her company at such a time, except to show off her new mare. Just in time, the recklessness that wavered on the brink of her anger was dissipated by the arrival of the two ladies. Waving a hand to the spaces by her side, she smiled up at them. "Come, come and join us," she said.

"Ladies." Sir Bastien held out a gallant hand. "I was just asking Lady Marietta about Beckington Manor down the road, there. It's your father's property, is it not, m'lady?"

Marietta looked at him in amazement, not only because

of the suddenness of the relatively uninteresting topic but also because of his assumption.

"No," she replied, "it isn't."

Hoping that this would conclude the enquiry, she turned her attention to Lady Mary's lively face bordered by gleaming red hair, plaited and coiled. "Have you left your family in good hands, Lady Mary? How old are they now?"

Deftly, almost fervently, she kept the conversation moving between her three guests, steering around their interests and away from her own as though on an obstacle course, knowing that any wandering into her doings, however trivial, would invite personal questions she preferred not to answer.

But there was to be no escape, for when Mistress Jean spoke of her magical ride on Mist, it was then only one step away from silly Dulzelina, and Monksgrange, and then her family, and then…Beckington, brought back with all the determination of a trained fighter.

Skilfully, Sir Bastien avoided asking the question he most wanted to ask, but left it to Lady Mary instead.

"This place, Beckington, is it? Who did you say it belongs to?"

"I didn't," Marietta said, by now too far gone to care a damn who knew her business, too unused to fending off questions to know which information mattered and which did not, "but since you seem so interested, I will tell you. It belongs to me."

"You?" Sir Bastien looked as though he was about to fall over.

"Why the surprise?" Lady Mary asked him.

"Well, I…er…"

Mistress Jean laughed. "Come now, Sir Bastien, surely you don't think that the only people who own property are men, do you? My husband and I are in business together. Women can do anything that men can do, you know.''

That, of course, was a signal for them all to fall about at the sheer absurdity of it, attracting the attention of the other guests.

Marietta was persuaded to explain.

''Well, it's always been passed down the female line to the first one to marry. And that's me. But it's no cause for excitement; it's in a terrible state. We're going to renovate the place any day now.''

''You've been, have you?'' Though Sir Bastien flicked a lady bird off his knee with studied casualness, his question was sharply put.

''Oh, yes. Alain and I were horrified. It's been sadly neglected because we've been so far away, but now it has to be attended to. Come…'' she spied Lord Alain walking towards them, alerted by the hilarity ''…it's getting dark already. The midges are out, look.'' They danced in tightly packed clouds in the last rays of the sun.

She would have turned to walk with Sir Bastien but, in two strides, Lord Alain had caught up with them and taking her arm firmly in his, escorted the party back into the courtyard and then into the great hall for a last nightcap before bed. His grip was painfully tight.

Intent on releasing herself as soon as possible, Marietta wondered if she could reach Emeline's room without him noticing her absence, but the chance did not arise, for he summoned Emeline's servants to escort her away and finally, when all were gone, he followed Marietta to her solar as though to emulate the candle's shadow.

She knew what was to come. She sensed his tension.

''What is this, my lord?'' She wheeled on him in anger as the door closed behind them. ''Why stick to me like a leech in the last half-hour before bedtime? Is it only now you've remembered my existence? I did not strong-arm you away from the person you've been close to all day."

"So you admit you've been close to Sir Bastien all day, do you? Well done, my lady, that's a start. Now we can make some headway." He walked to the door of his chamber and called to the squires who awaited him. "Get out!" he said to them.

Marietta heard the far door close and watched as he began to undress, wondering what was in store. "Well, of course, I've been with my guests. What did you expect me to do? Ignore them?" she said.

"Sir Bast—"

"No!" she yelled. "*All* of them! I'm not surprised you didn't notice who I was with. You've not seen anything of what I did from morn until now."

"Yes, I have, my girl. I've seen everything you did. I saw how you got out of showing off your new mare, too. That was not well done, Marietta." He came to stand near the window where she could see the last orange rays of the sun on his face and chest. "You know what I expected of you."

"Yes, my lord," she snarled, "and I also know it's the only time you spoke to me all afternoon, and even then it was not a request, politely couched, but a command. You think I respond to that, do you? After only a few weeks of marriage and it's come to that, already?"

"I told you to trust me, Marietta, to have faith. I know what I'm doing."

"Oh, no…" She was hoarse with rage now. "Oh, no, you don't. You don't know what you're doing to *me* at all. Insensitive…boorish…" She strode to the door, ready to go anywhere, to find a room with her maids.

But he reached out and pulled her back. "Come back, I

haven't finished. There's to be no more flirting with that jackanapes. Do you understand? No more!''

Like a wild animal, she flung his hand away from her arm.

"Hypocrite!'' she yelled. "You've known that...that jackanapes...how many years? You must have known what he's like. He actually boasted to me of going for his hosts' wives because it's more of a thrill—''

"...What?'' He twisted round to look at her, frozen. "What? He boasted of taking his hosts' *wives?*''

"Yes,'' she hissed, bending to him to push the words home, "that's what he said. Don't tell me you didn't know that.''

"No...no, I didn't know it was like that.''

"Liar!'' she spat.

She thought he was going to hit her, then, for his eyes narrowed, his cheek muscles tightened and the skin of his forearms rippled as fists were clenched. She braced herself but it did not come.

"You *knew!* And yet all day, and yesterday, too, you left me alone like bait while you dallied with my sister. And then you have the *gall* to chastise me for enjoying his attentions. Well, yes, I did enjoy them. And what's more, I shall enjoy them again tomorrow. And the next day, too.''

"Marietta, let me explain. I think it's time you knew...''

"Take your hands off me...I don't want to hear any more. You are beneath contempt! Yes, my lord. *Beneath* contempt!''

She saw how, for once, his shoulders dropped and sagged, how his eyes, once hard and challenging, now emptied into bleak dark pools. This was the first time ever that she had seen that look. She had wounded him. The temptation was to say more, to inflict on him what she herself had suffered.

But she could not. The joy of hurting him lasted a mere moment; it was replaced by a longing to hold and comfort him, to say how much she loved him. But he had never spoken of love to her, only of want and desire, and she understood that whether she loved or not was unimportant to him.

"Then if you don't want my explanation, my lady, kindly explain to me what else this…jackanapes…told you about his methods. Presumably you were not talking about that when Lady Mary and Mistress Jean were with you? Or did he have designs on them, too?"

Marietta thought back to their last topic of conversation.

"We were talking about Beckington, my lord, if you must know. I'll make a full record of our topics tomorrow, if…"

"What? Beckington?" He pulled her back once more. "You talked of Beckington…Christ! I don't believe it! Did you tell him it was yours?"

Again, she shook him off. "Is there some law that forbids me to talk of my own property? You will not talk of it with me. He did not know it belongs to me."

"No, little idiot! He thought it belonged to your father."

She blinked, thrown off course a little. "Well, what if he did? What does it matter who it belongs to?"

Instead of answering directly, he wanted to know more. "And when you told him that you are the owner, what then? Startled, was he?"

Remembering the man's look of sheer amazement, she would have said that "startled" was putting it mildly. But why all this fuss about something which he had so resolutely refused to discuss? "Yes, he was startled. But only because he'd not expected a woman to own it."

"Because he'd not expected *you* to own it, lass," he

snapped. "And did you tell him your father had bought Monksgrange, too?"

She knew both by the question and its tone that he had the answer to that already. Tired of this conversation and totally confused by his alternating rejection and concern, it was impossible for her to know which of them was genuine, or indeed whether both were genuine, but for the wrong reasons. Reaching beneath the large curtained bed, she felt for the wooden truckle-bed, pulled it out and began to shove it across the floor with one angry foot, picking up a blanket and shaking it out.

But Lord Alain saw what she had in mind. "You can forget that," he said. "You're sleeping in there." Before she could dodge him, he had caught her in one scoop and deposited her face-down on the bed. Then, ignoring her wild struggles, he held her hips down with one hand while he unlaced the ties of her cote-hardie from neck to below the waist, something she would have found it difficult to do without the help of her maids.

"I'm not sleeping with you…ever again…no, I'm not!" she yelled.

"Come on, get this off. You can't sleep in it."

"Yes, I can! Let me up!"

"I will in a minute, come on…other arm…but you're going to tell me what else he asked you. I want to hear what damage has been done, then I shall know how to proceed."

"Proceed with what?"

"With my plans. Lift your hips up…that's better." He threw the gown to one side and began to unpin the gold mesh cauls that held her coiled plaits to her head.

"Let me up!" she gasped, her words spitting into the bedcover.

He continued to loosen her hair with deft fingers as

though he was unbuckling his own armour. "Yes, we'll get rid of this thing first."

"I'm not going to sleep with you!"

"What else did he want to know? Tell me!"

"About what?"

"Beckington."

"Nothing. I told him we were going to renovate it, that's all."

His fingers stopped their unplaiting. "Renovate it?"

"Yes, don't worry, you know as well as I do that it's a lie, isn't it? You've no intention of putting the place straight, have you?" she growled, twisting round to look at him.

"Did you say when?"

"Oh, for heaven's sake, why all this? What does it matter? I said any day now, or something like that, because it sounded good, even though I knew it to be a lie."

Suddenly, his hand was removed from her hips and she was allowed to roll over at last and away off the bed, wearing only a fine linen kirtle and the long waving dark brown hair like a satin hood.

"Do you want me to explain?" he asked.

He sat on the bed and finished his own undressing while Marietta stood over by the window, watching him, still boiling with anger at his treatment of her, both now and during the day. What had he meant when he'd said that he didn't know it was like that? Like what? Was he saying that he didn't know Sir Bastien was attracted by the idea of taking wives? Had he expected him to flirt with Emeline, perhaps? But how could he when *he* had hovered around her all day?

"No! I don't want any more explanations. They're worthless. I've made every effort to make your damn horse-fair a success and this is all the reward I get...your pretences! Pretend concern. Pretend ignorance of your guest's well-known lechery. You're a sham, my lord.'' The lump in her throat barred further words and she turned her head so that he'd not see her tears.

On silent feet he stalked her, picked her up and carried her, now sobbing hoarsely, back to the bed where he held her to him, rocking her and stroking her hair. Still protesting that she'd not sleep with him, not ever, she listened with half an ear to his whispers that the day had been a huge success, that her planning was a miracle, that she had looked magnificent.

Tomorrow, he told her, he would not allow her to stray a hand's-breadth away from his side and, if that toadying little pipsqueak so much as looked at her, he'd geld him. For some unaccountable reason, that consoling thought brought on a lethargy so profound that sleep could be held off no longer.

For many more hours, Lord Alain lay awake, caressing her back from time to time and brushing her hair away from the hot damp forehead. She had every right to be angry, he thought. For that, and other reasons, he would not put her through such anguish again.

What was more, if he had known that it was not so much the colouring that attracted the man but the fact that he found excitement in the idea of stealing another man's wife, he would never have put her in that position in the first place. He'd been a fool. Blind. Ham-fisted. His plans would have to be adapted accordingly.

Chapter Ten

Not surprisingly, Alain's assurances that he would keep her close from now on were discounted by Marietta as soon as they were uttered. After all the pledges that he would seek her, find her, and bring her back to him, then his apparent unconcern, it was not to be wondered at that even a good night's sleep failed to convince her of his sincerity.

"You will forgive me, my lord, if I don't take your word too seriously," Marietta said, scathingly. She sat up against the pillows, watching the way the muscles of his back rippled when he ran a hand through his hair like a giant comb.

He had allowed her a justifiable anger last night, but she had better learn how far she could go. Slowly, he turned his head to look at her, showing his displeasure. "Don't dare to challenge my word, wench," he snapped.

Recklessly, she pursued her course. "It's not your word that's being challenged, is it? It's your ability to protect your own wife from the attentions of a man you know to be a rake."

"That's enough! You sail too close to the wind, woman!"

She stopped at that, still vexed and disbelieving, but not

foolish enough to venture further. Pulling up the covers, she waited in sullen silence for her maids.

Iveta joined her for breakfast in her solar while Lord Alain attended to business in the hall. Usually bubbling with an account of her activities with her new friends, Iveta was now subdued, nibbling absent-mindedly at her honey-cake and watching the maids tidy the room and dressing Marietta's hair with excruciating slowness.

She loved Marietta's willowy darkness, the hint of full curves beneath the deep pink surcoat and palest green cote-hardie, the olive skin and luscious dark eyes. Marietta was like a golden fruit, she thought, good enough to eat. Her friend Ian had told her that she, Iveta, was like an apple, sweet like a girl but quite tough. It could have been worse, but she would rather have been a peach.

At last the maids left them alone. "Now, little one," Marietta said, "are we ready to go? We're to hawk today; a picnic dinner. Will you like that?"

Iveta shook the crumbs from her yellow gown into the rushes and raised her bright blue eyes, launching without preamble into her secret. "Marrie, I've heard some men talking about horses. Lord Alain's horses. And they mentioned Beckington Manor, too. That's yours now, isn't it? Do you think I should tell him?"

Marietta stared, not quite understanding. "Talking where, love? Downstairs? When was this?"

"Last night." She looked sheepish and staved off Marietta's next remark that she should have been in bed. "Yes, I know, but it was hot and I couldn't sleep. You know how my little room faces onto the courtyard?"

Marietta nodded.

"Well, last night there was a full moon and I saw two men go into the doorway in the corner of the courtyard where the bakehouse and brewhouse are."

"The door that leads up to these apartments. Yes."

"Yes, that's where I thought they'd be going. Ian showed me a passageway that leads from that stairway to the granary and malting-house."

"Yes, that's right. They're immediately above the bakehouse and brewhouse. It's where the grain and malt are kept."

"Well, did you know that there are big wooden shutes up there so that the grain and malt can be tipped down to the floor below? Did you?"

"Er...yes, I suppose I have seen them. Why, Iveta?"

"Well, after I'd seen those two men go into that doorway, I went down to the passage on the floor below this one and then along to the malting-house, and when I got to the shute, I heard them talking."

"Men? In the brewhouse? At that time of night?"

"Yes, their voices were coming up through the shute. I could hear every word they said."

"And who were they? What did they say?"

"I'm quite sure one of them was Sir Bastien Symme...the one who was hanging around you all day. I don't know who the other one was, but he seemed to know a lot about Lord Alain's horses. They were talking about a stallion called Pen... Pen-something."

"Penda?"

"Yes, that's it... Penda. He said it was their last chance, that he dared not leave it later than Tuesday because he'd be off Wednesday morning. He told the other man he'd have to get a message to Longleigh."

"To Longleigh? Where's that?"

"No idea. Perhaps it's somewhere around here. Could be anywhere. And then he told him to get over to Beckington, that *that* was his last chance, too."

Frowning into each other's eyes, the two sisters puzzled

over the words, shaking their heads in mutual bewilderment.

"What on earth does Beckington have to do with it, I wonder? He was asking me about it...seemed shocked when I told him it belonged to me. What's going on...?"

Her words were not so much for Iveta as for herself. "And why does my lord get so angry when I mention wanting to put it straight?"

One thing is certain, she vowed silently, if he can't tell me what he's up to, I shall not tell him what I know, either. If he won't discuss Beckington with me, I'll keep the information to myself until I've made my own discoveries. Then I'll tell him what I know and save myself the trouble of having to ask.

Whether she had been too tired and distraught last night to hear him offer—twice—to tell her, or whether she wilfully discounted that, no one would ever know. Perhaps there were few enough ways for her to take revenge for the indignities she had suffered. If it cost him a stallion, it had cost her much more than that in humiliation and frayed emotions.

"Don't tell Lord Alain, Iveta, please. Don't mention any of this. I'll tell him myself when we have some time in private, but, for now, forget it...will you?"

As soon as Iveta had left, Marietta's first desire was to go along to the malting-house to look again at the great wooden shute that sloped to the floor below, but it was not to be.

With barely a knock, Emeline entered. Like Iveta, she knew little about pleasantries or preambles.

"Well?" she said. "Did it work?"

Marietta saw no need to pretend innocence but neither did she want to complicate the issue with all that had transpired last night. As far as Emeline was concerned, it must remain a straightforward campaign to pay Lord Alain back in his own coin.

"Yes," she said, "I suppose you could say that it did."

"Did he beat you?" Emeline was avid for drama, it seemed. She was prettily dressed in blue and mauve with grey-squirrel inside her long sleeve-tippets and down the edges of her surcoat. The neckline was wide, showing an expanse of white skin right up to her ears, for she wore no veil, as Marietta was now obliged to do. It would be a cool flirt, Marietta thought, who could remain unmoved by that.

But she could not portray Lord Alain as one who would beat his wife, even to feed Emeline's appetite.

"No," she said, "we quarrelled, but that's nothing new. He knows I'm angry with him and likely to remain so."

"Good." Emeline's eyes sparkled. "Does that mean he'll make you stay with him all day? I hope it does, because I want to be free to…enjoy myself." She bent to stroke Faith's head.

"Flirt, you mean."

"Well, yes, I suppose so. Has he not told you to stay with him? You won't go off with Sir Bastien, will you?"

"I'm not going to make it easy for him, Emmie. If he wants me to stay with him, he'll have to work at it. But I'm not going to go anywhere with Sir Bastien. I don't particularly enjoy having to work so hard at double-talk. Lord Alain comes straight out with it, and I prefer that."

He did come straight out with it…always had done, whether she liked it or not. Was such a man capable of duplicity then? she wondered.

Once in the courtyard, there was no time for Emeline to wonder who her escort would be; as soon as Sir Bastien Symme saw Marietta's hand being held in the vice-like grip of her husband, he made a bee-line for the fair-haired beauty in blue and mauve, lifting her into the saddle before anyone else could reach her and staying close enough to ward off other gallant young men with whom she had thought to have fun.

In one respect, it was a relief to Marietta not to have to take her flirting with Sir Bastien any further; the danger had been stimulating yesterday, but now it had already begun to pall and she was more than content to leave the chase to Emeline. On the other hand, she was by no means ready to let Alain off the hook.

Her flirtation had had the desired effect but she could not help thinking that his about-face had as much to do with Sir Bastien himself and *his* preferences as about her own humiliation. And that was not the background against which either an explanation or an apology should be made. If he thought the episode was over, he could think again.

Iveta's disclosure had also put a different colour on things since yesterday: if it had truly been Sir Bastien's voice she'd heard, then he must surely be the one Alain had wanted to entrap. But today was only Saturday and there was plenty of time to find out more before the guests departed. Perhaps she'd make some enquiries on her own account.

But today, nothing could have been further than yesterday's marked rejection of her company by Lord Alain, nothing could have been more calculated to prove how he wished to make amends, to show how he valued and cherished his wife, how he enjoyed her company. So much so that in the end they began to assume that his interest in Emeline had been no more than that of a host for a young guest, and that her resemblance to his former wife was coincidental.

Only he and Marietta knew how her polite responses to his observations were cool to the point of being icy. Only they knew that his insistence on her closeness was more enforced than voluntary. To the guests, it looked as though all differences had been resolved, but Marietta was wary enough to notice how her husband watched to see where Sir Bastien was at all times, and could not help construing this as a continuation of his vigilance over Emeline. It was an easy enough mistake, for they were together all the time.

Supper in the great hall was a merry feast, extending well beyond the music-making into story-telling, riddle-guessing, charades and blind-man's-buff where Emeline conspired to be well and truly caught by Sir Bastien while appearing to be indignant and red-faced. In the still balmy evening, they sat in Marietta's pleasance by the fountain and listened to the lute and to each other's tales then, when Iveta's yawns reminded them how late it was, Emeline took her away, leaving the others to follow as they would.

Marietta seized her chance to dart along the passage to the malting-house without being seen, while Lord Alain gave last instructions to his chamberlain about arrangements for the morrow. Intending only to look and be back in her solar before he could begin to wonder where she was, she searched the gloomy little room for the shute where the malt was tipped to the brewhouse below. In the dimness, she found it, but all was still and dark.

Through the thick malt-dust, she tiptoed on into the granary next door where the floor was white with flour. Sacks were piled high next to the square shute in the floor where they were sent, unopened, down to the bakehouse below. This floor even had a flour-covered hole as big as a coin through which one could see what was happening, but here, too, all was silent, though the warmth rose upwards from the slumbering ovens and she could not resist a guess at the number of lovers who had chosen this place for a private assignation.

Smiling at the imagery and on the point of turning away, she caught the sound of whispers; thinking that someone was coming towards her from the malting-house next door, she stepped forward to make herself seen. If it was a serving-man and his maid, they had better see her before it was too late.

But the malting-house was still empty, and the whispering, a giggling cry of half-protest, a gruff insistence, passed beneath her to somewhere under the floury boards, sounds so sharp that it was as though they came from the same room. The temptation to discover who had entered the bakehouse was irresistible, and lowering herself gently onto a hard sack of flour, she leaned towards the shute, clamping a hand over her mouth in horror as she recognised the woman's voice immediately. It was Emeline's.

"This is not the way…no, not here…!"

"Ssh!"

There was a soft thud as bodies landed on sacks of flour below the shute, a stifled yelp and protesting squeaks.

"Come on, you little tease, you've been asking for this."

"No, don't!"

Marietta was horrified, wavering between curiosity and a desire to go down and rescue her sister. But who was the man with her? Should she calmly walk away and mind her own business? Would Emeline thank her for interfering? Was she in any *real* danger, after all?

There was a silence. Marietta slithered off the sack and knelt on the floor, placing her eye to the hole at the side of the shute. It was too dim to see much except the grey-black tones of garments, pale hands and shoulders hunched over someone who squirmed, their heads just beyond her vision, maddeningly out of reach. She could only assume that this was Sir Bastien, but there was another whose involvement could not be discounted and, so far, the voice had not been clear enough to make her certain.

"Stop, go away. I don't want..."

"Oh, yes, you do, my lass." The man's voice was adamant. "You've been eyeing me all day long, wondering if I would...yes, I know. Well, now you can have what you've been waiting for."

"I was *not!*" Emeline whispered though Marietta could see how one pale hand rested lightly on the man's shoulder. "I was not even looking at you," she giggled softly.

"Little liar!"

There was another silence broken by sighs and the little noises that Emeline made, combinations of surprise, pretend annoyance and pleasure, and even now, Marietta was torn by guilt at the watch she was compelled to keep.

"That's enough," Emeline was saying. "I have to go."

"Not yet. I haven't started," the deep voice whispered, teasing. *Was* it Sir Bastien's? Could it equally well be Lord Alain's? Every word he'd said could have been his.

"I *must*...please! I shall tell my sister—"

"Leave your sister out of it. I can take her any time I feel like it."

"You needn't think I'm going to let you..."

"How are you going to stop me? Eh?"

Marietta saw her sister's hand move downwards then, to her dismay, saw the man's hand slide into the front of Emeline's gown and push away the fabric to expose her breast. She could watch no more.

With a gasp, she pushed herself away from the hole and sat back with a bump, feeling a heavy pulse somewhere beneath her jaw that vibrated into her soft kid shoes. Emeline, not yet fifteen, behaving like that with...with whom? That man? Or with *her* husband? Which?

The sounds of their love-making rose up through the

shute, single words, a cry, then silence. Was that how *she* sounded? And which of the two men had said he could take her any time he felt like it? Sickened, confused and fearful for Emeline's safety, she tiptoed through the doorway into the malting-house and from there along the passage to the stairwell, then upwards to her own solar.

She paused with her hand on the latch, unwilling to know for certain that it was him, the man she had come to love. How was she going to bear it? Slowly, very slowly, she slipped inside where the light from the setting sun hurt her eyes after the dimness of the inner courtyard rooms.

Lord Alain stood by the window, watching her furtive entrance. There was no warm greeting, no continuance of the gentleness that had kept her by his side all day with barely a respite. This greeting was hard and all too ready to disbelieve. "Well, my lady? Which route did you take to get to your solar? A lengthy one, it seems."

Marietta made no answer. The relief at having him here before her was so great that words failed her. Though Emeline was in mortal danger, at least it was not from her husband. How could she ever have doubted him?

"Well?" He looked her up and down.

"No…nowhere…I, er…" She could not tell him what she had thought nor what she had seen. It was disgraceful to watch such an intimate spectacle.

He strode forward, his mouth set in anger, his eyes dark and glittering. "Well?" he snapped again. "I asked you where you've been. And don't give me lies. Just take a look at yourself. Look!"

"What?" she frowned, not understanding.

"Look at yourself!" He grabbed her shoulder and yanked her forward to the light of the window. "Look!" He nodded towards her deep pink surcoat, her shoes, her hands. They were covered with white flour.

"The granary…" she whispered.

"Who with?"

"Nobody. I was there on my own."

"On your own? For pity's sake, woman! Don't tell me you've been rolling on sacks of flour on your own at this time of night. Between now and three of the morning when the bakers start again, there's only one thing people go to the granary for. Who were you with? That wretch who couldn't get near you today? Eh? Him, was it?" He shook her arm, making her wince with pain.

"Leave me! Let go! I was on my own, I tell you!"

Now aware for the first time of how it must appear to him, the full absurdity of the situation changed her relief at finding him here into indignation that he should believe of her what she'd believed of him only moments ago. Yet she could not explain that she'd unwittingly spied on her sister; he would never believe that her spying was accidental, nor would she tell him why she'd gone there in the first place.

Disinclined to argue the point, Alain was quite sure that what he was seeing could not be explained in any other way, and aware of how she had balked at his restrictions all day, how she had assured him she would thwart him, just to anger him, he had no choice but to believe that this was how she had chosen to round off the episode, with a show of her self-will. With that creature!

"Well, then, my lady…" he went to pick up his whip from the chest, cracking its snake-like lash across the room, flicking its tongue expertly towards her feet "…in that case, you'll have time to change to the truth while you're nursing your new stripes. I'll not be as tender as he was…"

"Who? In God's name, Alain," Marietta snarled, unafraid of the whip but angered by his assumption, "do you think I'd roll around the granary with that sniggering whelp? That *toad?* I'm not as free with my favours, my lord, as you are with yours. And if I'd been in your shoes this last week, I'd have deserved to have my hide red-raw by now…!''

She hissed in pain as the lash stung through the fine fabric of her garments across her thighs, catching the back of one hand. Refusing to flinch, she stood rigid, bristling with the injustice of his punishment and waiting for the next cut without showing him the pain of it.

But it was as though that single lash had been an un-stoppable overflow of his fury, for now he heard her words and held back, staring at her with a new doubt clouding the brilliant certainty of the moment before. Then, without an-other word, he threw down the whip and left the room, slamming the door after him.

With shaking fingers and with tears rolling silently down her face, Marietta summoned her maids to help her and, without asking any questions, they salved the red weal with comfrey, shook out the clouds of flour from her cote-hardie and surcoat and made up the small wooden truckle-bed with soft sheets and a blanket and pillow from the big bed.

Curled up, silent and alone, she wept with relief that he had not been the one with Emeline and that he cared enough about her to be angry at her supposed inconstancy. Then, as reason took another turn, she wept some more because she had no idea whether it was his honour he cared more about, or her. Sleep came while she was in the middle of debating whether he would return to his own solar or to hers.

Stealthily, his feet making no sound on the floury planks, Lord Alain followed the whispering, even in the darkness. The granary was empty but still the whispering went on as he bent his ear to the dark shute to catch every word.

"I don't know," the voice said. Alain knew it was Emeline's.

"Well, you've got to persuade him to let you go before Wednesday. I can get you out of Monksgrange easy enough, but I can't get you out of this place. It's like a fortress when the gates are down."

"Will we have a manor of our own, Bastien?"

There were sounds of nuzzling and soft shuffling noises. Alain stared into the darkness, every sense aware, angry and relieved, too, sure that Marietta had been here where he was sitting, alone and upset with no one to confide in, unsure of his reaction to what she'd heard. Sweet, lovely girl.

"A manor, horses, servants, gowns…all yours…as long as you let me have what I want…now…"

"Not again, Bastien," she whined.

Alain cringed at the sound.

"Didn't you like it?"

"You were rough…"

"I'll be gentle, then. Like this, eh? You liked that, didn't you?"

"Mmm. But we have to go. Someone will come…"

"In a minute. Time yet. Put your hand there…"

"No!"

"Go on, put your hand on it…"

"What will you give me if I do? A carriage and six horses, new gowns?"

That laugh. Alain knew that laugh so well; his hackles rose at the memory of the damage it had done in the past, damage waiting to be paid for. The dilemma now was that this silly baggage was in danger sooner than he'd anticipated. A fifteen-year-old virgin was hardly expected to run the length of the course at the first try. He might have known she'd be that stupid. The other one had been clever, devious, cunning. This one was brainless. Too dim even to say no. Should he put a stop to it now, for Marietta's sake?

Instantly resolved, he stood, picked up the sack he'd been sitting on, ripped open the top with his knife and shook the contents down the shute. Then he walked away, along the passage and back up the stairway to the solar without waiting to savour the yelps and indignant howls of the two lovers below He was still chuckling as he opened the door to Marietta's room.

Even at this hour, the west-facing room was not so dark that he could not see the truckle-bed with its sleeping cargo. Smiling, he undressed and pulled back the bedcovers then, bending to the form of his damp-browed wife, he picked her up in his arms and carried her to the bed.

She murmured in her sleep. "No…no…"

"That's what I thought you'd say, sweetheart. Beautiful girl, go to sleep now. You're safe. Sleep, sweet thing."

Everyone, except Emeline and Sir Bastien, attended mass in the small but well-appointed chapel the next morning. Perversely, Marietta had not allowed Lord Alain to make a full apology for his too-hasty assumptions last night; her wounds were too deep to be healed by a few contrite declarations, and she had gone to mass with anything but forgiveness in her heart and had come away not too surprised to feel as hostile towards Alain as she had before. It was wrong, she knew, but until he showed some consistency, it was impossible for her, in her present state, to warm to him. Loving him was one thing; liking him was altogether different.

Combining concern with curiosity, Marietta went to Emeline straight from chapel. Emeline was in a bath of steaming water.

"I needed one, Marrie," she said, almost defying her sister to scold. "I had to have one."

Marietta peered into the tub. "Water? It looks more like milk. You're not bathing in asses' milk, are you?"

"Flour!" Emeline pouted. "Some fool left an open bag by the staircase to my room and I tripped over it."

"By your room? Out there, you mean? I'd better find out—"

"No, don't bother, it's all been cleaned up now."

"But who's carrying sacks of flour along here?"

"Oh, some new scullion got lost, I suppose. Wrong passage."

"But it's in your hair, too. Emmie. Look." She held up a matted strand and showed it to her sister, whose scowl would have frightened the devil. "Did you fall into it head-first?"

The tightly pursed mouth showed that any retort was being held in check. Emeline scrubbed. The maids hovered nervously.

"Where did you get to last night, Emmie?"

Emeline looked discomfited. "I was with Sir Bastien."

"Where?"

"Oh, Marrie, you sound just like Mother. Just talking, that's all. Don't you get all nosy like she does, for heaven's sake. At least I had a day doing what I wanted to do, and that makes a change. Thing is, Marrie, I think Iveta and I have been here long enough now. It's time we were going home." She did not appreciate the contradiction of her two statements.

"You want to go home, even though you're enjoying yourself?" Had things gone badly for her? Marietta wondered. "You haven't been foolish, have you, Em?"

Emeline would not meet her eye but stepped out of the bath and turned her back. "No, course not."

"He's quite a rake, you know. He does this flirting act all the time. Did you know that?" When Emeline made no reply, she went on, gently. "He's the kind who seduces a woman, promises her everything and then disappears."

Emeline fired a quick barb over her shoulder. "What did he promise you?"

"Nothing. We never got as far as that before Alain dragged me off. Maybe if I'd shown more interest I might have discovered."

"He seems to think you *were* interested, Marrie."

"He would, wouldn't he? Can you imagine a man like that telling you that a woman was not interested in him?"

"Huh. No."

"Course not. Look, Em—" Marietta reached out and took her sister's hand "—perhaps you'd better tell Alain that you're ready to go now. Out of harm's way, eh? Before things get too serious."

Emeline nodded. "Yes," she whispered, "I think I'd better."

Suddenly, Marietta felt saddened by events, by Emeline's pretty pouting face which, by rights, should have been glowing with excitement and secret happiness. She could not ask her sister what had happened; they had never been on such intimate terms where experiences were shared, but Emeline did not look as though she had enjoyed Sir Bastien's intimacies too well.

Back in her own solar, Marietta puzzled over Lord Alain's attitude towards this man. Why had he invited him to stay under his roof while knowing him to be a woman-iser? Why this sudden change of attention from Emeline towards herself? Where did Alain go last night after another sudden change of mind? Had he gone to the granary and heard what she had heard? Surely he'd not wanted that to happen?

She sighed. It had been a mistake to marry him. It was not what she had wanted. She gazed out of the open window towards Monksgrange and her eyes strayed upwards towards the cave on the hillside above where she had been trapped, compelled, coerced. How different had it been for her, then?

Impetuously, she whirled round and grabbed the whip that lay coiled on the chest, strode back to the window and hurled it with every ounce of strength way out beyond the garden and over the crenellated wall into the treetops, oblivious to the sound of footsteps behind her.

"Well done, sweetheart. The fire still burns, does it?"

"No, my lord," she whispered, putting her hands behind her to avoid his outstretched embrace. "A healthy flame can soon be quenched by rough treatment, by lack of care. I was just admitting to myself that I made a terrible mistake." She struggled to keep her voice level, for he was handsome in his Sunday-best, so strong and graceful, his dark hair inviting her fingers to push deep into its silkiness, to caress his face.

"A mistake? You mean last night?" He bent quickly to retrieve her hands, looking sadly at the thin red line across the back of one and raised it to his lips to kiss it. Then he closed the window.

"No, my lord, not last night. Long before that, when I agreed to marry you. That was my mistake."

"Marietta, if it's any comfort to you, you did not agree. Remember how you did everything in your power to make it impossible. You defied everyone. You ran away and hid, and I found you and brought you back—"

"To *this!*" she yelled, snatching her hands away, tears flooding anew at his reasonableness. "You brought me here to this…this…madhouse! Where you alternately shore up my confidence and knock it down the next day. Where you offer hospitality to people you appear to dislike and rail at me when I react perfectly naturally to their foibles. You whip me when I tell you the truth, you ignore me one day and insist I cling to you the next. No one, my lord, no one has ever laid a whip to me before, not even my father, and God knows he had reason. It was a mistake. I should have taken your dagger…and…killed…killed…!''

"Who?" Ignoring her beating fists, he pulled her to him roughly. "Who would you have killed, sweetheart? Yourself?"

"You…you! I never wanted you," she sobbed, "and I don't want you now. I was happier without you. Go! Go!''

She swung a free arm but it was grabbed in mid-air and held against his shoulder. Through her angry tears she could see how he enjoyed her storm of temper, how he understood the fearsome contradiction of words and emotions. Even from her limited experience of him, Marietta knew that he would not be quelled by such an assault.

"You," she yelled. "I could do…I could!''

"Brave, wench! That's good," he laughed, "as long as you don't turn a dagger on yourself you can fight me any time. That shows you're still on fire, in spite of you telling me that the flame's died. Still, sweetheart…still! This is only a squall, not a storm. The first days are always unsettling for a lass.''

"Unsettling? I'm not unsettled…*you're* unsettled!''

"Yes, love…" he gathered her up into his arms "…I am indeed. So let's have a contest to see who's the most unsettled. Come with me to the butts, now, and whoever gets the most bull's-eyes out of ten wins. Eh?''

Through her rage, the idea appealed to her. "And when I win," she growled, "what's the prize to be?''

"If you win, sweetheart," he grinned, "you can do with me what you will.''

That was an offer she could not refuse; the ideas already crowded in.

"And when I win—" he continued.

"You won't!"

"When I win, I shall take you to that bed over there and make up for two nights of lost loving. So be warned, my girl, it could take some time."

"I shall win," she snapped. "Come and see."

He was not the only one to come and see, for when it became known that the lord and his lady were to contest their skills at the butts, the entourage grew until it seemed as though half the castle were behind them. And, not un-naturally, there were many who felt that Marietta needed their support and would have been happy to see Lord Alain lose, for once.

Good-natured from the spectators' point of view but deadly earnest from the contestants' standpoint, the contest buzzed with the sounds of advice—even young Bruno whispered in her ear from time to time as he held her ar-rows and checked their feathered flights.

The Master-at-Arms, knowing she could not win, soberly chose the best bow for her and applauded loudly at every score she made, but when every single one of Lord Alain's arrows landed with a soft thwack in the dead-centre of the bull's eye and when Marietta's strayed by a few fingers beyond that point more than once, the anticipation of the prize he would claim could not be held at bay.

The cheers were as much for Marietta as for the victor.

"A gallant and chivalrous knight would have allowed his lady to win, my lord," she rebuked him, her eyes danc-ing with reluctant mirth.

Before them all, he opened his arms and made her come to him. "Would he now, sweetheart? Well, this gallant and chivalrous knight wants his prize too much for any of that nonsense. Come on. Your surrender, my lady, if you please.''

"Proud woman," he whispered into her neck, tasting the perfumed softness of her skin and hair, "beautiful, proud, courageous woman."

Tenderly, Marietta smoothed her fingers over his shoulders, feeling the heat and moisture generated by his vigorous loving. He had not spared her, had not taken a whit less than his due, nor had she held back or complained, having accepted his challenge willingly. It had, after all, cost her little except in pride and physical energy, and they were both instantly renewable.

"What was your prize to have been, sweetheart? Can you remember?"

She felt his smile beneath her chin. "Arrogant brute," she said.

"Well, can you?"

There was a pause as she sought an answer that would sting him. But a heavy drowsiness was stealing over her and the careful weight of his body on hers banished all thoughts of revenge. "No," she said.

Chapter Eleven

The arbour was a delight, even before all the foliage had closed the gaps or covered the curved roof. From the raised floor, the four women peered through the crenels of the great wall, fully able to appreciate how secluded and pretty it would be by the end of the summer, how enticing it would be to sit on the turf benches and see without being seen.

"It was never like this before…oh, dear…!" Lady Isobel bit back the words, aware of her indiscretion.

But Marietta took it as a compliment. "Before I came," she concluded. "No, well, it took an army of men to have it ready for now. It was a wilderness."

"It was a wilderness last time I came with Sir Richard," Lady Mary told her, honestly. "We stayed in the castle then, but there was no pleasance, no garden, nowhere to walk except over by the shooting-butts. We went hunting…"

"We went hunting for beds, too, I seem to remember," Lady Isobel retorted. "What a business!"

"What?" Mistress Jean sat on the chamomile and brushed a palm along its feathery fronds. "Hunting for beds?"

"Yes," Lady Mary agreed, "nothing had been prepared the way it is this time. Hardly any servants, no bedding. It was chaotic. Isobel and I slept with some other guests all in one bed and the men slept in the hall."

Marietta frowned. "But that's…tch, tch! Was she not experienced, this first Lady Thorsgeld? There are plenty of beds in this place."

"Experienced?" The two guests looked steadily at each other as though to assess the lengths to which they dared go in explanation of the evocative word. "Aye, Jayne was experienced all right. But not at running a household of this size."

"Tell me," Marietta said. "Please."

Again, they hesitated on the brink of causing offence, but their hostess was insistent. Lady Isobel twisted a heavy gold ring around her plump finger and regarded the back of her hand. "A silly, pretty thing," she murmured, "thought more about her looks and men than anything else. And hunting."

"And hawking," Lady Mary added, staring into the sky.

"Aye, and hawking. Anywhere men went, she'd go, too."

Marietta waited for more, then prompted, "Were they in love, then? She and my husband? Was he sorely grieved when she died?"

Lady Isobel sighed, and told her, "No, Marietta, anybody could see that they were not. It was not a marriage of love but of property, that's all. A childhood thing, like many another.

"And I suppose," she added philosophically, "that if they'd both put their minds to it, it might have grown into regard, at least. But she appeared not to care what he thought of her and it looked as though he stopped bothering. He never showed her as much affection as you show that pup on your knees, Marietta. And as for having a shooting-match with her like he did with you this morning, well, you can see now why everybody was so interested: that was a real novelty, I can tell you. Especially the end bit!''

The end bit had been her public surrender to his kiss, something none of them had ever seen before, except Emeline and Old Adam. He had picked her up then and carried her as far as the garden, taking no heed of her laughing protestations but reminding her instead of a previous time when he'd carried her and suffered her anger for his pains.

Marietta laughed, remembering the direct progress to her solar without the slightest deviation or concession to the presence of his guests. Barefaced. And he had called *her* brave.

''But surely,'' she said, ''he must have been saddened when she died of the pestilence? That must have been shocking for him.''

''Pestilence? Around here?'' Mistress Jean said. ''Surely not. We had it around York, but it didn't reach as far as this.''

''No, Jayne died in the same year, but not of that, I think,'' Lady Mary agreed.

''Not that?'' Marietta was puzzled. ''What, then? Childbirth?''

They shook their heads, unable to help, and she was bound to let the matter drop rather than dwell on the subject indefinitely.

She did, however, long to know what part Emeline played in all of this, for she had no need to ask them if she and the first Lady Thorsgeld were alike; she already knew that for certain, though she also knew that Emeline's attempts at coquetry were those of the novice rather than of the fully fledged wanton.

It had crossed Marietta's mind more than once that Emeline was being used as some kind of decoy, but that idea had been dismissed when she remembered how Alain had begun his attentions towards Emeline before their guests had arrived, not afterwards.

But he had not been in love with his wife, apparently, nor she with him, so what reason did she now have to suppose that he could suddenly have fallen in love with Emeline? The more she thought about it, the more unlikely that theory became, even when she tried to recall her other reasons for believing it. And after this morning's display, how could she doubt that indeed it was herself that he wanted?

Strolling towards the stables with her three new friends, Marietta found it difficult to keep her mind on their chatter as a new image of Alain took shape in her mind—not the devastated widower seeking a replacement for his first lost love, as she had believed, but a saddened and lonely man who had recognised in her something he had never had. And he had been prepared to whip her when he believed she'd misbehaved.

Had he punished his first wife in similar fashion? Probably not, if he cared as little about her activities as these two had told her. What a way to live, uncaring, unloved and unloving. Poor man.

The men stood in a group over by the stables, thoughtfully discussing the destriers as they were brought out to parade before them again. They barely noticed the four women slip through the gate behind them, nor were they aware how they themselves were being scrutinised every bit as closely as the stallions.

Sir Bastien Symme stood a little apart with one of the older grooms, a stocky man with massive shoulders and a shock of black hair falling into his surly face. It was the first time Marietta had noticed him among all the others and she watched with interest as the two men talked, the one languidly handsome, listening, nodding, but keeping his eyes on the horses at all times, the other lively, his eyes roaming, disapproving and contemptuous.

Marietta, attracted by a snort from one of the stable-doors behind her, went to stroke the nose of a grey who was not part of the proceedings. Turning back to the company, she saw that Sir Bastien and the groom now stood with their backs to her, close together, and before her eyes had time to move on, she saw the groom's hand dive furtively into the open leather pouch which hung on the baldric across Sir Bastien's body, grab something and pull it out, then shove his closed fist into the pouch hanging from his own belt.

The strange part of this transaction was that Sir Bastien must have felt the firm tug on his pouch, for it was not done so stealthily that it could be called a theft. Yet, the very next moment, the groom walked away, swivelling his head round to see who watched, but seeing only Marietta's back as she quickly turned and renewed her attention to the horse. The next time she managed to catch a glimpse of the pouch at the knight's back, she saw that it was firmly buckled.

"Your sister is not with you, Lady Marietta?"

Without looking, she knew who asked for Emeline. "No, Sir Bastien, I think she may still be resting."

"Tires easily, does she?" His smile, she was sure, indicated another meaning to the words than mere concern. "We have a hunt tomorrow, do we not? I hope she'll be with us then. And you...? Do you hunt too, m'lady?"

"Indeed I will."

"And are you as skilled at the hunt as you are with the bow?"

"You shall judge for yourself, sir."

He took her arm and gently eased her towards the group of guests. "It is not so easy to judge for myself, lady, when your lord and master keeps you so firmly under lock and key. Does he allow you no liberty?"

She laughed at the plaintive questions, relishing the security of Alain's powerful presence only an arm's length away. "All the liberty I desire, sir. The lock was one of my own choosing, and the key is his to do with as he wishes. He guards me well."

"Tch, tch! Then I am doomed to make do with your pretty sister," he whispered. "Too bad. I had hoped for a more exciting ride."

In spite of herself, the hair on Marietta's head bristled. His thinly veiled reference to the episode with Emeline was audacious and she, Marietta, was not supposed to know of it. She could scarcely contain her annoyance.

"You are referring to the hunt, of course, Sir Bastien. I'm sure Alain has something to your taste. My lord..." she called. "Sir Bastien needs an exciting mount for tomorrow. What about Dulzelina?"

Lord Alain understood her message immediately. "Oh, we can do better than that, love." He turned obligingly to Sir Bastien. "Leave it to me, my friend, you shall have the very finest mount. Now, if we've finished business for the day, I believe it's time for supper." He took Marietta's hand firmly in his, smiling.

"You're looking pensive, sweetheart. What is it?" He closed the door to the solar. "What was all that about a horse for Bastien? Was he trying it on again?"

She told him what Sir Bastien had said to her.

"Well done. You took him at his word. I can guess what he was referring to, so I'll make sure he has an eventful day on Atlas. *That* should work off his appetite, eh?'' Atlas was a bad-tempered and headstrong old war-horse who was kept on only because he had been Alain's first stallion. He would leave Sir Bastien little to think of except how to stay aboard.

Marietta sat on the bed. ''My lord, I am growing concerned about Emeline. Do you think, for her own sake, that you might allow her to return to Monksgrange now?'' She had made so few requests of him since their marriage and yet he was as likely to refuse as if she made them daily. Already he had refused this one only a few days ago. Beckington, too. ''Please,'' she whispered, reluctant to wheedle but not knowing how else to move him.

''You're concerned, are you? Why?''

''She's not yet fifteen, my lord. That man is far too experienced a rake for her to handle, and I don't want her to run into trouble, especially here, of all places, under my care. I've played nursemaid to her for long enough now and I think my father should be the one to keep her safe, not me. Iveta…'' she flopped backwards ''…Iveta is different. I'd have her to live with us. She's never a problem, but I think Emeline would be happy to return now.''

Alain went to the other side of the bed and flopped backwards, too, and looked at her, upside down. ''For your peace of mind, sweetheart, I have already sent to Monksgrange to ask Lady Alice and Sir Henry to come here and take her back with them.''

''What?'' Marietta sat up and leaned over his head. ''You've already asked them? When? When did you do that?''

''Last night, love. I sent a messenger. They should be here in time for supper.'' He was smiling broadly at her astonishment.

''Alain, you didn't tell me! That's any moment now, and

I have not had rooms prepared...or extra food... Oh, why didn't you tell me before?'' She made to roll away, but he pulled her back.

"No need—'' he held her across him, laughing "—they're sharing Emeline's solar. D'ye think that'll keep her safe enough?''

"Oh!'' A radiant smile broke through her previous concern. "Oh, thank you, Alain. Thank you.'' She leaned over and pecked his nose, and when she would have made her escape, she found that his arms were locked about her.

Marietta would like to have had more notice of her parents' arrival but was bound to admit that this would have made no difference to the arrangements, only to her peace of mind. Everything was organised to perfection, clean rushes on the floors, more tables laid for supper, more silver and gold on view, more food and wine.

Only Emeline looked sour at the disconcerting news that they were to share her bedroom, not because she resented any threat to her freedom but, having begun to lord it over the servants, she was loath to hand over the power to Lady Alice.

Neither Emeline nor Marietta had anticipated the arrival of Sir Nicholas Bannon, though they might have known he'd not miss a chance to ingratiate himself with other landowners in the hope that one of them would discover his attributes and offer him their patronage.

To his credit, he made himself instantly affable to Lord Alain's guests and Marietta could not help noticing how sensibly he greeted her and how he appeared genuinely interested in the people around him, asking questions and, for once, dispensing with the overtones of contempt which so often concealed his feelings of inadequacy.

Instead of complimenting Marietta on her new estate or

making her blush with remarks about her personal appearance, he told her what she most wanted to know, about what had been happening at Monksgrange: the state of the garden, the sow and its new litter, the argument about common land and boundaries, the rebuilding of barns. As though the short separation had supplied a lifetime of news, they talked as friends as never before, even noting with shared laughter how Lady Alice had already taken Emeline firmly in hand.

Only a day or two ago, she might have been tempted to flirt with him merely to salve her bruised pride, but now the suspicion that Alain had perhaps received enough fickleness from one wife held her back. She would play no more games. She would give her husband no cause to doubt her virtue, no reason to exclude her from his protection. She would not sink so low in his esteem.

The idea of a day's hunting brought out the best in the men; there was not one of the company who could think of anything he would rather do on a fair day in May than sit astride a bold horse and head for the vast deer-park in good company. Sir Henry Wardle was in his element, beaming across his handsome face at the antics of Sir Bastien's mount who had it in mind to be the first out of the courtyard.

"Hah!" he grinned at Marietta. "He'll be on his way back before the rest of us have started at that rate. Is that his own stallion?"

"No, Father, it's Alain's first. He's old now, and set in his ways. He doesn't take kindly to anyone except Alain."

"So why has he put that young buck on him? Ah! Don't tell me. It's to keep him busy, I take it; warm his backside, eh?"

He had not agreed with Lady Alice last night that Eme-

line's admirer was a charming young man; he knew a rogue
when he saw one, even if she didn't, and had told her that
it was just as well Lord Alain had invited them when he
did before the young gallant got too frisky. Emeline's
blushes had been mistaken for embarrassment rather than
a sign of guilt, for they were not to know how their concern
for her safety was already too late. She prayed they never
would.

For everyone except Sir Bastien, the day was a huge
success, though not without adventure. It did not take him
long to realise that his request for an exciting ride had been
a regrettable lapse of good sense which he would never
have tossed casually in Marietta's direction if he'd known
she would pass it on with such devastating effect. The massive Atlas, all bone and war-hardened muscle, had his own
ideas about where he wanted to go and in which manner
he wanted to get there, ideas which rarely accorded with
those of his rider.

In no time at all he was in danger of overtaking the
fewterers with their straining greyhounds, and it took all
his strength and some oaths before Sir Bastien could hold
the brute back to take his place with the others. Consequently, the ride he had so looked forward to at Emeline's
side and the planned chivalry towards Lady Alice barely
had time to materialise before he was swept away from
them like a boat on a tidal wave, heaving and cursing under
his breath, arms aching and temper shortening.

Emeline did nothing to ease herself away from her parents' presence, not even to see his brave chase and his
attempt at a kill. Unfortunately, his arrows went nowhere
near the hart, even as it stood at bay in a river, for Atlas
had no mind to stand still at that moment.

For Sir Nicholas Bannon, however, whose mount was
not so wayward, the opportunity arose which was to place

him for ever in Lady Isobel de Rhennes' debt, and that of her husband. It happened as the ladies, following at a more sedate pace, came to a shallow brook between steep banks which the men had taken at a stride but which stalled the smaller palfreys until an easier crossing was found.

Downstream a little way, Sir Nicholas called to them, "Here, ladies! Try this…the bank is shallow here." He kept his mount in the water as they came forward, Lady Isobel first. "Keep clear of the hogweed, lady."

Busily chattering to those behind, Lady Isobel took no notice, looking neither at the hogweed nor at the water. It was Emeline's yelp that stopped her dead.

"Lady Isobel! Lady…stop! Look…get back! Back!"

Sir Nicholas had seen it, too. A boar stood barely hidden by the tree-like stem of the giant hogweed, its head lowered, its mouth agape with a set of tusks that curved upwards with terrifying efficiency. Two tiny vicious-looking black eyes glowered at their intrusion.

"Back, lady," Sir Nicholas yelled, "go back to safety!"

But Lady Isobel was by now steeply inclined towards the water and could not back away, nor would her mount move on, having smelt the threatening boar and heard its grunts of anger. She was stuck on the bank, aware that the great bristling creature would not turn and flee but would attack in a frenzy of slashing tusks as able to bowl over her horse as it would a hound.

Marietta's young greyhound, sitting in the safety of her mistress's saddle, yapped, and at that moment the boar chose to charge, lowering its head and rushing in ominous silence just as the arrow from Sir Nicholas's bow hit it squarely behind one ear. The momentum of its gallop hurled the heavy body head over heels through the air, cannoning into the hindquarters of Lady Isobel's mount and sending the stricken animal plunging sideways down the bank and into the water, almost on top of Sir Nicholas and his horse.

By some miracle, Sir Nicholas managed to stay in the saddle and reach out as Lady Isobel fell, lifting her bodily off her falling horse. Pulling her across his saddle-bow, he put spurs to his stallion and sent it up the opposite bank to safety. It was the neatest bit of deliverance from certain death the women had ever seen and even before the foot-huntsmen reached them, their applause was echoing through the trees and mingling with cries of relief and admiration.

Sir Nicholas made light of his heroism, preferring to jest that he had personally organised the event in order to catapult Lady Isobel into his arms, even though the lady was no sylph. But there was no disguising the body of the boar with an arrow in its head, nor was Lady Isobel stinting in her praise and gratitude. Apart from a bruised rib and one wet foot, she was quite uninjured, only shaken.

If Sir Henry Wardle was the first that day to kill a hart, then Sir Nicholas was the first—and only one—to take a boar, becoming the hero of the day and the talk of the feast that evening, sitting between Sir John and his lady and looking, for once, self-conscious at all the attention.

Chapter Twelve

Different entirely was the picture Sir Bastien presented. He could not appreciate the jovial feast for the brooding thought that his mount had been especially chosen to serve him ill, and it was only the eyes of two very young people who noticed his early departure from the hall before the gleemen had finished their songs and the last toast had been drunk.

It was relatively easy for Iveta and her friend Ian to saunter, unnoticed, towards the mews in the late-evening sunshine, chattering about the new pups, the hunt, the adventures of the day, then to disappear inside and work their way back towards the stable end.

A ladder led upwards towards the hay loft, where the youngest grooms slept in summer on an open floor that overlooked the horses' stalls. Here, with all the audacity of youth, they lay flat on the sweet-smelling hay and peered through the stalks down to where Sir Bastien leaned against the door-frame, waiting.

Before long, they heard the footsteps approach him from the stable-yard, heard the man turn into the stable below and lean against the very same wooden pillar that held up the platform on which they lay.

They stared at each other, unable to believe their luck, but now aware that their slightest sound would be heard unless it was one which could be mistaken for the occasional thud of a horse against its stall. Simultaneously, they lowered their heads as the first words floated upwards, nodding seriously to each other as they recognised the same voice speaking to Sir Bastien.

"When's it to be, then? Tonight?"

"No, fool. I told you Tuesday, not today."

"Had a good day, did you?" the voice sneered.

"Whose idea was it to put me on that bloody old stallion?"

"His. I tried to argue, but he wouldn't listen. Spite, was it? D'ye think he's getting wise to you, after all this time?"

Sir Bastien remembered the sack of flour. Few people would know of that trick unless it was someone who worked in the bakehouse. "I don't know, but I wouldn't be too surprised if he had his own ideas. I've got to be ready and packed for this last one; I shall have to disappear for good after that."

"You mean this'll be the last one? Nay, sir, never."

"It will. The last."

"What about…her…the lass? You're taking her, too?"

Iveta could almost hear his smile and the look of scorn. "Hmph! What do *you* think, numbskull? She's a child. It's the bloody horses I want, man, not that silly bitch. She's got less sense than Jayne had."

There was a silence at that last remark as though both men were remembering someone. Someone called Jayne.

"What d'ye want me to do, then?"

Sir Bastien's voice became urgent. "You've got to get rid of those three, Rigg."

"What, now? Or afterwards?"

"Tomorrow. Get a message to Longleigh…you'll need

some help…hide the bodies up in the wood behind the house.''

''I can't be gone for that length of time, sir! He'll miss me.''

''If you want your last bag o' gold, you'll have to, won't you?''

''But you gave me your word…''

''Bah!'' Sir Bastien pushed himself away from the pillar, causing the two in the hay above to duck down even lower, flat to the floor. ''My word stretches as far as your honesty, fool. Now, listen to me…'' They walked slowly towards the stable door, out of hearing.

Iveta regarded Ian in silence to glean what she could of his reaction. This was far more serious than either of them had thought. Killing. Bodies. Those three. Which three?

''What are they going to do?'' Iveta mouthed.

''Kill somebody,'' Ian replied, silently.

''Who?''

Ian's mouth bunched up into a negative bow and he shook his head. ''Come on,'' he said, slithering backwards, ''we must tell Lord Alain.''

''No!'' Iveta grabbed at his arm to hold him back. ''No, I promised Marrie I wouldn't. She prefers to tell him herself. We must go to her.''

''Don't be daft, lass,'' Ian's Scottish brogue spilled out in scorn, ''this is serious. What's the use of telling Lady Thorsgeld? She can do nothing.''

''If they're talking about Beckington again, she will. It's her property, not Lord Alain's. They said something about a wood behind the house. Well, that must be where they meant, Beckington Manor.''

Ian sat up straight and frowned at her. ''Well, why would they want to kill whoever lives there? And who's Jayne?''

''Somebody who's got a bit more sense than Emeline,

by the sound of things. Could be anybody…'' she added, innocently.

"Listen, Iveta, if Lord Alain finds out that I knew something of this and didn't tell him, he'll send me straight home to my father. For good."

"He won't find out. I'll say I was by myself."

"A girl? In the stable? Alone? Hah!"

"No, I could have been in the mews when I overheard. And Marietta believed me before when I said I was alone in the malting-house…with you."

Ian pulled pieces of hay from her fair hair, thoughtfully. "He musn't ever know," he said, "or I've had it. I shan't be given a second chance."

Iveta tightened her lips and looked away. "I know how to keep my mouth shut," she said, "you need not fear."

"Nay, lass, don't be angry…I didn't mean…" Clumsily, he reached out and pulled her to him and kissed her on the lips, nose to nose, until he remembered that it was better to turn his head sideways. Then, drawing away, he looked down at her hands. "You're pretty," he said, "much prettier than your sister."

"I love you, Ian."

"Aye, lass. Me too," he replied, somewhat ambiguously. "I'll marry you when I'm a knight. I'll wear your ribbon in my helm, and we'll live in a grand castle like this, shall we?"

She nodded with enthusiasm. "Yes…oh, yes. Only… how many years?"

"Only seven," he replied, nonchalantly, pulling her up.

Not until the next morning was Iveta finally able to pass on to Marietta what she and Ian had heard the previous evening, for Lady Alice's strong hand had ushered her up to bed as soon as her face had appeared around the hall door. Protests had been ignored.

Now, Marietta knelt on the window-seat, staring out across the valley and wondering what to do with the extraordinary information Iveta had at last revealed to her. The last time, she had done nothing. This time, she must act, for people's lives were at stake. Her tenants. The Fullers.

Iveta's recollection of what she had heard had lost something of its clarity during her hours of sleep. She could remember that the man had said something about "it" being on Tuesday, whatever it was, that it would be the last, and that the man called Rigg had to get rid of those three and to hide the bodies in the wood behind the house. Tomorrow. That was today.

But why? If it really was the Fullers at Beckington they'd been talking about, why did they have to be killed? Was that what the old couple had been afraid of? The more Marietta mulled over the facts, the less the whole thing made sense except that she must protect them, whether Alain wanted her to be involved or not.

It would be no use telling him; he would fly into a rage and tell her to leave it to him. And he would do nothing, just as he'd done nothing to relieve their plight so far. She must take matters into her own hands. If the men were going to steal horses, they'd do it anyway, and if Alain had been so foolish as to entertain a man he knew to be a rogue, then surely he must be well prepared for something to happen. He would be on his guard.

But with a house full of guests, how could she go flying off to Beckington? Who could she take to give her some support? Bruno? Uncle Nicholas? Her father? Yes, that was the answer; Sir Henry would be glad to see the place.

She was mistaken. Sir Henry was her husband's ally in

this and refused point blank to accompany her without Lord Alain's permission. Angry at his unhelpfulness, Marietta could only be relieved that she had not confided in him her reasons for wanting to go. Her most pressing need was to go immediately and get back to the castle before Alain discovered her absence, for her father would no doubt tell him where she was, if there was any delay. Damn these men! Why did they always know best?

Waiting until Alain and his clients were discussing business in the stable-yard and the ladies were in the pleasance, she took a horse from the ground-floor stable of the castle and shrugged off the offer of an escort. She hated this subterfuge—it was something she had never had to indulge in before her marriage—and she found it particularly distasteful and disturbing to be obliged to ask permission, to explain her reasons or to be prevented from doing what she knew must be done. Alain had been unreasonable in his attitude towards these old people and if he would not do anything for them, then she would.

The young lass, Milly, was in the herb-garden as Marietta rode up to the house and started in fright, her hand full of green leaves. Even as she dismounted, Marietta could see that Milly had been crying.

She held out a friendly hand. "Shh! Milly, don't be afraid. You remember me, don't you?"

Milly nodded.

"Where shall I put my horse? Round the back?"

Milly strode over the untidy garden and led her along the rough dry track round to the back of the old stone house, a part that Marietta had not seen on her last visit. Here were tumbledown stables, though on one of the doors she noticed that the bolts were strong and free of rust and that horse-dung was piled to one side. They tied the horse to one of the rings in the wall.

"Who's been, Milly? Have you had visitors?"

The girl shook her head, wiping her cheek with the heel of her hand and refusing to look at Marietta. "No," she whispered, moving off.

Remembering John and Betty Fuller's attempts to stop their daughter speaking, Marietta took advantage of this time alone to find out what she could, and taking Milly's arm gently in her hand, she held her back. "What herbs do you gather, Milly? Are they for the pot? Will you show me?"

Unwillingly, Milly raised the bunch of leaves, turning them this way and that so that Marietta could identify them.

"Foxglove leaves, Milly? Is that what these are? And wolfsbane?" This was a pretty pale yellow tall-growing plant with hoods like those of the monkshood.

"Aye," Milly said, "bees like it."

"And this one?" Marietta asked, by now highly suspicious. She took hold of the long stemmy plant with small white flowers. "I don't think I know this one."

Milly pointed to the gaping space in the limestone wall at the side of the track where the plant bushed out from between the stones. "There," she said, "it's that one. Baneberry. Some call it Herb Christopher."

"God in heaven, Milly! What are you about? These are all—"

"I know, m'lady. I know they are." A tear rolled down her cheek.

"Milly, will you tell me…please…what are you going to do with them? One alone is enough to kill a cow. But three together…!"

A woman's voice came from behind them. "Don't ask her, m'lady. She doesn't know how to tell you. She knows plenty about herbs and things but she can't put too many words together." Betty Fuller hobbled painfully towards them, neither angry nor welcoming. "Come on in. I saw you coming."

"Betty," Marietta began, still appalled by this lethal handful, "I thought it was you who grew all the simples."

"Aye, I meant you to. It's me what has the reputation as wise-woman but it's *her* what makes up all concoctions. I can birth women and weave spells, but it's Milly who gathers my herbs." She gathered up the corners of her apron and held it out, inviting Milly to throw them in. "That's it, is it, lass?"

Milly nodded and walked ahead of them to the stone steps.

"Then why…?"

Old Betty anticipated the question. She was still sharp. "Nay, lady, you know better than to ask that. How many folks would've come to *her* for their potions? Eh? Her being simple. Nobody would. Me neither."

That could not be denied. It also explained why, at Marietta's last visit, Betty had confused two relatively well-known plants and why Milly had felt bound to correct her.

The old woman hobbled off after Milly, leaving Marietta to trot after her, still bursting with curiosity about the apronful of poisonous plants. "Tell me, Betty, please. Who are they for? Someone in particular?"

"Aye, someone in particular. Us."

"What?"

"Us," Betty replied, testily. "You've come at a bad time, m'lady, but come on in just the same. I reckon if anyone has a right to know why, it'd better be you."

Suddenly it seemed that the Fates had it in for the Fullers. If Sir Bastien and this man Rigg didn't manage to kill them, they'd manage it for themselves. Marietta began to wonder if she was dreaming.

The upper room was every bit as messy as before, though this time a layer of steam hung like a heavy cloud across the rafters, pouring from a large cauldron on the fire. The heat was overwhelming. Betty crossed straight to the cauldron and allowed Milly to remove the plants from her apron and toss them in, poking them down with a well-stained stick.

In the dimness of the room, Marietta saw that John Fuller lay flat on a pallet over by the far wall, his thin frame almost disappearing into the tattered grey blanket, his face creased with pain, his skin deathly pale and tightly drawn. One leg was bound by rags to a board, still scabbed with blood. She did not need to ask what had happened. Only how.

"Down t'steps," Betty said, pulling out a stool and tipping a hen off it. The creature looked affronted and stalked off. "Here, m'lady, sit you down. Like I said, you've come at a bad time. He's not going to mend now, not with that." She nodded to his leg. "And he can't do nowt. And I can't. And *she* can't." Staring at the cauldron, she sniffed and went silent.

This was terrible, Marietta thought, angered, saddened and racked with guilt that she had not defied her husband and seen to supplies for these poor wretches. That they should contemplate suicide was beyond belief. "But, Betty, surely, why can't Milly do most of the work? She's strong." It was a feeble thing to say. The lass was simple and not up to the task of caring for the two elderly parents in such circumstances. She regretted the suggestion.

"Aye, she's strong. She's breeding too."

"What?" There was no need for Betty to repeat it; Marietta had heard. But could she not be mistaken? Did the lass have a lover? Had they not tried to abort it? Wise-women knew about such things. Milly herself would know what plants to use: rue, lad's love, laurel, pellitory-of-the-wall.

Again, Betty forestalled her question. "Aye, we tried to get rid of it, but it were too late. She doesn't know, you see. She can't count and she'd no idea she were breeding until it were too late. And we can't feed ourselves, let alone a bairn."

Marietta's head swam with the bitterness of their poor lives. How could she ever have grumbled about her own woes? But the details had yet to come. "Is John asleep?" she asked.

"Aye, Milly gave him something for his pain. It knocked him out."

Too efficient by half, whatever it was, Marietta thought. The lass could neither count, nor measure, nor read a recipe. How many cures had she effected? How many deaths? "Betty, I've come to warn you of danger."

The old lady turned her head from contemplation of her husband and swept Marietta with a glance of patent unconcern. "Danger? Hah! There's nothing about danger that I don't already know, m'lady."

Thinking to stir her with the fear they'd displayed at her first visit, Marietta told her, nevertheless. "Yes, there is, Betty. There are men up at the castle who mean you harm…"

"Hah!" The scathing laugh burst forth like a snapping twig, dry and brittle, "they've done all harm they're going to do, that lot. That's why they're going to find us dead, next time they get here. Hah!" She beckoned Milly to give the cauldron another poke.

Hardly able to believe what she had heard, Marietta could only probe into the implications of this and hope to come up with some facts. "Next time, Betty? You mean they've been here before?"

"Mother...please..." The words were whispered over Milly's shoulder, but her entreaty was disregarded.

"Aye, they've been here before, all right. Fer years they've been coming here, on and off. Devils, the lot of 'em. How do you think *she* got like that? Eh? A lover? Hah...hah!" Her cackling verged on hysteria.

"Mother!" Milly held a hand to her mouth, the tears now welling into her reddened eyes. "Don't tell... don't..."

Marietta went to her and placed an arm about her shoulders and with the end of her veil wiped Milly's tears. "It's all right, love, we're all women. I'm here to help you. Let your mother tell me what happened, then I shall know what to do. Don't weep, Milly, please."

Milly stared at the veil in Marietta's hand. "You're not like her, are you?"

This time, Marietta knew what she meant. "No, Milly. I'm not like her. Not in any way." She returned to the stool and leaned towards Betty. "Betty, there isn't much time. Please tell me what's been going on. Years, you said? Who's been coming here for years? Who are these devils you speak of?"

"Thieves, m'lady. That's who. Horse-thieves. Lay-brothers from Monksgrange, and that bailiff."

"The Monksgrange bailiff? The one who's there now?"

"Aye, Longleigh."

"Longleigh? He's my father's—"

"That's it. Your father's bailiff. I wanted to tell Lord Alain when he asked how often he'd been used to visiting, but John shut me up. Said we'd be killed if we said too much. They used to bring horses here from all over the place and hide them here until the lay-brothers and the bailiff came to fetch them and take them up to the caves above Monksgrange. Then they'd go off to the buyers over the moor road. Clever, eh?''

"So that's it! And they used Beckington and the caves as exchange points. And you had to agree and keep quiet about it. Oh, Betty!''

"Aye, m'lady, that we did. It were no use old John there making a fuss, they just clobbered him and threatened us, and every time he protested…he's a pig-headed sod is my husband…it were poor Milly that got it,'' she nodded towards Milly's back.

"Got it?'' Marietta frowned. A cold shiver ran down her back.

"She were ony eleven when they first had her. Here, on the table, in front of our eyes. Lay-brothers from Monksgrange, bailiff, that filthy groom from up at Thorsgeld, too. Eleven, she were. A child…'' Her voice broke and she clamped a hand to her mouth, holding it together while she rocked backwards and forwards.

"Lay-brothers, too?''

"Aye, them too. If Prior had found out, they'd have been sent packing, that's for sure. They were all in it together, the lot of them. An' your father never came near, not from one year to the next. Then it got like every time they came they'd take their sport with Milly, pretending like she were that simple she were enjoying it when she howled. Fiends!''

"God in heaven, Betty, was there no one who could see what was going on? What about Lord Alain? Were his horses being stolen too, at the beginning?''

Again the scathing look. "Him? It'd be no good going to him! It were his wife who came with them. She were worse than any of them. A slut, m'lady. She were a slut!''

This was getting worse by the minute. Marietta looked

around her at the dirt and disorder and began to realise how the place must have been systematically wrecked, over and over again to keep the Fullers under their brutal yoke, how poor old John had tried to defend them with his scrawny arms but been beaten, his wife and daughter humiliated, raped.

"Who did she come *with*, Betty? Why?"

"At first, she came here to meet Longleigh and that groom from Thorsgeld, Rigg."

"You mean to help plan the thefts?"

"Nah! She weren't bothered with that. It were *men* she wanted. Men. The ony man she didn't want were her own husband. Everybody else's, but not her own. She were rotten, rotten to the core…filthy bitch! She'd do it here, on the table, in front of everybody…one after t'other, all of them, screeching and howling like banshees…" Her voice became harsh with disgust. "Animals? I've never seen animals behave the way they did. At least animals get on with it in private!"

"In front of you…and John…and Milly? Saints!"

Viciously, Betty stabbed the table with one finger. "There, in front of everybody! There, where we eat! Then they'd get Milly. And then that whore came with Sir Bastien Symme, and they'd plan how to get horses away from Thorsgeld down to our stables, and who'd collect 'em. And they'd laugh that Lord Alain never found out how he lost his horses. And that Sir Bastien, he were worse than the rest of them. He'd take Milly while he were waitin' for his woman, then he'd have *her* as soon as she got here and carry on talking business when the others arrived, still at it. I've never seen anything like it. It was like they was possessed with devils. And she'd be lying there, telling them what to do. You'd never believe it, lady."

Marietta was dizzy with shock. She'd had warning that

the first Lady Thorsgeld was man-crazy, but this was not what she had expected, a she-devil, a whore. What on earth had Alain been thinking about to marry her? Why had he not seen what was happening?

It explained much, of course, but not enough. She had already deduced that Sir Bastien had stolen Alain's wife and horses, but this put a different slant on things, a bitter-tasting, distorted, vile slant, illustrating a sequence of events she could never have imagined. Not even in a night-mare. That man...she had almost flirted with him herself, laughed with him; he had held her around the waist, she had put her hand into his. Monster! Her hair bristled and her throat constricted with unexpressed fear.

And Milly, poor inarticulate Milly, now pregnant.

"But the woman died, did she not, Betty? Do you know what happened?"

"Two years ago, aye. The whore died. I thought it might be better for us after that, but it didn't make a lot o' difference. They just used Milly more, that's all. Now it's best if we all die, that'll put a stop to it, once and for all."

"Betty...no! Don't think of it, please. It's not the answer. It can't be. I can help." But the words carried no conviction in her heart, for she knew she had already over-stayed her time. She should have gathered them away to safety by now and hurried back to the castle. If they came while she was here, she'd be one more for them to dispose of, that's all. But curiosity lured her onwards. She had to know. "How did she die, Betty?"

"It were my fault. They know it were my fault. They've threatened to have me hanged for a witch, for murder, if I don't keep my mouth shut about what they're up to. There's nothing I can do. They'll take Milly too, as my accomplice. They'll say she's possessed o' the devil." She shook her head, forgetting that, absorbed in her pain, she had not an-swered the question.

"Tell me, Betty. How did it happen?"

Instead of responding immediately to the probing, she stood and, taking a large basin, stretched a greyish-green piece of cloth across it and carried it to the cauldron. With-out the need for instructions, Milly scooped the limp, al-most blackened, leaves out of the boiling water and heaped them into the bowl. Clouds of steam billowed upwards as Betty carried them to the table, gathered the cloth and be-gan to twist it, squeezing more dark green juice from the leaves. This, she poured back into the cauldron.

"She got herself pregnant, didn't she?" Betty talked as if to herself. "Get them bits o' chicken in there now, Milly, and them onions and leeks, and throw in what's left o' the barley to thicken it. It won't taste so bad." She glanced at her husband. "We'll get some down him first. If anybody grumbles, it'll be him! Hah! Best not tell him we're eating his one and only cockerel, had we?"

Appalled, Marietta prayed that Milly would not taste it. Poisoned broth. So that was how they were going to put an end to their lives. A last meal. Holy saints, please make something happen to prevent it.

"Pregnant?" she prompted Betty. "Not surprising, but did she die of that, or…?"

"She told me to make her a potion. She had to get rid of it, well…naturally, Lord Alain would know it weren't his. He never went near her. So I left it to Milly and I gave it to her ladyship when she came on't next time. Ony I gave it to her too strong, I think, 'cos…"

"No!" Milly's voice cut through the explanation like a knife.

Both Betty and Marietta watched as the lass threw the stick into the broth and strode across to the window, standing with her back to them as before. Clearly, she was agitated.

"No, Milly? What, then?" Marietta said.

Just as they feared that her words had dried up again, Milly spoke. "It was not Mother. It was me. I knew...I knew what to get for a potion to start a flow. Rue, and lad's love, and..."

"Well, that's what you got, you silly wench!" Betty snapped at her.

"Yes, and...and something else," Milly retorted, over her shoulder. "That stuff you noticed, m'lady..." she turned to Marietta "...it has little black berries in autumn. They're even more poisonous than tops. It only grows up here, in the limestone. I put some of them in. That's what killed her. T'other stuff didn't have time to work before she died."

Speechless, Marietta held a hand to her forehead. Poisoned, by this simple lass who had suffered so much at the woman's hands. "She got back to the castle then?" she asked Betty.

"Oh, she didn't take it here, m'lady. She took it off back home, and they all thought it were the pestilence, or something. Sir Bastien took himself off with horses and didn't come near for weeks till it were all over. T'others kept away, too, then they all came back and started up again, but they wouldn't leave Milly alone, poor lass. They thought it were my fault...she never said it were hers... she'd be scared..."

"It didn't matter whose fault it was, Mother," Milly found her voice in anger, "did it? They thought it was her own fault, but they blamed you to keep us quiet."

Betty, clearly surprised by this coherent outburst of reasoning, simply thrust the bowl of soggy leaves into Milly's hands, ripping away the cloth and shaking the bits into the rushes. "Here, shut your mouth, lass. Take this round to the back and throw it out. Keep it away from m'lady's horse."

Any warning that Marietta could give about imminent danger now seemed superfluous, especially so when old John lay unconscious on the pallet, unable to move, let alone flee to safety. How she wished she had asked Uncle Nicholas to help. A poor substitute, but better than being alone at a time like this. The revelation about Lady Thorsgeld's activities with all those men, here at Beckington, her mother's property at the time, was almost too much to take in.

There were gaps in the story, plenty of those, but this was a mess of huge proportions, involving Lord Alain's property, her own, and her father's, too. No wonder that Alain felt he must bide his time. Was this why he had wanted her to leave the place alone? To catch them red-handed? If so, she had now put the cat among the pigeons and he'd not thank her for that. Not after all the planning he'd done.

"Betty—" Marietta prayed that a plan would form while she was talking "—don't eat that broth, please. Don't give any to your husband and daughter. That's not the way…I'm sure of it."

"What is, then? I'll not run off and leave him here on his own and I've taken as much as I can o' their vicious ways. If they come and start again on Milly, like they always do, it'll kill her anyway. That groom were here two nights ago, and that bailiff; it were them what threw John down the steps."

"They threw him? Oh, my God…I thought he fell…!"

"He tried to protect Milly. She were screaming and he come at one of them with a stool, but it were no use. I'm not having that happen again, m'lady. We're better off dead.''

"But the property is mine now, Betty. It won't happen again, not now."

"Aye?" Betty's voice was heavy with sarcasm. "I haven't noticed no great change since you were here last, m'lady."

The accusation of neglect was difficult to refute. "I had no idea that this was going on…"

What use to explain? She had tried, then she had left the subject alone to keep the peace. Her garden had come first, then guests had arrived, her hands had been full of other problems.

"I'll stay here with you," she said, purposefully, "then whoever comes will have me to settle with." She looked along the table for possible weapons. "Do you have a knife, Betty? A large one? Sharp?"

"Here, this one. This is sharp. Where do you want it?" She picked up an old worn carving knife with a blade now so narrow that it was more like a spike. "Look here, I'll put it in here and hide it behind this great jug," and she inserted the point up to the handle between two planks of the table where the wood had shrunk. "There, look, you can grab at that if you need to, eh?"

"Good. And you'll not take that poison, Betty?"

"Wait 'n see, m'lady. Where's Milly got to?"

Milly had not returned from emptying the boiled leaves.

Marietta went to the window to see if she was in the herb-patch, then pulled back sharply, her heart almost leaping from her breast. "Saints!" she whispered, "it's that bailiff from Monksgrange, my father's bailiff…what's his name…Longleigh."

"Vicious, he is," Betty hissed. "Now he's got no lay-brothers to 'elp him, he wanted more money for his part. Threatened to stop, he did.''

"He's coming up..oh, why didn't we see him coming? We could have put a barrier across the door.''

"Wouldn't do no good. They'd find a way in.''

There was no time to do anything. The door flew open with a crash and Longleigh stood silhouetted in the doorframe. He hesitated, obviously not expecting to see a visitor at Beckington for he had tethered his horse at the front, by the stone steps. "We…e…ell.'' He frowned. "Lady Thorsgeld now, isn't it? Coming up in the world a bit, aren't we?'' He took a few paces into the room. "Come to view your property at last, 'ave yer?''

"I've already viewed it once, Master Longleigh, some time ago. And what gives you the right to walk in here, uninvited?''

For an answer, he looked her up and down, smiled at his thoughts and moved further into the room, his attitude and bearing insolent without the presence of Sir Henry at his side. A burly man, broad-chested and heavy, he had been respectful enough to her at Monksgrange on the few occasions they'd met, but so seldom that she had not picked up his name, only his dire warnings that the caves were dangerous places to be near. Demons and devils, he had told her. He had not been far wrong.

The day was warm, the stuffy room even warmer, and dark patches of sweat had formed under the sleeves of his russet woollen tunic. Meaningfully, he scratched at his groin and turned his attention to old John, still lying motionless on the pallet. "Dead, is he?'' he asked, casually. He might as well have been asking after his health.

"No…but near enough, thanks to you,'' Betty snapped, moving to stop him approaching the pallet.

Longleigh sauntered across, pushed Betty out of the way

like a feather and peered down at John Fuller then, before
Betty could recover her balance, nudged the broken leg
viciously with his toe. John made no movement.

"Master Longleigh! Have some pity, for heaven's sake,"
Marietta cried.

"He's dead." The man straightened and turned away,
unconcerned.

"Nay…he's not!" Betty yelped. "He's sleeping. I gave
him a potion. He's sleeping, I tell thee. John…John, wake
up!" She went and lowered herself painfully to the floor at
the side of her husband and shook him, gently at first and
then more urgently. "John…come on…wake!"

Longleigh let out a bark of laughter. "Aye, well, we all
know what happens when you give potions, don't we? Eh?
You've done it again, old crone, you've done it again. Hah!
Just as well to practise on your own family once in a while,
eh?" He laughed, looking at Marietta as though to share
the jest. His teeth were blackened and yellow and a fine
line of foam showed at the corners of his mouth. Piggy
eyes glinted viciously.

"Master Longleigh, go back to Monksgrange," Marietta
commanded. "If you do not leave my property this instant,
I shall see that Lord Thorsgeld and Sir Henry both know
of your involvement here."

He stopped and lowered his head, poking his face at her
belligerently. "Aye? Is that so, *Lady* Thorsgeld? Is that so?
Tell your menfolk, would you? And what makes you think
you're going to get out of this alive, then? Eh?" He extended one huge finger to touch her cheek but she slapped
it away and moved nearer to the table.

"You've done enough harm here. Go…get out!"

"Where's the lass?" he said, scratching again.

"I don't know. She went out some time ago."

"Hiding, is she? Well then, you'll have to do instead won't you? You should know what it's all about by now."

The breath tightened in her lungs, fear racing through every limb. "Touch me, Longleigh, and you'll get a knife in your belly," she snarled.

"Eh? Oh...!" He laughed. "Then I'll wait till I've got some help. Shouldn't be long now. Meanwhile—" he looked at the table, then at the cauldron over the fire "—what's there to eat? I'll need some energy, won't I?"

"Broth," Marietta pushed the word into a whisper.

"Broth?" He went to the cauldron and peered into the steam, poking with the stick at the contents. "Who made it? Her?" tipping his head towards Betty who now lay half over her husband, moaning in anguish.

"No. Milly." Marietta held her breath.

"Did you see her make it?"

"Yes, before she went out. I saw her put the chicken and vegetables in."

"Chicken? Well, there's a luxury. *He* won't want any, will he? Not now, eh? Put some in a bowl, my *lady,* and I'll have some while I'm waiting for reinforcements." He smiled again.

Vicious swine. Yes, I'll put some in a bowl for you. Gladly. Marietta could barely control the trembling in her hands, aware of the power over this man's life, power to pay him back for the suffering to this family and old John's death.

Betty lay still now, her head in her hands resting over the body of her frail husband. It was as though she was listening to what Marietta was doing, seeing it in her mind, seeing the bowl filled with barley-thickened greenish-grey liquid and chunks of vegetables and chicken, speckled with herbs. Steaming. Appetizing. Nourishing.

The stool scraped on the floor as Longleigh sat and

reached for a spoon, breaking the silence after Betty's brief weeping. She turned as the bowl was set before him. "That were for my John," she said, resentment and anger making her voice quaver.

Longleigh stirred, then took his first mouthful, blowing as the heat caught his tongue. "Was it, crone? Tell him it tastes all right, then."

"He's not needing it now," Betty mumbled, "not now."

Marietta could not drag her eyes away from the spoon but stood rooted to the spot as each mouthful was gobbled, each spoonful blown at and shovelled in with an audible gasp, unfaltering, rhythmic, untasted. Nothing was chewed, everything was swallowed whole until the bowl was empty. Was it not poisonous then, after all? Not enough? Slow-acting? Might it take hours? There had been no point in asking, at the time. "More?" she asked.

The spoon clattered into the bowl, making her jump.

"My mouth…lips…tingling…" He rubbed at them with his wrists.

"It was too hot for you," Marietta said.

"Too…too…hot…" The wrists rubbed around his throat. "Burning me…burning my…argh!" He tore at the neck of his tunic, throwing himself away from the table and grabbing at his throat, then at his stomach. "Burns…" he gasped, "burns…my god…what has she…the bitch…help—" his body doubled over as the burning pain seared through him "—help…argh!" He tried to stand, kicking over the stool, his face visibly reddening and pouring with sweat, his hands clawing at the collar of his tunic, the piggy eyes now almost black as the pupils dilated. "What…what is it?" he croaked.

"It's good chicken broth, meant for my John, that's what it is." Betty rose painfully to her knees and stared full at Marietta, no trace of gladness or jubilation, no mad desire for vengeance. Rather it was as though the women took on the aspect of two mice with an aged and infirm cat, staying out of his range and watching his futile attempts to find his legs, to sight them, to do them harm while losing power, moment by moment.

Keeping out of his range, they watched him stagger towards the door, clutching first at his stomach and then at his throat. Betty was less affected than Marietta. "Quick, m'lady, get that bowl and spoon. Hide them! If the others come, tell 'em his heart's burst, or summat."

"Oh God, Betty, he's dying, isn't he?"

"Aye, best thing that's happened to him since he were born. The swine."

"And John...your husband...he's...?"

"Gone. A life for a life."

Longleigh smashed into the door but was pushed back hard against the wall as it opened in his face. "Help...me..." he gasped at the man who entered.

It was Rigg, the groom from Thorsgeld. "Stop playing games, you great fool," he said, pushing Longleigh away. "There isn't time for that."

But Longleigh fell with a crash onto the floorboards and lay groaning and retching violently into the filthy rushes.

Chapter Thirteen

Rigg needed no introduction; Marietta recognised him at once as the black-haired groom she'd seen talking with Sir Bastien in the stable-yard only a few days ago, the one whose hand had delved into his friend's pouch when he thought no one was looking. The look he gave Marietta now showed that he was not surprised to see her again.

"Yes…" he said, softly. "Yes, you would be here, wouldn't you? Interfering…nosing about. I saw your horse around the back."

"This is my property and you are trespassing…" Her words went unheeded, for Rigg was staring at Longleigh who shook and moaned, his knees pulled up to his chin.

"What's been going on? How long has he been like this?"

Marietta was shaking with fright. It was her doing. He was dying because she intended him to. She must keep a grip on herself or she'd be no use to Betty and Milly, none to herself, either.

"You must have followed him here. He…he just collapsed. Betty thinks…"

Betty interrupted, "It's his heart. I told you what it is. His heart. I've seen it before."

"His heart? Vomiting? Don't be daft, woman," Rigg said.

"Aye, I've seen it before, I tell thee. It's been coming on. Seen it in his face lots o' times. Too red," she said, finally.

Still, Rigg could not bring himself to believe it. Here, of all places. This would complicate things, as would the extra presence of Lady Thorsgeld.

"You'd better go," Marietta said, once more moving towards the table. "Lord Alain is sure to know you've gone and he'll come looking for you. He knows what you've been up to, you know."

"Ah! So, my lady, you told him what you saw, did you? Well, that was not very wise of you, but I might have known you would. But he doesn't know I'm here, does he? Any more than you knew I was coming."

"Of course I knew. Betty told me everything…yes, everything," she countered, "and Lord Alain knows exactly what you've been up to."

"Up to? I'm not up to anything, my lady. I shall be back up at the castle as soon as Sir Bastien arrives to take the horses away and I shall deny any knowledge of it.

"The old chap's had it, by the look of things," he looked pointedly at the grey blanket that now covered the entire body of John, "the old crone will have a dagger in her belly, and the lass, wherever she is, well, nobody's going to take too much notice of her, are they? A half-wit? A babbling fool? And you…you can say what you like about Sir Bastien… I expect he'll be miles away by the time you get back wrapped up like old John."

"What do you mean?"

"Mean?" His eyes moved over her lasciviously. "Well, that's not too difficult for you to understand, is it? You know full well what Sir Bastien wants from you before he goes, and now you've made it easy for both of us. But you don't suppose he'll allow you to go yelping it all the way back to Thorsgeld, do you? I shall blame the whole thing on Sir Bastien. *You* won't be able to blame it on anybody, will you? Perhaps you should have co-operated with him a bit sooner instead of being so snotty-nosed. You had chance.''

When Marietta did not reply immediately, as he'd expected her to do, he looked more intently at the direction of her eyes and saw, too late, that she stared over his shoulder towards the doorway. He whirled. ''Sir! Holy saints, sir! You gave me a shock.''

Sir Bastien kicked at Longleigh in passing and moved further into the room, his feet making no sound on the rushes. ''That's obvious, Rigg. Presumably, if you'd known I was here, you'd not have been so eager to blame the whole thing on me, would you? I hope you're not going to blame me for *that* too, are you?'' He tipped his head towards the writhing man on the floor. ''And that over there? Died peacefully in his bed, did he, or what?''

''Er…broke his leg…er yesterday. Look sir, I don't want you to get the wrong idea about what I said just now…'' Rigg blustered, watching the handsome newcomer warily.

Sir Bastien ignored his attempted explanation and approached Marietta instead, smiling courteously.

''My Lady Marietta, you appear to be somewhat out of place here. Have these churlish creatures been offending you? Forgive them, they know no better. What he says is only partly true; I have no intention of doing away with you. On the contrary, I shall need your help now we're a man short.

''Rigg…'' he turned to the groom ''…get that to the top of the steps and give it a shove over the edge, will you? We can't have him making that clamour while we…amuse ourselves, can we? Go on, man. Get on with it!'' He waved a hand imperiously at the prone Longleigh. ''What happened? You didn't fix him with one of your famous arrows, did you, lady? Or is it a stab wound?''

''Neither, Sir Bastien. Betty says his heart's burst, but I don't know.''

''Ah, well, in that case we'd better be sure. We don't want him recovering and messing up our plans, do we?''

Before Marietta could guess his intention, he strode to the door, straddled Longleigh's body and plunged his dagger up to its hilt into the man's chest. Then, carefully withdrawing it, he wiped it clean on the man's clothes and helped with his foot to push the body over the vertical edge of the stairway.

Rigg straightened and gave a puff of relief. ''That should finish him off.''

''Where are the horses?''

''Stables, sir. Behind.''

''Both of them?''

''Both,'' Rigg nodded. ''Look, sir…let me explain about…''

''No need, Rigg.''

Sir Bastien half-turned as if to go inside then, with a speed too quick for the groom to anticipate, swung back and thrust the dagger upwards towards Rigg's heart, knocking him off balance and sending him hurtling down over the edge on top of Longleigh. The dagger came out as the body fell.

''There, if that doesn't look as though two men had a fight and fell, I don't know what will. Easier than I thought. No arguments, no payments and…'' he wiped the dagger on a tuft of stonecrop and entered the room ''…no silly tales about who did what. Eh, my lady? You didn't particularly want an audience, did you? No, you're not the kind to show off, are you? A quiet private time we'll have, just you and me…oh, and the old crone…and a corpse. Best I can do, I'm afraid. Come now, let's waste no more time.''

The nightmare worsened. The heavy blanket that enclosed the darkness and would not allow her to wake, to break through, now weighed so heavily upon Marietta that she could scarcely determine what was real and what imagined. Men lay dead, one at her own hands, poisoned at her invitation. Another man was casually butchered by this suave creature who, only a day or two ago, had sat at her side.

And now he intended to possess her while his hands were still sticky with blood. A corpse lay in the same room, and a frightened old woman she barely knew, while outside…somewhere…a terrified and pregnant girl roamed about. Stolen horses waited in the stables and Alain was nowhere near. Help was a million miles away.

The incredible revelations of villainy would have been quite enough to turn her stomach, the bestiality, the indignities wreaked upon poor people, without any further events. She had made the decision to stay and help to protect them without knowing the consequences and yet, if she had fled, both Milly and her mother would have been dead by now, if not by these men's hands, then by their own.

The horrors must be shut out. This beast must be dealt with by her alone. She must win. She was Alain's. He loved her courage; he had said so, often. It must not desert her now. She prayed. Holy Mary, help me.

Seth waited until Lord Alain had finished speaking to two of his guests in the courtyard, standing respectfully to one side until he was noticed.

''You'll not regret it, Mistress Jean,'' Lord Alain was

saying, "they're thoroughly reliable. Three of my very best—in fact, I wouldn't be ashamed to ride 'em myself."

Mistress Jean smiled. "I'm tempted to keep them for myself, Lord Alain. But look…isn't your head groom waiting to speak with you?" She nodded towards Seth.

Lord Alain swung round, "Seth, ah, what news, man?" They moved apart, not willing to be overheard.

Seth's whisper was urgent. "As soon as you'd left the yard, my lord, he took Penda and Apollo down the lane instead of to the croft. He had a horse waiting there, did you know?"

"No. Then what? Off, was he?"

"Aye, my lord, off across the fields. Short cut to Beckington, I reckon. One horse on each side of him."

"Didn't waste any time, did he? Good timing, too, just when we'd finished business and he knew he wouldn't be missed. Right, saddle up and I'll be with you straight away. Thomas!" he yelled to the young page who crossed the courtyard with a jug of ale in each hand. "Put those down and run to the Master-at-Arms. I want him here, fast. Fast!"

The lad placed the jugs on top of the mounting block and flew through the gate-house arch as though demons were after him.

"Where's Lady Marietta?" Lord Alain asked Bruno. "She was supposed to be here to take the guests in. Have you seen her, Sir Henry?"

"Not for several hours, my lord. She asked me if I'd go to Beckington with her, but I refused to go without your permission. Didn't want to override your wishes—"

"Beckington Manor? She asked you to go with her? Did she say why?"

"No." Sir Henry looked thoughtful. "She didn't give a reason but she would surely not have gone alone without your approval, would she?"

"Oh, yes, she would, Sir Henry. Did she always rely on *your* approval?"

"Nay, you know the answer to that, my lord."

"Bruno! Go search our apartments and the garden. See if you can find her."

The chaplain hobbled over to the group and caught at Lord Alain's arm before he strode off. "My horse," he said, pointing to the courtyard stable, "my horse was taken an hour ago. I've been waiting for someone to bring it back, my lord, I was about to go off on a visit..."

"Damn the girl, she must have taken it! Did nobody see her go? For heaven's sake...is everybody blind around here? Master, there you are! I want twelve men ready to go with me. Now. Here. Lady Thorsgeld's gone to..."

"Aye, my lord." He ran to the gatehouse where the garrison were roused, his voice bellowing loud enough to wake the dead. Horses and soldiers began pouring into the courtyard; swords were buckled on, Lord Alain's stallion was brought in, then Sir Henry's; others followed.

Bruno appeared with Sir Nicholas at his heels. "No, my lord, her maids say she's still not returned."

Lord Alain snarled at him in anger. "What the hell is your sister doing, going off without my permission? She knows damn well I don't want her to go near the place."

Feeling the sting of injustice, Bruno's caution slipped. "She's *your* wife, my lord, not mine!" Automatically, he ducked as the back of Lord Alain's hand swung at his head, then dodged away to collect his horses.

The blow was delivered more in frustration that Marietta had not only spoiled his plans to catch the men red-handed but had put herself at risk, also. A side-effect more dangerous than the theft. The secondary plan to discover more about his wife's death had had to be abandoned when he'd seen how close Emeline had come to danger.

Marietta had drifted close to danger, too, due to his care-lessness, and now she had sailed right into it, probably be-cause she thought he'd be too busy to notice what she was up to. Headstrong, proud lass. But this was sheer disobe-dience. What could have possessed her?

"Yes, you young whelp! She's my wife, as you say. And it looks as though I shall have to remind her!"

Seth came running back through the gateway. "My lord…it's as you thought…he's been followed. About ten minutes ago…while I was here with you…Sir Bastien…"

"Ah! He followed? Was he alone?"

"Yes, my lord. He took the road."

"Well, something's going according to plan, anyway. Good, Seth. We're ready for off. Don't worry, we'll get 'em. Pray God we get my wife back unharmed, that's what *I* care about." He swung up into the saddle and turned to catch Sir Henry's eye. "Come, Sir Henry, we'll retrieve your daughter yet again."

They rode cross-country in a tight pack, keeping to the trees, then spreading out as they neared Beckington, encir-cling the house stealthily to cut off all escape, finally mov-ing in like a tightening band. They found it strange to see no men preparing to leave, to hear no voices. Only horses were at the back of the house; the chaplain's, Sir Bastien's and another from Thorsgeld. So, Marietta was still there.

Silently, Lord Alain motioned to Sir Henry, Sir Nicholas and Bruno to follow him round to the front of the house, but their caution was arrested when two crumpled bodies lay across their path, one almost on top of the other.

"God's wounds! That's my bailiff…Longleigh!" Sir Henry exclaimed, "What's he doing here?"

"Not a lot, Father," Bruno said, flippantly. "But why is his face purple, I wonder, and his eyes wide open? Was he stabbed?"

"This one was. This is my groom, Rigg—" Lord Alain looked up towards the open door at the top of the stairway "—and it looks as though they met their match. Come, we must find Marietta." He darted round to the steps and bounded up them, two at a time, blinking into the foul dimness of the room at the top.

If the room had been a mess on his last visit, now it was a shambles of smashed stools, broken pottery, wooden bowls and implements everywhere, blood-soaked straw and, almost under the table, the figure of Sir Bastien Symme bent double, clutching his ribs and moaning, speechless with pain.

Over by the wall, the corpse of old John lay covered with a blanket, and Betty, staring blankly and registering no surprise, sat by his feet, rocking gently back and forth. There was no sign of Marietta.

"Mistress Fuller," Lord Alain called to her. "Betty! Where's Lady Thorsgeld? Where is she?"

"Dead," whimpered the old woman, "all dead."

"Dead? Lady Marietta?" He turned on Sir Bastien like a wild animal, yanking his head back by a handful of hair. "You've killed her, swine? Where is she…what have you *done?*"

"No…God in heaven…mercy!" he moaned. "No, she's not. Argh! The woman thinks you mean…mean Jayne… argh! My lord, oh, have mercy, let me go, I'm wounded. She stabbed me and fled…ah, I'm bleeding." His face, contorted with pain, was ashen, his well-cut tunic was stained darkly with blood that seeped through his fingers. His face, too, was bloody as though there had been a struggle, though clearly he had suffered worse than the victor.

Lord Alain had no mercy, shaking him like a rat. "Where? Where…you filthy, lying whoreson? Where is she? Tell me or I'll throw you down on top of the others, cur! Where?''

Almost unconscious now, Sir Bastien moaned. ''No…no…she ran off…I don't know where, she ran oh… stop…leave me.''

''Did you harm her, rape her?''

''No…no, I swear I did not…'' He fell hard onto the floor again as Lord Alain threw him down, his head making a sickening thud. He lay still.

''Sir Henry, will you stay and find out what you can here? Sir Nicholas and Bruno, come! We must find her. God knows where to start looking.'' This was nothing like he'd expected. Three men dead, another lying mortally wounded, old Betty now fast losing her wits, Marietta fled. But where was the girl? He doubled back into the room. ''Betty! Betty!'' he shouted. ''Where's your daughter? Did she go with Lady Marietta?''

Betty shook her head, her face still a blank. ''No…o…o.'' she crooned, ''she's dead. All dead…''

''Oh, for pity's sake!''

''She's out of her wits, my lord,'' Sir Nicholas said. ''Take no notice. We'll find her. Marietta wouldn't just run away, would she? Perhaps it was the girl who ran off and Marietta's looking for her.''

Bruno agreed. ''Yes, there are woods behind here, and high rocks. There has to be an explanation. Marrie wouldn't run away without a good reason. She knows our voices…'' they tripped down the steps ''…we can call. She'll hear us, my lord.''

''Yes, you're right. Pray God she's not harmed. Come.'' He stopped briefly to speak to the Master-at-Arms then, still calling to him over his shoulder, he broke into a trot behind Bruno and Sir Nicholas and, on foot, entered the dark shadowy woodland.

* * *

Dazed and covered with blood, her legs trembling and shaking with fatigue, Marietta wandered upwards through the thick elders that sprouted like arms out of the rock face, providing foot-and hand-holds for her to cling to. Panting with the effort of the climb and with the even more arduous effort of containing her terror after the most recent events, she searched through the trees for a sign of the drab grey kirtle that Milly wore, calling softly, for she had no energy to do otherwise. "Milly, where are you? Milly, don't be afraid…it's me. Milly."

The silence was like a drug, tempting her to sit on the mossy boulders and give in to its embracing calm, to lie under the green canopy and sleep, forget, obliterate the chaos in her mind, to do what Milly had no doubt done and lose herself in the peace as an antidote to the awful events down below her.

But the lass had to be found, for her nightmare had lasted years, not less than an hour, and her reaction was sure to be proportionately greater, especially as she had less to live for—no protection, no loving, no means of sustenance and a bairn on the way. One that had been forced upon her. Poor wench. She must be desperate. Frantic.

Another push through the high brambles, another torn cheek and then she saw her. "Milly, don't move! I'm coming. I'll help…you're safe."

Milly was sitting poised on the edge of a sheer drop where the limestone cliff, topped by hawthorns, rose out of the woodland. Her legs dangled over the side and, on her lap, the bowl of soggy black leaves was hugged by bramble-torn arms. Wild eyes stared ahead, recognising nothing.

"Don't move, Milly, I'm coming," Marietta called, wondering how she could sound so confident about a move fraught with difficulties. But if Milly had managed it, so could she, and after watching one of her shoes hurtle down-

wards over boulders and into a giant bramble, she managed
to reach the shivering girl without alarming her or sending
her leaping away in fright.

Talking all the time, Marietta crawled along the deeply
fissured rocks and sat by her side. Then, very carefully, she
took hold of the bowl with its noxious contents and slowly
eased it away from her. "Let me have it now, Milly. You
don't need it, you're safe, they've all gone. Dead. They
can't hurt you any more."

It was not the meaning of the words that soothed Milly's
fear but the sounds of gentleness and calm instead of her
mother's harshness. It was the feeling of warmth and sympathy to which she responded and the knowledge that,
somehow, she was being understood. Without moving, she
listened to Marietta's voice in silence. And when Marietta
wondered if she had heard any of what had been said and
took her hand to hold it warmly in her lap, Milly clasped
it and allowed it to stay there.

"You're not like 'er, are you?" was all she said.

"No, Milly. I'm not like her. I'm nothing like her."

She heard a horse neighing in the distance and wondered
whether that could be Alain come to find her or whether it
was only one of those already there. And how would he
find her? How would he know where to look? How was
she to get poor Milly, who had carried a bowl of poisonous
leaves here, alone, to eat them and put an end to her life,
away from this place? How long could they wait for help
to come?

"Do you want to come back down with me now,
Milly?"

Milly shook her head.

"They've gone. The men are all dead now."

"You're saying that…saying that…to get me…" .

"No, Milly. I mean it. Rigg came, and then the others—'' She was about to explain, but Milly would have none of it.

''No!'' She bunched up, ready to spring away, but Marietta held onto her hand.

''All right…all right, stay here. Lord Alain will come and he will lead us down. You'll come and live with me, Milly, at the castle.''

The wide eyes turned to Marietta at last. ''Live? With you?''

''Yes, with me, at the castle.''

''Not my mother…and father?''

''Just you, unless you want them…?''

''No…no! With you. Live with you.''

''I shall look after you.'' She was not to have known, at that moment, how valuable her invitation would be in keeping the poor wench by her side until help came.

Each moment seemed like a lifetime during which questions came and went, mostly concerning Alain and his first, unfaithful wife. His attitude to her, Marietta, led her to wonder how he would regard this interference into his affairs and into her own property here at Beckington after his express command that she should wait on his approval. He would be angry, no doubt. She had disobeyed him. He would have every reason to beat her.

Strangely, her concern was less for herself than for him. She could understand how he must have felt, betrayed in his marriage by a woman whose appetite for men knew no bounds. Insatiable. No wonder he was so intent on laying claim to *her,* having seen her unequivocal dislike of the idea of marriage. Undoubtedly, that was an over-reaction on his part, but understandable.

They heard the calls first, faint and muffled by the wind in the trees, then two voices, then three. ''Marietta! Marietta!''

The hand she held in hers squeezed tightly, the tattered body stiffened in fear and Milly seemed to shrink. Her eyes widened, but she made no move.

"Stay with me, Milly. I'll call to them. You'll come with me." Then she called, feeling the girl's trembling as the invisible net tightened on her. "Here!" she yelled. "We're up here."

"Marietta!" It was Alain's voice.

"Here, Alain! Up here!"

There was a silence as they tried to pinpoint the sound, but Milly could bear the tension no longer. Any man's voice was a threat. Pulling at Marietta's hand, she scrabbled backwards, slewing her captor round in an effort to escape.

"No...Milly, stay with me...please, come back...!"

The voices returned. "Marietta, where are you?"

"Milly...no...stay." Marietta heaved on the girl's wrist, lost it and made a wild grab at the hem of her kirtle. Pulling her down into a heap, she threw herself on top of the girl's body in a tangle of skirts and legs and, in combined anger and desperation, rolled her face downwards, ignoring her cries, and straddled her hips, holding her shoulders to the bare rock. It was the only way; they were inches from the cliff face. Now, with all the air left in her lungs, she screamed, "Here! Here, Alain! We're here, on the cliff!" Tears of desperation rose with her cries.

She heard them shouting to each other, heard the crashes as branches were broken, then Alain's voice again. "Where? I can't see you..."

Exhausted, she fell on top of Milly. "I'm here," she muttered into the girl's neck. "I'm here and I want to go home. Come and find me."

"On the cliff, my lord—" it was Bruno's voice "—up on the top." Then the shouts were behind them, close at hand, calling, whoops of discovery, panting and grunts of effort as the men scrambled over towards the two prostrate bodies. "Here, my lord. She's here!" Bruno yelled.

"Oh, holy saints, no...Marietta!" Gently, hands lifted her upwards, pulling her off Milly and hauling her backwards into the comfort of two strong arms. "Blood...she's wounded...sweetheart, speak to me.."

"Alain," she said, "take me home."

"You're wounded, sweetheart. Where are you hurt? Show me."

"No, not badly. This is not my blood, it's...oh, Alain." As relief poured through her, the enormity of what had happened flooded back again, threatening to drown her joy in the dark memories of terror and conflict.

"Don't cry, my love, you're safe now. Safe. I'll take you home." He held her close to his chest, smoothing her wild hair and searching her eyes for signs of pain. "Did he wound you, sweetheart? Did he...?" He could not say the word to her for fear she would tell him the worst.

"I fought him off. Is he...did you find...?"

"We found him, and the others. He won't survive, but tell me what this lass is...she's not dead, is she?" He looked up at Bruno and Sir Nicholas.

"No, my lord. Swooned."

"Thank heaven," Marietta said. "She's in far worse shape than me. I had to sit on her to stop her running off. Carry her down quickly before she wakes. Look..." she pointed to the bowl of wet leaves "...she came up here to eat...oh, saints in heaven, the broth...don't let anyone eat it!"

"Sweetheart, what are you talking about? What broth must not be eaten?"

"It's poisoned, Alain—they were going to poison themselves when I got here. That's why I had to stay...! Oh

Alain, quickly, the men must not sample it. It's in the cauldron over the fire.''

''They won't,'' he assured her. ''I know it.''

Sir Nicholas and Bruno lifted Milly. ''We'll take the maid down between us, my lord,'' Nicholas said.

''Good. Come on, my love, we'll wait for the other explanations till later. Put your arms around my neck. Lost your shoe, did you? Hold on. Gently now.''

He lifted her safely into his arms and carried her easily over the rocks while she nestled her head into his neck and closed her eyes to relish the feel of his arms and the closeness of his body, the warmth of his skin and hair, even the smell of his sweat.

He chided her gently as they went. ''This is a habit I'm going to have to break you of,'' he murmured, kissing her damp forehead, ''or I shall be spending the rest of my life searching for you and bringing you back. Shall I put a leash on you? Eh? Shall I?''

''I didn't run away from you, my lord,'' she replied. ''I had to find Milly. She took the leaves to empty them away but she didn't come back and I suspected she'd gone off to eat them.''

''Why ever should she want to poison herself?''

''She's pregnant, my lord.''

Alain stopped dead in his tracks. ''What? How? I mean…who?'' When Marietta didn't answer, he understood. ''That swine?''

''It could have been. It's a long story. I think you'll have to hear the whole of it before you understand what the family have been through.''

''Then it will wait, sweetheart, until you're safe home again.''

Down below, at Beckington, the men had already begun to clear away the evidence of carnage which had greeted them a little while earlier. The stolen Penda and Apollo were already on their way home, the murdered men were wrapped and slung over horses—only old Betty could not be moved.

To Marietta's confusion, the men broke into spontaneous applause as the three men and their prizes emerged from the woodland.

"Blood? She's wounded, my lord?" Sir Henry's face registered alarm as he took her hand. "Did that fiend…?"

"No, Father, I'm all right, really, no more than a few bruises. Is…is that man still alive?"

"No, Marietta, he died only a short time ago. Was it you who stabbed him?"

She nodded, her lips tightened, remembering the act.

"That's my brave, fierce woman," Lord Alain whispered to her, settling her before him on the wide saddle, "my courageous tigress. Well done, my beautiful girl. More than a match for any man, eh?" Tenderly, he tucked her into his arm and held her close.

"Where's Milly? She must come too." She turned her head to look, but Milly was already on Sir Nicholas's saddle.

"Yes, sweetheart, everything shall be just as you want it now. The place is yours and you'll be allowed to say what happens to it, and the Fullers. We've held off for long enough, too long, to wait for that monster to give us the evidence we needed. I'll send men down to see to old John and his Betty. They'll be tended, don't worry. Home now." He kissed her.

Home. She had never realised how sweet the sound could be.

Chapter Fourteen

The feast, originally meant to be a farewell to the guests on the last day of their visit, was a celebration that paid little heed to the multiple deaths of the day, only to its more than satisfactory conclusion.

Rested, bathed and tended with loving hands, Marietta's fears that Lord Alain would be angry at her interference in the affairs of Beckington were quickly dispelled by his attention to her superficial wounds. Bruises and a few nasty scratches claimed as much sympathy as a broken limb would have done while Alain did his best to assure her that she had saved them all a great deal of trouble by defending herself so proficiently. Sir Bastien deserved no less.

But Marietta wondered, as he soothed her guilt, whether he was aware of Sir Bastien's part in the affairs of his late wife, not merely as a lover, though that would have been serious enough, but as a man of bestial habits who repeatedly raped a defenceless girl and terrorised her parents.

Later, after the feast, and once more alone together, she sought to broach the subject in a roundabout manner, asking him how badly his plans had been spoiled by her involvement.

Half-naked in the warm solar before the sun disappeared completely, he sat on the pillows of the great bed and pulled Marietta backwards into his arms.

"Come to think of it, sweetheart, very little. The reason I didn't want to make it look as though we were about to renovate the place or move the old couple out was because I suspected something of the scheme when we saw horse-dung there, and tracks. And a newish bolt on the stable door. I knew the old couple were not telling me the truth and that they were scared stiff of something, so I decided to let things take their course. In fact, I tried to make things easy for the thieves to steal again; your father being away from home helped, too."

"You knew about Longleigh, then?"

"No, I didn't. I'd no idea your father's bailiff was involved, even before Sir Henry bought Monksgrange, but I was fairly certain that the caves in the hills above were being used as staging-posts for horse thieves. Do you remember when we saw the dung there, too?"

"Yes, and I told you I'd heard travellers in the mist? Were they horse thieves?"

He took her face in his hand and turned it to his so that she could see his laughing eyes. "They, my sweet runaway girl, were horse thieves."

"Taking your horses?"

"Taking my horses while there was a heavy overnight mist and my back was turned."

"But I saw Thorsgeld Castle above the mist that morning."

"The mares and colts were in the lower pastures," he whispered.

"And you were at Monksgrange."

"And I shall expect compensation, my lady, for their loss."

"Were they very valuable?"

"Very, *very* valuable."

"Oh, I have little to pay with. You'll take payment in kind, will you?"

"That was what I had in mind." His hands caressed.

"Would more information do, instead of what you had in mind?"

"What information?"

"That the lay-brothers who worked at Monksgrange before my father bought it were also involved."

His hands stopped their exploration. "The lay-brothers? From Bolton Priory? Are you sure?"

"Yes. They breed horses too, you know."

"Yes, but not destriers for war. Palfreys and draught horses."

"Nevertheless, they went to Beckington to collect horses for Longleigh and take them on up to the caves."

"Who told you this, Marietta?"

"Betty Fuller."

He paused, taking in the implications. "What else did she tell you?"

"That your groom, Rigg, was involved, too. Did you know?"

"Only recently I discovered that. I knew that one of the men in the stables was up to something. It had to be someone who knew where the horses were going to be at any one time, but I didn't realise it was Rigg until I saw him with Sir Bastien. Then I knew. Thick as thieves, right under my nose."

Marietta had it in mind to tell him what she'd seen and what Iveta had heard, but there was nothing to be gained by that. It could not be used in court now, it was too late.

Come to think of it, it was too late to tell him anything except those parts that would help her understand him. But she had opened the door to her source of information and she knew he would ask.

"What else, sweetheart?"

Instead of answering him directly, she asked a question of him. "Will you tell me, Alain…?"

He sensed her reluctance and knew what was to come. "What is it you want to know, sweetheart?" he said into her hair. "About my first wife?"

"Yes."

"You have a right to know. I've treated you harshly, and unfairly, too. It was all part of a plan to discover more about what happened two years ago, but it went wrong because I misunderstood the facts and so I don't understand any more than I did before. It serves me right for abusing your trust of me. All I discovered was that he…that man…was as evil as ever, and that I nearly lost you as a result of my stupidity. And I discovered that you are as unlike her as it's possible to be, and I thank God for that."

His voice dropped to a whisper in her ear and his arms pulled her closer as though to cushion himself against the pain of discussing past events.

"Why did you marry her? Was it arranged?"

"It had been arranged since we were both fourteen, to bring property to my family and connections to hers. It was seven years before we were married and I'd heard rumours that she had already broken our betrothal vows by associating with other men. But I thought it was jealous talk and I took no notice. I was busy winning my spurs and squiring. I couldn't believe it. She was so fair."

"Like Emeline?" It was the same question she had asked her father.

He sighed. "You knew, then?"

"I knew that much, yes."

"And that's why you were so insistent I was for her, rather than you? Because you thought I wanted a replacement?"

"Yes. Partly." She turned and kissed his bare shoulder.

"Nothing could have been further from the truth, sweetheart."

"But she was fair, and you married her."

"Yes, I married her, thinking that whatever I'd heard would be changed, that she would settle down and be the perfect wife. But she didn't, and she wasn't, and there was little I could do about it, except lock her up in here and keep her captive. That was not the solution."

"Was there a solution?"

"No. None that I knew of. I was young and I suppose I did not pay her enough attention. It was a marriage we both drifted through and such marriages need careful nurturing to make them blossom. I hadn't the sense to do that, and she ran wild in a place like this, with men everywhere."

"But she died, two years ago."

He nodded and shifted her round to sit in the crook of his arm, taking a strand of her hair to wind around his fingers. "Yes, love. She died."

"Do you know how?"

"That was something I hoped I might discover during the last few days. But I didn't. All I know is that she came home one day from a ride, went to bed and became violently ill, and by the time I'd sent for the wise-woman from the town, it was too late."

"There was no enquiry about the manner of her death?"

"No, it was the year when the pestilence took so many of those officials who attend to such things, and it was easier and less painful to write it off as the same thing, though it didn't seem to me to be the same in every respect. No one else here caught it."

She quailed at telling him, but he wanted to know. He had said so. "You knew that she and Sir Bastien were lovers, Alain?"

"Is that something you deduced over the last few days, or did you learn it some other way?"

"I had already worked it out when Betty confirmed what I had thought."

"What does that old crone know about it?" he asked, sharply.

"More than you'd think, my lord. She told me about it today."

"What? What did she tell you? Tell me what she said."

She took his hands in hers and held them, anxious not to hurt him more than he had been already but knowing that, if he wanted the truth, it was a risk she would have to take. So she repeated, after all, the story of what Iveta had heard of the threat to the Fullers and how she herself had decided that she must risk his displeasure by warning them. They were her tenants, she said, and what would have been the use of telling him when he had not wanted to speak of Beckington?

He said nothing to that. It was too true to deny.

She went on then to describe how she had found the Fullers on the verge of taking their own lives, at Betty's insistence, and then the full story of how they, and Beckington Manor, had been used for Lady Thorsgeld's evil pleasures, horse thievery and torment by all the men involved.

"Lay-brothers, too?" Lord Alain was incredulous. "And Rigg…and Longleigh? All of them? Good grief, I can hardly believe it!"

He was as appalled as she knew he would be when she told him of the attempt at abortion—always a risky business, with as many failures as successes—of how Betty was not reliable with the correct herbs, of how Milly always made the potions and how, on that occasion, she wreaked her vengeance on the woman who had so brutally assisted in her torment.

"Merciful heavens! I had no idea," was all he said. "No idea."

Choosing her words carefully, Marietta told him how she herself had contributed to Longleigh's death, not by stabbing as it had seemed to the men, but by poison. Then she broke down and wept, for she had been responsible for two men's deaths that day, and as much as Alain insisted she feel no guilt for defending herself against the one, two souls in purgatory weighed heavily on her conscience.

He allowed her to weep; few women ever killed one man in a lifetime, let alone two in one day.

"You killed in self-defence, sweetheart, not in cold blood. They deserved everything they got. They were beasts, and they would have had *you,* and killed you, if you had not got them first. I'm proud of you."

He kissed her tears away. "You have courage, and beauty, and intelligence. I was wrong to have taken advantage of you over this business. You were hurt, I know, and confused, and I was set on seeing my plan work so that I could catch that beast and hang him."

"What…what was your plan?" She snuggled her

damp face against his chest and ran a hand softly across the undulations of his muscles and ribs, delighting in the firmness of his skin and the hardness below it.

Alain laughed softly. "If you're going to do much more of that, tigress, you're going to have to wait some time before I can remember." He placed a large hand over hers. "Which do you want first, proof of my irresponsibility, or proof of my love for you?"

Love? That was a word she had never heard from him until now. She tipped her head back to look up at him, meeting his dark eyes with wonder. "Love for me?" she whispered. "Is that what you said, or was I dreaming?"

For an answer, he lowered her backwards onto the pillows, spilling her luxurious dark hair around her like a rippling sea. "I made so many mistakes in my first marriage," he told her, "you'd think I would have learned a few lessons in what women need from a man, love, security, respect. Few men bother with that, but I don't intend to spend my life without love, Marietta. I've tried it, and it's a barren place. And yet, when I fell in love with you the first moment I saw you…"

"No, Alain, you forget—"

"Hear me, wench. I do not forget. You lay on the ground, yelling at me to leave you alone, taking a swipe at me…" he smiled at that, making her blush "…and I couldn't keep my hands off you. And when I fell in love with you, as I said, something warned me to have a care. I'd been caught once. I dared not tell you I loved you, only that I wanted you and that I would have you.

"So we got off to a bad start, didn't we? With not a little help from your dear stepmother and half-sister. And for some reason, there never seemed to be a good time to tell you that I've loved you like a madman since that time you fell off that stupid horse."

Tenderly, she caressed his face, but he caught her palm and kissed it. This was something she had never thought to hear. "I thought…my father said you liked my courage…and my looks…and I was not very flattered—" she smiled at him, shyly "—but I thought of you day and night. I think that must have been love, too. Do you think it might have been, Alain?"

His grin broadened. "I think it might have been, darling girl. And now? Has the feeling gone, after all you've suffered at my hands, or is there still a bit of it left?"

The temptation to punish him rose in her like a bubble about to burst with the first huff of laughter, so she held the expression of it in her eyes while she reverted to the question he had still not answered.

"Tell me what this grand scheme was first, then I'll decide whether you shall know of my love for you or whether I shall keep it to myself for another hour or so."

"I could get it out of you in less than an hour, woman." He lowered his head to hers and took a kiss that confirmed his boast.

"I know you could, brute, but allow me to keep you in suspense for a little while longer. It's a delicious feeling."

"Very well, but I believe you must already have drawn some conclusions about what I was trying to do. It was when I saw Emeline here at the castle and realised how much like my first wife she was."

"But you must have noticed it before, surely?"

"Only distantly, love. Here, at Thorsgeld, she seemed to have bloomed. It's strange, but in *this* setting, where *she* had been, the resemblance seemed to be more pronounced, and it occurred to me, at that moment, to use her to trap Symme. It was not so much that he'd had my erring wife that rankled, but that he'd made a fool of me by taking my horses, too. And yet I'd been unable to prove anything. No trace.

"In my innocence, I thought it was merely the blonde good looks that he was attracted by, so I had to do what I could to keep Emeline from bolting back home after her arguments with you. And the surest way of doing that was to be nice to her. I'm afraid it looked bad, sweetheart. Didn't it?"

"Yes, it looked *very* bad," Marietta said, remembering the pain. "But go on. You wanted her to stay while you got Symme here and saw his reaction to her. Is that it?"

"I thought he'd be sure to make a bee-line for her, especially if he thought she was what I wanted."

"Ah, I see. So you made it look as though she was yours."

He had the grace to look shamefaced. "Yes, sweetheart."

"And that was why you kept her by you, to entice him."

"Yes. I know it was putting her in some danger, but I thought there were enough of us to keep her safe. And I thought, foolishly, that somehow if he showed an interest in Emeline, it might help me to find out what happened to cause my first wife's death and, at the same time, give me some idea of how he was taking my horses. I had an idea about Beckington by then, and the caves, and I knew that if he was with Emeline for much of the time, she would blabber to me about what he was up to."

"Especially if you kept being nice to her," Marietta snapped.

"Yes, my love, except that I didn't realise that he was more interested in you than in her...no, don't protest, it's true. It was men's wives he preferred, not particularly their colouring. You discovered that and told me. Remember?''

"Yes, I remember. So then you had to switch allegiances.''

"Sweetheart, no. It had already got out of hand. That day when I kept Emeline by me, I expected that he'd hover round like a frustrated wasp, trying to get her away. But he didn't. He stayed at your side instead. It was one of the worst days of my life. That's why, by the end of the day I could stand no more of it and pulled you away. That's why I was so angry and unreasonable. I realised I'd put you in danger and discovered that my plan was flawed from the beginning. I'm sorry, sweetheart: forgive me.''

"You thought I'd been with him the next evening, didn't you?''

"Yes, I saw you covered in flour. I was livid.''

"You cared enough to beat me. Did you beat *her* when she misbehaved?''

"No, sweetheart, she was not worth the effort.''

"Alain…''

He caught her to him and buried his head in her throat, moving his mouth over her in a wave of remorse that broke loose over her lips.

"Sweetheart, I'm sorry. That I should harm you after all you suffered.'' He told her then what had happened, how he had gone to the granary and tipped flour over the lovers and Marietta hooted with laughter and told him how Emeline had still been trying to get rid of it the next morning. It had sobered her down too, she said, for the lass was by no means as ready for Sir Bastien's forceful advances as she had thought she was. By that time, she'd been ready to go home.

"Alain, did that man…did he…you know?''

"Sweetheart, I don't really know. It's possible, but only time will tell if it had any effect. Say nothing. Just pray that she doesn't have to pay the price of her foolishness, or mine."

"I think I might ask her."

"Will she tell you?"

"Mmm…mmm…we've come to a better understanding over this you know. She discovered she needed my help and I found I needed hers and now we've called a truce; she learned a lot while she's been here."

"Especially how not to fool about in your pleasance," he teased her. "Are you going to become the wisewoman of Thorsgeld Castle?"

"Yes, I am. And what's more, I have a new assistant. Milly's going to be very useful to me. You'll allow her to stay, won't you?"

"After all that's happened, sweetheart, I would climb up to the moon and reach it down for you if that's what you want. You have only to ask."

Marietta thought that that was the loveliest offer anyone could ever make. She wrapped her arms about his neck.

"Thank you. I won't take advantage of that immediately, my lord, but I do want some of that loving, please."

"You shall have my loving until you cry out for me to stop, but first, dearest love, there is something you're going to tell me, is there not?"

Teasingly, she frowned and pretended puzzlement.

"Stop teasing me, wench. I've waited long enough to hear it," he growled.

"Ah, now I remember. I love you, Alain. I love you desperately…" She got no further with the long-awaited endearments, his lips stole the words from hers and added his own when they stopped for breath.

"I didn't want another wife like her, sweetheart, believe me. I saw you and knew by your very first resistance to me that you were as unlike her as it's possible to be. You fought me off, you ran away, you tried to talk me out of it, you wanted none of me, did you?"

"My body wanted you. My heart wanted you. But…"

"But what? Courage? It let you down, did it?"

"I felt sure I was second best, and I was angry and insulted."

"Sweetheart…ah, my fierce, proud woman, second-best never. You're the brightest star in the sky. The only one I want, ever. Love me now. Love me and let's start again, shall we?"

"No more misunderstandings. No more schemes."

"I swear it. I love you too much to risk your scorn again."

"Then let's forget…"

He took her offer and locked her into his arms as the light slowly faded from the room and a cooling breeze brought the faint scent of rain through the open window from the west. And when she gave herself, utterly and completely, her thought was that, if this was the difference it made to their passionate loving, it had perhaps been worth striving for. If she had given up when she had thought of doing, she would never have known this, the bliss of complete freedom from doubts and nagging fears.

"About those fierce sons and wild daughters," she whispered.

Alain lifted his head in the dim light and studied her face. "You like that idea, do you, after all?"

"Mmm." She smiled. "Shall we start with the sons?"

"He'll be magnificent," he whispered, "truly magnificent."

The day of the guests' departure was cool and misty-moist with a layer of low cloud hanging into the valley bottom, shrouding the road to Monksgrange. But none of this dampened the hearty farewells and shouts of advice, laughter and parting shots as groups, augmented by newly bought horses, made their way out of the courtyard. Marietta had made new friends; they had promised to visit again before summer was over.

Sir John and Lady Isobel's retinue was augmented by more than horses, though. Since the hunting adventure when Sir Nicholas Bannon had saved her from a wild boar, Lady Isobel had so much taken a fancy to Marietta's uncle that she had persuaded her husband to take on a new Horse-Master, a younger man who reacted quickly to danger and was strong enough to serve them as a retainer should. Sir Henry Wardle needed little persuasion to let his brother-in-law go; it was what he had hoped would happen this many a year and Lady Alice agreed, Nicholas must seek advancement further afield.

Lady Alice's smile was genuine enough. "We shall miss him," she simpered, hoping that the words, at least, would have a genuine ring. "The girls, especially."

Emeline turned her eyes towards Marietta and pulled a face. "Which girls do you think she means, Marrie? Not me, for sure. There's nothing I shall enjoy more than not having his advice thrust at me all the time. He's as interfering as Mother. That wild boar was a godsend."

The new friendship between the two half-sisters appeared to be founded on conspiracy, but neither of them saw any harm in that and Marietta took the chance to offer a suggestion along the same lines. "Emmie, would you miss Iveta very much if I asked Lady Alice to allow her to stay here with me at Thorsgeld?''

Emeline's face lit up. "Perfect!'' she breathed. "Then I can have the maids to myself!'' It was a typical response.

From the castle wall in Marietta's garden, they watched and waved as the winding retinue snaked down through the mist into the valley towards Monksgrange, savouring the strange emptiness of the green place which, until today, had thronged with their guests. The sun now spread its bright light through the whiteness, promising warmth after the rain, twinkling on the leaves that covered the arbour and catching the glossy white coat of the greyhound pup that sniffed and pranced at a stalwart frog beneath the box hedge, yapping at its stoicism.

"Look,'' Marietta said, snuggling closer to Alain, "we shall be able to take her hunting soon. It's time she was…''

"Time enough for that, love. But look over there, at your assistant.''

She followed his gaze towards the end of the garden where Milly, now clean and white-coiffed with a basket at her feet, snipped and tidied the herbs and flowers in the beds, totally absorbed and at peace. "I shall care for her, Alain, and her babe, and her mother. Is there a cott somewhere nearby where Betty can live, where I can keep an eye on her?''

"No need, my little protector, your father is finding her a place in his village where Lady Alice can watch over her. He insisted. She was Lady Alice's tenant, after all, and they both regret not managing Beckington as they should have done. We'll soon put the place to rights. We'll make it our next task, shall we?''

"Oh yes, it could be such a pretty place, with some

attention. And the garden's complete now, Alain, come and look.''

She led him to the corner of the herb-plot next to the self-heal where, after the overnight rain, tiny green shoots had begun to push their spears through the soil. ''See…'' she bent to touch them ''…it's the love-in-a-mist that Old Adam gave us.''

Alain pulled her up into his arms and held her gently, smiling at the aptness of the name. ''He must have known, the old rascal. Love-in-a-mist. Perfect.''

* * * * *

MY ENEMY,
MY LOVE
by

Julia Byrne

Prologue

Tracy Castle, Herefordshire
March 1136

"Edmund, I swear if you tear your clothes again, climbing that wall, I won't sit up half the night to mend them before Dameta sees the damage you are wreaking."

The grubby face of a young boy, not more than ten summers in age, peered down at the speaker through the tangled mass of overgrown shrubbery atop a high stone wall.

"I'm scaling the ramparts of a castle in Anjou," he protested somewhat breathlessly. "And you're the Empress. Prepare to be taken prisoner, lady."

"A fine ambition," scolded his victim, unmoved by the fate about to befall her. "What has the Empress Matilda ever done to you, pray tell?"

"'Tis not on my own behalf," claimed the would-be hero. "I am for King Stephen." He scrambled over the wall and fell with more haste than skill into the enclosed, sun-warmed garden below. Jumping to his feet, Edmund swung a makeshift wooden sword in a reckless arc.

"Yield, thou troublesome female," he commanded in a youthful treble. "You are my prisoner."

The young lady thus addressed jumped back a prudent pace or two. "By our Lady, Edmund, you nearly had my head off!" she exclaimed indignantly. "Go and take a few more lessons from Osbert."

Edmund heaved a disappointed sigh and let his sword arm fall. "Sisters are no fun," he complained. "You'd better take care, Isabel. You're becoming as prim-faced as Alice and Constance."

Isabel elevated her small nose with all the hauteur of a young lady who had attained the lofty age of thirteen, and had therefore ceased climbing walls and brandishing wooden swords herself.

"I'm sure if King Stephen ever did have the Empress in his power he would not wave a sword in her face," she declared severely. "He would be more gallant. And, moreover, we still don't know if our father will shift his allegiance to the King."

Edmund dismissed this remark with another perilous sweep of his sword. "Of course he will. A man such as Sir Guy fitzAlan would not be acting as the King's messenger if Stephen was not confident of Father's support. We de Tracys will never back a woman."

Isabel decided to ignore this annoying example of male arrogance. "What is Sir Guy like?" she queried curiously, not having been present in the hall when their visitor had arrived.

Her brother heaved another long-suffering sigh. "You're *worse* than Alice and Constance," he declared. "They, at least, confined themselves to giggling like village idiots when they watched him from the tower. Girls! No wonder we don't want one on the throne. Take heed!" he shouted, reverting to his character of besieging knight. "Stay here in Anjou and leave England to the rule of a man.''

Before Isabel could retort in kind, Edmund scrambled nimbly back over the wall with the assistance of its thick covering of climbing roses, putting a long slash in his white linen shirt in the process.

''You horrid little toad,'' his sister yelled after him in exasperation, foreseeing a long night of sewing ahead of her. ''I hope you turn into an eel and Tom puts you in a broth.''

''I can't be a toad and an eel,'' floated back the voice of her brother. ''And if that's the best revenge you can think of, we definitely don't want a woman on the throne.''

Inside the ancestral home of the de Tracy family, a more serious discussion of the same subject was under way.

''As a man of the Church, I must object,'' stated a portly cleric in the bombastic tones of a man accustomed to a respectful, if not enthusiastic, audience. He folded complacent white hands over his considerable girth and frowned at his two listeners. They remained unimpressed by either the measured words or the frown.

''Let me remind you, Brother, that your own superiors have recognised the Count of Mortain as King. Stephen is crowned and consecrated, by William de Corbeil, no less.''

The man who spoke was enough like the priest in face and build to indicate their relationship, but, instead of the severe black habit and tonsured head which proclaimed the cleric to be of the Benedictine order, he was dressed in all the splendour of a prosperous baron. His knee-length red woollen tunic was lavishly trimmed with fur, and the chain of solid metal links about his neck gleamed with the sheen of precious gold.

He was the only one who matched the colourfully embroidered wall-hangings and solid oak furniture of the private solar. The youngest of the trio was severely, even ominously garbed in chainmail over serviceable brown woollen leggings and tunic. A sword hung at his side and a plain iron helmet lay close to his hand on a nearby table. The afternoon sunlight, shining through the western window embrasure, highlighted the number of dents in the cone-shaped headgear, testifying to its effective and frequent use.

"We had heard 'twas so, of course," muttered the priest in answer to his brother's statement. But, despite the unwilling admission, he looked across the room at the soldier rather in the manner of one who hoped he had heard incorrectly.

The younger man nodded polite confirmation. "Aye, Brother Prior, the Archbishop of Canterbury blessed the King this last December, just before Christmastide, and had the support of the Bishop of Winchester and Roger, Bishop of Salisbury, the justiciar. Stephen also held the treasury," he tacked on drily, a slightly amused gleam in his eyes.

The Prior didn't notice the amusement. He sank down on to a convenient chair and shook his head dolefully. "Of course Stephen had Henry of Winchester's approval," he grumbled. "The man is the King's brother, and we all know of his ambition. Don't tell *me* Henry didn't plan Stephen's dash for the throne down to the last detail, because I'll never believe it. The Bishop is more statesman than priest."

"But a good one," murmured the soldier, unable, this time, to hide a smile as the priest shook his head again.

Baron de Tracy grinned openly and grabbed a drinking-horn, splashing some wine into it from the jug on the table. "Here, William, you look as though you need a drink. 'Tis not so bad that Stephen is King. Would you rather have a woman on the throne of England?"

"Matilda is the late King's daughter, Hugh, and we all took that oath to recognise her as the future queen after her brother went down with the White Ship," protested the Prior. But he accepted the proffered wine and took a long draught, letting a thoughtful silence fall. After all, he reminded himself, he was Prior William now and had his eye set on further promotion. One must tread cautiously, however, when kings, or, in this case, a king and a former empress, squabbled over the crown.

"An oath sworn nine years ago and under considerable duress may become invalid in certain circumstances," stated Hugh firmly. "What say you, fitzAlan? You know more than we who live in this backwater on the Marches. There is rumour abroad that King Henry disinherited Matilda on his death-bed. And who can blame him? The woman was at war with her father at the time."

The young soldier looked carefully from one man to the other. His host he could count on, he thought. Like so many others, Baron de Tracy knew which way the wind blew and where gain was to be had. A churchman's conscience over a sacred oath was the stumbling-block here. But he would not lie. There were too many stories flying from one end of the country to the other that Stephen's rapid seizure of the throne, before the late King was even decently interred, was based on lies and deceit.

"There was a knight who swore that King Henry disinherited Matilda," he admitted. "But to say truth, sirs, 'tis doubted by many. What is more certain is that the Bishop of Salisbury claims the oath sworn years ago was conditional upon the King's not marrying his daughter to anyone outside England. Since Matilda is now the wife of Geoffrey of Anjou, your oaths are no longer binding.''

"Well said," nodded Hugh de Tracy. "Besides, in times such as these, men must be practical. Stephen has shown himself capable thus far.'' He turned to his brother. "Could a woman have beaten back the Scots, forcing King David to come to terms before he plundered the entire north?''

"Matters of warfare are not fathomed by such as I,'' countered the Prior, taking refuge behind his priestly garb. "Although one assumes David only crossed the border because his niece had been cheated of her crown and gave him no peace until he avenged her, haranguing him with letter after letter. Besides,'' he added, descending from these dramatic heights, "Matilda's husband would have led the army.''

Hugh made an impatient sound. "We don't want Anjou here, interfering in England's affairs. Keeping him from snapping at the heels of Normandy is bad enough.''

Although worry still clouded his face, Prior William nodded immediate acceptance of this statement. Man of the Church he might be, but no Norman worthy of the name wanted any truck with Geoffrey of Anjou. Apart from the fact that Anjou was the hereditary enemy of the Normans, the man was a cold-blooded brute who hadn't hesitated to let his army of barbarians ravage the Norman countryside even while his father-in-law was still alive. If Henry, King of England and Duke of Normandy, *had* disinherited his daughter, as Stephen claimed, one could understand why.

"And remember,'' Hugh continued forcefully, "Stephen is as much a grandchild of the Conqueror as Matilda.''

"On the female side," the Prior felt impelled to point out. Another thought occurred to him. "But what of Matilda's son? Young Henry was the joy of the King's last years and—"

"A child!" scoffed his brother. "A babe scarce two years old. Don't tell me you can see *him* on the throne. Even Robert of Gloucester would be preferable."

"That was suggested," murmured young fitzAlan, moving restlessly in his chair. He was growing impatient with the argument, deeming it useless. The Prior would eventually have to obey his superiors, no matter what his private thoughts on the matter, and he couldn't see de Tracy going against the majority of England's nobility.

Stephen's quick action in marching to head off David of Scotland had impressed most of the barons and the King looked forward to a well-attended Easter court, which would confer upon his kingship the final confirmation of acknowledgement by his nobles. It was Guy fitzAlan's task to deliver Stephen's invitation to de Tracy and to persuade him to accept the inevitable—if such persuasion was necessary. He hadn't counted on the opposition of Hugh de Tracy's priestly brother, who should have been safely at home in his monastery, where he couldn't cause any trouble.

The subject of this exasperated thought sent him a look of enquiry, bringing him back to the present debate.

"While King Henry lay in state in Normandy, several barons went to the Earl of Gloucester to ask if he would be willing to take the throne," Guy elaborated. "He is the late King's son when all is said. But he refused on the grounds of his illegitimacy."

"Not because of the oath he swore to Matilda?" queried Hugh interestedly. "I remember how he and Stephen quarrelled over who should be the first to pledge alliance to her. The jealousy between them was the talk of the Court at the time. Stephen won, as I recall.''

"Aye, again on the grounds that a legitimate nephew of King Henry came before an illegitimate son. But, though Gloucester refused the crown, he did attend a meeting of the barons in Normandy to discuss an alternative to himself. After all, Robert mistrusts the Count of Anjou as much as anyone.''

"I believe Stephen's elder brother, Theobald, was put forward,'' said Hugh briskly. "Until they were told that Stephen himself had already been crowned. You see, William, that Matilda has precious little support in Normandy *or* in England. Where is the problem here?''

"The problem, Hugh, is that England will be torn apart by strife and ill deeds. Matilda has the reputation of being a shrew—do you think she will stay tamely in Anjou? You only have to cast your eye on Normandy. 'Tis already in a state of uproar, ready for that ambitious husband of hers to pluck it like an over-ripe plum, rotting and falling from the tree, and—''

"God's holy fingernails,'' burst out Hugh, impatiently interrupting his brother's flowery passages. "That is precisely my point. Mark my words, before the month is out we shall have Earl Robert crossing the Channel to make his peace with Stephen along with the rest of us. As for his sister, the woman is tied to Anjou, producing infants, and we have a competent man already on the throne, and one,'' he added shrewdly, "who has promised to confirm all the liberties of the Church.''

The Prior had opened his mouth to state that, in his opinion, Robert of Gloucester was unlikely to throw casually aside his loyalty to his half-sister, no matter what councils he might have attended, but this statement made him close his lips on the words. Seeing that the priest was carefully considering the Church's position in the situation, fitzAlan stood up abruptly, ready to put an end to the debate. His host quickly crossed the solar and laid a conciliatory hand on the younger man's arm.

"Leave the rest to me, Guy," he said softly. "William can be as stubborn as the devil when he chooses, and the sight of a soldier will only make him dig in his heels further. Let him take a favourable tale back to his abbot when he leaves us tomorrow. Meanwhile, stretch your legs outside before supper. I warrant you've seen nothing but the road between your horse's ears for days."

FitzAlan laughed and agreed. A brisk walk around the bailey to work up an appetite sounded good, and a glance at the Prior, who was still shaking his head gloomily over his drinking-horn, convinced him that there was no more to be gained by pushing the issue. Let Hugh de Tracy handle his brother, and the tricky question of broken oaths. He wanted to study the fortifications more closely in any case. It never hurt to know in advance what well-provisioned castles could be put at the King's disposal at short notice.

An hour later Guy refreshed himself with a jug of water drawn from the well and wondered how his host would take a few suggestions. Like most strongholds which dated from the Conqueror's day, the original Saxon palisade enclosing the large compound had been replaced by a stone wall, with a barbican protecting the gate, but the place was assailable. There was no moat, and though the hall was constructed of stone the other buildings within the bailey were of wood and thatch and therefore vulnerable to fire.

His eyes wandered further. In a grassy corner a large eel pond lay smooth and serene beneath the branches of a chestnut tree and, near by, several pigs rooted contentedly in the muddy shallows. A girl emerged from the dairy with a pan of milk and was instantly surrounded by the stable cats, mewing pleadingly as though they had not caught a single mouse for days. It was a peaceful scene. The girl bent to stroke one of the cats, murmuring to it, and from somewhere behind the hall came the cooing of doves.

Aye, peaceful, thought Guy. The harmless noises of the countryside surrounded him. But he knew how quickly peace could be overcome by strife and warfare, how quickly the cooing of doves could be silenced beneath the clash of arms. Prior William had been right about one thing. Anarchy *was* rife in Normandy. As soon as King Henry had breathed his last the barons had turned on each other like ravening wolves, attacking their neighbours and ripe for every type of lawlessness. A strong man was needed there, as well as in England, and those loyal to the King needed strong fortresses.

Guy turned to consider the stone hall. It was flanked by two towers and its entrance was reached only by a narrow stairway, but by no stretch of the imagination could it be called a fortress.

And Guy was uneasily aware of another fact. No one could say for sure if Robert of Gloucester would support Stephen, or if he would remain in Normandy to throw the considerable weight of his position, wealth and experience behind his half-sister. And if he landed in England with Matilda, estates such as Hugh de Tracy's were at risk, placed as they were in Herefordshire and Gloucestershire, where the majority of castles were held by men who owed fealty to the Earl rather than the King.

However, it was no use pondering on unanswerable questions. The King was steadily gaining more support. One could only hope that the Earl of Gloucester would realise the futility of remaining isolated in Normandy when Matilda's cousin was already annointed and crowned, an act that even the Pope acknowledged as irrevocable, despite his disapproval of Stephen's methods.

As Guy sat contemplating this conclusion, a fair-haired child came racing around the corner of the north tower. A short wooden sword was clutched in one grimy hand and the boy's shirt had been well and truly ripped. He scampered up the outer staircase and disappeared into the hall.

Guy grinned suddenly. The imp was either fleeing from female reproaches or about to fall into that trap. He wondered where the boy had come from. There was little behind the main building apart from the usual outdoor privies and midden heaps, and the little devil wasn't *that* dirty.

Still idly curious, Guy got to his feet and strolled across the bailey and past the hall. He really should go in search of his squire and order some hot water so he could wash away his own grime before sitting down to table. He'd been on the roads for days and they still retained their winter mire, despite the advent of finer spring weather. But instead he wandered past the neatly laid-out kitchen garden, strangely reluctant to give up this rare moment of peaceful solitude in the sun.

Then, from somewhere beyond the imposing stone wall, came a sweet voice singing a haunting ballad. Guy paused, spellbound. The poignant melody made him think of soft feminine sighs, warm arms and whispered words of love in the dark of night.

By the Saints, he must have been without a woman for too long, he thought wryly. And he'd probably have to resign himself to that situation until he returned to Winchester. His host had mentioned three daughters, but they were definitely not the sort of girls one could tumble into bed and then forget.

On the other hand, maybe that soft, slightly husky voice belonged to a nicely rounded wench willing to indulge in a little loveplay as well as sing about it. And as this notion made his mouth curve upward in amusement at his optimism, he found what he was searching for.

A small wooden door, set into the stone wall, and half hidden beneath the hanging tendrils of a climbing rose. If it had been later in the season, and the roses in full bloom, he might have missed the portal altogether, but there was just the one unopened bud on the bare branches, of a delicate peach shade with hints of rose which made him think of a girl's skin. A country girl, he decided, with the bloom of health and youth.

On impulse, Guy reached up and plucked the bud, avoiding the surrounding thorns. Still grinning faintly at such unaccustomed fancies, he grasped the iron handle and carefully pushed the gate open.

Isabel loved her great-grandmother's garden, although she had never known that lady, who had expired bearing her lord a son, the present Baron's father. Thus, when the stone ramparts had been constructed years ago, there had been no mistress of Tracy Castle, and the pleasance had been abandoned and left outside the boundaries of the bailey. Its crumbling wooden fence and the wealth of overgrown shrubs was considered useful only in shielding the postern gate from any but the most discerning eye.

Every few months Hugh de Tracy would mutter about seeing to the building of a proper barbican over the postern. However, under King Henry's harsh but effective rule, England had remained peaceful, so nothing had ever come of her father's plans and Isabel was free to indulge her girlhood dreams in the quiet haven, shut off from the bustle and constant noise of castle life.

When Edmund had left her she had wandered as far as the orchard, and had just pushed aside the crooked wicker gate to re-enter the garden when she heard the latch of the heavier postern rattle. Isabel paused, the refrain she had been absently singing fading away as the soldier stepped into the pleasance at the same moment.

Across the warm, sun-filled expanse of wilderness their eyes met with an impact that held them both motionless. In the sudden silence Isabel thought she could almost hear the life of the garden, preparing for its spring blossoming. Every other sound that she had hitherto been conscious of—the distant bleat of sheep in the field, the wind in the trees, the mewling cry of a hawk far above her—disappeared, vanished from her awareness.

Then her hand clenched involuntarily on the gate and she jumped, a startled murmur on her lips, glancing down at her finger where a splinter had pierced the skin.

''Don't be frightened,'' Guy said at once, his own hand still grasping the postern gate. He had never seen such a beautiful girl in all his life. So unexpected was her appearance that, for a moment, until she'd moved and cried out, he'd wondered if she was real. No sturdy country wench this, but a slender, fairy-like creature who seemed part of her wild, otherwordly surroundings. He was hardly aware of moving, but when he pushed the postern closed behind him she stepped back into the gateway, eyeing him with very human caution.

''Don't be frightened,'' he repeated softly, not daring to move again in case she fled. Or vanished. In the shadowy corner where she stood, she seemed almost insubstantial. ''Who are you?'' he murmured, only half expecting her to answer. Perhaps he really *had* dreamed her up after months of travelling.

"Isabel de Tracy," she whispered, and, releasing the gate, took a tentative step forward into the sunlight, the skirts of her close-fitting blue kersey gown swaying gently about her ankles.

Guy caught his breath all over again, so captivated by the sweet face upturned to him that he missed the strangely puzzled wonderment in her wide-eyed gaze, his own eyes tracing features drawn with exquisite delicacy, though her gently flushed cheeks still retained the rounded curves of youth. Her long, sable-dark hair was confined in two braids, each as thick as his wrist, but several shorter tendrils had escaped and curled enticingly over her brow and temples, almost mingling with the sooty lashes feathering luminous grey eyes that would probably show her every emotion. And her soft, full-lipped mouth was made for kissing.

She was tiny, he saw. He could have spanned her waist between his hands and, had they been standing closer, the top of her head would not have reached his shoulder. Guy had always liked tall women, preferably those built on rather buxom lines, but right now he couldn't for the life of him remember why. In fact he would have had trouble recalling his own name. He remembered hers, however.

"Isabel," he murmured, making the name sound like a poem. Then, as his eyes fell to the way she was cradling one hand in the other, he added, frowning, "You're hurt."

Isabel glanced down at her injured finger. "'Tis only a splinter…" she began, but her voice died away as the soldier moved swiftly towards her.

She stifled a desire to turn and flee, wondering what was wrong with her. She was in no danger. She was not afraid of the soldier, who was probably one of Sir Guy fitzAlan's men and therefore no threat to her.

This thought reminded her that he hadn't volunteered his own name, but somehow it didn't seem to matter. She knew him. He was a complete stranger, and yet she knew him. The shocked sense of recognition made her breathless; her heart fluttered in her breast like the trembling of a captured bird.

It wasn't supposed to happen like this, Isabel told herself, trying to regain control of her disordered senses. She wasn't supposed to have this kind of tremulous reaction to a soldier encountered so casually. Especially one who looked glaringly out of place in the still serenity of her garden. He wasn't right.

He wasn't what she had expected.

She had dreamed, as very young girls did, of a handsome knight who would one day arrive at her father's castle, fall in love with her, win her heart by some brave deed, and carry her away across his saddle-bow. But he had ridden up on a valiant steed with all the trappings of chivalrous knighthood. He hadn't just appeared from nowhere. And, though Isabel hadn't really pictured a face, she had known that he would be gently bred, slender, a little taller than herself, perhaps, and handsomely clad in the raiment suited to his station.

Not so tall and powerfully built that she felt as though she might break if he so much as touched her. Not dressed in travel-stained wool and dusty chainmail with his sword hilt gleaming harshly in the sunshine. And definitely not with several days' growth of beard on an aggressively masculine jaw, or with so much...so much compelling *strength* in his face, in his ice-blue eyes.

Her knight would be gentle, kind and chivalrous. This man looked big, tough and slightly dangerous.

But the strange feeling of recognition persisted.

"'Tis really nought," she whispered nervously as he reached her and held out his hand. Then she stared, amazed, at the fragile rosebud lying across his palm. It was flawless, completely unbruised for being held in that strong, long-fingered hand.

"See, I won't harm you," he said, smiling down at her bemused face.

Isabel looked up at him quickly, startled anew as she realised he was much younger than she'd first supposed. Somewhere in his early twenties, she decided, fascinated by his unexpectedly boyish smile. But the smile was the only thing he had in common with her fantasy knight. Close to, he was even more intimidating. He must have stood at least two inches over six feet, and his obvious physical strength caused an unfamiliar quivering to start up deep inside her.

"Give me your hand."

It was a command, but his deep voice was so soft that Isabel hesitantly held out her wounded finger. Her hand hovered above the rose, not quite touching it.

"I think you will not be able to remove the splinter, sir," she said, struggling to recover her usual practical common sense. It took an amazing amount of effort. "But Dameta will easily do so. She is my maid and her fingers are much smaller than yours and then she'll want to put a salve on it and…"

Under the soldier's intent gaze Isabel subsided abruptly into silence as she realised how she was babbling. She was behaving like a fool. And to think she had always poured scorn on her older sisters when they had put on such fluttering airs in front of a man. For the first time Isabel wondered if those airs had been caused by the same stupid helplessness which seemed to be gripping her.

When she made no move to take the rosebud, Guy tucked it into one of the mail links on his hauberk and captured her hand before she could withdraw it again. The flash of heat that surged through him as their fingers touched took him completely by surprise. Desire, immediate and powerful, tightened his entire body. It took every ounce of self-control he possessed not to crush her fingers with his and pull her into his arms.

Had she felt it also? Her little hand trembled in his much larger one, but Guy was too stunned to notice that she didn't pull away, although he continued to hold her as though she were as fragile as glass. Never, *never* had he felt such a violent reaction to a woman.

Isabel raised questioning eyes to his face. "See, 'tis but a scratch," she murmured, in a voice so shy and uncertain that something else shuddered deep inside him.

He wrenched his gaze away from hers and glanced down. The jagged sliver of wood piercing her finger caused a peculiar chill to sweep over him. He found himself rocketing from desire to protectiveness in the space of seconds, and felt suddenly impatient with such irrationally see-sawing feelings. God's teeth, he must be more tired than he knew. After the wounds he'd seen in his time, how could one little splinter have such an effect? How could *she* have such an effect?

"You're right," he said brusquely. "I won't be able to grip it."

Her face clouded over in confusion at his curt tone, and another set of emotions rioted through him.

I'm not ready for this, he thought almost desperately, not even knowing what "this" meant. He couldn't even begin to untangle the sensations buffeting both mind and body. The only thing he recognised with any surety was intense desire, so intense that the vague awareness at the back of his mind of something wrong was stifled.

Holding her captive with his eyes, he raised her hand quickly to his mouth.

Isabel gasped, her eyes widening in shock as warm lips enclosed her finger. She felt his teeth against her skin for a split-second, then the splinter was gone.

And, with it, the image of her bland, faceless knight. If she dreamed of him again it would be this man's face she would see. Isabel looked up at him and knew every feature was indelibly impressed on her mind. His fair, almost silvery-blond hair, the broad, high cheekbones, the strong aquiline nose, the firm line of his mouth. And his eyes—piercing, vividly blue, and glittering with a light that she was yet too young to understand, but which called to something very feminine within her.

"The splinter is gone now," Isabel managed, finally breaking the spell of his gaze. She gave a tentative tug at her hand. He didn't release her. "My finger is not even bleeding," she pointed out uncertainly.

"No, it isn't," he agreed, not even glancing at the small wound. His other hand retrieved the rose. Very carefully he placed the flower in her hair, just above one silky dark plait.

Isabel had meant to ask for her hand back, but now her breath seemed to have been stolen as well. A strange anticipation held her completely immobile. Unable to meet his eyes, she stared at the garden, wondering vaguely why it looked the same when she felt so very different.

She felt the soldier's hand gently cradle her face. His thumb tilted her chin up.

"The rose is for you, little maid," he said, his voice husky, deeper than it had been before. "And this is for me."

He bent and brushed her mouth fleetingly with his, before lingering for a heart-shakingly tender kiss.

It was the kiss that finally brought Guy to his senses. Her mouth felt warm and soft—and totally unawakened. *Hell, what am I doing?* he groaned silently. *She's only a babe.*

The swift understanding cleared his mind for a moment. He drew back immediately, only to stifle another low sound of longing at the wondering expression in her eyes.

She was too young, and, even if she was not, she was his host's daughter. Not for him. He had to leave the garden. Before he forgot where he was and why he was there. Before he did something he'd regret for the rest of his life. Before the quick rush of protectiveness was swamped by the passionate need growing more insistent the longer he stayed.

She's barely more than a child, he told himself again. *But sweet. So innocent and sweet. How long ago was it that I looked on the world with such innocent eyes?*

"Is-a-bel."

Several seconds passed before Isabel realised her name had come from beyond the wall and not from the man whose fingers still gently caressed her cheek. The intrusion of the world brought her back to reality with a thud.

Blushing hotly, she sprang out of reach and hurriedly backed away. "I must go," she whispered, avoiding the soldier's eyes, watching his hands fall to his sides instead. Merciful saints, she had let a complete stranger hold her, kiss her...

Had not her sister Alice cautioned her of the dangers in being alone with a man, now that she had reached marriageable age? Had Alice not warned of men who took advantage if a maid was compliant? But she had forgotten all the warnings. She had stayed willingly in the secluded garden with the soldier, had not voiced a single protest at his boldness. She went hot all over at the thought, too upset to understand that she had only escaped his hold because he had let her.

Without so much as a glance back to see his reaction to such an abrupt departure, Isabel scurried to the postern, yanked it open, and fled. She wondered wildly if a scratched finger would excuse her from supping in the hall so she wouldn't have to face the soldier again.

Chapter One

Empress Matilda's Headquarters, Gloucester Castle
October 1141

The flames of the rushlights burning in the gallery over-looking the great hall flickered gently, as though reaching out warm fingers to caress the girl passing beneath them. Their lambent glow danced over her sable-dark hair, touched her face briefly, then slid reluctantly away as she moved into the shadows between each one.

The last was more fortunate. At the end of the gallery the girl halted, gazing down into the hall through one of the archways cut into the wall. The flames seemed to burn brighter in her presence, illuminating her finely etched profile and the hand resting on the stone wall beside her. It was a small hand, with slender, tapering fingers. The hand of a lady, unmarked, but for a tiny, crescent-shaped scar on the middle finger. In the light of the flaring sconce the girl could see the scar quite clearly. As clearly as she recalled that spring day so long ago when she had received the small wound.

She hadn't needed to offer such a weak plea as a

scratched finger after all, Isabel remembered. Dameta had taken one look at her heated countenance when she'd emerged from the pleasance, and had ordered her to bed, muttering about fevers and the carelessness of wandering about in gardens without a mantle. And she had climbed between the sheets without a murmur, another circumstance which had convinced her nurse that she was about to succumb to a chill.

The memory hurt.

Determinedly Isabel tried to shut off the thoughts of Dameta, of home and family. For some reason it wasn't so easy tonight. She lingered still beneath the rushlight, the mark on her finger drawing her eyes irresistibly. It was odd how the scar had remained all these years. It had been such a little hurt. And yet today she had glanced again and again at her hand, and found herself remembering.

Remembering how she had stood on the tower battlements the next morning, watching her knight ride away. She had known who he was by then, had known that he was returning to the King with assurances of her father's support.

He had looked different. With a safe distance between them the impression of strength and toughness was not so overwhelming and, now that he was washed and shaved, with the morning sun turning his fair hair to gleaming gold, she had seen that he was handsome. His clothes had been brushed also, and the harness on his magnificent black destrier had been cleaned. Isabel remembered how the horse had tossed his head and sidled playfully, like a huge, overgrown puppy, when Guy had tried to mount him. She remembered his laughter, and her father's voice shouting farewell.

He had ridden away without a backward look.

"You are reluctant to go down to the hall, *demoiselle*? Allow me to escort you."

Roused abruptly from her memories, Isabel looked around to see one of the young knights from the castle garrison. He liked her, she knew, although he never seemed to gather the courage to do anything about it. Just as well, she thought thankfully. She would never marry a man such as Sir Richard Fiennes. But at least he respected her. She was glad not to have to hurt his feelings by spurning any deliberate advances.

"My thanks, sir," Isabel murmured, turning to walk with him. The noise of conversation from the hall below bounced off the walls around them. It seemed louder, more raucous than usual, and she sighed at the prospect of another evening spent listening to the same arguments and bitter reproaches.

The boy keeping pace beside her must have heard the sigh; he glanced at her, his expression concerned. "I regret I must leave you at the door, Lady Isabel. I'm on duty tonight. But you need have no fear. You are under the Sheriff's protection here."

A faint smile crossed her face, but she remained silent until they had descended the stairway and stood at the entrance to the great hall. It stretched before them, appearing huge, despite the crowd gathered for the evening meal.

Off to one side, several men, still wearing their mail hauberks, were warming themselves before the fire. Drinking-horns were passed around, and a burst of laughter greeted the end of a tale being recounted by one of the soldiers. On the opposite side of the room another fire burned brightly behind the high table, and a page was carefully setting the finger bowl in its place. Though the benches at the lower trestles were filling up quickly, Isabel saw that none of the nobles had as yet put in an appearance.

Fiennes glanced doubtfully into the room. "Would you rather wait for the other ladies?" he ventured, obviously torn between his duty and the thought of her sitting alone in such rowdy company for several minutes.

"No one will accost me," she assured him, and smiled with gentle irony. "After all, as you just reminded me, I am under the Sheriff's protection."

The irony was lost on Fiennes. Like all men, he saw only the smile and not the sadness that lay behind it. She didn't mind. It was safer that way. He bowed reluctantly, and took himself off to his post.

Isabel forgot him instantly. She glanced down at her hand, wondering yet again why the memory of that day should be so insistent tonight, then her lovely face became expressionless as she wrapped herself in the familiar cloak of indifference. A remote, cool air enveloped her that caused more than one man to think twice about approaching her as she walked slowly down the length of the hall.

Entering a room full of rough soldiers, unescorted, and sitting alone at the high table, exposed to their speculative eyes and lewd jokes, held no fears for her.

It was raining again when he reached Gloucester. The hollow clatter of his mount's hooves on the castle drawbridge mingled with the heavy splash of water rapidly filling the ditch. Further along the embankment a few miserable beggars huddled close to the stone ramparts, seeking the meagre shelter afforded by a jutting tower.

Ordinary sights and sounds on a night like this, mused Guy. There was no logical reason why they should add to the vague tension he'd been conscious of all day. His mission was going well, and he had even managed to save some precious time by arriving before the curfew was rung and the drawbridge raised for the night. Instead of having to seek shelter at an alehouse, he would be able to deliver his messages immediately and leave in the morning.

He spared a glance at the ragged specimens of humanity crouched against the wall and wondered how many of them had once been prosperous farmers or innkeepers or tradesmen. How many had been beggared while the war between the royal cousins had swept across their fields or through their towns, while the barons who should have protected them looked only to their own gain, shifting loyalties so often that the ordinary common man found himself constantly besieged and attacked by both sides?

Of course there were those who remained staunch, Guy reminded himself, as he reached into his tunic for a few coins. Men who had stayed loyal to Stephen throughout his misfortunes, and, on the other side, men who followed the Empress Matilda unreservedly.

This fact was abruptly brought home to him by the commanding voice ringing through the gloom of the overcast evening.

''Hold there!''

A young soldier appeared beneath the arched gateway, flanked by two men-at-arms, wielding pikes. ''Let me see both hands—slowly,'' he instructed, his voice strained.

Guy's mouth kicked up at one corner in a wryly amused smile. Despite the fact that the war had ground to a halt while the commanders-in-chief of both armies languished in their respective prisons, the young sprig confronting him obviously took his guard duty seriously.

''I'm fitzAlan of Ashby Chase,'' he announced quietly, withdrawing the hand concealed in his cloak. The other retained its firm grip on the reins. He wasn't going to risk having his horse spooked into the ditch by a nervous sentry. "I carry letters from the Queen to the Countess of Anjou."

He noted the awed curiosity on the younger man's face on hearing his name, but the boy came back with a swift answer. "You mean the Empress, sir. I'll see that she gets the letters, if you'll be good enough to wait in the guardroom."

Guy muttered darkly and dismounted. "I mean the Countess of Anjou, boy," he snapped with barely concealed impatience. "Where's your commanding officer?"

As he had expected, the sentry came to attention automatically at the suddenly terse voice.

"I'll take you to him, Lord fitzAlan," he responded stiffly. "You'll understand our caution, I trust."

"Very commendable," Guy growled. "But since it's obvious that I don't have a bloody army at my back you can take me directly to the Countess, or the Sheriff of Gloucester, if he's here."

"Aye, sir." More rigid than ever, the boy turned to lead the way.

Guy followed, taking the time to throw the coins in his hand to the beggars. They scrambled to retrieve them, croaking out blessings and thanks.

At least he'd made someone happy, he thought drily, regretting that he'd snarled at the lad in front of him. The boy was only obeying orders. But the odd tension which had been nagging at him seemed to be increasing.

He looked up at the formidable stone keep of Gloucester Castle towering three storeys above him and wondered if there was danger within, although his task was straightforward enough. Behind him, along the road leading down to the town, he could see lights start to glow as home fires were kindled against the cold night. No danger there, either. And yet, as the sentry yelled for a stable boy to take Guy's horse before they mounted the outer stairway of the forebuilding, he felt every muscle in his body tighten.

Shrugging off rational assurances, Guy let the warning sensations roll over him. More than five years of rebellions and civil war had honed his instincts to a fine edge, and he knew better than to ignore them. No matter what awaited him tonight, he was braced and ready.

"Isabel, look!"

"What is it, Adele?" Isabel didn't trouble to glance up from her stitching. Repairing her already threadbare clothes was not her idea of an entertaining evening, but she had learned that if she appeared busy no one bothered her.

Sometimes she even managed to shut her ears to the arguments going on around her. They were always on the subject of war anyway. She was sick of battle plans, plots and schemes that never succeeded, and the angry railing against failure. Why couldn't the Empress Matilda see that she was beaten?

It had been a different story earlier this year after the Battle of Lincoln had seen Stephen's army defeated and the King himself taken prisoner. King Henry's daughter had been triumphantly proclaimed Lady of England until she could be crowned queen. Even the powerful Bishop of Winchester had turned his back on his brother and had acknowledged Matilda.

But the tide had turned. Unable or unwilling to curb her arrogance while her star was in the ascendency, the Empress had alienated nearly all those who had abandoned the King. Her overweening imperiousness had finally driven the Bishop to send a message to the Queen, begging for her forgiveness and her help. Furious, Matilda had besieged the Bishop in his own castle, but the surprising determination of Stephen's gentle wife had prevailed.

Only too glad to regain the support of her brother-in-law, the Queen had gathered her army and surrounded Winchester. The besieger had become the besieged, and Matilda had only escaped because of the gallant rearguard action of her half-brother, Robert, Earl of Gloucester, as they fought their way out of their castle before they were starved out. Robert had been taken prisoner in his turn and, for the time being, hostilities had ceased while both sides licked their wounds and took stock of the situation.

But had the Empress been grateful that her brother's sacrifice had meant her freedom? No, thought Isabel. Matilda was still ranting and raving against the absent Earl for getting himself captured. She was beginning to hear that strident, angry voice in her sleep.

Adele's softer tones were a welcome change.

"Oh, Isabel, do look. He's so handsome."

Isabel finally turned to regard the girl sitting next to her. Adele was in a similar position to herself—caught up in the middle of a war, alone, and without the protection of close family. But she was also distant kin to the Sheriff of Gloucester, and thus treated with more consideration than Isabel.

"Who have you fallen in love with this week, Adele?" she asked, smiling indulgently.

"No one," protested Adele indignantly, then blushed. "I mean, I haven't changed my mind about Philip, you provoking creature. I'm talking about the man who just came in." She cast a glance down the table from beneath her lashes, and added, "I see our lady is quite interested, also."

Isabel's eyes followed the direction of Adele's to rest

on the woman seated midway along the high table. She was flanked by two men. Men whose stern faces and seasoned appearance proclaimed their experience in war and hardship. And yet the woman's personality overshadowed them both.

Matilda, Countess of Anjou and Princess of England, occupied her great, carved chair as though she sat upon the throne she stubbornly insisted was hers. She was a tall woman, dark of hair and eyes, still considered strikingly attractive, although she was nearing forty. But there was a hard veneer to her, a cold ruthlessness, which repelled many who came into contact with her.

"One doesn't think of the Empress as being interested in men," observed Adele in a gossipy whisper. "She is usually so impervious to any softer womanly emotions, and we all know her opinion of her husband. Philip tells me they fight like cats every time they come within sight of each other, and Count Geoffrey is so occupied with annexing Normandy that he refuses to help her cause here."

"Matilda argues with everyone," Isabel pointed out.

"I think she has other plans for this man," murmured Adele. "Perhaps he has come to offer his support. Why else would anyone come here?"

Why else, indeed? wondered Isabel. *She* certainly wasn't in this forbidding place by choice.

Her curiosity mildly aroused by Adele's close interest in the stranger, Isabel glanced across the table, her gaze sliding past the sentry announcing the visitor.

Big, was her first impression. The man stripping off his helmet as he strode down the room was tall and broad-shouldered, and moved with the leashed power of the hunter. A hunting wolf, she thought, shivering suddenly. That lithe, muscular grace told of awesome physical strength under perfect control. Intrigued almost against her will, Isabel shifted her eyes to his face—and, in the space of a heartbeat, five and a half years vanished from her life.

It was her soldier!

Guy fitzAlan.

Not a longed-for dream, but the man himself.

For a breathless instant, made dizzy by the fierce uprush of joy sweeping through her, Isabel could not think beyond the fact that he had come. He was *here*. Almost within reach. She was conscious of nothing else. She heard nothing else, saw nothing but his face, felt nothing apart from the out-of-control pounding of her heart. The entire world shrank to the mere fifteen feet separating her from the man she had thought never to see again.

"Isabel? Are you all right? You've gone as white as snow."

Isabel stared blindly at Adele's concerned face. "A...a sudden toothache," she improvised wildly, hardly knowing what she was saying. Reality swung back with another dizzying rush that made her head swim. Without understanding why, she knew she had to distract Adele's attention away from her. "It must have been those honeyed cakes," she added hurriedly, and gestured to the Empress. "Hush, Matilda is speaking."

Adele turned away, apparently satisfied, and Isabel shrank back on the bench, half hidden by Adele's body as the other girl leaned forward to hear what was going on. Struggling desperately to regain control of her senses, Isabel forced herself to listen also, to silence the clamouring questions in her head.

Matilda was contemplating the man before her, tapping the letters in her hand against the table. "So, my cousin is becoming anxious to have her husband back, my lord."

The tone of voice was gently musing, but Guy wasn't fooled for a minute. This wasn't his first encounter with Stephen's rival and he knew the woman seated on the other side of the high table was a formidable opponent, probably more dangerous than the King, and possessing in full measure the strong will and harsh determination that had characterised her father and grandfather.

It was her misfortune, Guy reflected briefly, that Matilda hadn't also inherited the Conqueror's skill at diplomacy. If she had, she might now be wearing the crown of England instead of being holed up in Gloucester Castle, her supporters scattered and dwindling, and what little popularity she had once possessed destroyed by her own hand.

Guy stared into hostile eyes, his own gaze ice-cold. "No more anxious than you are for the return of the Earl of Gloucester, madam," he countered.

He felt a sudden sharp impulse to look to his left, but controlled it, his eyes never leaving the Empress. Her face took on a mask-like stillness at the lack of title with which he addressed her. She'd better get used to it, Guy thought inflexibly. Matilda was the Countess of Anjou. Damned if he was going to call her Empress when her first husband, the Holy Roman Emperor, had been dead for years. And she was no longer Lady of England.

"I seem to recall that you don't believe in wasting time on gallantry, Lord fitzAlan," Matilda bit out, her eyes narrowing to hazel slits. "You have not changed, I see."

"Gallantry is wasted, madam, when 'tis repaid with threats and ill treatment. But I am not here to bandy words with you," Guy continued, ruthlessly forestalling another angry retort. "The Queen *is* anxious for the negotiations between our two parties to be concluded satisfactorily. It is the natural anxiety of any wife who is concerned for

her husband's well-being. Since more formal arrangements seem to be delayed, she has ventured to address
you herself, one woman to another.''

Even if it's useless, Guy added to himself. He caught
the eye of the man seated on Matilda's left and nodded
curt acknowledgement. ''My lord.''

Miles, Sheriff of Gloucester and Constable of Gloucester Castle, nodded back. ''Lord fitzAlan. 'Tis some time
since we met.''

Guy didn't bother with any further conversation. He
and Miles had last faced each other across a battlefield
strewn with the dead and dying. Miles had managed to
vanish before Guy could get to him. Apparently his escape
from the rout of Winchester hadn't been so easy. Guy had
heard that Miles had finally reached Gloucester on foot
and practically dead from exhaustion, his weapons and
armour long since abandoned so he could travel faster. He
had not been alone in fleeing thus ignominiously. The
field had been littered with riderless steeds and discarded
equipment. As a result, Earl Robert had not been the only
valuable prisoner taken, a fact that obviously rankled with
Matilda.

''Such arrangements as are proposed take time to consider, Lord fitzAlan,'' she pointed out. ''My brother is but
an earl, and yet you expect us to give up a king in
exchange. I believe the release of all your prisoners for
my cousin's freedom would better suffice.''

Guy raised a mocking eyebrow. ''In that case, are you
freely acknowledging that Stephen should remain King,
madam?'' he asked smoothly.

Matilda's eyes flashed. ''Never!'' she cried angrily.
''That false perjurer and defiler of oaths stole the crown
from me. He has no right to it!''

''Then, madam, the exchange of one commander for

another is fair, is it not? The other prisoners will be re-leased on payment of ransom, as is the custom.''

Isabel couldn't help it. No one spoke to the Empress like that and got away with it. She leaned forward to see Matilda's reaction to Guy's brutal logic just as he turned his head slightly in her direction, as though he sensed her watching him.

Their eyes collided with a force that deafened and blinded Isabel to everything else. She vaguely heard Ma-tilda's angry voice, but it came to her from a great dis-tance. She glimpsed the Sheriff's movement, but through a blurred mist. The only thing Isabel saw with any clarity was the startled recognition in fitzAlan's ice-blue eyes. Transfixed by the sudden intensity of his gaze before he turned back to the Empress, she was totally unprepared for what happened next.

''I see you are still human enough to be attracted by a pretty face, my lord,'' Matilda purred with patently false sweetness.

FitzAlan narrowed his eyes at her. ''I once knew the girl's father,'' he said abruptly. ''How does she come to be here?''

Matilda's smile was mocking. ''Why, Tracy Castle is held for me, of course.'' She cast a glance at Isabel's still face. ''This dear child's loyalty is my greatest pleasure, and *so* useful. Men will often behave…rashly, shall we say?…when the reward is thus sweetly packaged. You see, I give you fair warning.''

It was Adele's indignant gasp that wrenched Isabel out of her frozen state. Her eyes flashed swiftly to fitzAlan, only to recoil at the look of blazing fury and contempt he turned on her. She shook her head slightly, making a move as if to rise, but Adele grabbed her arm.

''No,'' she whispered in Isabel's ear. ''Let it go. You

know Matilda is always looking for a reason to punish you.''

Sick and shaking, Isabel obeyed, slumping back on the bench and gazing helplessly at fitzAlan. When he at last looked away from her, she felt as though she had been seared to the soul by the scathing dismissal in his eyes.

Oh, how could she explain? How could she tell him why Matilda had made such a spiteful remark? She would never be allowed to see such an important visitor, let alone speak with him. Oh, God, what was she to do? The prospect of Guy leaving, thinking the worst of her, was unbearable. The idea that she might be able to leave with him didn't even occur to her.

''Isabel? You really *are* in pain. And no wonder, after that. Poor girl, you must retire.''

Barely hearing Adele through the strange roaring in her ears, Isabel gazed blankly at her friend.

''Go up to our room,'' instructed Adele firmly. ''I'll send a serf with some vinegar, oil and sulphur to rub on your tooth.''

This practical suggestion got through the haze. ''I…I can't,'' Isabel stammered, not wanting to leave the hall while Guy was there. Then she realised that he had gone, and she hadn't even seen him leave. Had shock held her deaf and blind for so long? She glanced distractedly around the room. He was nowhere in sight.

''Where…?''

''Oh, don't worry about our visitor. Uncle Miles suggested that Lord fitzAlan retire for the night while he and the Empress read through the Queen's letters. I wager they've put him in the meanest, coldest room, without even a brazier, after the way he spoke to Matilda. I thought she would have a fit on the spot. And she obviously didn't like the way he looked at you.''

"Me? Adele, what…?" Frantically Isabel gathered her wits, trying to suppress the sudden queasiness in the pit of her stomach.

"Well, she might have been angry with him," Adele chattered on, "but he's not the sort of man one can ignore, is he? Matilda would love to have him on her side, and not only because of his reputation."

"Reputation?" She felt sicker than ever. "You mean with women?"

"Heavens, no! I don't know anything about *that*. But I remember Philip telling me of a man he admired a great deal, and 'twas Guy fitzAlan of Ashby Chase. It must be the same man. Apparently he fought with incredible bravery at Lincoln, only retreating when the King was captured. And he is one of the few who have never changed sides. Of course, that doesn't mean he won't take a woman if he fancies her, especially after what Matilda said, but…"

Adele saw Isabel's pale face turn even whiter and broke off, patting her hand consolingly. "Don't fret," she advised kindly. "I'm sure Lord fitzAlan will be kept much too busy to accost you. Although I have to admit, if he had stared so at *me*…" Adele shivered dramatically. "Holy Mother, those eyes!" She seemed to realise that this comment was not exactly reassuring and hastened to make amends. "But keep to your room if you fear him, Isabel. And, see, Matilda is retiring also. Now that she's vented her spite for the evening, she won't even notice you're missing, but if anyone asks I'll tell them you're suffering from toothache."

"Aye," gasped Isabel, remembering her hastily manufactured excuse and rising. "My thanks, Adele."

Hurrying from the hall, she stifled her guilt at deceiving her innocent friend, knowing that Adele had entirely misunderstood her fright. But the need for solitude to pull herself together was too imperative. She would confess her deception to the castle priest later, Isabel promised her conscience, and then wondered if, in fact, the chapel might provide the privacy she craved. It would be empty at this hour. Then she saw that, in her haste to leave the hall, she had fled to the nearest exit, which opened on to a passage running along the side of the great-room. It was seldom frequented since only the Empress's suite of rooms lay here in the south-west tower.

Isabel hesitated, considering her choices. She could reach the chapel from here, but it was situated in the fore-building, beyond the staircase turret at the other end of the corridor, and, though a rushlight burned in its sconce above the steps leading to Matilda's rooms, the rest of the passage lay in heavy darkness.

She hated the dark.

But the alternative of returning to the hall, and travers-ing its crowded sixty-foot length to gain the opposite stair-case leading to the upper storey, where she shared a tiny chamber with Adele and two of Matilda's ladies, was just as unappealing.

It would have to be the chapel, Isabel decided, scolding herself for her cowardly hesitation. The only danger in the dark passage was the risk of a collision with the odd piece of furniture, and surely she was not afraid of a table? Placing one hand on the cold stone wall for guidance, she plunged forward.

Blackness closed around her instantly. But there would be lights in the chapel, Isabel assured herself, peering ahead for a sign of them and flinching from the feel of the rough stone beneath her palm. The chill from the bare wall seemed to penetrate to her bones. Surely it was odd that no light at all shone in the corridor? It was Matilda's private route to the chapel, after all.

That's if the woman ever prays, Isabel reflected, holding on to the random thought to steady her shaky nerves. Matilda was more likely to rant at her Maker than supplicate, even when she hadn't been put into a rage. She found herself wondering how long Matilda would rant against Guy, and another stray thought flashed through her mind.

Everyone had called him *Lord* fitzAlan. Some time, then, during the intervening years, he had been granted a barony. A reward for unswerving loyalty, no doubt. Despair washed through Isabel again as she remembered the cutting disdain in fitzAlan's eyes, too distressed at the moment to be angered by his instant acceptance of Matilda's explanation. So many families had changed sides, and she was not imprisoned, nor even a slave. He had seen her sitting at the high table among the other ladies of noble birth who served the Empress.

Oh, God, she prayed silently, show me a way to let him know how wrong he is. I but saw him the once, and yet cannot bear for him to despise me so.

"He despises me! Did you see the scorn in his eyes? I'll not endure it! Do you hear me, Miles?"

It took a moment for Isabel to realise that the low, passionate words, so like those inside her head, had been spoken aloud. She stopped immediately, her heart thumping in sudden fright as she saw that the chapel was occupied. At the same time her groping fingers felt emptiness and she knew where she was.

Ahead, a narrow sliver of light showed where the chapel door had not been properly closed. The shadowy form of a woman crossed it before the Empress moved out of Isabel's line of vision. To her right, as her eyes adjusted to the faint lifting of the darkness, she could just make out the first steps of the spiral tower staircase. Then, before she could decide whether to retreat and wait for the Empress to leave, a man murmured softly. Isabel couldn't hear the words clearly, but she knew the voice. And she knew who it was they were discussing.

Matilda was with the Sheriff, and there was only one reason why they would be here, seeking privacy like herself: to plot against Guy.

Holding the skirts of her worn grey woollen gown close about her legs, Isabel glided into the darkness of the stair turret, hugging the wall. She no longer felt the cold, or worried about the unlit passage. Every sense strained to hear the low-voiced conversation in the adjacent chapel. For the first time she was grateful for Matilda's notorious temper, which made it impossible for the Empress to keep her voice down.

"How dare he speak to me like that? 'The natural anxiety of any wife for her husband's well-being.' Did you hear him, Miles? And look at this letter. That puling creature has the gall to remind me that Stephen is a consecrated king and should not be treated as a felon. What else should that perjurer expect, but to be chained in a dungeon? Do you tell me that my brother is not treated in a like manner?"

"You forget, my lady, that the Queen has treated Robert with the utmost honour."

"Honour? *Honour*? They offered him the highest position in the land, second only to that traitor, if he would forsake me! Is that honour?"

"I meant the way he is housed. My lady, try to calm yourself and consider carefully. Do you think it wise to continue to hold Stephen bound and chained in that dungeon at Bristol? The reports of his health are not good."

"Then let the man sicken and die." The words dropped into the darkness like shards of ice.

Isabel, listening in the tower, shivered at the implacable hatred in Matilda's voice. She saw a shadow move across the wall opposite her as the other woman paced violently.

"If that happens while he is in our custody," continued Miles, "you can give up any hope of getting your brother back; and we need him."

"Don't tell me my business, Miles," stormed the Empress. "God, why did Robert have to be captured? Why am I served by incompetents who can only advise surrender?"

"'Tis not surrender, my lady. 'Tis true that releasing Stephen will put him back on the throne, but our army can do nothing without my Lord of Gloucester at its head. Holding Stephen is no longer an advantage."

The shadow suddenly stopped moving. "That may be," said Matilda, and her voice was now soft and deadly. "But we can hold him for a while yet. Time enough, perhaps, to break his health so that he does not long survive his freedom."

"And how do you intend to convey a delaying answer to the Queen, my lady?"

"Very simply," replied Matilda silkily. "Even that whey-faced simpleton who calls herself Queen will understand a message pinned to fitzAlan's dead body. Where did you put the arrogant lout?"

"In one of the chambers off the gallery, but you can't…"

Isabel did not wait for more. Reluctant to brave the corridor again in case the conspirators emerged and caught her, she turned sharply and fled up the tower stairs, just one thought uppermost in her mind.

She had to warn Guy. He must leave at once. Matilda

must have run mad to suggest such a thing. To murder a man while he was under her roof...

Shivering with fear and the need for haste, Isabel stumbled up the narrow stone staircase, slipping once and bruising her knee when she fell. She hardly noticed. At last she reached the floor above the hall and began to cross to the diagonally opposite tower, grateful that there were lights here to guide her way. A room off the gallery, the Sheriff had said. But which one? There were one or two built into each thick wall of the rectangular keep. How could she find fitzAlan without anyone becoming suspicious? Apart from disturbing the wrong occupants, the gallery was open to the hall below it in several places and she might be seen.

But then, if she waited until everyone slept, she might be too late.

The idea of Guy being killed while he lay sleeping quickened Isabel's steps. She hurtled down the north-west turret staircase with a reckless disregard for life and limb, and emerged at the point where she had entered the hall earlier that night—was it only hours ago? She felt as though she had been running forever. Her legs quivered and her chest heaved as she struggled to control her breathing. The north and west galleries stretched before her; every door was shut. Below her, the hum of voices was reassuringly loud. She should have brought a wine jug from the hall, she chided herself as her breathing steadied. It would have given her an excuse to be searching for a particular room, but she had been so frightened...

And she must not hesitate now. The memory of the fear induced by Matilda's vindictive rage spurred Isabel towards the nearest door. She would just glance quickly into each room and hope she didn't encounter anyone who knew her.

It was not only fear that drove her forward. Guy's safety was the only conscious thought in her mind, but deeper, in a dark, secret place in her heart, Isabel knew she was also impelled by the urgent need to see him again. To speak to him. Perhaps, by her action, to convince him that she had not turned traitor to the King. The barely acknowledged hope caused her heart to beat faster as she reached for the first round iron latch.

Then every drop of blood drained from her face as a man's hand reached past her. Strong fingers clamped brutally around her wrist, staying her action, and she was swung roughly about to meet the hard, questioning glare of one of Matilda's Angevin guards.

Chapter Two

"Ungrateful wench! Thankless creature! For years have I housed and fed you, and this is how you repay me! Traitorous slut!"

The vicious epithets struck Isabel's ears like blows. She stared stoically at the tapestry wall-hanging in front of her. It was the only concession to comfort in the Empress's room. The bed, table and stools were of plain, sturdy oak, rushes covered the floor, and the fire had not been lit. Matilda lived as hardily as her men.

"I have sworn no oath to you, my lady," retorted Isabel, refusing to cower. "Nor did my father."

"You dare to answer me so?" shrilled Matilda. "Fool! Ignorant wench! You will soon learn the penalty for your disgraceful conduct."

"I have committed no disgrace," insisted Isabel. "'Twas you, my lady, who would have been dishonoured by killing a guest." She didn't have to wonder where such reckless courage was coming from. The worst had already happened to her. She had been intercepted outside Guy's room and would be severely punished, perhaps even killed.

The Empress was right, she thought wretchedly. She

had been a fool not to anticipate that a guard would be keeping a hidden watch on fitzAlan's door. Her despair at this belated realisation had rendered her only half aware of being dragged down the gallery stairs and across a hall humming with surprised murmurs. She had vaguely noticed Adele's startled, anxious face, before she was shoved roughly across the threshold of Matilda's chamber to be confronted by the Empress, the Sheriff and the one man who thought Matilda could do no wrong—Brien fitzCount, Lord of Wallingford, who, except for her half-brother, was the Empress's most devoted follower and, some said, her lover.

But he was also a man of fixed principles in matters of warfare. When Matilda had demanded an explanation, Isabel had given it to her, omitting nothing. She might not have succeeded in warning Guy, but she didn't think Brien fitzCount would stand by and allow the Queen's equerry to be murdered while he was on official business.

Matilda's harsh laughter cut through this hopeful belief.

"Are you telling me you were concerned for my soul?" she mocked. "Look to your own, girl. Skulking about in private passages, listening at doors, betraying your rightful queen." She paused in her furious pacing and thrust her face close to Isabel's. "I should despatch you to hell this minute, where your soul will be justly rewarded."

Determined not to show fear, Isabel stood her ground before the rage in Matilda's eyes, staring back at the other woman defiantly. With a strangled sound of frustrated fury, Matilda drew her arm back.

"My lady, wait!"

"Don't try to stop me from punishing this ingrate, Brien. I'll make sure the drab never interferes in my plans again."

"You will do as you see fit, my Lady of England, but am I right in thinking this girl has a brother?"

Matilda's arm stayed. She turned slowly towards Brien. A look passed between them that Isabel, braced for the blow and hardly daring to breathe, couldn't decipher.

"Don't we hold him at Tracy Castle?" fitzCount continued with careful emphasis. "The girl would not like any harm to come to him, I warrant."

There was a long, heavy silence. Isabel felt her defiant bravado disintegrate like shattered glass. She watched, numbly, as Matilda lowered her arm and stepped away.

Miles of Gloucester, who had remained quietly in the background since Isabel had entered the room, now moved forward. He carefully closed the door to the antechamber where some of Matilda's ladies sat, trying to ignore the scene going on in their hearing. "What do you have in mind, Brien?"

"The girl was going to warn fitzAlan of the danger to his life, presumably so he could escape." FitzCount's voice held no inflexion of either censure or approval of Matilda's plan. "Perhaps we should allow her to go ahead with her virtuous deed. Under certain conditions, of course."

Another look passed between the three. "Why?" asked Matilda at last.

She seemed to have completely forgotten her rage, or perhaps it had been channelled into a more dangerous, calculating form, thought Isabel in dread. Terror caused her heart to jolt sickeningly, and her hands became damp. She had not cared about risking her own life, but Edmund... Her mind shut off the thought. She must not show fear. She must listen and wait.

"The last man I sent to Winchester has had more success in gaining entrance to the castle than the others," explained fitzCount. "But he can't get close enough to anyone of importance. He needs a contact—someone who can listen and not be noticed, someone whose presence is unremarked. A lady-in-waiting to the Queen herself would be the perfect answer."

"You're saying I should let the wench escape with fitzAlan?" Matilda swung around and stared narrowly at Isabel.

Isabel stared back, trying not to let her flimsy hope show in her eyes as Matilda's appraising look swept down to her feet and back again.

"The creature has possibilities," the Empress pronounced consideringly. "Aye, 'tis more than time that she made herself useful. How will your fellow know her, though, Brien?"

"I'll send Rainald a message," responded fitzCount. "Telling him to expect word from this—what's your name, girl?"

"She's Isabel de Tracy," Matilda answered for her, still thoughtful. "A rebellious family, but their blood is good enough. My tender-hearted cousin will not refuse to take such a nobly born orphan into her household." The Empress nodded once and became suddenly brisk. "You are spared, girl, to carry out your self-appointed task and one of greater importance. My Lord of Wallingford's man will tell you what information to listen for, but know this: one false step and your brother's life will be forfeit. One word from Rainald that you are not proving useful to us and young de Tracy dies. Do you understand me?"

Isabel nodded carefully. She would agree to anything to save Edmund. There was only one doubt in her mind.

"What...?" Her voice came out as a hoarse whisper and she had to clear her throat. Matilda's satisfied expression at the betraying sound roused Isabel's pride.

"What if my lord fitzAlan refuses to take me with him?" she managed to say quite steadily.

"Because of what I said earlier?" Matilda laughed scornfully. "Look in a mirror, girl, and you'll see what that insolent cur saw in the hall tonight. Of course, he'll be suspicious, but he's a man just the same." She looked over her shoulder at the other two, smiling archly. "Don't you agree, gentlemen?"

Brien fitzCount didn't even glance at Isabel. He sent Matilda an answering smile that immediately caused Isabel to suspect that the gossip concerning the pair was true.

The Sheriff, however, remained grim-faced. "FitzAlan may be a man," he argued, "but he's a man on a mission—not likely to saddle himself with female company on a hard ride. The girl's still a maid, isn't she? Do you think she'll be persuasive enough?"

"With her brother's continued good health at stake?" derided Matilda. "She will do whatever she has to, won't you, Isabel? After all, what is your maidenhead compared to his life?"

Isabel didn't reply. There was no answer anyway. Her growing indignation at the way they were discussing her as though she were so much merchandise was abruptly swamped by misery at the thought of giving herself to the man she had dreamed of for years in such a cold-blooded manner. She had survived much. This might finally destroy her.

Through a haze of despair she noticed that the Sheriff was still frowning at her.

"Can't you look a bit less like a nun?" he demanded with masculine vagueness. "Loosen your hair...and what about that poor excuse for a gown?"

"We don't want to overdo it," objected Matilda, gesturing to Isabel to unfasten the braid hanging down her back.

Feeling like a puppet, Isabel obeyed.

"The dress can stay," continued Matilda. "If seduction doesn't work, she can play on fitzAlan's sympathy, if he has any." Her lips curved suddenly in an unpleasant smile. "And just to help arouse it…"

The vicious, open-handed blow landed on Isabel's cheek before she had any warning of the Empress's intention. It was hard enough to make her stagger and fall to her knees. Her eyes filled with tears of pain and shock, but Isabel refused to let them fall. She would not give the other woman that satisfaction.

Pushing herself upright again, she met Matilda's triumphant expression with impassive calm. "How do I contact Rainald, madam?"

It was very late. In the hall a few sleepy serfs cleared away the debris left from the evening meal. Others, their duties finished, were settling down for the night on their pallets in front of the fires. The castle dogs crept closer to the flames also, snapping lazily as they squabbled for their accustomed places near the warmth.

Despite the almost empty room, Isabel had been taken back to the gallery by a circuitous route through little-known passages deep inside the castle walls. It was a trip she would rather have forgotten—the cold was biting and the whispering patter of rodent feet made her heart jump every few minutes—but she knew she would have to face it again when she and Guy escaped from the keep. Matilda had told her that their escape had to look genuine if fitzAlan was to believe her story.

At the moment, however, as she stood outside the door she had intended trying before, one trembling hand hesi-

tating over the latch, Isabel could only think as far ahead
as the next few minutes. She did not have any idea, she
realised abruptly, of what she was going to say to fitzAlan.
The breathless warning she would have uttered earlier
would at least have had the ring of sincerity, but now she
was only too conscious of having to play a part. And the
fact that she wanted nothing more than to entrust herself
to fitzAlan's protection made her nervousness all the more
acute.

What if he didn't believe her? Worse, even if he accepted her warning, what if he refused to take her with
him, thinking what he did of her?

The impatient gesture of the guard who had escorted
her caught Isabel's eye. No doubt he wanted his task over
with, so he could return to his companions and his ale-
cup in the soldiers' quarters. The man was ignorant of the
Empress's scheme, but when Isabel glanced back at his
face she saw only too clearly his opinion of her visit to
their guest's room. And by morning the entire barracks
would share his belief.

Suddenly Isabel knew she *had* to succeed. If she did
not, and survived the failure, her life here would be unen-
durable.

Unable to bear the lustful, knowing mockery in the
guard's eyes any longer, she closed her hand over the
latch, pushed the door open, and slipped into the room.
The door shut again on pitch-blackness. Isabel stood
pressed back against the wooden panels, trying to listen
for the sound of breathing over the drumming of her heart.

It seemed an age before she thought she heard movement over to her left. Her feet felt like leaden weights,
but she eventually managed to take a step, and then another, one hand held out in front of her to feel for the
bed. She only hoped there *was* a bed, and that she

wouldn't fall over a low pallet. Why hadn't the man left a sconce burning? Was there an economy drive on rush-lights tonight?

Then, just as this nonsensical question darted through her mind, something huge and heavy slammed into her back with all the force of a boulder slung from a catapult. She was flung violently forward, to land face down in a heap of blankets, the crushing weight of her assailant forcing all the air out of her body.

It was a woman, Guy realised in surprise.

When the door had opened to admit her, the waiting tension still gnawing at him had finally transformed itself into swift action, and he'd been too busy quitting the bed and judging the right moment to attack to identify the intruder. But there was no mistaking the soft fragility of the body beneath his, or the fragrant silkiness of the long tresses brushing across his throat as she tried to turn her head.

At her desperate movement, Guy promptly shoved his unexpected visitor's face into the bedding with a large, relentless hand before she could let loose a scream.

"Make one sound when I release you and I'll break your neck," he growled in her ear.

Isabel barely heard him. Almost fainting from lack of air, she could only answer in choked gasps. Apparently it was enough, because the heavy pressure on the back of her head eased and she could turn her face to the side, dragging air back into her lungs.

It took a couple of deep breaths before she recovered enough to grasp what was happening. The oppressive weight above her had lifted slightly, and she was being searched. Systematically and with devastating intimacy.

Her faint scream of shock was abruptly stifled by a hand clamped over her mouth. She tried to struggle, flinching away from that intrusive touch. It was useless. Sobbing with rage and fear at her utter helplessness compared to the superior weight and strength of the man above her, Isabel could only submit. When fitzAlan had satisfied himself that she didn't carry a weapon, she felt as though no part of her body remained untouched.

"Don't move a muscle," he ordered.

Too dazed by the rapid succession of shocks to disobey, Isabel stayed prone on the bed. She heard a flint strike and, a moment later, light flickered, dimly illuminating a small area around her head.

"Now, then, let's have a look at you," came fitzAlan's voice, and she found herself flipped over on to her back to encounter a pair of hard blue eyes.

In the ensuing silence she could have heard a flea move in the rushes on the floor.

Then, with a rough jerk, fitzAlan pulled her to her feet. "Just what the hell are you doing in here?" he snarled, towering over her.

"I..." Isabel's voice was scarcely a whisper. She had to stop and try again. Before she could utter a word, however, he suddenly slid his hand down to hers and raised it to the candlelight. His eyes scanned her bare fingers and returned to her face, their icy glitter freezing her to the floor.

"You're still unwed?" The words were flung at her like an accusation of felony.

Thrown mentally off balance by such an unexpected, seemingly irrelevant question, Isabel could only nod, her attempt at speech failing completely.

FitzAlan uttered an impatient curse and pushed her down on to the bed again. She went easily, her trembling legs no longer capable of supporting her, watching in silence as he strode over to the table next to the window embrasure and stood with his back to her, leaning both fists on the oak surface. Isabel saw the powerful muscles of his shoulders flex beneath his tunic as he controlled whatever emotion was driving him.

Dear lord, she had to speak, she told herself, staring down at her hands gripped tight in her lap. But she was being battered by so many conflicting emotions that her brain felt numb. She had never experienced such roiling confusion before in her entire life. A strange mixture of dread and tremulous joy at seeing fitzAlan again battled for supremacy with outrage at his rough treatment of her. What had happened to the icy indifference with which she had surveyed the world for the past few years?

"Well, you've certainly come a long way from the child who ran from me in that garden."

The contemptuous tone of the words brought Isabel's head up. FitzAlan had turned and was now half sitting, half leaning against the table. He was still fully dressed, she noted distantly. For a moment they stared at each other—and, though the anger and hostility in the room were almost visible, the memory of that long-ago day hung in the air between them.

He looked bigger, thought Isabel. Stronger. More powerful. It was not only physical strength. She saw now that his tough appearance, which had so overwhelmed her five and a half years ago, had then been tempered by his youth. But if there was any softness, any tenderness in his nature now, it was buried too deeply to be easily discernible. Though still handsome, he looked hard, ruthless, and twice as dangerous as Isabel remembered.

What, Guy wondered, furious with himself, had possessed him to bring up that day? It was too dark in the small room to see by her expression if Isabel remembered also, but he knew she did. He could *feel* the memory they shared. Damn it, he hadn't meant to betray that he'd never been able to forget that afternoon, and the sweet innocence that had touched something very deep within him. Because she was certainly far from innocent now. Her presence in his room at this hour confirmed her role in Matilda's household only too plainly.

Well, if Isabel had any ideas of playing on that one unguarded remark she could think again, he vowed grimly. She might still be the most beautiful woman he had ever seen, but it wasn't going to affect him. Guy pushed the image of innocent vulnerability out of his mind and forced himself to look at Isabel objectively.

She was taller, of course. No longer a child. And although her slenderness gave her an air of fragility, Guy had felt the gentle curves of her body when he'd searched for a concealed weapon. She was all woman—soft, warm and enticing. He ruthlessly banished that memory as well, concentrating on the rest.

Her hair was loose, falling in thick waves to her waist, a dark frame for her exquisite face, with its delicate bone-structure, softly curving mouth and expressive clear grey eyes. No, not expressive any more, Guy acknowledged, as the candle flared briefly in a gust of air from the open window. She stared back at him now with an indifference that almost rivalled his own. For some reason that angered him. He said the first thing that came into his mind that would eradicate any suspicion she was harbouring that he might soften towards her.

"If Matilda sent you here after warning me of your 'usefulness', she must be losing her mind."

Isabel ignored the scornful statement. The long silence had given her time to pull herself together. Dragging about her every shred of the detachment she had learned over the years, she forced herself to concentrate on the immediate future. If she had to lie to get herself and Guy out of this place, she would lie. If she had to beg, she would beg.

"I am not here for Matilda. I came to warn you," she said, and her voice held determination.

"Another warning," Guy observed sceptically. He might as well have said, Don't bother with the rest.

"Aye. Your life is in danger."

He gave a short laugh that sounded genuinely amused. "That's nothing new," he informed her, and added sarcastically, "'Tis one of the hazards of warfare."

"But you are here on honourable business, not to fight," persisted Isabel, beginning to lose some of her composure in the face of his blatant disbelief. "Matilda planned to kill you and send a message back to the Queen pinned to your body."

His eyes narrowed. "Planned?" he questioned, in a voice of such ominous quiet that Isabel's heart leapt into her throat. Holy Mother, she had blurted out the wrong thing already.

"I...I mean she *plans* to—"

She was abruptly cut off. FitzAlan strode forward and captured her face in one powerful hand. His long fingers held her in a grip that Isabel knew she could not escape without hurting herself—and probably not even then.

"You don't lie very well, little schemer. Try again. The truth this time. What was your task? Seduction and murder? Or just plain seduction to serve the Countess's ends?"

This was so uncomfortably close to the truth—at least as Matilda had ordered it—that Isabel flushed guiltily. Though her face was in shadow, she knew fitzAlan could feel the betraying heat beneath his fingers. This time his laugh was unpleasant.

"'Tis true," she cried as vehemently as possible with her jaw clamped in his hand. "Her plan to kill you, I mean," she stammered. "Not…not…"

"'Seduction' was the word I used," he mocked her hesitation. Releasing Isabel's face, he stepped away from her, his hard eyes raking her up and down with casual appraisal. He grinned insolently. "Don't let me stop you from trying, though. I might enjoy sampling what I was touching a few minutes ago."

And suddenly, unexpectedly, out of the whirlwind of Isabel's emotions, anger gained the upper hand. Furious, reckless anger.

How dared he speak to her so insultingly?

She remembered her fear for this man's life, the way she had fled through the castle to warn him, her useless defiance of Matilda's wrath and the threat hanging over her head if she refused to co-operate with the Empress. She also remembered five and a half years of girlish dreams and fading hopes.

So much for that gallant, knightly rescuer, she berated herself with sudden savagery. You may put *him* out of your mind. He doesn't exist in this man, if he ever did. Matilda was right for once. He *is* a lout. A sneering, arrogant, unchivalrous *lout*.

"You fool!" she cried, leaping to her feet and gesturing frenziedly with both hands. "I came to help you escape from here. I am *not* lying! You *will* be killed! And I wouldn't care now. I wouldn't—"

This time the words were stopped by his mouth. She was seized and held in a crushing embrace before she could do more than tense at the look on his face. Anger emanated from fitzAlan in waves, the force of it completely overwhelming her, even as the physical impact of that ruthless kiss stunned her into frozen immobility.

Then, before she could struggle, before she could even unravel her wildly mixed reactions, Guy broke the kiss and, with one smooth movement, picked her up and tossed her on to the bed.

Isabel bounced once against the plump straw mattress, then made a frantic bid for freedom. She got as far as the other side of the wide bed before being dragged back and pinned beneath fitzAlan's forceful weight for the second time that night.

"I wouldn't like you to think your visit was wasted, pretty traitor," he grated tauntingly, and lowered his mouth to hers.

Struggling would be useless. Her soft feminine frame was no match for fitzAlan's solid muscularity. Heart pounding, Isabel waited until his mouth had almost reached its goal, then jerked her head to the side.

She half expected Guy to wrench her face back up to his and braced herself to resist, but to her astonishment he laughed softly. There was no harshness or mockery in the sound now. Rather, his low laugh held a note that sent unexpected shivers down her spine. Quite involuntarily Isabel began to tremble. Then she stiffened, a startled gasp escaping her lips when his mouth began to string a row of tiny moist kisses down the side of her throat.

"Is this what it takes to silence you?" he murmured, the movement of his lips sending waves of heat along her neck.

The heat didn't stop there, but spread lower, stealing her breath and jolting her heart into an even wilder rhythm. The rest of her body seemed to have melted into a useless tangle of arms and legs. The iron grip Guy had used to subdue her had relaxed into a hold that now cradled rather than constrained, and yet she couldn't lift so much as a finger to defend herself, could barely summon the will to press her face harder against the bed in a futile attempt to escape that warm, spine-tingling touch.

"That's better, little one," he whispered against the junction of her neck and shoulder. "I've kissed you before, remember. Do you remember, sweet deceiver? You were only a child then, but now you're a woman, and this time I'm going to take what you came here to give me."

Sweet deceiver?

The murmured words finally pierced the haze of unfamiliar pleasure induced by those hot, insistent kisses. What was she doing? Isabel wondered in bewilderment. Exactly what the Empress ordered, a cold little voice in her head replied. But she couldn't. She *couldn't*. The man despised her, hated her. And she—

With a muffled cry of rage at her own weakness, Isabel shoved furiously at fitzAlan's broad shoulder with one hand and brought the other up and around with the full force of her arm behind it. The slap landed against the side of his head with a crack that echoed around the room. Her wrist felt as though she'd broken it, but she didn't wait to find out. Taking advantage of Guy's momentary stupefaction, she wriggled out from under him and leapt off the bed, everything forgotten but the need to escape from something she dared not put a name to.

Panicked, angry and perilously close to tears, Isabel sprang for the door.

She had not taken more than two steps before fitzAlan caught her. Both arms wrapped her in a bruising hold, and when her mouth opened her scream was smothered by his hand.

"Quiet!" he spat, ignoring her futile attempts to push his hand away.

It was like trying to push a fully harnessed plough

horse. Isabel abandoned the attempt and fought to regain her control instead.

As if sensing that she had given up fighting *him* for the present, fitzAlan released her immediately, frowning down at her distraught face. "You'll have the guard in here if you continue with that racket," he growled. "Was that your plan? To have me accused of assaulting you? Were you going to provide the Countess with a legitimate excuse for murder?"

The last word was like a pail of cold water dashed over her. Rage and panic at her muddled, turbulent emotions vanished. They were replaced by a chilling mental picture of Edmund as she had last seen him. Saints have mercy, she was making an appalling mess of everything.

Tears of desperation sprang into her eyes. "No. *No*! Oh, please, you must believe me. I was outside the chapel when I heard them…the Empress and my lord Sheriff… 'Twas such a strange place to…but Matilda said she would have you killed and…I didn't wait to hear more… Oh, please…"

"God, not tears as well, you little traitor."

"I'm *not* a traitor," she protested huskily, roughly swiping at her face with her sleeve. The tears stubbornly continued to flow, but, driven by fear, intent on making fitzAlan believe her, Isabel ignored them. "I hate this place. 'Tis true that I came to warn you, but also to beg you to take me with you."

Something flickered in his eyes before they went hard and cold again with suspicion. "I'm returning to the Queen; your home is in the other direction."

Isabel's gaze slid nervously away from his and back again. "I…can't go home."

"Why not?"

"You heard the Empress earlier. My brother holds our

castle for Matilda and sent me here to serve her. He won't take me back." Oh, Edmund, forgive me.

Guy stood still, glittering eyes narrowed on Isabel for a long, tense minute. There was something wrong with her story. Something he felt but couldn't pinpoint. It sounded plausible enough on the surface, but...

"All right," he said at last. "You've warned me. I'll be ready if any attempt is made on my life. As for taking you with me—forget it. I'm not on this trip for pleasure. You'd never be able to keep up."

"I can ride hard if I have to," protested Isabel. "My lord, please—"

"No, damn it!" he broke in roughly. "What in God's name would you do in Winchester? What's left of the town is full of soldiers and Flemish mercenaries... 'Tis no place for a woman. Hell! Why am I even discussing it?" Guy added disgustedly, turning away from her.

"Do you think the soldiers here are any different?" cried Isabel on a sob of despair. "I can't stay here. I *can't*!"

"Don't be ridiculous."

Isabel heard the impatience in his voice and fear lanced through her. He was standing there as if he'd dismissed her already. In another moment she would find herself on the other side of the door, facing disaster.

Whirling suddenly, she grabbed up the candle burning near the bed. "Look," she cried, holding the light close to her bruised cheek. She wondered crazily if she should thank Matilda for inflicting the injury.

FitzAlan glanced over his shoulder, turning fully when he saw the ugly discolouration along her cheekbone and the narrow line of dried blood where she had been cut by a ring. Whoever had struck her had come perilously close to her eye.

"Who gave you that?"

"The Empress, and only because I refused to cower at her anger. If she discovers that I've been here, I'll be killed."

"She doesn't have to discover it," he retorted in exasperation. "Damn it, girl, I can't take you with me." There was a short silence. "Where's your father, for God's sake?" he demanded tersely.

"Dead." The answer came out baldly, unemotionally. Her face went blank, but this time Guy saw the effort it cost her to regain that air of remote calm, and her eyes still held a mute appeal that stabbed him to the heart.

God, how could she have such an effect on him? First he'd been crazy enough to subdue her with a kiss which, though it had begun in anger, had aroused a need for her so hot and instant that it had stunned him more than her slap, and now this.

Furious at the strong wave of protectiveness that washed over him, despite all his suspicions, Guy bit out a curse that, in normal circumstances, he wouldn't have dreamed of using in the hearing of a woman.

He saw Isabel flinch, but she continued to hold his glowering gaze, oblivious to her dishevelled hair, mussed clothing and the tear-stains glistening on her bruised cheek. Guy cursed again, silently this time. It was extremely likely that she was pleading with him to escape so she could lead him straight into a trap which would result in accusations of spying or some such thing. If he wasn't careful he would find himself in the dungeon—or dead.

And yet, to his utter disgust, he wanted to believe her, to believe that her fear and distress were as genuine as her outrage at his slighting advances. He did believe in that. Her slap had had real anger behind it. His head was still ringing. But any woman would have reacted with anger to his insults, he reminded himself, especially if the barbs he'd slung at her were accurate and she was trying to convince him otherwise. If he wanted to survive—or retain his sanity—he would do better to get rid of the wench. By the Saints, Matilda herself had warned him!

"I must be out of my mind," he heard himself say instead. "All right, I'll take you to Winchester, but you'll have to get out of the castle on your own and meet me on the road tomorrow."

Isabel's eyes widened in renewed dismay. "But…I can't do that," she protested. "Not alone. I—"

"Why not?" Guy asked inflexibly. "You had the guts to come in here alone. Why so insistent that we leave tonight? Unless there's a party of soldiers waiting for us somewhere along the route. Is that it? Am I to be killed in this mysterious attempt to escape?"

That final question was too much. Isabel replaced the candle on its spike and slumped down on to the bed in despair. "Why won't you believe me?" she whispered pleadingly. "I came to warn you, not to lead you to your death. I swear it on the blood of Christ Jesu."

FitzAlan didn't move for a moment. Then he strode over to the table and picked up the ale jug standing there. Splashing the liquid into a goblet, he carried the drink back to the bed and shoved it brusquely into Isabel's hand.

"Here, drink this," he ordered gruffly. "I'm assuming, of course, that 'tis not poisoned."

This cynical aside went right over Isabel's head.

He waited until she had obediently taken a few sips of the ale, before propping one knee on the bed beside her and jerking her face up to his. "You really believe Matilda would have me killed—tonight?"

"Aye!" Isabel answered fervently, and closed her mind to her conscience. "You don't know her. She—"

"I know what she's capable of. And you would go against your family? You realise what that means? You'll cut yourself off from them completely."

"I know that."

FitzAlan held her face still a moment longer, staring down into her eyes. "Very well," he continued softly. "We leave tonight. I'll take you to Winchester and let the Queen decide what to do with you. But listen well, Lady Isabel de Tracy…" His fingers tightened with a menacing precision that kept her absolutely motionless. "You'll obey my every order. And if you've betrayed me, if I find my head in a noose, I swear to God yours will be right there along with it. Understand?"

His grip relaxed enough to let her nod.

"I understand," she whispered. And suddenly, despite fitzAlan's merciless vow of retribution, a fatalistic calmness descended on her, bringing a return of the cool impassivity that had served her so well in the past. What was another threat, after all? If she failed in her task she would probably be killed anyway, after first watching Edmund die.

When fitzAlan stepped away from her and sat down on a nearby chair, hooking one booted foot over his knee and regarding her with grimly assessing eyes, her mind was clear once more, ready with the plan Matilda had outlined.

"We can leave in an hour or so when everyone is asleep. I know a way through the keep that will take us out near the stables and the postern. The gate is guarded, but there is only one sentry, and no one guards the stable so you should be able to get your horse out." She paused, regarding fitzAlan with slight misgiving at the expression that crossed his face. He didn't appear overly impressed

with the scheme. In fact, he now looked downright scep-
tical.

"One—" he cocked a thumb "—when you're trying
to creep out of a castle *no one* is asleep. Two—" a finger
joined the thumb "—I know another way through the
keep that will take us out to a side-gate which, if we're
lucky, won't be guarded…

"I've been in this part of the country before, remember," he broke off to explain at Isabel's surprised stare.
"I examined this place years ago."

He went back to counting objections off on his fingers
before she could reply. "Three, horses tend to make a
considerable noise when they're disturbed late at night,
and four, if the stable lads didn't hear us every sentry in
the bailey would. Matilda is no fool; this place is well
patrolled."

Isabel looked at him. "Do you have a better idea?"

FitzAlan lifted a derisive eyebrow. "Co-operative little
wench when you get your own way, aren't you." It wasn't
a question. "First, we leave right away—"

"Right away? Are you mad?"

"Probably. Now shut up and listen." He ignored the
affronted expression that crossed Isabel's face at this sardonic rejoinder, and continued. "Getting outside the castle isn't a problem. I'll leave you in the ditch near the
gate I know of and go back for my horse."

"But—"

FitzAlan scowled heavily, and Isabel subsided again.

"If I go openly to the stable no one's going to question
it. 'Tis only furtive behaviour that draws attention. The
stable boys and sentries won't know I'm not supposed to
leave until tomorrow. I can ride out of here quite safely."

"What about me?" she asked in a small voice.

"We'll have to ride double. Once I'm across the drawbridge and out of sight I'll circle around and pick you up. Thank God there's no moat," he tacked on matter-of-factly. "Although if it's still raining the ditch won't be too comfortable. Still, you'll be safer right under the wall until we have to make a run for it."

But Isabel wasn't concerned with her own safety. The thought of Guy walking into the stable as calmly as you please, asking for his horse and riding out in full view of the entire garrison was utterly nerve-racking. She determinedly erased the alarming pictures from her mind.

"Don't worry," he said sardonically, as if privy to her thoughts. "I'll get you to Winchester, my lady. That is, if you're tougher than you look. You're going to have to leave in the clothes you're wearing, and 'twas damned wet and cold out there when I arrived earlier."

Isabel almost laughed. He was worried about the *weather*? She might have been housed in Gloucester Castle for three years, but before that...

No. She wouldn't allow herself to think of the past. Except to be thankful for the strength it had given her.

"A shower of rain won't kill me," she retorted, as that derisive eyebrow lifted again in mocking challenge at her apparent hesitation.

The eyebrow quirked further, but fitzAlan merely rose to his feet and reached for the pack on the floor beside the bed. "In that case," he said blandly, "we only have to worry about the guard outside my door."

Chapter Three

"He patrols the gallery," Isabel explained quickly, not bothering to ask how Guy knew the sentry was there. "We can slip out when he has turned the corner. But the entrance is on the other side of the keep," she added worriedly.

"Aye, as far away as possible from this room," fitz-Alan agreed ironically. "But it doesn't matter. We're going down the north-west staircase and past the garderobe passage."

"Doesn't that...doesn't that lead to the dungeons?" Isabel asked cautiously.

Guy flattened himself against the wall and opened the door a crack before answering. "Aye," he murmured absently. "The passage we want runs right past them."

He closed the door again and looked at Isabel. "There are grilles high up in the walls, so whatever happens don't make a sound or we'll be in a cell so fast your head will spin."

He didn't wait for an answer, but strode forward to snuff out the candle, then edged the door open again. In the dim light from the gallery Isabel saw that all traces of mockery had vanished; his profile was grim and hard, the look of danger very pronounced. She heard the regular tramp of the sentry's boots against the floor. He passed down the gallery, the sound growing fainter.

''Stay close behind me,'' ordered fitzAlan, his voice a mere breath in her ear. ''And go on my signal—*now*!''

Isabel knew that that progress through the castle was destined to become part of her nightmares. She was still trembling half an hour later, as she huddled beneath a small gateway, trying to keep her footing on the wet grass of the embankment.

The descent of the empty turret staircase had been un-eventful enough, but the garderobe passage had seemed to her anxious gaze to teem with a constant flow of traffic. Had everyone chosen that night to drink more than they could hold? she had wondered dementedly. And then, in-stead of hiding until the passage was clear, fitzAlan had given her a shove and told her to wait in the last cubicle.

''Just act as you usually do when you have to visit the privy,'' he had instructed, with a grin that Isabel could only describe as fiendish.

That had been bad enough, but worse was to come.

The sconces burning in the passage had at least pro-vided some light, poor though it was. The narrow staircase that had been revealed when Guy had removed a grille from the wall of the tiny chamber had been so black that Isabel had forgotten her embarrassment at their surround-ings. Only her determination not to betray weakness in front of fitzAlan had enabled her to grit her teeth and step into the seemingly bottomless pit. She had thought long-ingly of the candle left behind in Guy's chamber, but had known better than to mention it.

FitzAlan had replaced the grille and taken her hand. For guidance, Isabel knew. There was no comfort in the hard, impersonal touch of his fingers. Well, that was all right, she'd decided. The man had escape on his mind, not dalliance. The absurd thoughts had got her as far as the foot of that horrible stairway, then she had felt the level floor of another passage beneath her feet. The darkness had been unrelenting.

Isabel shuddered at the memory and wrapped her arms about her waist. She couldn't stop shivering, but whether it was caused by cold or the strain of waiting until fitzAlan won free of the castle she didn't know. She didn't doubt that he would find her. She had discovered that he possessed the eyesight of a cat. How else could he have got them out of the keep? Disorientated by the smothering blackness surrounding them, she herself had completely lost her sense of direction—until they had been midway along the passage.

A constant eerie keening sound, which she had been only vaguely aware of until then, had suddenly risen to a blood-chilling shriek, before being abruptly cut off. A loud clanging, accompanied by a rough, shouted curse, had answered the shriek, and Isabel had known they were passing the dungeons. She had immediately closed her mind to all thought, not even realising how tightly she had been gripping fitzAlan's hand.

Moments later he had led her up a short stairway, through the heavily bolted door at the top, and out of the building, and Isabel had recognised the alley leading to the wash-houses and pressing-rooms, which lay between the towering keep and the curtain wall.

And now here she was outside the gate used only by the laundresses. It was indeed unguarded, apart from the sentry patrolling that section of the wall, since there was no bridge across the ditch, and the land on the other side dropped gradually to meet the swiftly flowing waters of the Severn.

In fine weather the steep, grassy embankment was a colourful patchwork of clothes and sheets spread out to dry. Isabel wondered why she hadn't thought of using the laundry gate herself, before she realised that it would have been kept locked. That thought then raised the interesting question of how fitzAlan had managed to open it—and the door leading up from the dungeons.

She was still pondering on this mystery when a low whistle came from the other side of the ditch. At the same moment, the moon appeared briefly from behind its cover of cloud and Isabel saw the indistinct shape of a horse. She plunged instantly down the slippery incline.

The rain had stopped. Guy knew it would make hard riding easier, but any noise they made would no longer be muffled by the downpour. He had waited until the sentry reached the tower at the end of his beat, knowing, after watching the man from the bailey, that the guard would pause to exchange a few words with another man-at-arms before they separated to retrace their steps.

He estimated that Isabel would have about one minute to negotiate the treacherously wet embankment, cross the ditch, and scramble up the other side. Less, if the men weren't feeling talkative at that particular time. Then they had an open patch of land to cross before reaching the shelter of the woods about a hundred yards away.

It was risky—the sentry would be sure to hear their horse as it picked up speed—but crossing the dangerous waters of the Severn at night was riskier, and would point them in the wrong direction for Winchester. Guy could only hope that Isabel was quick and that the sentry wasn't inclined to shoot at an unseen target.

He heard a splash and a muffled gasp, and grinned faintly. She had reached the ditch. In his experience women did not like getting their feet wet and muddy, and were apt to have plenty to say on the subject. Well, she'd badgered him to let her come along; she could take cold, muddied feet and be thankful it wasn't worse. He rather hoped she would complain so he could point out that incontestable fact.

Isabel didn't even notice her wet feet as she encountered the pools of water left by the rain. The last one had caused her to slip and she had jarred her already sore wrist by flinging out a hand to save herself. Gritting her teeth, she climbed the far slope towards the point where fitzAlan waited, ignoring the throbbing ache.

"Here," he said softly, as she reached the summit.

The moon scudded across a gap in the clouds again, just as Guy reached down to haul Isabel up into the saddle before him. Barely giving her time to find her balance within the circle of his arms, he spurred the horse towards the beckoning trees.

The animal responded at once, quickly lengthening its stride into a gallop. Almost immediately a confused medley of sounds followed. Isabel heard a yell from behind and above them, swiftly running feet, and then a sinister rush of air. An instant later she felt fitzAlan's arm jerk and slacken about her.

"You've been hit," she cried in horrified comprehension.

"Shut up," he grated through clenched teeth. "Just hang on and shut up."

"We have to stop and get that arrow out of your arm."

It wasn't the first time Isabel had said the words. In fact she'd been repeating them every mile or so. She didn't know how far they had come from Gloucester, but surely after an hour at a steady gallop they had put enough distance between themselves and the castle to halt for a few minutes.

It wasn't only the pain fitzAlan must be enduring that worried her. The longer the arrow remained in the wound, the greater the danger of infection. Especially with the rough treatment it was being subjected to. And it was beginning to rain again. That was all he needed, Isabel thought. A chill on top of an arrow wound.

"If your arm festers you might lose it," she pointed out, desperate enough to try shock tactics. After all, he was a warrior. They tended to need two good arms. "Perhaps even die," she tacked on for good measure.

He muttered a curse that Isabel thought it best to ignore. "Worried that you won't make it to Winchester on your own?" he asked unpleasantly.

"I'll make it," she answered, refusing to rise to the bait. "But you won't with an arrow sticking out of you all the way."

"God! *Women!* Think, you little idiot. 'Tis more than likely that we've got a party of Matilda's soldiers after us. Hell, I should have remembered that she makes a habit of greeting emissaries with violence."

"I think 'twas more in the manner of a farewell," Isabel murmured, and then wondered if she was growing light-headed after the events of the night. However, levity would not help her to convince fitzAlan that they were not being followed. "What would be the point in chasing us?" she demanded reasonably. "If the rain gets heavier there won't be any tracks to follow, and, even if there were, 'tis too dark to see them."

There was a moment of silence. Then, sighing slightly, Guy reined in the horse. Before he could change his mind, Isabel slipped to the ground.

He dismounted also, his left arm held stiffly by his side.

Beneath the trees where they stood it was too dark to see much, but Isabel could feel the tension in fitzAlan's body and knew his arm must be hurting terribly. Her own body flinched at the thought.

"I can't reach back far enough to pull it out cleanly." Guy's voice, tight with frustration at his own helplessness, came to her out of the darkness. "You'll have to do it. And for God's sake don't swoon before you've finished the job."

"I'm not the swooning type," Isabel bit out.

"Thank the saints for small mercies. Get a cloth out of my pack, and be ready to press it to the wound as soon as the bolt comes clear."

Isabel obeyed, suppressing various retorts. This was not the time to object to his tone. She had to pull the arrow out. Their very survival might depend on it. And if he was still alert enough to be insulting, his wound might not be so bad after all.

"It will be easier if you sit down," she suggested, gently feeling for the place where the arrow protruded. He sucked in his breath when she found it.

"For once I agree with you," he murmured, sinking to the ground.

"I'll try not to hurt you too much," she said. "But 'tis difficult in the dark."

"Just do it," Guy muttered. "And don't waste any time with a fancy bandage. We have to keep moving. Even if we're not being followed, Matilda's men hold most of the castles in this part of the country. I want to win past Malmesbury tonight before—"

He broke off, clamping his teeth together. The damn thing was in deep, he thought, as Isabel's little hand closed around the shaft of the arrow. He was probably going to start bleeding like a pig the instant the barb was out, and he only hoped—

His thoughts were abruptly cut off by a blinding flash of pain. His whole arm seemed to be afire, a searing contrast to the cold sweat he felt break out on his brow. Then he felt a cloth being held against the wound. The pressure only added to the fiery torture. "Are you satisfied now?" he growled. "Can we be on our way?"

"I hope this is clean," Isabel muttered, again ignoring his temper, knowing pain was causing him to lash out like any wounded animal.

"Never mind. Just bandage the thing and be done with it."

"You can't mean to keep riding," she protested, firmly winding the cloth about his arm. "You need to rest, and your arm should be washed and tended properly."

"And just how do you propose to do that?" The question was savage. "Do you see a convenient castle near by?"

"Then we'll just have to stop at the first one," Isabel declared. "At least I'll be able to see what I'm doing."

"Stop at the first one?" he repeated disbelievingly. "Do you think they're going to have a sign out, telling us which side they're on?"

"There must be a village somewhere," she insisted, tying a final knot and stepping back. Her foot nudged the discarded arrow and, unthinkingly, she bent to pick it up. "Where are we anyway?"

Guy rose slowly to his feet. "Heading towards Winchester," he replied unhelpfully. "Get on the horse."

"Very well," sighed Isabel, obeying only because she knew they had to find shelter, and there was none where they stood. She stuffed the arrow absently into Guy's pack, gathered up the reins, and mounted. "I can afford to wait. At the rate you're going, you'll probably swoon before too long.''

''I'm not the swooning type,'' snapped fitzAlan, quoting her own words back at her. ''So don't count on it.'' He mounted behind her and ruthlessly removed the reins from her hands.

Isabel sighed again as the horse moved off at his signal, breaking easily into a canter. Now she'd made him angry again.

An hour passed in silence, and then another. The horse had gradually slowed as it tired, until the animal now moved forward at a resigned walk.

We must be well past Malmesbury by this time, Isabel thought. But the fortress there was an outpost, virtually surrounded by enemy castles. It would be miles yet, probably another day of travelling, before they reached safer country, and even if fitzAlan stubbornly insisted that he could travel the horse wouldn't go forever.

And the weather had grown steadily worse. With the disappearance of the moonlight, they had had to abandon the forest and find the road. It was easier to follow in the darkness, but exposed them to the full force of the wind and rain. The relentless downpour had soon saturated the cloak Guy had wrapped about them. She wouldn't have to worry about his wound, Isabel decided. They were both going to die of exposure.

''Or lung rot,'' she grumbled aloud.

''What?''

His deep voice after miles of silence made Isabel jump.

''Nothing,'' she answered. ''I was just… Why are we stopping?''

''There,'' Guy said very quietly, as the weary horse plodded to a standstill and let its head droop against the driving rain.

Isabel peered ahead. At first she only saw the dark shape of the forest beside the road, then as her eyes adjusted to a faint lifting of the gloom a narrow laneway appeared between the trees.

"Do you think it leads to a village?" she whispered.

"Perhaps. 'Tis too narrow a road to be guarded by a castle." FitzAlan seemed to hesitate for a moment, then turned his mount on to the barely discernible path. "The horse needs to rest," he said, as though in explanation.

And so do you, thought Isabel. But she didn't dare say it.

A quarter of a mile further on the lane widened out into a small clearing in the trees. Several small huts stood in a roughly circular pattern, as dark and silent as the rest of the countryside.

"What are we going to do?" asked Isabel, still whispering. "Knock on a door and ask for shelter?"

"No need," returned fitzAlan aloud. "The doors are all open. Look. The place is deserted."

He was right, Isabel realised, staring hard at the black hole that marked the entrance to the nearest hut. Glancing around at the rest, she could see that none of the small hovels was secured against intruders. The doors were all wide open, and one hung drunkenly from its rawhide straps. It must be almost dawn, she thought absently; an hour ago she had not been able to see a thing.

Guy urged the horse over to the largest of the mean shelters and dismounted. The second his cloak was gone, Isabel was buffeted by the heavy rain. She slipped hurriedly out of the saddle, and then had to grab for it when her legs threatened to buckle. She was numb with cold, and bone-weary.

FitzAlan was fumbling in his pack. "Here," he said,

producing his flint. "Go inside and see if you can find a light. I have to tend to my horse."

Isabel eyed the inhospitable rectangle of darkness in front of her. "What if there is someone in there?" she asked warily.

"Then we can spend what's left of the night discussing the lousy weather with them," was the disagreeable reply to this nervous question. "Use your head, woman. If the villagers were driven out today, the rain would bring them back. They wouldn't spend a night like this in the forest with women and children to think of."

Isabel wanted to ask why not. After all, fitzAlan hadn't seemed to worry about exposing *her* to the elements. Why would peasants be more considerate of their womenfolk? Unfortunately another possibility occurred to her which drove the question of chivalry out of her mind.

"They might all be dead," she whispered.

To her surprise he answered this quite gently. "There would be bodies out here as well as inside if there had been a massacre. They wouldn't all have been killed in their beds. Go on, you're starting to look like a drowned kitten."

Charming, thought Isabel indignantly, as she cautiously felt her way into the hut. How could he tell what she looked like in the darkness? Though dawn was approaching, he had only loomed as a huge shadow to *her*.

"Eyesight of a cat," she muttered aloud, then immediately uttered a pained yelp as she bumped into a rough-hewn table. Her hand skidded across the wooden surface and collided with a small round object. A bowl, she decided, exploring with fingers that were almost too frozen to feel anything, with something inside it that felt like a tiny lump of candlewax—and a wick.

"Saints be praised," she murmured. But, of course,

there was nothing on which she could strike the flint. A fireplace? No, a peasant's hovel wouldn't have such a thing, but surely a fire would have been needed for cooking?

Dropping to her hands and knees, Isabel crawled gingerly forward across the earthen floor, clutching the candle-bowl. Despite fitzAlan's assurances that she wouldn't encounter a corpse, she held her breath with trepidation every time she swung her free hand in a groping semicircle. At last she felt stones. A small circle of them, enclosing a heap of cold ashes and dried leaves.

Within seconds Isabel had a twig alight, its crumbling leaves quickly shrivelling in tiny flames, but with fire enough to light the candle. However, her heart sank when she examined the bowl more closely. The wick lay almost flat in a perilously small amount of wax. She had to find something else before its feeble light expired.

Shielding the flame carefully from the draught sweeping in through the open door, Isabel glanced about the single room. It was small, but seemed surprisingly well stocked for a peasant's shack. The table stood to one side of the doorway with a stool beside it. Another stool lay on its side some distance away. On the other side of the stone circle, against the wall, a wide bench for sleeping was covered with a thin woollen blanket, and high up on another wall a shelf had been fashioned, hand-made and crooked, but functional nevertheless, and holding an assortment of objects and jars that drew Isabel at once.

Her spirits rose considerably at the sight of an uneven blob of wax. She had seen such lumps before. Whoever had lived here had been given the remnants of used candles and had melted the stubs down to make a crude light. Which meant, she reasoned thoughtfully, that there was a castle or town near by where one of the vanished occupants of the hut had probably been employed.

She decided against mentioning this little fact to fitzAlan. He would probably insist on leaving again. And she refused to go another step until his arm was properly cared for, Isabel vowed, as she dug a small hole in the top of the misshapen lump with her thumbnail. She carefully poured the melting wax around the wick into the larger candle, and balanced it in the bowl.

"There," she said to herself, replacing the bowl on the table and feeling inordinately pleased with the result. "My lord fitzAlan is not the only one who can be useful."

But the lonely sound of her own voice in the emptiness of the hut immediately made Isabel wonder why Guy was taking so long. He'd had time enough to get ten horses under shelter. Had he collapsed? Should she venture out to search for him?

A mental picture of fitzAlan lying senseless out in the rain sent Isabel hurrying to the door. Guy met her on the threshold, only just managing to avoid knocking her over. He dropped his pack, unbuckled his sword and propped it against the wall, then turned to rake Isabel with eyes as sharp as the wicked-looking blade behind him.

"Going somewhere?" he queried interestedly.

"We'll need wood for a fire," returned Isabel with aplomb, not about to admit that she had been worried about him.

That piercing blue gaze made a comprehensive sweep of the room and fixed unerringly on an untidy pile of wood in one corner. "I think the dry stuff will be better, don't you?" he asked smoothly.

Taking Isabel's disconcerted silence for assent, Guy turned and pushed the door closed. The abrupt cessation of the draughts blowing into the room was a welcome relief, although Isabel was so chilled by now that she was conscious of no great change in the temperature. They had to have warmth immediately. Her gown was almost wet through and water dripped from her long hair to the floor. FitzAlan didn't look any drier, she thought critically, his blond hair darkened with rain, his tunic drenched, and his boots squelching with every step.

"I'll build a fire," he said, not mentioning the light Isabel had managed to produce.

She made a face at his back, but her expression quickly changed to concern when she caught sight of his arm. The rough bandage was saturated, and not only with rain.

"You're bleeding," she cried. "Leave the fire for the moment. Let me tend to your arm."

"It's been bleeding on and off all night," he responded coolly. "Another few minutes won't make any difference, and we're both soaked."

He took the candle from the table and bent over the fireplace, setting the twigs ablaze. The sudden warmth, meagre though it was, drew Isabel like a magnet. She held her frozen hands to the flames as Guy fed the fire with more kindling before placing a log from the woodpile on to the blaze.

"It looks as if they were interrupted at their meal," he remarked, righting the overturned stool and using it to indicate a soiled trencher and several dusty earthenware mugs on the table. He pulled the table closer to the fire and draped his cloak over it to dry, but his movements lacked the usual lithe, co-ordinated strength Isabel had hitherto seen in him, and she noticed that he wasn't using his left arm at all.

"Here," she said gently, pushing forward the stool he had set down. "Sit near the fire and let me bandage your arm properly."

"In a minute. Get out of that wet gown."

The brusque command brought her widening eyes up to his.

"There's no need to look at me as though I'm about to rape you," he barked impatiently. "I didn't ask you to strip to the skin."

Isabel went completely white. Even in the dim, flickering light cast by the fire Guy saw all the colour wash out of her face. He wondered what the hell was wrong with her now, but it was becoming strangely difficult to think clearly. And the cramped hut was becoming too damned hot.

Stepping away from the fire and dismissing the odd behaviour of his charge, Guy removed the makeshift bandage and his sodden tunic and undershirt. The fact that he could barely move his wounded arm didn't improve his mood. When he turned back to drape the garments alongside his cloak, and saw that Isabel was still clothed and beginning to shiver visibly with cold, his precarious patience snapped.

"Strip!" he roared.

She flinched once, then started to obey, unfastening the ties at the neck of her gown with shaking fingers. Guy watched her through dangerously slitted eyes.

There was no lecherous anticipation in his expression, however, Isabel realised. He was doing it to punish her. For not immediately obeying him, or for her very presence? she wondered briefly, then gave a mental shrug. What did it matter? She had survived this indignity before; she could survive it again.

And her hesitation hadn't even been caused by the grim memory his words had stirred up. Common sense had already told her they had to get out of their sodden clothes, but, for an unexpected instant, the sight of fitzAlan half naked, the firelight burnishing tanned skin over strong muscle and bone, had made her suddenly, acutely, aware of the differences between them. The differences between male and female; between hard masculine power and yielding feminine softness. He was so much bigger than her. So much stronger. He could force her to do anything. And yet the vulnerability she felt seemed strangely *inward*—as though danger lay within her own body, and not in the raw strength of the man before her.

Shaken off balance by her startling thoughts, Isabel glanced away, stepping out of her gown and hanging it over the table. She sent up a brief prayer of thanks that her shift was still dry, although it could hardly be described as a significant covering. The once fine linen had thinned and shrunk with frequent laundering, with the result that the garment only reached just past her knees and did little to hide the curves of her body.

She could still feel fitzAlan's eyes on her and flushed slightly, steeling herself before she could look at him again, and fully expecting a remark that was sure to be unpleasant at best. She wasn't disappointed.

"You don't have to play the shrinking virgin for me," he mocked. "I'm sure you've stripped willingly enough for the men who have enjoyed your favours in the past."

Quick resentment surged through Isabel, deepening the colour in her cheeks. She let it build, momentarily forgetting the dangers in arguing with him. Right now there was more danger in the strange, yielding weakness that had just taken her by surprise. "You don't know anything about my past," she cried. "I've n—"

"Don't bother with the usual outraged denials," he interrupted scornfully. "You knew what to expect when you came to my room tonight. What's more, I could have had you. I felt your response. If you hadn't decided to retaliate for my plain-speaking, you would have been willing to pay the price for my escort to Winchester.''

Another affronted retort rose to her lips, but bewildered honesty forced Isabel to choke it back at the last moment. He was right in a backhanded sort of way. The Empress had ordered her to do whatever was necessary in order to leave with fitzAlan, and if she hadn't been so angry and confused that she had forgotten the threat to Edmund she would have complied.

But an odd sense of hurt washed over her at the scornful sound Guy made at her silent acquiescence. Ridiculous, she knew. He wasn't to know the truth, and yet, against all reason, she wanted him to believe in her innocence. Fool, she chastised herself, angrier than ever. Wishes would not help in this situation. Let him believe what he liked.

Isabel lifted her chin, pride and defiance turning her eyes a stormy grey as she stared back at fitzAlan coldly.

''If we had more time I'd take you up on that challenge you're issuing, my lady,'' he growled, in a voice that had gone dark and soft. ''But, until we do, you can make yourself useful by binding up this hole in my arm before I give you the pleasure of bleeding to death.''

His death, give her pleasure? A sudden spasm of pain pierced her heart, subduing her anger. She quickly suppressed it. She would not allow his insults to touch her. She would not care what fitzAlan thought of her. He was a callous brute, and if she didn't need his protection on the journey to Winchester she wouldn't care if he bled to…

But she couldn't finish the thought. Despite her outrage and hurt, Isabel knew she *did* care if fitzAlan lived or died.

Turning away, she determinedly refused to acknowledge why. Exploring that path would take her to the edge of a precipice over which she did not wish to step. Instead she would tend his arm, make sure she did not become a hindrance by falling ill herself, and refuse to acknowledge his barbed remarks. She knew how it was done. You just made your mind very cold and distant. You retreated to a place where harshness or cruelty couldn't touch you. A place where you felt nothing.

Only…this time it was not so easy.

She had drawn back from a direct confrontation again, Guy realised. He was beginning to recognise the signs. Her face was remote and serene; her eyes showed only calm resolve as she began to inspect the jars on the shelf.

"What are you looking for?" he snapped, perversely unwilling to let her resume her cool composure. He kicked the stool further away from the fire and sat down. The action didn't seem to stop the room from spinning. Guy wondered vaguely when he'd first noticed the wavering movements of the walls.

"Ale," she answered briefly, turning with a jug in her hand and sniffing experimentally. "It smells a bit stale, but there's no wine so it will have to do. Come closer to the fire."

"I'm not cold," he said shortly, bending to unwind the thongs from his boots.

The words caused tentacles of fright to curl around Isabel's stomach. He should have been as frozen as she was herself. Blessed Mother, was he feverish already? She looked at Guy more closely. He did appear flushed and his eyes held a strange glitter. And she had nothing, Isabel remembered. No herbs, no clean linen, no water. Unless…

Searching through a scattered pile of utensils, she found an empty pail, opened the door, and shoved it outside.

Water, at least, could be obtained, she told herself sternly, before the frightening sensation of helplessness got the better of her.

"Leave the door open a little. 'Tis like a bread oven in here."

Isabel ignored the curt order. "You have a slight fever, I think," she replied with the quiet firmness she would have used towards any sick person. "I'll have some water for you to drink soon, but you must keep warm. Now sit still and let me see to your arm."

"Aye, my lady," he responded with mocking compliance. But Isabel saw genuine humour flash briefly in his blue gaze.

She turned her attention to his injury, relieved to see that he was now losing very little blood, and that although the area about the wound was reddened and irritated the edges of the gash where the arrow had entered were not jagged, which would have delayed healing.

She was about to report this piece of good news when fitzAlan took the ale jug from her, and, before she could protest, tilted it to his lips for a healthy swig. He then up-ended the rest over his wound. She heard the air hiss between his teeth at the bite of the liquid.

"That should clean it," he grated, his teeth still clenched. He tossed the jug aside and reached for the discarded bandage with his good arm. "What does it look like?"

"I was about to tell you," retorted Isabel, "before you applied your own method of healing. It looks clean enough, but don't be surprised if your fever gets worse after that primitive treatment. It should have been washed with water and then a salve applied."

"Do you see one?" he asked sarcastically, shoving the soiled cloth at her.

Isabel eyed it with disfavour. "No," she admitted, unabashed. "But that doesn't mean I'm going to add to your foolishness by tying that filthy rag over the wound."

Ignoring the suddenly bright gleam in his eyes, she bent and grabbed the hem of her shift, tearing the flimsy material easily until she had enough for a bandage.

"Foolishness?" Guy repeated with a derisive laugh. "You think there's been *anything* that makes sense about tonight? I still haven't decided if you're really afraid of Matilda, or whether you have some other reason for leaving her."

Isabel refused to answer. She finished tying the bandage, stepped away from him, and indicated the bench. "You'd better rest if you want to be well enough to travel tomorrow," she suggested coldly.

FitzAlan stood up, immediately looming over her in the confines of the hut. Even the fact that he staggered slightly didn't lessen his menacing impact on Isabel's senses. "I intend to rest," he agreed, an unexpectedly devilish smile crossing his face. "With you."

Isabel reminded herself that he was mocking her, that his wickedly attractive smile didn't affect her one bit, and that keeping her own expression politely aloof wasn't at all difficult. It was less easy to convince herself that the thought of lying down on the bench with fitzAlan, with hardly a stitch of clothing between them, didn't scare the wits out of her.

"I am going to dry my hair," she announced, pleased that her voice sounded so calm and resolute. "Then I am going to fetch some water. Then I am going to sleep by the fire."

"You're damn well going to sleep with me," he countered bluntly, disregarding this comprehensive schedule. "So I can keep an eye on you. Don't worry," he tacked on sardonically at her rebellious expression. "Your questionable virtue will be safe enough. I've a feeling I'm going to need two sound arms for the task of taming you, my lady Isabel. 'Tis something I shall look forward to."

"You'll have a long wait," flashed Isabel, and immediately cursed herself when fitzAlan grinned again. How did he manage to ruin all her fine resolutions to remain cool and distant? she asked herself. She had never found it difficult before. It really wasn't fair. First the man insulted her, and now he seemed to be taking a perverse delight in taunting her.

Taking a deep, steadying breath, she tried to reason with him. "My lord, I am not such an idiot as to go fleeing into that downpour. How far, indeed, do you think I would get alone? Believe whatever you like of me, but please—"

Her assurances fell on deaf ears. Not giving her a chance to finish, fitzAlan's good arm shot out and snagged Isabel about the waist. She was lifted against his bare chest as if she weighed no more than a feather, the shock of his warm skin and the slight roughness of short, curling hair against her palms rendering her abruptly speechless. Taking a step back, he flung the blanket aside, cursing aloud as the movement wrenched his arm, and lowered them both to the hard bench.

By the time Isabel realised her position, it was too late to do anything about it. She was trapped between fitzAlan's solid body and the wall at her back. And when she opened her mouth to protest at this treatment she saw that her objections would have to wait. He had turned on to his stomach, flung his right arm over her—to make sure she didn't escape, Isabel assumed indignantly—and fallen instantly asleep.

Chapter Four

Isabel wished she could find the oblivion of sleep as easily, but though her body ached after the unaccustomed hours in the saddle her mind refused to rest. The hard bench under her wasn't conducive to restful slumber either, although she had known worse beds. No, it was not discomfort keeping her from sleep. She was too on edge, too nervous, too aware that their shelter was easily accessible and fitzAlan hurt.

She turned her head to study him, close beside her. Very close. She could see the dark gold lashes feathering his broad cheekbones, and the tiny lines radiating out from the corners of his eyes. His face looked slightly less hard in repose, but, even sleeping, he was still intimidating. That aura of compelling strength remained. Despite his wounded condition, Isabel had the distinct impression that to awaken fitzAlan would be dangerous. Rather like rousing a sleeping wolf, she thought fancifully, remembering her earlier comparison. Only a fool would risk doing so. A sensible person respected the sleeping beast and crept away.

So why did she want to stay? Why did she wonder if the wolf could be tamed?

Her eyes drifted from his face to the smoothly muscled shoulder near her cheek. Aye, dangerous. The arm lying across her was relaxed and heavy, but Isabel knew it could become an iron band, trapping her in an instant.

Her breath caught as a strange little *frisson* of excitement slid from her throat to her toes at the thought. The sudden sharp urge to lift her hand, to test the strength of that broad shoulder with her fingers, was almost irresistible. Isabel trembled, half afraid, half shocked, at such shameless, hitherto unknown longings. And yet still unwilling to creep away, still wanting to arouse the sleeping wolf, wanting...

What? she asked herself almost fearfully. To feel that firm, beautifully drawn mouth on hers in tenderness rather than anger? To know the meaning of the weakness that had sapped the strength from her limbs when she had seen him half stripped earlier? To lie in his arms?

Isabel stared at Guy's face, her heart beginning to pound. Had she run mad? Had she not already decided that five and a half years of girlhood dreams bore little resemblance to the harsh warrior beside her? That a fleeting encounter in the past, no matter how romantic, had no place in the bleak present? Of course she had.

He was no different from the other men she knew. Perhaps not as brutal, although she had no doubt he could be if the situation warranted, but definitely arrogant, intimidating, ruthless. At best he did not trust her. In truth, he seemed to dislike her intensely. And if he knew of the wanton pictures chasing one another through her head his insulting opinion of her would no doubt be confirmed.

He was not to know that those pictures appalled her, that she had never imagined herself capable of such thoughts. On the contrary—she had sworn never to marry, never to expose herself to the mercy of a man's rough or abusive treatment. For years she had turned a calm, expressionless face on the world—quiet, distant, not even blatantly cold, because that would have been a challenge to some men. She had learned how to protect her emotions and thus her body.

So why couldn't she erase from her memory the image of fitzAlan, tall and strong and golden in the firelight? Powerfully, overwhelmingly male. He had looked almost...*primitive*, she thought. And she had *felt* primitive. As though she had been nothing more than a vulnerable female creature in the presence of her mate.

A five-year old memory did not explain *that* feeling.

Isabel wrenched her eyes away from fitzAlan and glared at the wall. She must be very tired to give room to such feeble-minded notions. She would go to sleep. No one would be abroad in this weather. They were safe enough for the present.

Clinging to this assurance, Isabel listened to the rain beating down on the other side of the wall and refused to think about her peculiar reactions to fitzAlan any longer. Tomorrow, when she was rested, she would be her sensible self again. In the meantime, there were far more practical things to consider. She would retrieve the pail soon, she promised herself, wriggling into a more comfortable position on the wooden bench. And the fire would need another log.

Her movement seemed to disturb fitzAlan. He shifted restlessly and Isabel raised herself cautiously to peer at his bandaged arm. No matter what else she thought of him, she could not ignore his wound.

There was no blood on the bandage, but as she glanced across the broad sweep of his back Isabel realised suddenly how close Guy had come to being killed. A few more inches to the right and the shot would have been fatal. The knowledge made her shiver.

Frowning thoughtfully, she pulled the thin blanket over them both and lay down again, her mind now busy on another track. Had the sentry panicked at the sound of a galloping horse and fired off a lucky shot, or was there a more sinister design?

The disturbing question brought the scene in Matilda's chamber flashing into Isabel's mind, and the odd looks exchanged between the Empress and her men. She had sensed the undercurrents in the room at the time, but had been too tense and afraid to take much notice. But now…she had to wonder. Had she been used for a purpose other than the stated one? Had Brien fitzCount's aim been to appease Matilda by killing Guy while he was apparently escaping, sooner than allow the Empress to murder her guest out of hand? Guy himself had suspected as much, she remembered.

Isabel shook her head. It didn't make sense. Why go to all the trouble of providing her with information about Rainald, which she could easily have related to fitzAlan? No, that wasn't right either. Matilda would be sure that any knowledge Isabel possessed was safe as long as Edmund lived. That silent communication had come with the mention of her brother's name, after all.

For a few minutes longer Isabel tried to sort out hard facts from vague suspicions, with little success. FitzAlan's misgivings had aroused her own unease about the Empress's true motives, but she was growing too sleepy to reason it out now. The warmth of the small hut was finally melting the frozen ice in her veins, and the ceaseless rain had become a distant cradle-song. Even the vague awareness of her assorted aches and bruises no longer had the power to keep her alert.

Unknowingly nestled against Guy's shoulder, Isabel slept.

* * *

There was heat and gentleness and safety. And she was floating.

Floating? That was strange, thought Isabel drowsily. She must be dreaming, but surely she had only just gone to sleep. From a vague distance she was aware that the rain continued unabated, but it couldn't touch her. She was so deliciously warm. Surrounded by warmth. Enfolded, sheltered, protected by warmth.

Her lashes fluttered, but it was too much of an effort to open her eyes. She just wanted to sink back into the dream and give in to the lovely floating sensation. The gentle caress of warm lips pressing her eyelids closed seemed part of the fantasy. So did the low, husky whisper accompanying those feather-light kisses.

"That's it, sweetheart. Just relax and let me love you. Don't run away this time. Not this time…"

Run away? How could she? Isabel wondered hazily. You couldn't run away if you were dreaming…at least if you did 'twas only part of the dream…not real… Somehow it seemed very important to make that clear.

"'Tis only a dream…" she whispered, almost inaudibly.

"Then dream with me, darling girl. Stay with me. You always disappear. Don't disappear… I need you so… I've needed you…" The words faded as those warm lips closed gently but firmly over her mouth.

The dream shifted with startling speed. Suddenly Isabel was no longer floating, she was falling instead, the sensation so swift and unexpected that she flung up her hands to save herself, and found them clinging to the source of the heat above her. It didn't help. She continued to fall.

Her head was spinning, she couldn't breathe, and when she clung tighter the kiss changed, as though keeping pace with the dream. Warm gentleness became heated demand. Against the hard, insistent pressure of Guy's mouth, Isabel's lips parted and a whimper of surrender sounded deep in her throat. But that was all right, she thought vaguely. She could surrender because it was her knight kissing her. She wasn't sure just how she knew that. But it didn't matter, did it? Because this was only a dream. Wasn't it?

She couldn't think properly. Her mouth was being taken with a possessive intensity that obliterated thought and left only sensation. It was almost terrifying—and yet wildly exciting. It felt so real. Surely dreams weren't *this* real?

Still drugged with sleep, struggling to free herself from her half-dreaming state, Isabel's eyes snapped open just as Guy released her mouth. She stared dazedly up into a wild, glittering gaze that held her helplessly captive.

"I'm not—" she tried to say, but his mouth descended on hers again, quick and hard.

"Don't talk," he commanded hoarsely. "Whenever I speak, you vanish." He groaned and held her closer. "Whenever I touch you, you leave me…Isabel… Isabel…"

He lowered his head to bury his mouth against her neck. His lips were fiercely hot, melting every bone in Isabel's body, despite the dawning knowledge fighting its way up through the mists of sleep still clinging to her brain.

Didn't it hurt his arm to hold her like this? she wondered distractedly, but then another tremulous whimper escaped her as the hand holding her against him moved to cover her breast. The heat of his caressing fingers through the thin linen of her shift made Isabel gasp. He was burning her. And the fire went straight to a place deep inside her body that she hadn't even known existed until this moment. Then her breath was lost completely when Guy's mouth left her throat and closed hotly over the tender peak cupped in his hand.

She had never known such deliriously exquisite sensations, never known that one could feel like this and still want more. The pleasure was so intense that Isabel thought she was going to swoon. A soundless cry parted her lips and her body arched, instinctively seeking his, but when his hand lifted to unfasten the neck of her shift and she heard a sharp, tearing sound a shaft of fear lanced through the delirium, wrenching her abruptly into full wakefulness.

"No! Wait—"

"Don't stop me," he pleaded thickly. "God, Isabel, please don't stop me. I don't care if 'tis only a dream. I—"

"But it isn't," she cried, frantic now as her words brought home the enormity of what was happening. "'Tis real!" She pushed against fitzAlan's massive chest, her fear escalating into panic when she saw the hot, unfocused glitter in his eyes. Suddenly the significance of the warmth surrounding her exploded on to her consciousness. Her hands slid up to his shoulders, his skin dry and hot to her touch.

He was burning up with fever, probably not even fully aware of what he was doing or saying.

"My lord..." she quavered, trying to form a plea in her mind.

His eyes went hard, though the fiery heat remained undimmed. The combination was frightening. Mother of God, how was she to get free of him? He was between her and the edge of the bench and was half lying over her anyway, imprisoning her between his arms. One long, heavily muscled leg had been thrown over hers, pinning her beneath him. She would never be able to fight him off physically. She was trapped.

"Are you going to refuse to pay the price, after all?" fitzAlan grated harshly.

Isabel's eyes flashed back to his face. Surely he hadn't been using that tone with her a moment ago? Bewilderedly she struggled to remember the words Guy had been muttering, but they had been lost in the half-sleeping state which had dulled her mind, and, later, barely heard over the unfamiliar demands of newly awakened desire. All she could recall with any certainty was the tender, soothing voice in a dream that was rapidly becoming a nightmare. Oh, why had she fallen asleep?

"I didn't...you can't...you're out of your mind with fever," she stammered wildly.

"I'm out of my mind, all right," he snarled. "Out of my mind for wanting a traitorous little witch like you. But once I have you, by God, that will be the end of it!"

"No! You don't know what you're saying. You don't know what you're doing."

FitzAlan laughed unsteadily. "Oh, I know what I'm doing, little deceiver. Don't worry, I know what I'm doing. Before I'm finished you'll want me as much as I want you."

"I won't. I'll fight you," she cried in instant denial, wondering in despair if she could actually bring herself to hurt him to save herself. She might have to, Isabel decided, as he laughed again and his hand drew aside the neck of her shift, exposing the delicate lines of her throat and shoulders. "Would you rape me?" she choked, twisting aside in an attempt to avoid his seeking mouth.

But she felt his lips, hot and hard, caress the soft skin

he had bared. "It won't be rape, sweetheart," he murmured against the side of her neck, and, with bewildering suddenness, his voice was a soft murmur again. "Do you think I would hurt you, my lovely girl? Not you, Isabel. Never you."

Blessed Mother, should she try another appeal while he seemed more gentle...?

The thought never had a chance to become action. Isabel had one quick glimpse of the fire smouldering in fitzAlan's eyes as he lifted his head, then his mouth came down on hers in a kiss of such male dominance that she went completely limp. The yielding weakness was total, sapping her will and her strength.

He was right, a distant voice in her mind whispered mockingly. He wouldn't have to rape her. She was his. She had always been his. She might fight him, resent him, even hate him for condemning her on Matilda's word alone, but she couldn't deny his need or her longing to satisfy it. She had never felt like this before in her entire life, knew she would never feel like this for any other man. On some deep, primitive level, sensed earlier when she had gazed at him across the fire, she belonged to him.

But at what price?

The silent question was as instinctive as her moment of surrender, hardly a conscious thought, but it was enough to wrench Isabel back from the precipice. Enough to remind her of the consequences of submitting so easily to a man who despised her.

"No!" she sobbed aloud, when fitzAlan freed her mouth to rain kisses across her face and into her hair. The word was barely more than an anguished gasp, but Isabel felt strength begin to seep back into her. That instant of frightening acceptance was pushed violently aside, buried deep, deeper than her memories of a carefree childhood, deeper than the terrifying nightmare that had followed.

"I won't let you do this," she panted, pushing at fitzAlan's shoulders. Her desperation was now so great that she momentarily forgot his wound, striking out at him blindly. "You already hate me. You won't make me hate myself!"

There was no answer. Not even a movement to show that fitzAlan had heard her fierce protest. Gasping for breath, Isabel managed to twist her head away from him and look around.

He was out cold, his body a dead weight on hers, his face buried in the tangled skeins of her long hair.

During the countless terrifying minutes before she managed to wriggle free and scramble off the bench, Isabel neither knew nor cared whether it was she or his fever that had caused fitzAlan's loss of consciousness. She was too grateful for the reprieve. Her head smarted painfully where several strands of hair had been wrenched out by her violent struggles, the fragile material of her shift had torn further, and she was shaking uncontrollably and unable to stand upright. But she was free.

Heedless of the rough dirt floor, Isabel dragged herself over to the fire and crouched beside it, crying with mingled fright and relief. The racking sobs didn't last long; she was too afraid that fitzAlan would recover and come after her. But when she brushed her hair out of her face and peered cautiously over at the bench Guy lay in the same position, completely unmoving. If it hadn't been for his harsh, laboured breathing, Isabel would not have known that he still lived.

Her breath caught on another sob. Holy saints, the nightmare wasn't over yet. But fever, at least, was an opponent she could fight, and action would stop her from thinking. She would *not* think. She dared not!

Rising unsteadily to her feet, determinedly keeping her mind on what she needed to care for fitzAlan, Isabel opened the door of the hut. Daylight struck her eyes, momentarily blinding her. Then, realising that she was getting wet, she grabbed the pail and slammed the door shut again on the incessant rain.

The noise aroused fitzAlan. He muttered and stirred, flinging his wounded arm out, but his eyes remained closed.

Isabel crouched against the wall, watching him as though he were in truth the wolf her imagination had conjured up, and waiting until her fluttering pulse had steadied before moving again. Only when Guy had been still for several minutes did she cross to the bench and set the pail down. Her heart sank at the sight of fresh blood on the bandage, but she set about unwinding the strip of linen, praying that she had not opened up fitzAlan's wound too badly in her frantic efforts to escape. Praying even more fervently that, when he awoke, he would remember nothing of his fever-induced passion.

And it must have been the fever, Isabel decided a long time later, when she at last had time to sit down and rest. She knew, of course, that men were driven by lusts of the flesh, desires that they satisfied with little or no regard for the females they wanted, but, strangely enough, she would not have considered fitzAlan to be a man to lose control of himself for that reason. Especially with a woman for whom he felt nothing but contempt. He seemed too strong, too self-contained. And his reputation for honour was apparently widespread enough to have reached Gloucester.

But what did she really know of him? Isabel asked

herself broodingly. As Adele had pointed out, even men of integrity could behave differently when it came to women. The thought depressed her, but she told herself it was only weariness. She was exhausted; more so because of the alarmed way she had sprung out of reach whenever Guy had become restless, than from the number of times she had sponged him down in an attempt to cool his fever. Though he appeared no longer bent on seduction, nor even aware of her seeming absence, Isabel knew she was no match for his strength. He could have hurt her badly without meaning to.

When the burning heat in his body had at last broken, she had concentrated on his arm, washing the wound constantly by setting a bowl outside to catch the clean rainwater and then replacing it with the pail, changing the two receptacles again and again. Her whole body ached, but the treatment seemed to have worked. Guy was now sleeping more naturally, and his skin felt only slightly warm.

But though tiredness dragged at her mind and body, Isabel couldn't relax. The passing hours brought other tasks in their wake. She was hungry, and there was fitz-Alan's horse to check also, she remembered, reaching for her dress. It was still damp, though not uncomfortably so, and Isabel quickly pulled it over her head. After ensuring that the fire was safe and that Guy was still deeply asleep, she crossed to the door and slipped quietly outside.

The daylight, overcast and grey though it was, made her blink after the dimness of the hovel and caused her to hesitate while she got her bearings. The village was so small that it could hardly be described as such. There were only three huts and a couple of three-walled structures that Isabel had taken for huts last night. They were piled high with branches and logs, and the very old remains of a bonfire lay a few yards away.

Of course, she thought, still clinging to the dubious shelter of the doorway. Charcoal burners. They would live here while they gathered the leafless branches of the surrounding trees and prepared their charcoal for winter use in the local castle or town. At this hour the little clearing should be abustle with activity, huge mounds of logs being erected, smoke from the fires rising into the misty air.

Isabel glanced warily around at the silent forest, seeing nothing but dripping trees, ablaze with the autumn colours that even the dismal weather could not dim. Piles of fallen leaves carpeted the forest floor with gold, and the stillness was broken only by the steady rain. Whoever had been here had long since gone.

The air smelled clean and fresh after the smoky little hut, and she took a deep breath, feeling her spirits lift. In that moment, despite the grim task awaiting her in Winchester, she savoured the knowledge that she was free of Gloucester Castle with its dark atmosphere of frustrated anger and intrigue. Few there would miss her, she knew. Adele. Richard Fiennes, perhaps. But they would soon forget. She had been a silent, remote member of the household, retiring into the shadows as much as possible, quickly forgotten.

The whicker of Guy's horse interrupted her thoughts, and Isabel hurried across the clearing to the hut where the animal was tethered. It was a big grey, strong but fleet, built for speed. Isabel remembered the huge black warhorse fitzAlan had ridden before and wondered what had happened to it.

"Do you know?" she asked the grey. He flicked his ears at her and snorted politely.

"You're a lot friendlier than your master," Isabel informed the horse. "And you carried us both very bravely last night." She stood stroking the animal and murmuring to it for a moment longer before glancing around the hut.

There was evidence here, too, that the owners had left hurriedly, or been driven out. A mouldy lump of unidentifiable food lay on a table amid a pile of crumbs. The food was so hard that even the small denizens of the forest had left it alone. Isabel sighed and decided she was going to remain hungry for a while longer. FitzAlan's horse was better off, she saw. Guy had obviously carried a small bag of grain in his pack and had left some with the animal. And he had water, as well, since the thatch roof was leaking badly in several places. Isabel gave the grey a last pat and made sure the door was securely closed before speeding back through the rain to her own shelter.

FitzAlan slept on, she noticed thankfully. Quickly stripping off her gown, which had become soaked again, she sat down by the fire and began to comb through her wet, tangled hair with her fingers, holding the strands to the blaze to dry.

He had been watching her for a long time before she realised he was awake. Watching her and wondering. Wondering about her reasons for leaving Gloucester. Wondering why he had agreed to take her.

Her face was tilted, half turned towards him, as she dried the back of her hair. The bronze strands hung over her arm like a curtain, a silken backdrop for her delicate features. Her lashes were dark crescents against skin flushed rosy by the firelight. Not even the fading bruise high on her cheekbone detracted from her beauty; she only looked more fragile. Breakable.

But Isabel had plenty of spirit, Guy reminded himself, ruthlessly stamping down on the protectiveness the sight of her always seemed to arouse in him. She was no helpless, timorous female. Look at what she'd faced in the past twelve hours. Very deliberately Guy went through the list.

Whether or not her warning was genuine, she had come boldly to his room to ask for his escort to Winchester. She had fought him off like a veritable wildcat when he'd slung a few well-deserved insults at her, and then had had the gall to deny she had turned traitor, although her brother held his castle for Matilda, and God only knew what she, herself, had done for the Empress. If Isabel had hated the situation as much as she claimed to, she could have refused to serve Matilda and sought refuge in a convent.

What else? Ah, yes. While another woman would have had hysterics all over him because of the rain and his wound, Isabel had had enough presence of mind to realise they could not be followed in such inclement weather. She had unflinchingly wrenched the arrow out of his arm as if 'twas all in a day's work, and had argued with him all through the operation and while bandaging his wound later. And when she hadn't been arguing she had been calm, efficient, distant…

Exactly as she was now. Not raising her head, nor even starting, at the sudden clamour of birds squabbling out in the clearing. She was absorbed in the feminine ritual of drying her hair, as though there were no danger in their situation, as though she had not a care in the world.

Would a mere slap from an enraged mistress send such a woman fleeing from the shelter of Gloucester Castle?

Not unless there was another damned good reason for her flight, Guy concluded grimly. But as soon as he cursed himself for being taken in last night by Isabel's distress, two insistent memories shook his belief that it had been an act put on for his benefit: the way she had clung fiercely to his hand when they had passed the dungeons, her grip almost painfully strong, and the stricken expression on her face when he had ordered her to strip.

Try as he might, he could not get those two incidents out of his mind. They nagged at him. They didn't tally with the cool, distant woman he was looking at now. And other memories, fragmented and vague, began to torment him. Of Isabel lying soft and pliant in his arms, her slender body pressed to his. Of a burning hunger that only she could appease. Then of cool hands moving over him with teasingly light caresses, but quenching some of the fire, taking away the heat. Had he dreamed all that?

Guy found his gaze moving slowly over Isabel as if her body held the answers to the questions in his mind. The shift didn't hide much. With the fire behind her, he could see the shadowy curve of her breasts through the thin material, and its ragged hem now only reached to mid-thigh. Her legs were curled to the side, slender with dainty ankles curving to small, arched feet. There was something about those little feet, Guy thought suddenly, trying to pin down the memory. Then it came to him. They were supposed to be muddy.

"You've washed your feet," he rasped abruptly. Somehow it came out sounding like an accusation.

Isabel's head came up like a wary animal scenting the air, but her face was swiftly wiped of all expression. "They were dirty," she returned calmly.

An instantaneous, violent urge to shake that remote calm, to see emotion in those serene, fathomless eyes, surged through him at her cool reply. And while he was about it, Guy told himself savagely, he had better discover what little plot Isabel had in mind once she reached Winchester. Knowing Matilda, the girl could have been sent to do anything. And he was helping her to do it!

But she hadn't complained about her dirty feet.

Even more annoyed by that intrusive thought, Guy scowled furiously as Isabel rose and took a beaker from the table, filling it with water from the pail. She didn't seem in any hurry to resume her clothing, he thought cynically, considering her initial reluctance to shed the dress. Indeed, her pose by the fire had been that of the consummate temptress, and yet…there it was again, the feeling that something didn't add up.

He watched her graceful movements as she came towards him and tried to shut his mind to the sight of her bare limbs. She looked both vulnerable and infinitely desirable, and he didn't know which was more disturbing— or more dangerous.

"You must be thirsty," Isabel murmured, proffering the beaker.

Still frowning, Guy took it and downed the contents in one gulp. "My mouth feels like the bottom of a dried-up moat," he grumbled, handing the roughly crafted mug back to her.

Isabel refilled the beaker, then hoisted the pail and replaced it by the side of the bench. She didn't exactly replace it with a thump, but she saw fitzAlan glance at her before he sat up cautiously. Let him wonder about her mood, she thought, refusing to feel contrite. Obviously she wasn't going to get any thanks for nursing him. Then she remembered that he had been wounded because of her.

"'Tis the aftermath of your fever," she explained shortly. "You were… I tried to get you to drink, but…"

The explanation faded into silence when Isabel recalled the way she had spilled water all over her patient because she'd been so nervous of him. Even discussing the subject of last night made her nervous. So far fitzAlan showed no sign of remembering what had happened between them, seeming to be concentrating all his formidable will on remaining upright. She hoped such mundane matters would keep his mind occupied for a good while, because, if he ever discovered how helplessly she had responded to him, Isabel knew she would die of humiliation.

"I'm afraid water is all we have," she muttered, clutching at the first diversion that occurred to her. "I couldn't find any food here or in the other huts."

"You've been out?"

Her chin lifted. "Aye. To check on your horse and look for something to eat."

FitzAlan downed another drink, his lowering gaze on Isabel the whole time. The slight pallor beneath his tan and the white bandage high on his left arm did nothing to detract from the air of menace about him. The danger might be controlled, beneath the surface, but it was there nevertheless. Isabel wondered if he knew how intimidating he could be with just a look, and decided fitzAlan was fully aware of his effect on her. Determined not to betray her uneasiness, she turned away.

Instantly his free hand shot out, preventing her escape. She couldn't quite suppress a gasp of pain as those long, powerful fingers wrapped around her swollen wrist. Immediately his grip shifted to her hand, but he didn't release her. His intent gaze dropped to her arm, his firm mouth curling sardonically.

"The price of retaliation," he mocked. "You should have thought twice before avenging a few unpleasant truths, my lady."

"I care not for the hurt if it indeed avenged your *insults*, my lord," Isabel retorted. "I would do it again."

"Would you?" Guy's half-smile broadened into a grin that held arrogant masculine assurance and an equally arrogant challenge. His thumb began to stroke the inside of her wrist. "Then next time I'll try to be more gallant."

"There will be no next time," Isabel got out, desperately trying to keep her breathing steady while she struggled unavailingly to free her hand. She knew Guy could feel the sudden acceleration of her pulse, but she could do nothing to stop the traitorous throbbing. That stroking thumb was sending shafts of heat straight up her arm with every heartbeat.

"You think not?" he murmured, watching her efforts to escape with the lazy, slightly curious air of the predator who knew his victim was helpless. Then his eyes flashed to her face, their piercing regard anything but lazy. "You were willing to tolerate my touch last night. In fact, sweet traitor, you clung to my hand as you would to a lover."

Isabel froze, the insulting term scarcely heard. She stared apprehensively into fitzAlan's eyes, searching beneath the gleaming mockery for a sign that he was beginning to remember the events of the night. Then she realised he was referring to their escape and drew in a shaky breath of relief. "I don't like the dark," she managed, then wished she'd had the sense to keep her mouth shut.

Utter surprise crossed fitzAlan's face. Whatever he had expected her to say, it was obviously not that. "You're afraid of the dark?" he echoed in patent disbelief.

"I didn't say that," denied Isabel quickly, clinging to her dignity as best she could under the growing amusement in her tormentor's expression. "I just don't like it." She gave another tug at her hand.

FitzAlan ignored this attempt to free herself, as he had all the others. His amusement faded, to be replaced by narrow-eyed speculation. His next words, dropping gently into the tense silence, shook her tottering composure even more.

"Hmm. I suppose that answers one question. Now for the next—why is your shift torn?"

How many questions did he have? Isabel wondered agitatedly. She had to swallow hard before she could speak. "I...I needed a clean bandage for your arm. Do you not remember?"

"Your shift is torn at the neck," Guy elaborated, his voice even softer than before.

That gentle tone meant danger, Isabel thought, mesmerised by the way his eyes bored into hers. She suddenly knew how a rabbit felt under the hypnotic stare of the hawk.

With a final effort that she felt in every nerve of her body, she jerked her hand from his and turned away to the fire. "I...I tore it outside. On a branch."

Guy knew at once she was lying. But why? Why lie about such a trivial thing? Another hazy memory floated tantalisingly at the edge of his mind. Warm skin, as soft as silk against his mouth. Memory—or dream?

"Oh?" he murmured, watching her. "That's a relief. I thought I might have done it, since you had trouble getting me to drink when I was out of my senses."

Not even the crackle of the fire and the pelting rain could disguise Isabel's quick gasp. She whirled to face him, braced for further interrogation, her arms wrapped defensively across her waist. Then hesitated, unsure, at the waiting stillness in fitzAlan's body. The air was suddenly thick with unspoken questions.

He was engaging in a war of nerves with her, Isabel realised at last, but he didn't remember. She stared back at him, unable to speak, terrified of betraying the slightest clue that might jolt his memory, but conscious of a heartfelt sense of gratitude for the fever that had kept her so busy during the morning hours. FitzAlan might suspect that something had happened between them, but he didn't know for sure.

Trembling with relief, she bent quickly to add another log to the fire, using the small task to break the heavy silence. "'Tis fortunate we have the fire, isn't it?" she remarked in a hopelessly breathless attempt at chattiness. "Since we're stuck here until your...I mean until the rain stops, and—"

"Wrong both times," he growled behind her, frustrated anger plain in his voice. "We leave again in the morning, rain or no, even if you have to tie me to my horse. Which reminds me—is he dry enough?"

Isabel turned to look at fitzAlan before answering. She was not very much surprised to see him on his feet and opening the door, but when he swayed and put a hand on the wall to steady himself she was unable to prevent her own hand going out towards him. It was quickly snatched back when he shot a black look at her.

"Your horse is fine," she retorted, annoyed at that moment of weakness. "But you're not. At least sit down until you feel stronger."

"I'll feel stronger a damn sight faster if I move around a bit," he threw at her in a voice little better than a snarl. "And when I do, my lady, we'll get back to that interesting little conversation we were having."

The door slammed shut behind him.

Chapter Five

Isabel's shaking legs got her as far as the bench before she collapsed. She felt as if she'd already been questioned on the rack, and fitzAlan hadn't even tried to force any definite answers out of her. But he would when he returned.

The thought sent Isabel scrambling into her gown again, as though the garment might afford her some protection. Somehow it seemed easier to dress while Guy was absent. No doubt he would have made a nasty remark, and she didn't need to hear any more of them.

When he returned, however, fitzAlan made no comment on her clothing nor demanded any immediate answers. He was looking a little pale and the lines of strain around his mouth betrayed the pain his arm was giving him. "You're right," he said shortly. "Not a crumb of food in the place. But there are some strips of salted meat in my pack."

"Oh." Isabel gave a nervous little laugh. "I didn't think to look in there."

She was conscious of fitzAlan's sharp glance at her sudden murmur of laughter, then he sat down heavily on the bench, wincing at the jolt to his arm, and gestured towards the bulky pack by the door. "Go ahead."

Isabel didn't need a second invitation, quickly finding the meat and dividing it between them. But, despite her hunger, she took as long as possible over the simple meal, desperately trying to stave off the moment when they would have nothing to do except talk or sleep. She doubted she would ever sleep again while fitzAlan was in the immediate vicinity, but the prospect of remaining awake and having to keep her mask of aloof composure in place was daunting indeed. The questions she had feared earlier seemed to be taking physical shape in the shadowy corners of the room, phantoms waiting to trap her if she dropped her guard for so much as a second.

And yet the waiting silence was almost more than she could bear. When the lonely howl of a wolf carried to them through the forest, Isabel jumped, glancing at the door as if she expected to see the beast standing there.

FitzAlan rose and moved his sword nearer to the bench, where he could lay his hand on it quickly. "'Tis not four-footed predators we need worry about," he observed, and Isabel knew he had seen her nervous reaction. "I dare say we're safer here than in Gloucester. At least for tonight."

The shadows moved imperceptibly closer.

"My…father…once told me…a wild animal will not venture near a fire," she stammered. Anything to keep the conversation simple and unthreatening.

FitzAlan promptly turned it around. "Tell me about your father," he commanded abruptly. "When did he die?"

She withdrew immediately, retreating into her corner of the bench, her face expressionless but for the suspicious sidelong glance she sent him. "Why?"

Guy's brows rose. "Why not?" he countered. He continued to watch her for a moment, then murmured, "I liked him."

Isabel looked back at the fire, her tense muscles easing a little. "He had many friends," she said softly. "They all liked him."

"So how did Hugh die?" he persisted when she didn't say any more. "In battle?"

Alarm pulled her body taut again. Another quick guarded look told her he was still watching her. Why was he so interested in her father? Why did he have to ask all these questions? Perhaps if she flatly refused to give any details…

"There was a fight," she confirmed shortly. "'Twas a long time ago. My father was killed. I would rather not speak of it."

FitzAlan's brows drew together. "What would your ladyship prefer to discuss?" he enquired with heavy sarcasm. "The exact nature of your work for Matilda, perhaps? Is it possible that bolt in my arm should have been through my heart?"

She flinched. "If that had been my purpose I would not have tended your wound," she faltered, hoping he couldn't hear the tremor in her voice.

"Oh, really? Should I thank you?"

Her eyes widened, lifting to his face. FitzAlan was leaning back against the wall, seemingly at ease, but his eyes were narrowed and the muscles of the forearm braced over his raised knee were rigid. Despite the warmth of the fire, Isabel began to shiver. This was not the almost idle interrogation he had started earlier, but something darker, something dangerous. He had been angry before, he was angry *now*, but this time…this time he was *using* it, controlling it. Isabel's trembling increased as she saw what was happening. He was using a very real emotion, cold-bloodedly, deliberately, to taunt and intimidate.

Just like all the rest, she thought bitterly. Just like every other man. Was brute force and intimidation all they knew? Resentment flickered within her, a tiny flame, not yet warm enough to banish the chill of fear, but steady. "'Twas little enough payment for taking me to Winchester."

"And do you always pay your debts?" The question was soft with hidden menace.

"If…if I can."

"Hmm. A pity I didn't collect when I had the chance. Your skills might have been…interesting."

Isabel felt all the blood drain from her face. Merciful Jesu! He had remembered. The wolf had cornered his prey and was now moving in for the kill. She could almost feel the fangs at her throat, and knew the real cause of the choking sensation was fear. And she was so tired of being afraid. So tired of having to be careful. So tired of being the target of insults. So *tired*.

She stared into fitzAlan's hard, relentless eyes, and behind her fear that tiny flicker of resentment flared into sudden blazing life with the force of a rage as hot as his was cold. Rage at a fate which prevented her from screaming and railing at him for so misjudging her, rage at him for playing this cat-and-mouse game with her, rage at herself for letting him get away with it. She could not let him throw last night in her face. This time she had to fight back or be utterly shamed.

It occurred to her far too late that in a contest between fire and ice there could be only one victor.

"You seem to have your own particular talents, also, my lord. Getting us past two locked doors, for instance."

To her surprise he allowed the diversion. "'Tis easy enough to pick a lock when you know how." His eyes scorned her. "You should learn the trick of it. 'Tis a useful accomplishment for ladies who come creeping into a man's chamber late at night.''

''Is that so?'' Isabel snapped. ''Well, I am happy to say that my acquaintance does not run to thieves, so—''

''No,'' he shot back, his voice suddenly harsh. ''Only traitors. Tell me, how does the Countess pay you?'' He looked her up and down disparagingly. ''Obviously not with gowns. Is it your brother who reaps the rewards? Do you whore for him rather than for Matilda?''

Isabel gasped, jerking back as though he had struck her. For a stunned moment she couldn't believe what she had heard, then she leapt to her feet, dark eyes blazing from an ashen face. ''You know nothing!'' she spat, her voice shaking with such fury that the words were barely coherent. ''*Nothing*! You…'' She choked on a raggedly indrawn breath and had to stop, fighting for air.

FitzAlan stood up and took two slow, measured paces towards her, until she was forced to tilt her head right back to look up at him, or retreat, which she refused to do. Blue eyes, as light and as frozen as ice, stared into hers before his glance moved slowly downwards, deliberately insulting. Isabel's hands clenched into tiny fists at her sides as she struggled against the waves of savage anger threatening to sweep her beyond caution. He saw the movement and laughed. It was the final straw.

''Who is the traitor here?'' Her voice rose on a note that betrayed how near she was to breaking-point. ''Stephen swore a sacred oath to recognise Matilda as Queen. As you probably did yourself. So tell me, my lord, just who is the traitor here?''

The laughter was wiped from fitzAlan's face instantly. ''I swore no oath to Matilda,'' he grated. ''And Stephen was released from his promise by the Church—''

"Aye, on the condition of other promises, which he then proceeded to break," she cried recklessly.

She saw fitzAlan's eyes narrow to glittering slits, his jaw lock tight with fury. His hands lifted to her shoulders as though he would shake her, but clenched and fell back as he controlled himself. Isabel found her gaze fixed in unwilling fascination on one white-knuckled fist. No wonder he had laughed at hers, she thought distractedly. If he ever hit her with that, he would probably kill her.

"Well," he stated with deadly quiet. "Now I know exactly where your loyalties lie, my lady Isabel."

Her eyes flew back to his face. "No," she whispered, going pale again with fright as she remembered what she was supposed to be doing. Rage drained out of her with numbing speed, leaving her empty and cold. "No. I only meant—"

"I know what you meant," he dismissed contemptuously. "And if anger loosens your tongue I'll also find out what you mean to do in Winchester. Pretend to sell yourself to a higher bidder, no doubt." He gave a short laugh. "You won't be the first, but what do you think to offer the Queen? False information? We'll get the real thing out of you soon enough and you won't see a farthing for it."

"*No*! I…" Tears clogged her throat and she had to stop, fighting them back. What had she done? She had only meant to defend herself, but it had come out all wrong. And now her flash of temper had probably endangered Edmund. FitzAlan could prevent her from seeing the Queen…confine her somewhere in Winchester…

"I…only intend…to serve the Queen…" she faltered huskily, her eyes pleading with him.

The plea shattered his control as her anger had not

done. The words were barely out of Isabel's mouth when
fitzAlan grabbed her arms with bruising strength.

"*Damn you, don't lie to me!*" he roared, shaking her
hard. Her head snapped back. An involuntary cry escaped
her lips at the force of his grip. Far from relenting, his
fingers tightened even more, nearly lifting Isabel from the
ground.

The room started to spin. Her eyelids fluttered and she
went deathly white, but she fought back the dizzying
sensation, her hands coming up to brace herself against
fitzAlan's chest while the world righted itself. She would
not faint. She had to think of Edmund. But the only coherent thought in her head was an awareness that fitz-
Alan's heart was pounding violently against her palms and
his hands seemed to be shaking almost as much as she
was.

Then, as her eyes lifted to his, he shoved her roughly
away from him, wheeled about, and slammed out of the
hut.

Isabel dropped to the floor where she stood, one hand
gripping the edge of the bench. The firelight caught the
tiny scar on her finger and a long, whimpering sound of
anguish filled the hut. Her head fell forward to rest on her
fingers. Fool! she moaned in silent despair. *Fool*! Had the
past taught her nothing? Had she not learned the futility
of striking back? Why had she fought him? Why had she
uttered one word? And why did it tear her apart because
it was fitzAlan who had said those terrible things to her?

Why did he feel as though he had just run his sword
through the heart of something small and desperately
struggling for survival?

Guy leaned back against the hut door, dragging the cold
night air into his lungs, and tried not to think of the an-

guish in Isabel's white face, of the tears drowning her luminous grey eyes. He should be satisfied that he'd succeeded in destroying her calm façade. He should still be inside, keeping up the pressure until he forced the truth out of her. But instead he was feeling torn apart by his own emotions.

God, he'd never felt such savagely conflicting sensations. *Never*! He had seen her passionate anger and had wanted to kiss her senseless, had heard her lie to him and had wanted to shake the truth out of her, had almost caused her to swoon and had wanted to hold her close and tell her he wouldn't allow anything to hurt her again—all in the space of about half a minute.

And what did he have for it? *Nothing*! Oh, yes, he knew she was afraid of the dark. Wonderful! Very helpful! He was standing here on the other side of the door, knowing nothing of Isabel's plans. Hell! He didn't even know what had happened last night, although he was damned sure something had to make Isabel so nervous of him. She had been wary and guarded before, but not jumpy—not with that purely *feminine* type of nervousness.

His thoughts skidded to a halt. There it was again. That nagging doubt, the feeling that something was missing in the woman she was supposed to be. It wasn't reasoned. It wasn't logical, or even safe. It was sheer gut instinct. And that wasn't all.

Guy pushed himself away from the hut and strode across the clearing to make sure his horse was secure for the night. The anger in him slowly dissipated as questions raced through his mind. Isabel hadn't searched his pack. By design or in innocence? She hadn't taken his horse and left him when he'd fallen into a stupor last night. Because he was hurt, or because she needed his protection? There was passion in her, showing itself in anger, yet she fought to control it. And if she was not always cold and distant, what had made such a detached, unemotional mask necessary in the first place?

Questions!

He wondered suddenly what he would find when he returned to the hut. His cool, scheming enemy, or his hurt, fragile…

He found Isabel crouched by the fire, staring into the flames. She still looked pale, but she got slowly to her feet, watching him carefully.

Guy pushed the door shut, studying the uneasy expression in her eyes. "We have to let the fire die out tonight," he said quietly. "We needed it to dry off, but now 'tis dangerous if we're near enough to a castle for the smoke to be noticed. If 'tis known this place is abandoned, someone might investigate."

Her eyes widened a little, as though in surprise, then she nodded, glancing aside to the table and indicating the misshapen light with a hand that shook slightly. "I think there may be a castle or…or town…quite close. The candle…"

Guy found his eyes following the gesture. Such a little hand. And she sounded…defeated. He felt a sudden piercing need to reach out, capture her hand and pull her into his arms. God's blood, why did she have to look so damned vulnerable? And tired. The bluish shadows beneath her eyes made the eyes themselves look enormous. For the first time he wondered how long his fever had lasted, and how much sleep Isabel had got the night before. Enemy or not, she had nursed him.

"Come," he said, deliberately keeping his voice low and even. "We have a long ride ahead of us tomorrow. 'Tis time to sleep. You'll be more comfortable on the bench with me and we'll be warm enough under that blanket and my cloak, even without the fire.''

Isabel heard the words, but they sounded all wrong. Almost too afraid to hope, she repeated them in her mind. Had she been mistaken earlier? Did he still have no memory of the previous night? Oh, Holy Mother of God, let it be so.

''The hut will stay warm for a while yet,'' she ventured, despising the timid note in her voice, but powerless to disguise it. ''I won't be cold.''

''Maybe not,'' fitzAlan answered, and then an unexpected smile suddenly transformed that hard, handsome face. ''But I will.''

Isabel could only gape up at him. He had smiled at her. After his rage and sarcasm, he had actually smiled at her. In that fleeting instant she had seen the soldier of her dreams. For some inexplicable reason her mind went completely blank.

Then the smile was gone. ''Come on,'' he said more roughly, apparently regretting his good humour.

Once again Isabel didn't get a chance to argue, even if her brain had been working. In seconds she found herself arranged carefully within the circle of fitzAlan's good arm, her head cradled on his shoulder, and the blanket and cloak wrapped snugly around her. He made a surprisingly comfortable pillow, she thought bemusedly. And at least they were both fully dressed this time.

''Relax,'' he murmured in her ear, a thread of amusement in his voice. ''I'm in no condition to attack you tonight.''

Isabel went even more rigid.

''Jesu! I've felt drawn bowstrings less tense than you.''

''I'm sorry,'' she whispered, and immediately cursed herself for apologising. At this rate she might as well give him a blow-by-blow description of the last time they had shared the bench, and save him the trouble of remembering. Idiot! You've been given a reprieve. Say something harmless.

"Perhaps one of us should stay awake in case—"

"Go to sleep," he interrupted gruffly. "We're safe enough for another night."

This time she didn't answer. Guy lay still, trying to ignore the softness of her body against his, trying to ignore the urge to stroke her tension away. He knew only too well where *that* would lead. He should concentrate on his relentlessly aching arm instead. The only trouble with that idea was that Isabel was impossible to ignore. With every breath he inhaled the warm, womanly scent of her, and, as she gradually began to relax, *his* body began to tauten.

In an effort to distract himself, Guy considered all the questions about Isabel he was beginning to amass. Questions to which there were too few answers. But there was still time. Isabel needed his protection as far as Winchester, and if he didn't have those answers before they arrived he would keep her under restraint until he unlocked every secret she possessed. And his feeling of intense satisfaction at this conclusion was only because he was finally clear-headed enough to make some sort of decision. It had nothing to do with the soft, seemingly defenceless girl lying in his arms.

But, almost of its own accord, his mouth brushed across her silky hair and his arm tightened fractionally. "Go to sleep, Isabel," he murmured again, and this time his voice was gentle.

Outwardly Isabel obeyed, relaxing further into the warmth of their makeshift bed, lying docile and still beside him. But she didn't sleep. Instead she gazed into the dully glowing ashes of the dying fire and remembered a wild, enchanted garden and a tender, handsome soldier who had awoken her to approaching womanhood with one gentle kiss and a rose.

There was no sign of tenderness in the man who tossed her up into the saddle the next morning, but, seeing him now in the full light of day, Isabel was forced to concede that he was still handsome. If one liked that uncompromisingly masculine type of good looks, she thought, trying to tell herself she did not.

But she couldn't resist studying fitzAlan as he secured his pack, her eyes moving over his fair head, the strong planes of his face, the hard line of his mouth. With his long blue cloak fastened across his shoulders, his injury was hidden and his height emphasised. He looked powerful and tough, and yet Isabel found herself noticing that his lower lip was slightly fuller than the upper, and that his mouth quirked at one corner, hinting at a sense of humour.

Then fitzAlan mounted behind her and she was immediately aware of the unyielding strength of his body against her back, the restrained power in his hand on the reins. She forgot about hints of sensitivity or humour. He was too big, she told herself. Too overwhelming, too hard.

She thought back to his anger last night. The prospect of a man of fitzAlan's size ever losing control, no matter what the cause, was enough to make any sane woman run for the nearest convent. But instead, for a dizzying instant, as he wrapped his cloak about her, Isabel found herself savouring a delicious sensation of feeling small and infinitely fragile, enclosed within his arms.

Utterly dismayed, she wriggled forward a little, trying to put some distance between them.

"Be still, for God's sake," growled his deep voice above her. "Do you want to ruin my horse's back?"

Isabel sighed and subsided. She didn't bother to answer. FitzAlan would only snap at her anyway, as he had been doing from the minute they had risen in the half-light of a chilly grey dawn. Clearly his gentler behaviour when he'd returned to the hut last night had been an aberration. All she had done this morning was suggest that she bathe his wound again before they started out, and he had refused with a complete lack of gratitude or even common courtesy. Recollecting his churlish behaviour, Isabel wondered how she could be attracted to such a man even for a moment. As for his arm, she decided, it could just fester and drop off as far as she was concerned.

Fortunately the rain had ceased some time during the night. A weak sun shone through the dispersing clouds, sending misty rays of light dancing through the trees and turning their necklaces of raindrops into sparkling gems. A cool but bright autumn day promised, and at any other time Isabel would have enjoyed the ride. However, silent contemplation of the passing forest tended to pall after several unbroken miles of it. She finally admitted to herself that even the risk of another snub was preferable to her growing anxiety about what lay ahead.

"Could we not travel safely on the road now?" she asked cautiously, as they forded yet another stream. She felt fitzAlan glance down at her and resolutely kept her face to the front.

"Possibly, if 'twas Stephen you were fleeing from. Matilda tends not to yield what she considers her property so easily."

"'Twas *your* life the Empress wanted," she murmured. Sudden curiosity overcame her caution and she glanced up at him. "You've met her before, haven't you?"

"Aye." FitzAlan's eyes narrowed thoughtfully on her face. "When she landed in England two years ago. I was among her escort to Bristol when Stephen made the idiotic mistake of allowing the Countess to join her half-brother." His tone made it clear the job was not one he had enjoyed.

"You said Matilda repaid gallantry with ill treatment," Isabel remembered.

"Stephen can be too generous for his own good," fitzAlan said tersely, "and is all too prone to listen to well-meant but foolish advice. He's easily swayed." He hesitated, then gave a short laugh that held no humour whatsoever. "Incredible how a man of such undoubted physical courage can be so unsure of himself in other ways."

But you are not like that.

For one ghastly second Isabel thought she had spoken the words aloud. "Physical courage?" she questioned hastily. She wouldn't put it past fitzAlan to read her mind.

"Aye. Stephen is the most fearless man I've ever seen in battle. The odds were against us from the start at Lincoln—and he knew it. But even when he was surrounded he continued to lay about him with his sword, and then with an axe when his sword broke, until he went down from a blow to the head. 'Twas the same gallantry that prompted him to send Matilda to her most powerful supporter, instead of keeping her isolated at Arundel. Reckless, foolhardy, but it inspires men to follow him. 'Tis not a gift the Countess possesses."

"But there are men who consider her beautiful," Isabel remarked, and in the next instant could have bitten her tongue out. What had possessed her to make such a statement? *And* with a faintly questioning intonation that fitzAlan would have to be deaf to miss. Feeling hot colour rush to her cheeks, she quickly turned away again, but not before she had seen the sardonic amusement gleaming in his blue eyes. She braced herself.

"Surely you know men are blind to other women when you are present, Lady Isabel." The words were uttered with devastating sincerity.

They were immediately followed by a stunned silence. Isabel stared fixedly ahead of her, wondering if she had heard aright. She had expected mockery, and, judging by the unnatural stillness she felt in fitzAlan's body, he had *intended* to mock her. What had happened?

"I've no time to waste on Matilda's beauty or lack of it," he said shortly after a moment. "'Tis her fortitude and determination which bear watching. She is harsher than Stephen and won't be deflected." He paused, then added dispassionately, "Had she been born a man, those traits would have made her an excellent ruler."

Isabel's eyes widened in surprise. She had to make a determined effort not to look back. "That is very generous."

"I may wish destruction on the King's enemies—" his voice was still clipped "—but that doesn't blind me to their good qualities."

The russet and gold forest blurred suddenly before Isabel's eyes. Did fitzAlan hate her so much, then? she wondered. Did he consider her to have no good qualities at all, to be so scornful of her? He had judged her without question, but could attribute fortitude and resolution to Matilda despite the Empress's glaring faults.

Isabel blinked her tears away furiously. She could not be so generous. Not to the haughty woman who used helpless people as pawns in her ambitious games. She remembered Edmund, little more than a child, grave and courteous, thanking the Empress for her hospitality. And she remembered the answer he had received. She thought of the task awaiting her in Winchester, and the consequences of failure. The words were out before Isabel could stop them, despair and bitterness giving them a stark finality that was absolute.

"She is arrogant…and cruel!"

And that was what he got for testing her, Guy told himself disgustedly. Five little words that only raised a whole pile of other questions. He would have the answers, though, he vowed grimly. And before he had to spend many more sleepless nights like the last one. A good thing they'd be in Winchester tonight… Wry humour put a slight quirk in his mouth. Another night like the last, with Isabel in his arms, would try his control to the limits. And if he wasn't in control, how could he expect to control *her*?

Two sleepless nights, Isabel brooded as the silence remained unbroken, was not conducive to good sense. She felt as though control was slipping away from her in some obscure way. FitzAlan could not have made his opinion of her clearer, and yet for an insane moment there, shaken by his reasoned judgements of Stephen and Matilda, she had been tempted to confess the truth and beg for his help.

She must be going mad. He probably wouldn't believe her, and, in any event, what could he do? Turn around and make for Tracy Castle? Alone? Edmund would be killed the instant they appeared at the castle gates. What was the alternative? To toss Rainald into prison when they reached Winchester? There were sure to be other spies reporting to Matilda; Brien fitzCount had said as much. Again, Edmund's life would be taken. She simply couldn't risk it.

But as the day lengthened into afternoon the argument lurched back and forth inside Isabel's head until she could no longer think straight. Weariness and hunger were also taking their toll. When they crested a wooded hill shortly before sunset and saw cultivated fields stretching down towards a small village in the distance it took all her will-power not to beg that they stop there for the night.

FitzAlan reined in his horse just before the trees thinned out. ''The Test,'' he said, pointing past her to the silvery flash of sunlight on water beyond the village. ''There's another ford south of here, and then Winchester, about nine miles yonder.''

Don't cavil at another nine miles, Isabel ordered herself. If fitzAlan were alone, he would be in Winchester by now. I won't ask if we can rest. I won't ask if we can buy some food from that village. I won't... She suddenly realised that fitzAlan had turned his horse back into the forest, along a parallel course with the river, but out of sight of the small hamlet.

''Why are we going this way? That village looked harmless enough and your horse must be thirsty.'' There, she hadn't actually *asked* for any favours.

FitzAlan jerked his head back at the settlement. ''Men-at-arms,'' he explained succinctly. ''Four of them. Probably only collecting rents or some such thing, but it will be better if they don't lay eyes on you. Besides, I want to reach Winchester before dark.''

Isabel was still vaguely wondering if chivalry or haste was behind fitzAlan's decision to ride on, when the choice was abruptly taken out of his hands. The horse had barely stepped on to the gravelly riverbed at the edge of the ford when it stumbled, almost falling to its knees. The animal plunged to a halt, snorting and tossing its head nervously as water sprayed into the air around them.

Guy was out of the saddle instantly, backing the grey

out of the river and examining its hoofs. Isabel heard him mutter an oath.

"What is it?" she asked anxiously.

"Chalon has picked up a stone." He lowered the horse's left foreleg and came back to lift Isabel to the ground. "I can get it out, but it will take a moment. Hold his head, will you?"

Isabel picked her way carefully over the rough bank, the cramped muscles in her legs protesting at the exercise, and took the reins. While fitzAlan hefted the grey's hoof and set to work, she glanced about, absently patting Chalon's velvety muzzle.

It was peaceful by the river. Two swans glided majestically past and ripples spread over the breeze-ruffled surface as a fish captured an unwary insect which alighted above it. On the other side of the ford the trees grew almost to the water's edge, appearing shadowy and dim as the sun moved slowly westward. The air was growing cooler with the approach of evening.

Chalon whickered softly, as though recalling her attention, and Isabel murmured soothingly. "What happened to your other horse?" she asked on a sudden impulse. "The black one."

"Romulus?" FitzAlan released the grey's leg and glanced back. In the light of the setting sun his eyes glittered like blue ice.

Too late Isabel heard the unspoken admission in her question.

"I still have him," Guy said. She had watched him leave all those years ago, he thought. She had not seen him arrive at her home, since she had not known who he was when they had encountered each other in the garden—but she had seen him leave. From some hidden vantage-point she had watched him that morning, while he rode away with the image of her in his mind and his—

"If you've finished petting my horse we can be on our way," he rasped abruptly, annoyed at the direction of his thoughts. "I'd like to ford the river before dark if it won't inconvenience your ladyship too greatly."

"'Twas not my fault we had to stop," Isabel snapped back indignantly, the peace of the afternoon ruined for her. The sooner she was free of such a boorish escort, the better, she thought angrily, taking a hasty step forward.

She shouldn't have moved so quickly. The riverbank rushed towards her with dizzying speed as the stiffness in her legs caused her stumble and lose her balance on the uneven ground. But even as she flung out a hand to save herself she was whisked off her feet and pulled into the secure haven of fitzAlan's arms.

Isabel gasped at the strength of his grip, her senses reeling as she fought a wild impulse to melt into the crushing pressure of his embrace. He was so *strong*. It should have frightened her—she felt so weak by comparison—but instead she wanted to cling, to soften, to yield. Appalled, she pushed back, but the movement only succeeded in pressing her lower body more closely to fitzAlan's hard thighs. His reaction was immediate and unmistakable.

Isabel froze, staring into those glittering eyes only inches from her own. They seemed to have darkened, smouldering in a way that sent hot and cold chills chasing each other through her body. Suddenly she *was* frightened. Her heart was beating somewhere in her throat and she felt giddier than ever.

"Please," she whispered, forcing herself not to struggle, hardly breathing in her attempt to remain still. "Please let me go."

For a nerve-racking minute Isabel thought fitzAlan would ignore her plea. Then with excruciating slowness he relaxed his hold, allowing her to back away a pace. She was still imprisoned within his arms, but they no longer kept her clamped against him. FitzAlan shifted one hand to the nape of her neck, holding her still, while that probing gaze seemed to penetrate the very depths of her soul.

He was watching her, Isabel thought perplexedly, with the single-minded intensity of the hunter. She felt helpless. She could not look away, could only gaze back at him, wondering what he sought.

''Hell's serpents, lads! Look what we've found here. More booty for our lord.''

The loud, coarse voice ripped through the quiet air with shocking force, like a dagger through silk.

FitzAlan's head jerked up. One glance at the mounted soldiers emerging from the trees was enough. Uttering a low, violent oath, he grabbed Isabel's arm and yanked her behind him, drawing his sword at the same time. In that moment it didn't matter who or what she was. She was threatened, and the primitive male instinct to protect what was his brought his entire body to battle-readiness within seconds.

Chapter Six

Men-at-arms…four of them…better if they don't see you. The words echoed in Isabel's head as she clung to Chalon's saddle, where fitzAlan's shove had sent her, and watched the four soldiers size up the situation.

It didn't take long. Like a wolf pack scenting easy prey, they dismounted and spread out. Three of them moved forward, swords unsheathed, while the fourth held their horses, grinning evilly and calling encouragement to his fellows.

"'Twill be a good day's work if we can bring in this prize, lads. A wealthy lord to fleece and a tasty little wench for us to play with."

"You'll have to go through me first," warned fitzAlan, his voice low with menace.

Isabel couldn't see his face, but she could feel the murderous ferocity emanating from him. The foremost of the advancing men hesitated, a flicker of doubt crossing his rough features as he considered the size and strength of his victim. FitzAlan moved a pace to meet them, his free hand unfastening his cloak. He flicked the garment around his left arm and brought his sword up in a sweeping arc.

"Come on," he snarled. "Which of you vermin wants to be the first to burn in hell?"

Isabel gaped at him, horrified. Had the fever turned his brain? He was one against four—and already wounded— and yet he stood there deliberately inciting the men to fight. As if they needed encouragement! His aggression was going to get them both killed.

"We're on the Queen's business," she cried, in a desperate bid to avert disaster.

The soldiers' attention shifted to her immediately. One of them laughed, his eyes gleaming with anticipation. "You could be on th'devil'sh businesh, for ought we care," he slurred.

"Shut up, you little fool!" hissed fitzAlan. "He's drunk."

He was right, Isabel realised, watching the soldier lurch forward another step. Her eyes moved swiftly to the others. Were they in a like condition? Would it slow them down or make them more vicious?

"Stay with the horse," ordered Guy, without taking his eyes off his opponents. "Use him as a shield if you have to."

Isabel barely heard him. Sick with fear, she watched helplessly as, at a shouted signal, the three rushed at fitzAlan in a concerted attack that looked like succeeding through sheer weight of numbers.

Then, in a movement so fast that Isabel had to replay it later in her mind to sort everything out, fitzAlan flung his cloak over the drunk on his left and brought his sword slashing through the air to slice through the arm of the man on his right. The soldier howled in agony and staggered back, dropping his own weapon to clutch at the gaping cut that had opened his arm to the bone.

Ignoring him, Guy let the impetus of his powerful

swing carry the blade onwards to clash violently with the sword of the third soldier. Steel met steel with a force that sent a nearby flock of birds shrieking into the air. The man reeled under the shock of the blow, his blade wavering briefly. That instant of unguardedness was long enough for fitzAlan. His sword plunged into the exposed chest before him, aimed unerringly at the heart. The man was dead before he hit the ground.

Jolted abruptly out of her paralysis by this drastic reduction of their adversaries, Isabel suddenly became aware of the curses of the fellow untangling himself from fitzAlan's cloak. His struggles had brought him to within reach of Chalon's powerful hindquarters, and Isabel didn't hesitate. Pulling on the reins with one hand and pushing the big horse with the other, she backed him straight into the drunken lout just as he flung the cloak aside. He went down immediately, yelling and cursing afresh.

Already unnerved by the fighting, Chalon lashed out, catching the soldier a glancing blow before the man could roll free of the deadly, flashing hoofs.

FitzAlan swung about, ice-blue eyes blazing. A grin of unholy amusement slashed across his face. "Good girl," he said. "Keep him busy."

He's enjoying this, thought Isabel incredulously. But there was no time to enlarge on the idea. The fourth man had abandoned their horses to his wounded companion and was launching himself into the fray. He came in on Guy's unprotected left side, swinging a long pike, clearly hoping to cripple his opponent with the advantage of the weapon's longer reach. The solid oak staff caught Guy a brutal blow on his wounded arm.

Isabel screamed, almost feeling the agony of the blow in her own body. She saw fitzAlan stagger back, his face whitening with pain. The soldier swung again, this time aiming for the head. FitzAlan hurled himself forward in a low tackle, the pike whistling harmlessly over him. It flew through the air to land some distance away as both men went down with a crash that shook the ground.

Isabel heard the sounds of the ensuing fight only vaguely. Her scream had startled Chalon and she now had her hands full trying to control the plunging, frightened horse, realising with a renewed surge of alarm that he was much too strong for her. The threat of the soldiers was momentarily forgotten as she struggled to keep her footing and prevent the animal from bolting.

There was a sharp crack behind her, then a shout. "Get the girl, Raoul. Hurry! Use her to disarm the bastard."

At the same moment Chalon side-stepped, dragging Isabel with him. She lost her hold on the saddle. Her flailing hand slipped down to the pack, wrenching its cords open, just as cruel fingers seized her arm. There was a flash of steel. Hardly aware of what she was doing, driven by the blind instinct to fight for her life, Isabel grabbed at the falling object. It was in her hand when the soldier jerked her roughly around and pulled her against him.

Everything seemed to stop. Time stood still. The leering triumph on her captor's brutish features changed to a rigid mask of surprise. Isabel stared into muddy brown eyes, frozen with terror herself.

Then the eyes glazed, the sweaty, grasping fingers slid from her arm, and the man crumpled to the ground.

How very, very quiet it was. She wondered why she hadn't noticed the quiet before now. The birds had settled again. Even the breeze had died away.

"Isabel?"

She frowned, not wanting anything to intrude on the peacefulness.

"Sweetheart? Are you all right? Did he hurt you?"

The insistent, questioning voice wasn't going to leave. Isabel wrenched her gaze from the limp body at her feet. She found that muddy brown eyes had been replaced by alert blue ones. FitzAlan's eyes. She felt life begin to flow back into her limbs. *What* had he called her?

"Are you hurt?" he repeated, running his hands over her arms.

Isabel's eyes followed his progress downward. Nausea rose in her throat, threatening to choke her, when she saw the bloodied arrow clutched in her hand. With a stifled cry, she dropped the bolt, stepping back on legs that were suddenly made of water. If she hadn't cannoned into Chalon, now standing quietly, she would have fallen.

"Did I kill him?" she whispered, her face pale as she stared at the weapon. With seeming irrelevancy she remembered stowing the arrow in fitzAlan's pack when she had pulled it out of his arm. What had made her do that? she wondered.

"Not intentionally," replied Guy drily. "The fool ran straight into it when he attacked you. Come on, we've got to cross the ford and get away from here before—"

"I *did* kill him," Isabel whimpered, not even hearing this terse advice. "I killed a man—"

"*Listen to me!*" FitzAlan's voice was rough with barely controlled impatience. "We don't have time for this. I'll get the Bishop of Winchester himself to absolve you if it'll make you feel better, but first we have to get there. Now *move!*"

The barked command finally registered. Isabel dragged her eyes away from the ground and stared at fitzAlan. The first thing she saw was the fresh blood staining his sleeve. "Your arm…'twas struck…"

"'Tis well enough for now. Come on, up with you."

"The other man…the one you wounded…" Isabel

murmured, her mind still working only sluggishly, although she managed to grasp the saddle when she found herself sitting in it. Grey eyes still clouded and wide with horror, she glanced along the riverbank as though seeking the remaining soldier.

"He forgot about his bleeding arm long enough to get on a horse and run," fitzAlan said grimly, retrieving his cloak and swiftly re-tying the pack. "We don't know how far he has to go, but you can be sure others will be back for the horses. So we're leaving right now."

How could he be so calm and practical? Isabel asked herself as fitzAlan swung himself into the saddle behind her. Her own body and mind still seemed to be moving in slow motion, and she had a wild urge to—what? Laugh? Cry? Scream? She wasn't sure just how she felt, but she retained enough control to know that she couldn't give in to shock in front of fitzAlan. She had to push it aside, forget it. Because his mockery or contempt on top of everything else would devastate her.

But when Guy urged Chalon into the shallow water of the ford, she looked back again, as though compelled, to the bodies behind them. "'Tis very different, isn't it?"

Guy flicked a glance down at her, his eyes narrowed and intent. "What is?"

"Killing someone," Isabel whispered, her voice a mere thread of sound. "'Tis very different from seeing it done."

For a while there was silence between them. Isabel listened to the sound of Chalon's steady hoofbeats, finding a vague comfort in the monotony of the noise. It had almost lulled her mind to blankness when she felt fitzAlan's arms close tightly about her with the utmost care, bringing her nearer to the warmth of his body. As though he feared she might break, Isabel thought wonderingly.

"You had to do it, Isabel. He might have killed both of us," Guy said very gently. "Remember that."

She had been wrong, Isabel discovered. Wrong to fear fitzAlan's impatience or scorn. It was his unexpected kindness that caused her jaw to clench suddenly in an attempt to stave off the hot tears scalding her eyes.

So he *could* be tender.

The thought crept into her mind and lingered. Isabel forced herself to dismiss it. In that direction lay a hope too fragile to be exposed—even to herself. It was more likely that fitzAlan did not want a distraught woman on his hands. With the way she was shaking he probably thought she was about to fall to pieces at any moment.

'Tis only reaction setting in, Isabel told herself sternly, trying unavailingly to control the tremors rippling through her body. You're safe now. Safe!

She fixed her burning eyes on the road ahead of her and tried to believe her own words. A solitary tear trickled down her cheek and was quickly brushed aside. She would *not* cry. She would *not* be weak. They would be in Winchester soon. She had to prepare to meet the Queen, plan what to say…

But nothing came to mind. The orders she had been given whirled about in her brain in disordered, meaningless circles. If only she weren't so tired. If only she could sleep.

"You need to rest," murmured Guy's deep voice. "We'll stop here."

Isabel stared blankly ahead. Had he read her mind? The thought didn't bother her. Such was her exhaustion that she would not have cared if her traitorous purpose was emblazoned across her face for him to see. She had no idea where they were, had not even noticed that night had fallen. They must have been riding for a long time, but there was no sign of a large town, only a solitary light shining ahead. Then she vaguely remembered fitzAlan saying something about circling around to approach Winchester from the north in case of pursuit.

"Where are we?" she asked listlessly, not really caring.

"An inn near Winchester." Guy dismounted and lifted Isabel out of the saddle, keeping his arm around her. "The gates of the city will be closed by the time we arrive, and won't be opened until morning. We might as well spend the night in some comfort."

As he led her towards the wood-and-thatch building by the roadside, Isabel contemplated another night in fitz-Alan's company. She felt strangely detached about it. In fact, nothing seemed quite real. She was so tired. So terribly tired. Perhaps that was a good thing. She would probably fall into slumber tonight if the devil himself were to share the room with her.

But the dreams came when she was tired. What if—?

Guy's fist hammering on the door of the inn broke into Isabel's rambling thoughts. She could hear footsteps approaching and the sound of a bar being lifted. A strange sort of inn, she reflected, to be barred to customers. But it all came to her from a distance.

"Who is it?" demanded a suspicious male voice from the other side of the door.

"Travellers needing shelter for the night," fitzAlan called back. "We were on our way to Winchester but have been waylaid and robbed."

"Robbed! Saints have mercy! Wait just a minute, sir; I'll have the door open directly."

The muffled exclamations of horror continued, accompanied by the sounds of another bar being removed and the rattle of a key. Under cover of the noise Guy's voice was a soft murmur in Isabel's ear. He spoke just as the door opened.

"You're my wife."

Wife?

Wife!

"*What*?" Isabel squeaked, wrenched forcibly out of her apathy. Before she could say more, she was confronted by a flaring rushlight held in the hand of a wiry little man who peered into their faces.

"Save us! You have your lady with you, sir. And only the one horse and that small pack… Thieves! Rogues! But enter, enter, my lord, my lady, and welcome. Walter! Here, you scoundrel, take my lord's horse and mind you care for him properly."

Confused by the light in her eyes and the constant chattering of their host, Isabel found herself ushered into the house before she could correct the man's assumption that she was fitzAlan's lady. A rosy-cheeked, motherly-looking woman, as small and wiry as the innkeeper, bustled forward, adding her exclamations to those of her husband.

"Robbed, did you say, my lord? Aye, the roads are not safe for anyone these days. You poor child," she added without drawing breath, turning her attention to Isabel. She urged her into the centre of the room, where a bright fire burned. "Come, my lady, sit by the warmth. I swear you are frozen to the bone. Lucky you were to escape with your lives, let alone your horse. But you'll be safe enough here. We keep the door barred tight."

"Aye," agreed her husband. "A fine thing, is it not, sir? That a man cannot keep an open house for the benefit of travellers such as yourselves."

"Never mind your gossip now, Thomas," exhorted their hostess. "Fetch up some ale, while I put the broth

back on the fire. My lady looks pale nigh unto death and
you stand there gabbling like a half-wit.''

"A loose tongue to match a loose brain, eh, Thomas?"
chuckled a third voice from the shadows beyond the fire.
"I don't know why Dame Sybil puts up with you." The
speaker came forward. He was a youngish fellow, dark of
hair and eyes, and modestly clad in a plain green tunic
over buff-coloured leggings.

An apprentice or pedlar, Guy judged, removing his
cloak. Glancing about the big, lofty room, he saw an elderly merchant snoring gently in a corner, hands folded
over his well-rounded belly. Two younger men, serfs by
their garb, and most likely travelling with the merchant
for his protection, sat at a nearby table nursing ale-cups.
They looked up incuriously for a moment, then went back
to their talk. An open door opposite gave a glimpse of
rows of barrels, and next to it a short flight of wooden
stairs led to another door above the store-room. Probably
the landlord's private solar, he thought. The place looked
clean and secure, the yokels doltish but harmless.

Guy sat down on the bench next to Isabel, casting a
quick glance down at her. She looked confused, almost
dazed. He carefully draped his thick woollen cloak over
her shoulders, wryly conscious of the indulgent smile on
the face of their hostess. No doubt the woman thought
him a concerned, doting husband. Only Isabel knew that
the arm he kept around her was more in warning than
attentiveness.

He noticed the shrewd examination Dame Sybil gave
them, and hoped she would believe that Isabel's worn
gown and his stained raiment were the clothing of im-
poverished nobility. Their lack of baggage was easily explained away by his tale of robbery, as was his wound.

This thought had no sooner crossed his mind than the good dame noticed his bloodstained sleeve.

"Holy Mother save us!" she exclaimed, shocked into abandoning her broth. "You've been hurt, my lord. Ralf, instead of lolling there mouthing insults, fetch my pot of salve from the pantry and—"

"Later, perhaps, if you would be so good, mistress," interposed Guy firmly. "My lady needs food and sleep before anything."

Sybil favoured him with a keen stare, but obediently turned back to the fire. "A few more minutes will make little difference," she agreed, seizing a knife and cutting several thick slices from a loaf of bread. "Food you shall have, and your poor lady looks asleep on her feet. You shall have our solar, my lord. 'Tis but a simple place, but you will be comfortable and private there."

"But…we can't take your bed," objected Isabel faintly, although she wondered why the thought of sleeping in a bed with fitzAlan seemed worse than sleeping with him on a bench. "A pallet by the fire will be—"

"Hush, my love," admonished her supposed husband. "Dame Sybil is a better judge of what you need."

If Isabel had had the energy she would have wiped the solicitous smile off his face. As it was, she had to be content with glaring at him, subsiding beneath the Dame's amused chuckle. What was the use of arguing? If she denied fitzAlan's story so she could have the solar to herself, she would become lost in a morass of other lies and explanations, and her mind wasn't clear enough to cope with such a task. Besides, Isabel comforted herself, as she concealed her ringless left hand in her skirts, she would never see these people again anyway.

"Don't think you've talked your way out of Sybil's ministrations," Ralf warned fitzAlan, stretching his legs out before him. "She won't rest until she's seen to your arm. How did it happen?"

"There were four of them," Guy answered briefly.

"Four!" exclaimed Sybil. "Against one? Cowards!"

"You've come lately from Winchester, my friend?" fitzAlan enquired of the younger man.

"Aye, my lord. Ralf the pedlar, at your service. I was in Winchester for St Giles' Fair last month—" he paused and shook his head "—but 'twas a poor showing this year, half the town still needing to be rebuilt, and the other half with scarce two farthings to rub together. As for those Flemish mercenaries of the Queen's, they were as likely to wreck the stalls as buy from them. I'm hoping for brisker trade on the road."

"You'd do better to stay put," argued Dame Sybil, pouring a thick savoury broth into two large bowls as Thomas returned from his foray into the cellaret with a tankard of ale in each hand. She passed one of the heavy dishes to Isabel, whose cold, shaking hands nearly dropped it.

Instantly Guy steadied the bowl. "Easy, sweetheart," he murmured, the note of concern in his voice causing fresh tears to gather in Isabel's eyes. She knew he was only pretending for the benefit of their audience. Why did she have to respond so to his gentleness? Even the thought of sharing a bed with him didn't seem so threatening when he was being kind. She *wanted* to be held in his arms, to feel safe. If only for this one night.

Forcing back the tears, she watched Dame Sybil take a warm stone from the fireplace to put between the sheets of the bed. The small kindness nearly overset her again. Had she lived with fear and harshness so long, Isabel wondered, that even ordinary thoughtfulness from strangers undermined her strength? It had started with fitzAlan battering at the wall of indifference she had erected between herself and the world, and now every little thing seemed to hinder its rebuilding.

Fortunately Sybil came bustling back, distracting her, armed with clean linen, warm water and a pot from which wafted an ominous odour. Isabel wrinkled her nose. Thomas and Ralf both groaned.

''Sheep fat,'' pronounced fitzAlan, looking amused at these reactions.

''Aye, mixed with healing herbs,'' confirmed Sybil. '''Tis of my own making. Take no notice of these weak-stomached creatures, my lord. This will heal your arm in a trice.''

''I know,'' he agreed. ''But will my lady allow me to share her bed tonight if I smell like an unwashed ram?''

Isabel nearly choked on a mouthful of broth. How could fitzAlan say such things so naturally? He spoke as if they had been married for years, and could joke about sharing a bed. It was bad enough that they were deceiving these innocent, kindly folk—did he have to do it so well? There was a sinking sensation in the pit of her stomach, as though she was falling deeper into the morass of lies. What had he said about getting the Bishop to absolve her sins? At this rate they would both need no less a person than the pope!

And the wretch knew what she was thinking, Isabel realised, as fitzAlan threw a wicked grin at her under cover of the good-natured ribaldry from the other three. Oh, why did he have to look so irresistibly handsome when he smiled like that? Why was it so difficult not to smile back?

And when he stood to strip off his tunic and shirt to have his arm attended to, why did he have to look so big and strong? So like the protector of her dreams.

"Now, my lord, hold still, if you please," commanded Dame Sybil, obviously not a female to be overawed by a man twice her size. "This bandage is stuck fast, but 'tis clean enough, thank the Saints."

Isabel felt herself blushing, but either fitzAlan took pity on her or his arm was hurting too much, for he made no comment on where the bandage had come from. Thomas stood by holding the bowl of water and looking anxious.

"Sybil's right, you know, Ralf," he said. "If thieves have taken to the roads you're likely to end up with a hole in you like…" He paused enquiringly.

"FitzAlan," Guy murmured.

"I dare say thieves are no more frequent on the roads than in the town," argued Ralf, saving Guy from further introductions. "There was plenty a cutpurse at the fair. A man had to keep his money close. Not to mention a sharp dagger in case of attack."

"Of what use is a dagger against four?" demanded Thomas gloomily.

"These weren't common thieves," corrected fitzAlan. His keen eyes went from Thomas to Ralf. "They were soldiers."

"Soldiers, you say, my lord?" Thomas looked unsurprised. "Aye, 'tis easy to believe in these woeful times. But whose?"

FitzAlan shrugged, earning himself an impatient cluck from Dame Sybil, who was trying to separate the blood-stained bandage from his arm with as little pain to her patient as possible.

"There's been no trouble in these parts," Thomas continued, stroking his jaw thoughtfully. "And further afield—well, 'tis only rumour. You recall what that minstrel told us some weeks back, Ralf? Where had he come from?"

"Further east," supplied Ralf. "There've been villages looted, men killed, women carried off—the usual tale of barons who do as they please while the King is helpless. I can't remember this particular fellow's name. Eudo…" Ralf broke off, shaking his head.

"What matter the name?" put in Dame Sybil. "'Tis all of a piece. Travellers stripped of their possessions and disappearing into castle dungeons, never to be heard of again. Towns pillaged and burned, crops razed to the ground, even Holy Mother Church defiled and mocked. There's no law anywhere in the land, nor will be until King Stephen is free and that woman packed off back to Anjou."

She paused to examine Guy's arm, bending to sniff at the healing gash. "No poisoned flesh," she announced. "'Tis badly bruised, but a good, clean wound, my lord. You heal quickly, if I may say so."

"Aye," agreed fitzAlan non-committally. "My thanks, Dame Sybil."

"And mine," added Isabel, finishing her broth and coming alive under the beneficial effects of warmth and food. She could act the loving spouse as well as fitzAlan, she decided, succumbing to a rare mischievous impulse to repay him for his earlier comments. "He would not let me tend it properly before, stubborn man that he—"

FitzAlan took instant revenge by leaning forward and silencing her with a slow, gentle kiss. Stunned, Isabel could only sit there, ensnared by the caressing warmth of his mouth. And something else—a strange, almost seeking touch that made her tremble inside. By the time he drew back she was blushing, and completely incapable of further speech. She felt as though all her bones had melted and that everyone knew it.

Dame Sybil earned her everlasting gratitude by suggesting that it was time she retire. Unfortunately her attempt at a dignified exit was ruined by fitzAlan murmuring in a perfectly audible voice that he would not be long in joining her.

Cheeks still aflame, Isabel scurried up the stairs after her hostess, trying to ignore Dame Sybil's chuckles and the three grinning male faces behind her.

"If you give me your gown, my lady, I will have it brushed for tomorrow," the kind woman offered, ushering Isabel into a tiny chamber containing a bed and a low stool. Sybil gestured to a wooden rod protruding from one wall for the hanging of clothes. "I would lend you something of mine, were it not for the fact that everything I own would be indecently short. But if you sit here a moment, I will comb out your hair, and you may keep the comb. The brutes must have ripped the coif from your head to leave your hair so tangled. Ah, 'tis a sorry pass we are come to when a lady is robbed of the clothes on her back."

"You are very kind," murmured Isabel. She hadn't given a thought to her lack of coif; her mind was too occupied with trying to think of an excuse for remaining in her gown, and failing dismally. She handed it over, silently cursing fitzAlan for calling her his wife. Why couldn't he have said she was his sister—or even a cousin?

"You'll be going to join the Queen, I suppose," remarked Sybil chattily, drawing the bone comb through Isabel's long hair. "Poor, gentle lady. How she must fret for the King. Fortunate you are to have your man with you, my lady. Although 'tis easy to see that he could not leave you behind, nor take his eyes off you for a moment. You are not long married, I warrant." She chuckled again.

"Not long," repeated Isabel weakly. Not leave her behind? Not take his eyes off her?

"I knew it. And a strong, lusty young husband he must be, too." She smiled and wagged the comb at Isabel. "Oh, no need to colour up, my lady, when 'tis merely we women gossiping. You wouldn't think it to look at him now, but my Thomas was just such a one. Not so big as your man, but he was a comely-looking lad in his day, and kind of heart. We are fortunate, you and I; 'tis a rare combination in a man."

"Aye," agreed Isabel, bemusedly struggling to reconcile the description "kind of heart" with her image of fitzAlan.

The mental exercise proved impossible. Arrogant, aggressive, autocratic. Those were the words she would choose, she decided vengefully, after Dame Sybil had tucked her into bed and returned to the hall. *And* mocking. Embarrassing her like that in front of everyone. Her cheeks burned again as she remembered the kiss and her utter submission to it. He hadn't even used force, holding her with nothing more than the subtle movement of his mouth on hers.

Turning over, Isabel pummelled the straw-filled pillow into a more comfortable shape. She was a weak fool—the pillow received another thump—imagining things when he had only been intent on silencing her. Thump! Thump! Just as she had imagined that concerned endearment after the fight on the riverbank. She must have been dreaming.

No! Don't think of that! Dreams were dangerous. Better to remember that he had called her sweetheart tonight, and it had been as much a sham as his kiss. If she weren't so tired she would be angry with him, except that it was difficult to remain angry with a man who had saved her life.

Isabel laid her cheek against the abused pillow and her eyelids drooped. No, she couldn't remain angry with fitz-Alan. She might tell herself he was arrogant and aggressive, but she could not suppress another little voice whispering that those very qualities went hand in hand with others that drew her irresistibly—courage, strength, utter dependability.

And, briefly glimpsed, in a place she longed to reach, there still lay tenderness.

He heard the whimpering first.

Not really whimpers, Guy thought, holding the candle higher as he entered the solar so he could see Isabel more clearly. The sounds were those of a person weeping and trying desperately not to be heard. She was crouched in one corner of the bed, against the wall, her knees drawn up, hands over her face, oblivious to his presence.

Guy put the candle down on the stool and reached across the bed. He'd been expecting something like this since Isabel had killed the soldier. She had been on the verge of hysteria then; add to that a day of travelling, with him pushing Chalon as fast as the horse could go carrying a double weight, plus the previous day's tensions, and it was a wonder she hadn't given in to it. But then he should have known that her courage was equal to the task of remaining calm until she was alone.

A tiny shaft of surprise jolted through him at the realisation that, this time, he had imputed courage to Isabel's stoic control instead of calculated coldness. However, before he had time to dwell on the thought, another stronger jolt shook him when his fingers grasped her wrists and he pulled her hands away from her face. An icy chill slid up his spine, causing the hair at his nape to rise.

She was completely unaware of him. Her eyes were

wide open, but they stared straight ahead, gazing in anguish at sights he couldn't even begin to imagine. Her soft lower lip was caught between her teeth, stifling the sobs that shook her body intermittently. She made no attempt to prevent him from taking her into his arms, gave no sign that she knew of his presence.

What had happened to her, to cause such torment to visit her in sleep? It had to be more than the trauma of the afternoon. As Guy gathered Isabel close to him, her words at the ford flashed into his mind. It was different, she had said. Killing someone was different from seeing it done. At the time he'd thought she was referring to his slaying of the two men-at-arms. But now he had to wonder what other deaths she had witnessed, what other acts of brutality.

And what was happening to *him*, that he felt torn apart, rent violently in two, at the sight of her agony?

This was no act. Though rigid with tension, she was totally acquiescent in his arms, still asleep, and gripped by God knew what nightmares. An unaccustomed feeling of helplessness washed over him. He didn't know whether to wake her, or even if that was possible if her sleep was so deep that she could crouch in a corner, weeping, and not wake herself.

Before he could decide, a shudder passed through Isabel's body and her lashes fluttered closed. He felt her lips move, warm against his throat. "So dark," she whispered. "So dark."

"No, sweet," he answered very softly. "The candle still burns." He had hoped to waken her gently, but she drew in a small gasping breath. The little hand resting against his bare chest was suddenly ice-cold. Guy drew back so he could see her face. Her eyes were open again, but heavy-lidded now and dazed, unfocused. She was clearly exhausted and barely awake.

"What—?"

"Sssh," he soothed, folding her closer as protectiveness flooded him. "'Tis all right, sweetheart. Go to sleep. You're safe now."

"Safe?" It was a small, disbelieving whisper. She lay limply in his arms, those cloudy, fathomless eyes gazing up into his. Her next whimpered, broken words cut him to the heart.

"Where...were...you?"

Guy almost flinched. Did she know who was holding her? Were those words meant for him? She was looking straight at him, but...

Then her lashes closed once more, and Guy knew there would be no answers tonight. Her body relaxed against him in sleep and his arms tightened, supporting her instinctively. God, she was soft. Soft and small and hauntingly lovely. And he ached. Not only his injured arm, but his whole body throbbed with wanting her. He wanted to press his mouth to her softly parted lips and taste the sweetness within, he wanted to push aside the loosely tied neck of her shift and let his hand savour the warmth of her flesh, he wanted to lay her back on the bed and hold her against him as he had at the river-crossing; he wanted *her*.

With a careful movement at odds with the set grimness in his face, Guy shifted position so he could hold Isabel more comfortably. There would be no sleep for him tonight. Sleep was impossible while she lay in his arms like this, completely vulnerable. And twice as impossible while an insistent question, as tormenting as any nightmare, began to beat at his brain.

Despite all the evidence against her, despite her own words, her betraying silences, had he been wrong about Isabel from the start?

Chapter Seven

Isabel awoke slowly, reluctant to abandon the warmth
and safety of her snug nest of blankets. She had felt
like this once before, and recently, she thought with
sleepy vagueness. Secure and warm. Protected. Safe—
with fitzAlan.

FitzAlan!

Full awareness and memory returned in a blinding
flash. She remembered everything. *Everything!* Oh, not
the details of the dream, but that didn't matter. The nightmare had once been real and the spectres visiting her in
sleep were always the same. No, the picture tormenting
her mind was of herself waking in fitzAlan's arms and
staying there. Worse, she had fallen asleep again, cradled
to the warmth of his body, after asking him why he hadn't
rescued her!

Isabel almost groaned aloud. How was she ever going
to face him again? He knew of her weakness. What was
he going to do? What questions would he have this time?

She lay very still for a moment, trying to think. It was
very quiet in the solar. Dared she hope that fitzAlan had
already risen, giving her time to resume her protective
mask? Holding her breath, Isabel slitted one eye open to

encounter the crude, bare wall of the inn solar only inches away. She glanced down, to discover she was hugging the very edge of the mattress. Which meant that there was a lot of bed left to investigate before she knew if it was safe even to turn around. Listening carefully for any sound that might indicate fitzAlan's presence, she stretched out a cautious foot, ready to withdraw it immediately if she encountered so much as a hint of him.

Nothing. Exploring further, Isabel decided she was alone. Both eyes opened and her breath rushed out in a small burst of relief as she rolled over on to her back— and her heart slammed to a stop.

FitzAlan was sitting on the stool by the bed, back propped against the wall, arms folded across his chest, long legs stretched out in front of him, his brilliant light eyes fixed on her from under half-lowered lashes. Isabel wondered how long he'd been sitting there—intent, watchful, waiting. For a fleeting instant she felt as though she had woken to find herself in the lair of a dangerous wild animal. The wolf's lair, she thought. And he had her trapped.

Seeing that she was awake, fitzAlan sat forward, resting his forearms on his thighs, his eyes never leaving her face. "Did you sleep well?" Somehow he made the softly growled question sound incredibly intimate.

Isabel swallowed nervously, pondering her answer as if the fate of the kingdom rested on it. Could she pretend not to remember last night? Would he believe her? People did forget dreams. FitzAlan had done so himself, except that his had been caused by fever and… Oh, blessed Saint Elizabeth, help me.

Not trusting herself to speak, she nodded.

"Good. How do you feel today?"

"Why?" The suspicious query slipped out before she

could stop it. Isabel could have bitten her tongue when she saw one corner of fitzAlan's mouth kick up.

"You've endured a great deal, especially yesterday."

"Yesterday?" Her eyes shifted to his mouth, staring in fascination as the smile deepened. Then, abruptly realising what she was doing, she wrenched her gaze back to his. "Aye, yesterday!" she exclaimed accusingly, seizing on the distraction when his words finally got through the strange fog in her brain. "I thought we were going to be killed, and you *enjoyed* it!"

The smile vanished, leaving fitzAlan's face shuttered, almost brooding. "Action of some kind was long overdue," he muttered cryptically.

What did he mean by that? Another vivid picture, this time of herself standing by the ford in fitzAlan's arms, insinuated itself into Isabel's mind. She had a distinctly uncomfortable feeling that he was not referring to the fight which had followed that little incident. And if he thought she had endured a great deal, why hadn't he mentioned her nightmare? Where was the barrage of questions she had expected?

A discreet tap on the door reminded her that they were not alone, thank the saints. She made a belated grab for her wits while Guy rose and went to answer the summons, exchanging a few murmured words with whoever was on the other side of the door.

When he turned back into the room Isabel saw he had her gown in his hand. He stopped a pace or two away from the bed and regarded her with an unexpectedly teasing glint in his eyes. Another smile played about his lips as he held out her dress.

"Time to rise, my lady wife."

Not while he was standing there daring her with his eyes, Isabel vowed silently. She sat up, clutching the blankets to her breast and feeling faintly ridiculous when she recalled her lack of modesty in the hut. But everything seemed different this morning. Waking up to that penetrating ice-blue gaze was enough to throw *anyone* off balance for the rest of the day. Nor did she understand this new playful mood of fitzAlan's. The quick shifts from concern to curtness to mischief were confusing. And that lurking half-smile was doing peculiar things to her pulse-rate.

"I am not your lady wife, my lord," she pointed out as coolly as possible. "And I do not intend to entertain you by dressing while you watch."

FitzAlan tossed the gown carelessly on to the stool, where it promptly slithered to the floor. Isabel opened her mouth to protest at this cavalier treatment of her clothing, only to shut it again in alarm when he took a step forward and leaned over her, bracing his hands on the mattress and trapping her between them. She stared up into his blue eyes, trying to conquer the urge to scoot further up the bed. Apart from the need to preserve some semblance of pride, she knew such a retreat would cause her to lose her hold on the blankets.

"This new-found modesty is very admirable, sweetheart, but a little out of place when you've just spent the night in my arms."

Isabel's eyes closed for a despairing second. She clutched the blankets even more tightly. "I know we had to share a bed, thanks to your lies," she corrected, valiantly trying to stave off the dreaded interrogation.

It didn't come. Instead, fitzAlan leaned an inch closer. "For all I knew, the inn could have been full. You may not think so now, little one, but you were safer as my wife."

Isabel turned her face away. "That's a matter of opinion," she muttered beneath her breath. Then, afraid he might have heard, she added waspishly, "You mean you suspected I might run away. 'Tis what you thought in that hut, if you recall."

"Then, perhaps," admitted fitzAlan. "Not now."

This brief reply threatened to bring the argument to an abrupt halt. The distant sounds of the inn door being opened for the day sounded unexpectedly loud in the silence.

"Let me see your eyes."

The low, husky command sent a shiver down her spine. "No," she whispered stubbornly, keeping her head to the side. She would not look around. Not while he remained so close that she could feel his warm breath against her cheek. But then, as the silence lengthened and fitzAlan still didn't move, curiosity got the better of her. "Why?"

"Your eyes don't lie, sweetheart."

Sweetheart? Little one?

Slowly, as though pulled towards him against her will, Isabel obeyed. And was instantly caught, imprisoned, by the warmth of his gaze. His eyes were like blue flames, she thought, drawing her irresistibly into his fire. She had forgotten all about her dream and its consequences.

"I thought so," he murmured. "I saw it before, and felt it last night when I kissed you. Something missing."

"My virtue, I suppose," snapped Isabel, fighting a losing battle against the treacherous weakness creeping over her. He was so big. So warm. She was melting inside. How could she feel like this when he wasn't even touching her?

FitzAlan's eyes burned fiercely into hers for another second, then he straightened, stepping back. "The innocence I saw five years ago is gone," he said calmly, "and one day you're going to tell me how it happened. But that isn't what I meant." His expression gentled and he gave her a slow smile filled with a conviction that was very male and utterly sure. "Real experience hasn't taken its place."

Isabel was so stunned that she nearly fell back on the pillows. Still gripping the blankets as if they were a lifeline, she stared back at fitzAlan, completely speechless.

He reached out a big hand and touched her cheek fleetingly with the backs of his fingers. "Our breakfast is ready. I'll settle up with Master Thomas while you dress."

And he was gone, leaving Isabel to gaze blankly at the wooden panels of the door while she cudgelled her brain, trying to decide what had caused such an astounding about-face. Surely not one brief nightmare. She remembered uneasily that he hadn't said a word about it. Perhaps he hadn't understood her last night. She had been all but asleep and possibly incoherent. But that left only one alternative—that fitzAlan was beginning to trust her. That he believed her story.

A quick rush of hope surged through her, only to be instantly squashed when Isabel remembered the treacherous reality behind the truth. She felt sick. Of what use was the truth, she asked herself bitterly, when it could so easily be turned against her? Aye, she had told fitzAlan that she wanted to leave Matilda—but the Empress had planned her escape. She had denied his accusations of betrayal—but would spy on the Queen. She might have saved fitzAlan's life—only to use him.

Of what use was the truth?

The truth was sometimes very simple, Guy decided, as he led Chalon over to the open doorway of the inn. Isabel had grasped the opportunity of his presence to escape from Gloucester.

Of course that didn't alter the fact that de Tracy had changed sides. Nor did it remove the niggling suspicion that Isabel was hiding something. Whenever her family had been mentioned she looked as guilty as hell. But he could handle that. She was not responsible for the actions of her male relatives. The real problem lay in convincing her that he could be trusted with her secrets.

Guy grimaced, remembering the way he'd been treating her. It wasn't going to be easy. However, he didn't have time now for self-reproach, nor to wonder why Isabel's seeming betrayal had cut so deeply that he had instantly thought the worst of her, had immediately accepted Matilda's word though he'd known how vindictive and spiteful the woman could be.

Isabel's personal integrity had been there in her clear gaze all the time, if he'd been thinking with his head instead of with his emotions. Integrity, combined with wariness, pride, and the kind of stoic endurance that accompanied an understanding of suffering, a loss of innocence that went as deep as the soul. But Guy would have staked his own soul on the fact that Isabel had never lain with a man.

The knowledge sent a fierce surge of possessiveness through him, which almost translated itself into violent action when he saw Isabel emerge from the inn with Ralf hovering attentively over her. The younger man's voice carried clearly across the small space separating them.

''Dame Sybil mentioned that you have no ribbon to fasten your braid, my lady. You will honour me beyond measure if you accept so small a token from one who is your humble servant.''

Guy's fist clenched involuntarily, but, fortunately, common sense reasserted itself. Much as he wanted to pound Ralf into the mud, he contented himself with sending the fellow a narrow-eyed glare which brought a look of respectful caution to the pedlar's usually cheerful countenance.

"You're very kind—" Isabel began uncertainly.

"But there's no need to throw away your wares for nought when business is so poor," Guy interjected bluntly. He produced a penny, nicked at the side to denote its present value of a half-penny, and tossed it to Ralf.

The young pedlar cast him a wary glance and apparently decided on practicality over valour. He pocketed the coin.

Isabel, however, drew breath to argue. Before she got a word out Guy seized her gently by the shoulders and turned her around, so that he stood between her and Ralf. He felt her jump slightly when he slid his fingers beneath her braid. She started to move away, lifting a hand to stop him. "I can—"

A careful tug on her hair silenced her. "Keep still," he murmured, and bent to drop a warm kiss on the tender nape of her neck before tying the ribbon. He had to take a deep breath to stop himself tasting the delicate spot again.

Isabel felt the kiss clear down to her toes. A dismaying number of seconds passed before she could even move. And then, as though determined to keep her in a state of confusion, fitzAlan startled her again. Instead of lifting her into the saddle first, as he had always done before, he mounted Chalon, turned the horse in a tight circle to present its left flank to Isabel, and extended an imperative hand. One booted foot was thrust out for her to use as a stirrup.

Isabel stared at that strong hand for several seconds before lifting her gaze to fitzAlan's face. Piercing blue eyes, full of masculine command, gleamed down at her.

She went very still, the sensation of being poised too near the edge of a precipice sweeping over her again. This was no mere offer of assistance, she saw. FitzAlan was asking—no, *demanding*—something from her. It was there in the challenging tilt of his head, in the assertive reach of his hand. She had never felt the force of his personality more strongly.

Yet he was giving her a choice, Isabel realised suddenly. And it was not the option of walking behind all the way to Winchester. He was sitting far enough back in the saddle for her to mount without his help if she wished to. He might demand, but he was not going to force her.

That last thought prompted Isabel's decision. Placing her hand in his, she prepared to mount.

Something fierce blazed in his eyes for an instant. She saw the muscles in his thigh brace to take her slight weight, then his long fingers closed over hers, such overwhelming possession in his grip that Isabel gasped, suddenly, inexplicably, afraid, and tried to pull back.

It was too late. She was pulled upwards with startling velocity, the sensation of flying through the air causing the world to tilt so precariously that she found herself clinging to fitzAlan like a drowning woman. She stared into the handsome face so close to her, aware of his powerful body against hers with every fibre of her being, and all she could think of to say was a trembling, "Does this mean your arm is better, my lord?"

He grinned down at her. "Much better, sweetheart. Thanks to Dame Sybil's potion." He nodded in the direction of the inn.

A tide of crimson flowed into Isabel's face when she hurriedly disentangled herself from fitzAlan and saw that Ralf had been joined by Sybil and Master Thomas, who had come to the inn door to wave them off. Ducking her head, she busied herself arranging her skirts comfortably, fighting embarrassment and wondering how she could have forgotten all about their audience.

And she had also forgotten the stern lecture she had given herself earlier, she thought despairingly. The lecture had kept her mind occupied all through breakfast, and had contained a great deal of sound advice on the best method of dealing with fitzAlan, which had not included embracing him as if he were in truth her husband. But with those powerful arms enclosing her she couldn't seem to remember a word of it. Indeed, she had scarcely enough presence of mind to return Sybil's bright smile and bid farewell to the genial innkeepers.

Surely fitzAlan had not held her so close yesterday? She was practically draped all over him. She should move away, or at least sit forward, but the horrifying part was that she *liked* it. His arms were strong, his body muscled and hard. Her blood seemed to flow swifter, hotter, in response. She felt soft and vulnerable, scared and—*excited*. Obviously she was losing her mind.

As Chalon responded to Guy's signal to start, Isabel tried to remind herself of fitzAlan's arrogant judgement of her, his mockery, his taunting insults, the frightening force of his anger. Not to mention his probable reaction should he discover the truth.

She repeated the list again. And a third time. Nothing changed. Instead, her stubborn mind persisted in remembering the unexpectedly lighter side he had shown at the inn. Her body persisted in leaning into his warmth, seeking his strength—almost as though it knew something she did not. Even her skin seemed to recall the touch of his hands, strong but tender.

The last sensation was unnerving to say the least. It was not until they had rounded a bend in the road, and the echoes of Master Thomas's good wishes had long since died away, that Isabel managed to pull herself together enough to recall her resolution to put fitzAlan at a safe distance—and keep him there. She had a task to carry out. A task which made her his enemy, not—

"Did you have to behave so churlishly with Ralf?" she burst out, saying the first thing to enter her head. "He was only trying to help."

"He was drooling all over you."

Everything else was promptly pushed to the background. Isabel turned her head to stare up at fitzAlan incredulously. "He was not!" she denied. "How can you say such a thing?" Indignation showed clearly on her expressive face. "Ralf isn't a *dog*! 'Drooling', indeed!"

"Listen, my little innocent, I know what was in Ralf's mind."

"By our Lady," exclaimed Isabel, quite exasperated. "He's only a pedlar."

"That doesn't make him less of a man," countered fitzAlan. "Another smile like the one you were giving him and he would have been fastening that ribbon himself. And I don't want another man's hands on you," he added in a soft growl that sounded incredibly dangerous.

"Really, my lord." The protest came out weakly and Isabel strove to inject some firmness into her voice. It was difficult when she could hardly speak at all, but she couldn't let a statement like that go unchallenged. "You do not have the right—"

"You gave me the right when you accepted my protection, sweetheart."

"Don't call me that," she said crossly, aware that she was becoming side-tracked. She should be firmly denying his claim to *any* rights where she was concerned, not arguing about his habit of using unsuitable endearments.

"Ralf meant no harm, and, in any case, there is no need to keep up the pretence that we're married."

FitzAlan smiled down at her. "I'll kill any man who touches you, Isabel. You had best keep that in mind."

He might as well have knocked all the breath out of her body. The shocking contrast between fitzAlan's smile and the stark violence in his words turned Isabel's legs to water. She had to grip the saddle to prevent herself pitching forward on to the road.

What was happening here? Why this sudden show of possessiveness? It didn't make sense. Nothing made sense today. Even if Guy believed her tale, surely he couldn't change his opinion of her so completely? He had seemed to hate her, but now...

Now it was too late, Isabel reminded herself miserably. She could not let him get close to her. Already she was terrified of what lay ahead. How could she cope if fitzAlan was starting to like her? She must keep him away, keep fighting him, because as long as she fought with him she and Edmund were safe.

"There's no need to look so worried," he observed softly, yanking Isabel back to the present. "I know you would not behave dishonourably." He lifted one hand to her mouth and gently freed her lower lip from between her teeth, soothing it with a stroking, caressing movement of his thumb.

Isabel's mouth went dry. She hadn't even been aware of gnawing on her abused lip. Now it tingled under fitzAlan's touch. Her whole body tingled. She couldn't speak, could not even think while his thumb was brushing back and forth across her mouth like that. His touch was feather-light and yet deeply compelling. She wanted to part her lips and—

No!

Terrified that he would guess her wanton reaction to the heart-stopping touch of his hand, Isabel jerked her head away. FitzAlan slid his fingers into her hair, exerting just enough pressure to force her face back up to his.

Isabel knew her heart had ceased beating because now it shuddered into action again, racing so fast that she began to feel faint. She was unable to meet the intense look in his eyes, and her lashes fluttered wildly against her cheeks. His mouth was so close. Was he going to kiss her? A wild thrill of anticipation shot through her, shocking, frightening, exciting.

"Easy," fitzAlan murmured, his voice like dark velvet. His hand slipped down to encircle her throat.

Did he think she was a horse that needed soothing? Isabel wondered, half angrily, half hysterically. His hand felt so warm, so strong, pressed against the frantic pulse beneath his fingers. She swallowed and knew he must be able to feel the betraying movement. What was he doing to her? *Why* was he doing it?

Then all coherent thought fled as fitzAlan's hand lowered further. His right arm was suddenly rigid, holding her still, at the same moment as that warm, strong hand brushed across the upper curve of her breast.

The contact lasted barely seconds. Isabel had scarcely felt the fiery rush of blood to her cheeks, the quick involuntary swelling of her flesh, before fitzAlan wrenched his hand away, transferring the reins from the other as if that was the only thing that would prevent him from touching her again. His free arm tightened further, pulling Isabel hard against him.

"Hush," he whispered against her hair, although she had made no sound. "'Tis all right, sweet, 'tis all right."

Still shocked, utterly shaken at his action, Isabel forgot all thought of fighting him. Turning her heated face into his chest, she shrank into fitzAlan's embrace, her hands clinging to his tunic for support. She was vaguely aware of the irony of seeking safety from the man who threatened a danger far greater than any she had ever faced, but she pressed closer—needing him, wanting him, longing for him to hold her forever.

A minute crawled by. The intensity of the moment was almost more than she could bear. FitzAlan's heart thundered against her cheek and his body was strung as tightly as her own, the arm around her like iron. Isabel started to shake, fear for Edmund maintaining its clutch on her mind, and an increasingly urgent desire to trust fitzAlan tearing at her heart.

Then a shudder went through him and his arm relaxed. She felt him glance down at her.

"You don't have to be afraid, Isabel," he murmured softly. "Tell me what troubles you. Trust me."

"What do you mean?" she faltered, trying to summon the will-power to move. She wondered if fitzAlan had noticed that Chalon, taking advantage of his master's unusual inattentiveness, had stopped and was investigating a bush by the side of the road.

"I want to know why you left Gloucester," stated fitzAlan. His voice was still gentle, but the iron will behind the question was unmistakable. "The Countess of Anjou can't hurt you now. All you have to do is tell me the truth."

For several seconds Isabel remained absolutely still. Then as the meaning of Guy's actions sank into her brain she pushed herself back, glaring up at him and quite unaware that her hands remained splayed against his chest.

"The truth!" she exclaimed, too hurt and angry to remember that he still had every reason to be suspicious. "Is that what this little scene is about, my lord? Did you think I would fall straight into your arms, confessing everything?''

"I don't know," Guy replied, a strangely crooked smile curving his mouth. "Will you?"

"Why, you conceited, arrogant... I don't have anything to confess!" Isabel cried, her voice rising. She was so furious that she forgot that he had first asked for her trust. The humiliating knowledge that those tender, ardent caresses—indeed, his every action since she had awoken this morning—had been coldly calculated shattered her fragile composure in seconds.

Oh, how could she have let herself be so easily tricked, so eager to believe that he had changed? How could she have responded so instantly? And how dared he use such a method, and then have the gall to ask if it would have succeeded?

"I am not so easy a conquest!" she stormed. "Does that answer your question, my lord? And you won't get any more answers out of me just because you started to...started to..."

"Make love to you," fitzAlan supplied. There was an oddly grim note in his voice now, and all signs of humour had vanished.

"Love had nothing to do with it!" shrieked Isabel, almost beside herself with rage and shame. Suddenly noticing the position of her hands, she snatched them back, thrusting aside fitzAlan's supporting arm. Far from wanting him to hold her, she now wished to get as far from him as possible. Without stopping to think, Isabel leapt from the saddle.

The road was hard. She landed awkwardly, falling to her hands and knees. Small stones bit into her palms and an involuntary cry escaped her lips, to be quickly followed by another when fitzAlan's hand grasped her elbow. She had forgotten how fast he could move—he must have been off Chalon in seconds—but as soon as he hauled her to her feet Isabel began to struggle, swinging her free arm up.

Her hand was caught and held before it was anywhere near its target.

"Not this time, you little vixen," he grated. "Calm down before you hurt yourself again." He started brushing the dirt from her hands.

Isabel tried to yank them free. "I'm not hurt," she spat. Then immediately ruined the effect of this proud statement by adding, "You tried to use me," in a choked, husky voice that betrayed all too clearly where the real hurt lay.

FitzAlan gave a short laugh and released her. "Then perhaps we're even, my lady."

Isabel stared up at him, momentarily silenced, her eyes stricken. She wanted to cry out in protest against his charge, but her throat was too tight to allow the words to escape.

FitzAlan made a slicing gesture with his hand. "Isabel, I didn't mean that," he began quickly. "I only wanted… Oh, *hell*!" He turned away, raking his hand through his blond hair.

It looked more silver than gold on this dull, overcast day. How could she notice such a trivial detail when her vision was impeded by tears? Isabel asked herself. Worse still, she longed to reach up and smooth the ruffled disorder caused by his impatient gesture. She really was losing her reason. How else could he have the power to make her feel this way—angry and hurt and yearning?

Then fitzAlan turned back to her and the serious, searching expression in those piercing light eyes banished reason of any description. Isabel was very much afraid he was looking straight into her heart. Before she knew what she was going to say, the words were tumbling out, tripping over each other in her nervousness.

"I didn't use you like *that*. I couldn't…I've never… This morning you said you knew…"

"I do know," he said swiftly. "Isabel, I do know. I didn't mean to hurt you." He lifted his hand to her face and caught an escaping tear-drop on the tip of one finger. "Please don't cry," he murmured. "Why should you trust me, indeed, when I'm so clumsy with you?"

"I…I know I am in your debt," Isabel stammered. His gentleness had her utterly confused. Was this wry contrition yet another ruse to weaken her defences?

He shook his head, still stroking her cheek softly. "There are no debts between us, little one."

With a supreme effort of will Isabel swallowed the lump in her throat and forced back her tears. Her mind raced like a deer before the hunter. Did she dare trust fitzAlan? He had claimed to believe in her innocence, but had not apologised for misjudging and insulting her. He had started to caress her and had been enough in control to ask questions. Could a man feign desire to obtain the information he wanted? She didn't know, but she thought it might be possible.

Why did that conclusion hurt so much? The suspicion that fitzAlan might have cold-bloodedly used kindness, then seduction, for his own ends almost felt like a betrayal. But wasn't she about to betray *him*?

Isabel went cold. She stepped back, shivering slightly when fitzAlan's hand fell away from her face. Where had that question come from? It was the Queen she had to betray. Not fitzAlan. It couldn't be fitzAlan. It would destroy her to have to choose between Guy and her brother.

Sweet lord, what was she thinking? FitzAlan meant

nothing to her. She was confusing him with her old dreams. And she could not sort out her brain while he stood less than a foot away, watching her with eyes that gave away nothing of his own thoughts. She had to get to Winchester. Then she could decide what to do. She wouldn't think beyond that.

"We had best be on our way, my lord," she managed in a barely audible voice. "Before we become objects of interest to the passing traffic."

"There is no passing traffic," he contradicted, frowning at her. "Isabel…"

But, even as he spoke, two black-robed monks driving a small donkey-cart crested the hill ahead of them. Four men-at-arms rode alongside, and bringing up the rear was another monk herding a flock of sheep and goats. The Benedictines nodded genially as the procession clattered past.

FitzAlan looked after them, a wry smile slowly replacing the frown. "I stand corrected, my lady."

And, despite everything, a shaky smile tugged at Isabel's lips also. She couldn't help it. The prosaic sight of monks going about their everyday business, just when she needed them, was irresistible. But the smile lasted less than a heartbeat and vanished entirely when she saw that fitzAlan continued to watch the small party until it disappeared from view.

"What is it?" she asked, following the direction of his gaze.

He shrugged quickly. "Nothing. I was just thinking there might be something to that tale Ralf told last night, if the monks need an escort to move their flocks."

It was Isabel's turn to frown. A dim memory teased the back of her mind. She hadn't really been listening to the talk last night, but there had been—what? A word? A name? She shook her head, strangely uneasy, then the vague feeling that she had let something important slip through her fingers faded away when fitzAlan turned back to her. His eyes made a swift study of her face, before he cast a glance at the sky.

"Come. 'Tis beginning to look like rain again. The sooner we reach Winchester, the better."

He spoke with such calm practicality that Isabel felt her resolve harden. She had been right not to trust him. Surely if that tense moment had affected him at all he would not sound so cool and distant now as he reached for Chalon's reins. He pulled the grey's head out of a bush and gestured to Isabel to mount. Without assistance this time. Isabel told herself she didn't care. She didn't need his help. She would rebuild her defences and cope alone, the way she had always done.

Guy led Chalon back on to the road, casting another searching glance up at Isabel's closed face. She had managed to squeeze herself into such a small space in the saddle that there was practically room left for *two* men. Two days ago the sight would have amused him. Now it only increased his determination to find out what had made her so wary, so controlled.

But her trust would not be easily won. He was going to have to move with extreme caution. Not a pace he usually favoured. Especially when he knew he could push aside her doubts by making love to her. The urge to do just that was almost overpowering, but he wanted Isabel to come to him willingly, not because he had taken advantage of her innocence.

Unfortunately the discovery that he could make her respond to even his lightest caress was enough to make the ride into Winchester a damned uncomfortable one. He might be able to force his mind to forget the way she had felt in his arms. His body was another matter.

Swinging himself into the saddle, Guy turned Chalon's head towards Winchester and began to consider the various means whereby he could ensure that Isabel belonged to him while he was giving her the time she needed.

Chapter Eight

Winchester. Seat of England's rulers since before the coming of the Conqueror.

Isabel stared up at the royal castle high on its hill overlooking the town and wondered what the grim stone fortress would mean to her. Pennants fluttered in the breeze, indication that the Queen was in residence. A little distance away the spire of the old minster soared towards the clouds. Several shorter spires surrounded it, like chicks around a mother hen.

So many churches. How would she find the right one?

Anxiety fluttered deep inside her stomach, like thousands of tiny moths, but then they rode in through the north gate of the city and the clamorous bustle of the narrow, crowded streets assaulted her senses. It was like entering a whole new world, thought Isabel. She gazed, wide-eyed, at the first large town she had ever visited, for Matilda had not permitted her the freedom of Gloucester.

The noise was deafening. Street vendors called out the merits of their wares, shouting each other down in the hope of attracting customers from the goodwives who were out doing the morning marketing. The shrill tones of their voices mingled with the bawled instructions of a master mason, whose men were engaged in repairing the spire of a nearby church. Across the street a merchant cursed vociferously, shaking his fist aloft, as slops hurled from an upper room landed a scant inch in front of him.

Chalon picked his way nervously among the throng, tossing his head and splattering mud over the feet of more than one unwary pedestrian who was too slow to get out of the way. Nobody seemed to mind, thought Isabel. Or, if they did, they knew better than to remonstrate with the grim-faced man behind her.

An unexpected pang lanced through her as she realised that after today fitzAlan would no longer stand between her and the rest of the world. She stifled it immediately, straightening her spine. Once she met the Queen she would not need fitzAlan's protection. She had managed without it before; she would do so again.

They turned into a quieter street where open shutters gave a view of craftsmen bent over worktables placed at the front of their shops to catch the best of the morning light. Silversmiths, goldsmiths and moneyers seemed to abound. One fellow was haggling with a customer over the price of a heavy silver buckle.

"Why do they all wear yellow?" queried Isabel, noticing the bright clothing along the entire length of the street.

"They're Jews," fitzAlan told her. "'Tis their colour."

"Jews? But do they all live here in the one street?"

"Aye. 'Tis near the castle since they're under the King's protection."

"Why is that? Don't the townspeople like them?"

She felt fitzAlan shrug. "Sometimes there's trouble."

His voice had become more terse with each of her questions, and now his brief reply caused Isabel to fall silent. She wondered uneasily what was in his mind, but at that moment the main gate of the castle came into view and, as they started across the drawbridge, a new wave of apprehension assailed her.

Several buildings, showing signs of the recent siege, lay within the walls of the bailey, which was dominated by the huge stone keep built by the Conqueror. A whole street of houses had been demolished to make way for the edifice looming above her, Isabel vaguely recalled hearing. But then William had had to build the castle because he had permitted the defeated Harold's widow to remain in her own hall. Which just went to prove, she reflected, that there were two sides to every situation. Unfortunately, this conclusion didn't make her feel any better.

A loud hail from across the compound broke into her thoughts. With a start, Isabel saw that they were in the midst of the busy activity that characterised every large household. She watched, round-eyed, as several men-at-arms, pikes in hand, marched by on their way through the gate, and tried not to imagine herself a prisoner in their charge. Nearer, a plump, important-looking individual was tallying the stores being unloaded from a recently arrived wagon, and from the armoury came a steady clanging as the blacksmith hammered the dents out of the shield of a knight, who stood by watching.

And striding across the bailey towards them was a tall, dark man of about fitzAlan's age, dressed in businesslike chainmail and armed with both sword and bow.

"Guy! I expected you yesterday. How the devil did the Empress's messenger pass you? And you travelling across country. I would have thought—"

The words were broken off abruptly when the man saw Isabel sharing the saddle with fitzAlan. Keen hazel eyes under black brows widened incredulously, before sparkling with a quick mischievous gleam. "By every saint in the calendar! I don't believe it. You've been side-tracked by a woman. Wait until Joanna hears about this!''

"Put a gauntlet in it, Simon," recommended fitzAlan, his apparent imperviousness to this gleeful threat restoring Isabel's stomach to its proper place. Although why it should have plummeted to her feet at the mention of the unknown Joanna, she could not have said.

"What's this about a messenger?" Guy continued tersely. "And what are you doing here? Is the Bishop with the Queen?"

"Well, 'tis nice to see you, too," replied his friend indignantly. "Aye, the Bishop's within. The man won't step foot outside his castle without myself as escort, so I have to kick my heels until his business with Queen Matilda is done. I might as well move into the place."

FitzAlan dismounted and reached up to lift Isabel to the ground. He made no attempt to present her to the other man, however, apparently so deep in thought that he seemed to have forgotten her very existence. Isabel didn't know whether she was relieved or affronted. All of a sudden several unpleasant consequences of spending a large amount of time alone with fitzAlan, without so much as a spit-boy for chaperon, rose forcibly to her mind. Unless Guy came up with an acceptable explanation, the entire Court would be gossiping about them. And she was supposed to remain inconspicuous.

Their companion cast them exactly the sort of curious glance Isabel had just been anticipating. "As you may guess, his Grace's business is to do with the fellow who rode in here yesterday morning. I swear he must have ridden from Gloucester at the gallop to arrive before you. What's going on?"

"The Countess is covering her tracks," murmured Guy. "I can even tell you what her message says." He looked thoughtfully at Isabel. "So your warning was genuine also, my lady."

"What warning?" demanded Simon instantly. "What tracks? Will someone tell me what is going on?"

"Later," returned fitzAlan brusquely. "I have to see the Queen at once, and privately. Give me about ten minutes, then bring Isabel into the hall, will you?"

Before either of his listeners could reply to these curt instructions, fitzAlan shoved his reins into the other man's hands and strode off towards the forebuilding without another word. They continued to watch in stunned silence as Guy ran up the stairs and disappeared through the doorway, then turned to look at each other.

Isabel could not think of a single thing to say. The only words in her head were aimed at fitzAlan and they were quite unrepeatable. So much for explanations! Did he think she was invisible? And how dared he leave her standing out here in the bailey like a...like a *serf*?

Her escort seemed equally speechless, but he recovered first. "Uh...Guy met you on the road?" he queried delicately, with obvious caution.

Isabel shook her head. She would never forgive fitzAlan for putting her in this position, she promised herself. Her scowl was furious enough to cause her companion to revise his original opinion.

"No, of course not," he murmured hastily. "I'm Simon de Villiers, by the way. Um...Isabel, is it?"

"Lady Isabel de Tracy," pronounced Isabel clearly, finally retrieving her voice. If fitzAlan expected *her* to explain everything, he could cope with the truth, she decided angrily. It would be worth a little temporary gossip to see how he did it. "My lord fitzAlan agreed to give me his escort from Gloucester. Unfortunately, in times such as these, a lady must accept whatever ill-mannered protection is available at short notice.''

A grin appeared unexpectedly on de Villiers' face. ''Guy can be a little abrupt,'' he agreed. His bemused gaze shifted to the keep again. ''But I must say I've never seen him quite so—''

''Rude?'' suggested Isabel. ''Arrogant? High-handed?''

De Villiers made a noise in his throat that sounded suspiciously like smothered laughter. ''Something like that. I'll have to introduce you to my wife, Joanna. I seem to have heard her use several similar words when describing her brother.''

''Your wife is Guy's sister?'' asked Isabel, in her curiosity not even noticing that she had used fitzAlan's given name.

De Villiers eyed her keenly. ''Aye. In fact, she's staying at Ashby Chase. 'Tis safer for a woman than Winchester at the moment.''

The wistful note in this last remark produced a slight smile from Isabel. ''You miss her.''

''Aye.'' De Villiers grinned disarmingly. '''Twould not be so bad if I could get some work done so I could visit her now and then, but there's little chance of that with the Bishop running to the Queen every five minutes.'' He heaved a sigh, which was instantly belied by the droll look in his eyes. ''On the other hand, if she were here I wouldn't get any work done at all.''

Isabel nodded, although her mind was only half on the conversation. The knowledge that fitzAlan had a family had come as a strange shock. He had seemed so solitary, so self-reliant. Again she realised how little she knew of him. Why, he, too, could have a wife somewhere...even children.

A black depression descended on her at the thought.

"No," de Villiers said gently, with a shrewd glance at her face. "He isn't married."

"Oh…" If surprise hadn't made it impossible for Isabel to prevaricate, her quick blush would certainly have betrayed her. "How…?"

"I've seen women look after Guy like that before." He hesitated, looking uncomfortable, and appeared to pick his words carefully. "Forgive me, Lady Isabel, if I trespass, but you seem to be alone here. Don't depend too much on fitzAlan. He will stay for no woman."

"I take your concern most kindly, sir," Isabel responded politely, if a little coolly. Hadn't she already given herself that very same advice? "However, I can assure you I am in no danger of succumbing to my lord fitzAlan's rather blunt charms." She thought of the way Guy had left her just now without a word of reassurance or explanation. "No danger at all," she muttered grimly.

"Aye, well—" de Villiers' expression was a comical mixture of relief, guilt and boyish appeal "—I'd best take you inside. I don't know why we're standing here for all these fools to gape at. Here boy…" An imperious wave of the hand summoned a serf to take fitzAlan's horse, and with another apologetic smile de Villiers began to guide Isabel over to the castle forebuilding.

"What makes you think I am alone here?" she asked him, relenting a little as they mounted the stairs. After all, he had meant well, and he certainly had better manners than that…that…

"If you had family or friends in Winchester, Guy would have taken you straight to them," de Villiers answered, more at ease now. "But no need to fear the Queen won't make you welcome, my lady. She's a kind soul. Not like that she-wolf in Gloucester. You're well out of that den."

Isabel shivered suddenly. They had passed out of the daylight into the comparative dimness of the castle interior. She didn't know if it was the lessening of daylight, or Simon's mention of the Empress, but in a matter of seconds her entire body had become ice-cold, her hands and feet almost numb. The huge fire roaring in the hall beyond the small entrance chamber warmed her not at all. Indeed, the blaze did little to counteract the wintry draughts blowing into the room through the unshuttered windows, some strong enough to stir the heavy tapestries covering the stone walls.

Despite this chilly inconvenience, however, the place was crowded with people who all seemed to be talking at once. No one appeared interested in a new face, Isabel was relieved to see. She was just one of the many petitioners waiting for an audience with the Queen or her sheriffs. Trestles were being set up along both sides of the room, but only a few sombrely dressed ladies were seated, the rest of the company apparently preferring to mill about in the centre of the hall.

Broken snatches of conversation wafted around Isabel's head as she followed de Villiers around the perimeter of the room, interspersed with the thunk of wooden trenchers as the servants set places for the midday meal.

"And I told him the mud in the high street was an absolute disgrace. The bridges are meant to be kept in good repair. My best shoes lost forever, and the fellow only laughed. Wait until the Sheriff hears of this, I said…"

"Not there, you dolt. The finger-bowl goes on the high table. How many times…?"

"That hospital is nothing but a place for layabouts. Aye, the lepers and beggars must have somewhere to go, but why does it have to be on my front doorstep? The Bishop started the hospital; let *him* live alongside…''

''They say Stephen is failing. Not that anyone would repeat that to the Queen, but…''

The sound of the King's name sent another wave of ice water rushing through Isabel's veins. Her limbs began to feel heavy; it was an effort to walk. She was glad when de Villiers paused beside a colourful tapestry depicting a hunting scene, to indicate fitzAlan crossing the room towards them.

Somehow at the sight of him all her anger seemed to vanish like the wisps of smoke wreathing up the great chimney near by. Isabel found her eyes clinging to him, his height making it easy for her to watch his approach. She could not look away. He moved through the crowd with that long, prowling stride, the aura of leashed danger about him causing other men to make way automatically. Aye, he was big and tough and sometimes he frightened her, but in a world that had suddenly become alien and dangerous he was her only security. She wanted to run to him, to feel his arms close about her, to forget treachery and deceit and the choice that was coming inexorably closer.

''The Queen will see you in her private solar,'' he said without preamble when he reached them. ''Her counsellors will have some questions for you, then Matilda will speak with you alone.''

Isabel barely heard him, but she nodded. The voices buzzing all around them echoed in her ears. She felt as though she was going to be sick.

FitzAlan must have seen something in her face, because he took her hand briefly, his fingers tightening ever so slightly around hers in a gesture meant to reassure. ''I won't leave you," he murmured. Then, louder, "You'd better come too, Simon."

"Did you think I was going to be left behind?" responded de Villiers cheerfully, his bright, interested gaze going from one to the other. "I wouldn't miss this for the whole of Christendom."

FitzAlan sent him a look that would have pierced armour at a hundred paces.

His brother-in-law remained unscathed. Grinning unrepentantly, he strode ahead and rapped on a door at the far end of the hall. A gruff male voice bade them enter.

And in that instant the harsh reality of her task hit Isabel like a blow to the head. The choice lay before her. No longer was it a plan calmly discussed from a safe distance. No longer was it something she could think about later. It was here. It was now. It was *real*. There was no going back.

Hands tingling with fear, hearing only the thundering of her heart, Isabel stepped over the threshold to confront the wife of the man who had once come to her aid, and whom she must now betray.

She couldn't do it. Even if fitzAlan had not been involved, Isabel knew she would have to find another way to save her brother, because she could not deceive the anxious, sweet-faced lady who was gently explaining her new duties.

"And I shall look forward to having you read to me, my dear, while you are with us. My ladies find it a sad chore since reading Latin does not come easily to them, and after a day spent poring over official parchments my own eyes ache so."

Barely making sense of the murmured words, Isabel

responded with a weak smile. It was the best she could do. The last hour had left her mentally exhausted.

The minute she had entered the room a grim, tense atmosphere had fallen over the Queen's solar. It had not been lessened when William of Ypres, the surly Flemish commander of the royalist army, had begun to question her extensively about the size and strength of the garrisons at Gloucester and Bristol, the state of the Empress's exchequer, the loyalty of her supporters, and whether Geoffrey of Anjou was planning an invasion of England to help himself to the throne by right of his wife.

With fitzAlan, de Villiers and a chastened but still influential Bishop of Winchester listening to every word, Isabel had answered as best she could in the hope that by doing so she might appease her conscience.

It hadn't worked. For one thing, she knew very little of the Empress's plans and had sensed Ypres's disappointment in her replies. He had also been extremely suspicious and had made no secret of it. In fact, if Matilda's messenger hadn't carried a letter to the Queen explaining the ''unfortunate misunderstanding'' that had resulted in Isabel's ''ill-considered'' flight from Gloucester with fitzAlan's assistance, she was quite sure William of Ypres would have clapped her into prison until he had verified her story for himself. And when she realised that the messenger giving credence to her tale no doubt served the dual purpose of informing Rainald of her presence, Isabel felt wretched indeed.

Worse still, she had seen almost immediately that it would be the easiest thing in the world to listen for information. The two ladies in attendance on the Queen had been banished to a corner of the solar, where they sat talking quietly, half hidden by a carved wooden screen, but only the slightest effort would have been needed for either of them to overhear the interrogation going on by the fireplace.

It seemed that no obstacle at all stood in the way of the Empress's plans—unless Isabel were willing to sacrifice Edmund.

When the intensive questioning was at last over, fitz-Alan had left with the other men, looking as stern and thoughtful as the dour Fleming commander. As she watched him leave, without so much as a glance in her direction, such a feeling of desolation had swept over Isabel that she had almost cried out. And now, battered by guilt and indecision, desperate half-formed schemes jostling themselves about in her head, she could scarcely summon the wit to listen with a show of attention to the Queen.

"But carrying on the business of the realm is the least I can do while the King is so wretchedly confined," Matilda concluded.

"At least the Empress has agreed to the exchange of prisoners, madam," faltered Isabel. She sat on a stool beside the Queen's high-backed chair, her hands clenched tightly in her lap, eyes fiercely studying the fur-trimmed hem of Matilda's crimson robe.

The warm colour suited the Queen, she thought, daring a fleeting glance upwards at the softly rounded face framed by a white veil. A simple gold circlet held the veil in place, beneath which guileless blue eyes shone with a gentle womanly strength. Between Matilda the Queen and Matilda the Empress there was a world of difference, Isabel reflected. This Matilda had shown herself to be as resolute and intelligent as her cousin and namesake in Gloucester, but had forgotten neither compassion nor patience.

Isabel's eyes fell as guilt racked her again.

"Aye. And for that we owe you our thanks," acknowledged Matilda, unwittingly turning the knife in her listener's heart. "If the Countess of Anjou had not been so anxious to correct any false impressions we may have had about your arrival the negotiations might have dragged on indefinitely. The King's release is the last thing she must desire." The Queen sighed wearily. "I fear my cousin will never relinquish her claim, since she is fighting for a position that she considers to be her son's heritage as well as her own."

"But surely an anointed king cannot be put aside," murmured Isabel.

"Not put aside, perhaps," agreed Matilda, "but never given any peace while a rival cause serves the purpose of every malcontent in the realm. Even a king cannot please everyone, though, Our Lady knows, Stephen tried. 'Tis why loyalty such as my lord fitzAlan's is so appreciated. You did us a great service in warning him of the threat to his life, Isabel. Why, even William was forced to admit that his doubts about you were groundless."

Isabel shook her head. "I cannot blame him, madam. He has your safety at heart." The words were almost whispered.

Matilda laughed unexpectedly. "You mean he is a rough, unmannerly soldier who you feared would bring out the thumbscrews. But you answered his questions very well. I am sure William no longer thinks you've been sent here to poison my wine, or whatever dark thoughts he was harbouring." She leaned forward and patted Isabel's hand. "You must not mind his unpolished ways, child. The Flemings are not famed for their courtliness, but William's loyalty to Stephen is as beyond question as fitzAlan's. And as your own has proved to be."

Every word flicked Isabel like a whip. No torture devised by William of Ypres could be worse than this, she decided, still not daring to raise her head. Oh, what was she to do?

"But I can see you are still troubled, my dear," observed the Queen kindly. "Can you not tell me what it is? Something you could not mention before the men, perhaps?"

Again Isabel looked up, into clear, sympathetic eyes that seemed to offer understanding and infinite tolerance. Her lips parted—trembling—as she hovered on the brink of speech. Here was her opportunity. All she had to do was tell the truth and she would be free. Free of guilt. Free of the fear of discovery.

And Edmund would die.

If only she had time. Time alone to think. Time to plan. *Time...*

The glimmering of an idea flashed into Isabel's brain.

Stammering, feeling her way, she prayed for inspiration. "Perhaps they would not understand, my lady, being men and accustomed to..." She hesitated, took a deep breath, and plunged on. "You see...yesterday...there was a fight, and—"

"Ah, so fitzAlan explained," interposed Matilda. "But surely the soldier's death was by his own evil hand, Isabel. I will never believe you killed a man purposely, and nor will our most merciful Lord. A dreadful experience, to be sure, but you must put any thought of blame from your mind."

"And so I would, madam, if I could but confess," suggested Isabel tentatively. "I even know of a priest...at St Mary's Church... I once knew him..." Her voice died away as she resisted the urge to cross herself against the lie.

Matilda looked doubtful. "I don't know, child. Not that I would prevent you from confessing," she added hastily. "'Tis just that the town is no place for a lady at this time. My own confessor would absolve you, but he has taken alms and clothing to the hospital and, if I know Father Selwyn, will no doubt spend some time there, helping out…"

"Perhaps an escort," hinted Isabel, worried that Matilda was going to suggest she wait for the good father's return. "A serf, or maid, or some such person." The rider was tacked on as hurriedly as Matilda's had been. The last person she needed was fitzAlan, but an attendant of humble rank wouldn't matter, if it helped her to obtain permission to go into the town. And she sensed that the Queen, a deeply pious woman herself, did not like to deny her new lady's apparent need for immediate absolution after killing a man, albeit accidentally.

A flicker of hope stirred to life, although it was accompanied by a shiver of horror, as Isabel saw the evil hidden once again behind the truth. The conspirators at Gloucester could not have planned the soldier's death, of course, but still she shuddered. It was a chilling thought that the very circumstances she was using for her own purpose accorded only too well with the Empress's schemes.

Matilda's face had cleared. "Of course," she exclaimed. "A maid. I was going to arrange for one to attend you anyway." Suddenly animated, she clapped her hands to summon her ladies.

It was odd that she would have her own servant, Isabel mused vaguely. This was a very different place to Gloucester, where the Empress's ladies were virtually servants themselves, but in the flurry of introductions and orders for a place in the ladies' chamber to be made ready for her Isabel forgot about comparisons. Nothing seemed quite real. It was as though she had become two people. A shadowy image of herself stood there, nodding and smiling shyly, while the real Isabel remained in the cold, lonely place she had inhabited for so long and grimly decided that the first step was almost accomplished.

The Empress would receive word that she had made contact with Rainald, which would stay her vindictive hand for a while. If she could then convince Rainald that it might be a few days before she was granted another opportunity to meet him, and if she could discover how many spies the Empress had in Winchester, the precious time gained might be used to save Edmund. She was not sure, yet, how that might be accomplished, but at least she would have won a reprieve. And then—

"Lady Isabel will be staying with us for a short time. Pray you, Judith, pick out a likely girl to serve as her maid, and, Eleanor, fetch some of my gowns. She must look her best for my lord fitzAlan."

This jerked the real Isabel back to the Queen's solar with a vengeance.

"But madam, I am here to serve you," she began, belatedly hearing these commands. Matilda was speaking as though she was a guest, she realised, startled. And what did fitzAlan have to do with gowns?

"And so you shall, child." Matilda barely paused in her instructions to voice the smiling assurance. "Don't forget a cloak, Eleanor. The red woollen mantle with the hood will be the most suitable, I think."

Isabel could only watch helplessly as Lady Eleanor was set to scurrying back and forth between the solar and the Queen's wardrobe. Gown after gown was brought out and held up to her. And when Matilda finally pronounced in favour of a close-fitting robe of soft, unbleached linen, worn under a blue velvet over-tunic, laced at the sides to show the garment beneath, and trimmed with soft grey vair, her protests had quite died away. What girl could resist the lure of the first new clothes she had possessed in years? At Matilda's insistence she tried on the gown then and there, even forgetting her tattered shift until her old dress was whisked away.

"Merciful saints!" uttered Matilda. "You can't wear that! Quick, Eleanor, fetch a clean shift at once."

The door shut behind the hapless Lady Eleanor again.

"I needed something to bind my lord fitzAlan's arm," explained Isabel weakly, feeling compelled to offer an apology for the indecent state of her underclothing.

However, Matilda didn't appear unduly shocked, despite her horrified exclamation. "So he said. 'Twas regrettable, of course, though you obviously had little choice but to abandon modesty when the need was so imperative. And no need to fear that anyone outside this room will learn of it, my dear. FitzAlan is a man of honour, and would never let the slightest hint of gossip touch you." She smiled at Isabel. "Tell me, child, what do you think of him?"

This unexpected rider took Isabel by surprise. "What do I think of him, madam?" she repeated, nonplussed. "Why...I...I...don't know. I hardly know him. That is, we were together only a short time, and..." She stopped, aware that she was stammering like an idiot, and yet quite at a loss. Words didn't seem able to describe the confusion of her feelings for fitzAlan.

"My lord fitzAlan gave me his escort to Winchester," she tried again, cautiously. Was the Queen about to warn her in much the same way as Simon de Villiers had done? She was beginning to wonder if fitzAlan was in the habit of leaving languishing females behind him wherever he went. "There was nothing more between us than that. I mean, we didn't…he didn't…'' she faltered, not at all sure she was telling the exact truth.

"Faith, child! I know that," expostulated the Queen. "I merely wished to know if you…well, if you like him."

"Like him?" echoed Isabel. Could anyone apply such a bland, woefully inadequate word as "like" to fitzAlan? she asked herself bewilderedly. He had made her angry, afraid, excited. She had felt alternatively vulnerable and safe with him. But *like*?

Isabel found herself staring at Matilda's kindly face, completely at a loss.

"I see I have you thoroughly perplexed," the Queen said, laughing. "Forget I asked, my dear. I am sure Lord fitzAlan is more than capable of conducting his own affairs without any well-intentioned assistance from me."

The return of Lady Eleanor with a pile of fine linen shifts scarcely registered with Isabel as a rapid succession of images flashed through her mind: fitzAlan confronting the Empress with that cold, relentless logic; wounded and feverish in the hut, but still in control of both her and the situation; swinging his sword with savage, deadly grace at the ford; leaning over her at the inn this morning; holding her…

"Of that I have no doubt, my lady," she muttered, determinedly quelling that last thought. "But why—"

"'Tis nought, my dear. Merely, I have a great kindness for fitzAlan and would see him happily… But I go too far and too fast," Matilda broke off to amend hastily. "Think no more of it, I pray you, except—" she paused in the act of motioning Isabel behind the screen, and this time her smile was one of pure feminine conspiracy "—do not dismiss him as another rough, unchivalrous soldier, Isabel. He has known little but fighting these last few years, but I think, with the right wōman, he could be as gentle and tender a knight as any girl could wish for.''

It was fortunate, Isabel decided, that the screen shielded her from curious eyes as she changed her shift. She could feel heat searing her cheeks, and a strange trembling seemed to have seized her hands, making her fumble with the ties at the neck of the garment. What had fitzAlan told the Queen? What was Matilda telling her?

Nothing made sense any more. Words and pictures spun around behind her eyes with a speed that made her head start to ache. Edmund…Rainald…fitzAlan…the Queen…de Villers' advice…what to choose…whom to trust…whom to believe…

Weak and dizzy, Isabel slumped against the wall, wishing she did not have to move. The images swirled and danced in her head like figures around a maypole. Voices echoed in her ears.

"It won't be forever, Isabel. One day I'll be old enough…" *"He'll be waiting at the church for you, every day for an hour between noon…"* *"Why should you trust me, indeed…?"* *"as gentle and tender a knight…"* *"He will stay for no woman…"*

She could not bear it. She had to clear her mind. She had to think only of the next few hours. She had to be calm and distant just once more. Just one more time, Isabel told herself, straightening, just enough to get through the meeting with Rainald. Especially, she must not think of fitzAlan.

"Ah, here is Judith and your new maid."

The Queen's voice came from a great distance. Her maid. Another person to whom she must speak, at whom she must smile, with whom she must pretend.

Stepping from behind the screen, Isabel schooled her features into an expression of remote serenity. From that cold, emotionless void she watched herself speak kindly to the young girl introduced as Ellen, thank the Queen for her great kindness, beg to be excused from dining in the hall on the grounds of wishing to find her priest as soon as possible, and resolutely put all thought of fitzAlan out of her mind.

After all, he had left without a word to her. His task was done. He had delivered her safely to Matilda. There was no reason for him to see her again.

He was waiting for her in the hall.

The instant she saw him, leaning with careless masculine grace against the wall, Isabel's throat tightened. His head was bent slightly, listening intently to Simon de Villiers, who was speaking rapidly, and he was frowning. The frown gave a ruthless edge to his handsome face, as though the leashed danger in him had moved nearer to the surface, was more visible. She wondered what the two men were talking about.

Then fitzAlan looked up and saw her, and the hard look of danger vanished. A smile flashed into his vivid blue eyes, warming them instantly. Isabel felt the barriers around her heart shake. Not yet, she told herself desperately. Not yet! She had to meet Rainald first, she had to gain some time for Edmund, she had to—

"All right?"

Isabel blinked, coming back to her surroundings with a start. Simon had disappeared into the crowd still milling about the hall, and fitzAlan was standing before her. He had asked her something.

"Are you all right?" he repeated.

When Isabel only nodded silently, he glanced at Ellen, hovering behind her new mistress. "Where is my lady housed?"

Ellen dropped an awed curtsy, rounded eyes gazing up at him over the pile of red woollen mantle in her arms. "In the ladies' solar in the south tower, my lord. We were on our way there."

"I will escort Lady Isabel." A quick smile softened the brief statement. "Run ahead and make ready for her."

"Aye, sir." Flushed and eager, emboldened by fitzAlan's smile, Ellen prattled on. "The Queen has said that my lady shall have a place in the bed. No mere pallet for her, and—"

FitzAlan gently stopped the excited flow. "That is excellent…" He paused interrogatively.

"Ellen, sir, if it please your lordship." The girl curtsied again before scuttling off down a nearby passage.

Everyone from the Queen to the servants thinks he's wonderful, thought Isabel, and a flash of awareness rippled through her. A sense of urgency, of impending loss, of…

But fitzAlan spoke again before she could pin down the feeling.

"I believe you and Simon exchanged some rather uncomplimentary views about my deplorable manners." His blue eyes twinkled down at her with sudden, unexpected mischief and he offered her his arm. "Allow me to make amends, my lady."

"Oh…" Confused, flushing as though she had been found out in some guilty action, Isabel tentatively let her fingers rest lightly on fitzAlan's arm. Heat flowed over her, turning her bones to water. When he started down the corridor Ellen had taken she was surprised that her legs still functioned.

"The thing is," he murmured, sending her a smile that managed to be wicked and appealing all at the same time,

"I'm so used to trusting Simon completely that I forgot you didn't know him at all."

How could she resist him when he was like this? No woman could, Isabel thought. The combination of sheer male power and boyish devilment was too seductive. She glanced up at him, feeling oddly shy, almost as though she were meeting him for the first time with no doubts, no mistrust, between them. "I think I understood that," she whispered, admitting, "I trusted him, too."

It was the truth, she realised. Though she had been angry with fitzAlan, she would not have blurted out the bare facts to just anyone.

"I hope that means I'm forgiven."

"Of course," Isabel managed. Her pulse fluttered. Even barely touching him, she could feel the taut power of the muscles beneath her hand. His strength was compelling, drawing her closer until their bodies almost brushed with every step. The resulting sensations had the strangest effect on her thinking processes, she discovered. She didn't even seem capable of taking note of where they were going. They had reached a short flight of stone steps leading down to an open door, and she had no idea of how they had arrived there.

FitzAlan stopped just out of earshot of the room, his free hand covering Isabel's before she could remove it. "I have to leave you now," he said. "Tell Ellen to bring you something to eat. I don't want you dining in the hall unless I can accompany you, and I'll be busy at Wolvesey Castle with Simon until this evening."

"As you wish," Isabel replied vaguely. She was so busy absorbing the knowledge that fitzAlan would be safely occupied for the rest of the day that she only belatedly heard the possessiveness behind his instructions. Looking up, she saw his brows lift in amused surprise at

her meekness, and added hurriedly, "But I must attend
the Queen some time, my lord. You need no longer feel
an obligation—"

He stopped the words with a gentle finger against her
mouth. The finger was removed almost immediately, but
not before Isabel had felt the throbbing pulse against her
lips. She could not have spoken if her life depended on
it.

"'Tis no obligation, sweet lady," he said very softly.
"You are under the Queen's protection now—for a little
while." Gazing down into her eyes, he raised her hand to
his lips and pressed a lingering kiss into the soft palm
before releasing it. "Until this evening," he said huskily,
and turned to go back the way they had come.

Isabel stared after him, gripped again by that frightening sense of loss. She watched fitzAlan walk away from
her and saw him walking out of her life, saw the final
destruction of a young girl's dream that her mind had
rejected and yet her heart could not relinquish. She didn't
understand it. She had made the right decision to first
appease Rainald. Why this terrible fear that it could all
go horribly wrong, that a dream was all she would ever
know?

Without giving herself time to think, Isabel called out
Guy's name, and began running after him.

He stopped halfway down the passage, whirling about
to meet her. Even in the dim light of the narrow corridor
Isabel saw the flash of some powerful emotion in his eyes.
Unaware that she had called him by name for the first
time, she halted, still some feet away, gazing at him uncertainly.

"I just…I wanted to thank you…" she began, not really comprehending why she was so reluctant to let him
go. Then, as Guy reached her in one long stride, it no

longer mattered. This was her knight. The man who had
fought for her, who had killed to protect her. If he wanted
to claim her, she was his. For this brief moment in time
nothing else mattered. Lifting her hands to his shoulders,
she raised herself on tiptoe and brushed her lips across
his cheek.

His arms closed around her instantly, fiercely possessive as he pulled her against him. Isabel didn't have to
wonder this time if he was going to kiss her. Intent blazed
from his eyes, tautened the strong lines of his face. His
mouth descended on hers, hungry, demanding, almost
frighteningly rough in his unhidden need.

Overwhelmed by the force in him, trembling with the
intensity of her own response, Isabel parted her lips,
whimpering in feminine submission and an equally feminine fear of the total surrender he was wrenching from
her. Instantly he gentled. One hand came up, cradling her
face as he slanted his mouth over hers, softening the demand and yet deepening the kiss with a tender seduction
that was as devastating as his initial urgency.

When he lifted his head minutes later Isabel was completely helpless in his arms. She clung to him, dazed, her
heart pounding, her breath coming raggedly from between
slightly swollen lips, her legs barely supporting her. Her
lashes fluttered open to meet fitzAlan's darkened eyes
mere inches away. The stark desire in his face threatened
to take what strength she had left, nor did he make any
attempt to hide the blatant response of his body to that
consuming, passionate kiss, continuing to hold her so
tightly that she could feel him with every part of her being, could still taste him inside her mouth.

Then very slowly he put her a little away from him, his
hands holding her steady until he was sure she could stand
alone. He drew in a shuddering breath. ''Don't ever doubt

that I want you, Isabel,'' he said, his voice so hoarse that the words sounded as if they were torn from deep inside him. His eyes burned into hers. ''Don't ever hide from me.''

He put out his hand, as though he would touch her again, then turned quickly and walked away.

The hectic flush on Isabel's face gradually faded as she watched fitzAlan leave. She was still trembling, tiny aftershocks of excitement tingling inside her. If he had set out to prove that the passionate interlude on the road this morning had been genuine on his part he had certainly succeeded. In his arms all her doubts on that score had been obliterated.

But men wanted women all the time. It didn't mean anything. How could she have forgotten that? Isabel moved restlessly as bitter memories engulfed her. She had forgotten the dreadful price her own sisters had paid for that male greed and self-interest. As in that night in the hut, she had been conscious only of fitzAlan and the wild sensations he aroused in her. And she had not been half asleep and dreaming this time.

Isabel put her fingers to her lips. Her mouth felt soft and pliant; her lips still throbbed. She wanted to tell herself that fitzAlan had taken her by surprise again, but she could not. And he had not been brutal or selfish. He had sensed her fear of yielding to a man's passion and had reined in his desire immediately. Nor could she get his last words out of her mind. ''Don't ever hide from me.'' Was she a fool to hope there had been a deeper meaning in that fierce command?

Impatience, knife-edged and turbulent, gripped her body. She wanted it over with. She wanted it done. Until she met Rainald she could not think of a future, with or without fitzAlan. Somehow she must discover the extent of the threat to Edmund's life. And tonight…

Sudden resolve flowed over her, calming her, restoring her strength. Tonight she would see fitzAlan again. He would be with her. Tonight she would tell him everything.

Chapter Nine

"Are you sure the Bishop's castle is at the other end of town?" Isabel asked Ellen for about the tenth time. She picked up her skirts to avoid a particularly noisome pool in the road and wished they could move more quickly.

FitzAlan and Simon de Villiers were the only people in Winchester who knew her, but she still could not banish a feeling of trepidation at being on the high street in broad daylight. She had to resist a constant urge to glance back over her shoulder to make sure they were not being followed, although she had given fitzAlan enough time to be well ahead of her before starting out.

Ellen halted at a short wooden bridge, one of many which spanned the streams dissecting the main road through the town. "Aye, my lady. Look, you may see it past the abbey." The girl pointed eastwards, where a brightly coloured pennant could just be seen beyond the abbey's spire.

As the two girls stood there, Isabel dubiously eyeing the rickety-looking structure at her feet, a wagon rumbled to a stop behind them, filled with women. One raggedly clad individual shouted an incomprehensible greeting, cackling shrilly when Ellen quickly pulled Isabel away so the cart could proceed over the bridge. The driver yelled an order for silence over his shoulder and flapped his reins.

"Your pardon, my lady," apologised Ellen, "but we don't want those dreadful creatures following us all the way down the street."

"Who are they?" Isabel whispered, eyes round with curiosity.

"Harlots," replied Ellen repressively, waiting until the wagon was some distance ahead before stepping on to the bridge.

"But why are they in that cart? Where are they going?" Isabel persisted. The women had been crammed together like animals, she thought.

"Every few months they're rounded up and driven from the city," explained Ellen. "It doesn't seem to matter, though. They always come back."

Isabel was silent, unable to share Ellen's seeming indifference to the women's fate. She knew all too well by what circumstances a woman could be forced into using her body as a means of ensuring survival for herself or her family.

She shivered as a stray gust of wind whistled around the corner of a side-street, averting her eyes from the shadows cast by the encroaching house frontages. The upper storeys of the dwellings leaned out over the street, giving them a drunken appearance, and the dim caverns beyond the light of the high street seemed to Isabel to mirror the dark side of this city of churches. Evil behind the truth everywhere, she thought.

"Here we are, my lady." Ellen's voice broke into her grim reflections. "The church of St Mary."

Isabel looked at the small stone building in front of her,

then glanced up and down the street. It was almost deserted. A group of people were gathered at a mill two blocks away. Opposite, the fields of the abbey stretched to its grey stone walls. Several young boys were racing each other across the open expanse, leaping and shouting, and from the abbey itself the voices of monks chanting the noon office rose on the air. No one was near enough to accost her or wonder about her presence. The hour had been well chosen.

Drawing in a deep breath, Isabel pushed open the door. "Wait here for me," she said quickly to Ellen as the other girl began to follow her. She slipped into the church before her maid could protest.

Peace and quiet surrounded her. As her eyes adjusted to the muted light, Isabel saw that the walls had been limed to the height of a man, and that the windows were glazed, shutting off all sounds from outside. Rows of simple wooden benches drew her gaze towards the altar, where candles burned beside a tall, plain wooden crucifix. The place was empty, but for a cloak-shrouded figure bent over a rosary to the right of the door, and a man sitting alone in the front row. The latter turned his head as the door shut behind her, coming to his feet and raking her with a glance that was both sharp and insolent.

The church was tiny. Only a few steps brought him to within feet of her. He was short but built like a bull, with a thick neck and heavily muscled shoulders. Isabel wiped her suddenly damp hands on her gown. "Rainald?"

"Lady Isabel." His voice was harsh, uncultured, the slight emphasis on the "Lady" definitely mocking. "Torold's description didn't do you justice."

Isabel went to speak again, but he motioned her to silence, his eyes going to the figure shuffling towards the door. Enveloped by the cloak, it was impossible to tell if it was male or female, but the worshipper had evidently finished praying. The door whispered shut.

"Probably just an old peasant," Rainald said, "but 'tis better to be careful. You have news for me?"

"Not yet," she whispered, and cleared her throat. She had to be firm. "We only arrived today and—"

"We? You mean Lord fitzAlan? Is he a danger to us?"

"No." Isabel swallowed nervously. "I don't think he suspects me any more."

"You don't *think*?" Rainald's small black eyes narrowed maliciously. "You had better make sure, lady, or I send a message direct to Tracy."

"No, please…" She stopped. Pleading would not work with this creature. She must be firm. "I'll co-operate. But I'll need some time. I can't leave the castle every—"

Her halting explanation was cut off short. Behind her the door crashed open, flung against the wall with a force that rattled the windows and sent the candles flickering wildly. With a half-stifled cry, Isabel spun about.

And there, framed in the open doorway, long legs braced apart, blazing eyes flashing from her to Rainald and back again, stood fitzAlan.

For a moment there was utter silence. No one moved. At the edge of her vision Isabel could see Ellen peering fearfully around fitzAlan's arm. There was another man behind her, a stranger.

Then very slowly fitzAlan advanced into the church. Isabel could see the tension in his body, feel the waves of fury vibrating from him. The very air seemed to be alive with his anger. How had he caught her so quickly? She had been sure he had already left the castle before she and Ellen had ventured into the town.

The useless question had no sooner formed in her mind

when Rainald moved. The instant fitzAlan was free of the doorway he was through it, shoving Ellen roughly to one side and racing into the street. The man standing beside Ellen moved to go after him, but fitzAlan turned on him.

"*No*!

"Let him go," he added more quietly. "He won't get far. I've sent orders for the gates to be watched while Simon's men round up the rest."

Round up the rest? It sounded like the harlots, Isabel thought hysterically. Then wondered what she was thinking of. They didn't need her. Edmund did!

Jolted into action, she sprang forward and grabbed fitzAlan's sleeve, almost shaking his arm in desperation. "You can't let him go," she screamed. "You—"

"*Quiet*!" FitzAlan turned on her, flinging her off as if she carried the plague. "Not one word out of you!" he roared. "Not one word!"

The savagery in his face was such a horrifying contrast to his recent ardour that Isabel shrank back in terror, stumbling over one of the benches. She half fell, half collapsed against it, unable to stop the tears of fear and anguish pouring down her face.

Failed...failed...failed. The word repeated itself over and over in her head like a death knell.

FitzAlan ignored her. Glancing back at the young man waiting in the doorway, he gestured impatiently to Ellen. "Take this girl back to the castle," he ordered tightly. "And wait for me there."

"Aye, sir." Casting an unreadable look at Isabel, the boy obeyed, taking Ellen by the arm and urging her away from the church. Isabel could hear her maid's protesting voice fading into the distance.

"Get up!"

It was fitzAlan, looking down at her with eyes that

ripped her heart into pieces, speaking to her in a voice so hard that the words were like blows. Where was the man who had held her—kissed her…?

"You don't understand," she pleaded, nearly sobbing with despair. "My brother—"

FitzAlan reached down and yanked her to her feet. "Your brother?" he snarled, his grip merciless. "Are you going to tell me that he holds his castle for the Empress and won't take you back?" He laughed mirthlessly. "My God, you're good, I'll give you that. Even after what I just learned I couldn't believe you've been lying to me since we met—that I was coming back to ask you—"

He bit off the next words with an oath and pushed her away. Turning, he reached the church door in two steps, grabbed it, and slammed it shut. There was so much enraged violence in the action that Isabel knew she had missed being hurled across the church by that powerful arm only because of fitzAlan's self-control. Her terrified eyes gazed at him as she stood with his back to her, both hands braced against the door, staring at the ground between his feet.

"Ask me what?" she quavered. Anything was better than the terrible silence that had fallen.

He turned around slowly, moving like a man in pain. That last ungovernable action must have hurt his arm, she thought distantly.

"I had my answer before I entered this church," he bit out. A muscle jerked in his tanned cheek. "There was an old peasant in here when you arrived, was there not?"

Isabel's lips parted. She couldn't speak, but the answer was there in her horror-stricken eyes.

A mirthless smile, more like a grimace, twisted fitz-Alan's mouth. "Aye, you saw him. More to the point, he saw you. Heard you greet a known spy by name and heard

him acknowledge you.'' His voice had roughened, growing harsher with every word, but now it dropped to a flat
monotone. ''You left your maid in the street to no purpose, my lady.''

''You know Rainald,'' Isabel murmured dully. It wasn't
a question. What use were questions now? He had told
her the one thing of importance, even if nothing else made
any sense. She and Edmund had been doomed from the
start.

''We know him. And the rest. A cosy little nest of
vipers sent here by that bitch you serve. That peasant
was one of Simon's men. We've been watching them for
weeks.''

''And now?'' As if she didn't know.

''They'll be hanged.''

''Hanged,'' Isabel repeated almost to herself as she
worked it out. ''The Empress will hear nothing, and…''
Her eyes lifted to fitzAlan's. ''You don't know what
you've done,'' she whispered brokenly, tears running unheeded down her cheeks. ''Edmund…''

The name seemed to act on fitzAlan like a goad. His
right hand shot out and snapped around Isabel's arm. All
feeling left the limb, but she didn't struggle. Perhaps the
rest of her body would become lifeless, too. Then she
wouldn't have to see or hear…

''Don't use your brother's name to save your neck,''
he grated in a voice she barely recognised. ''God's teeth,
no wonder you were so convincing when you said you'd
go against your family. You were already estranged from
them!''

''What? *No*! I—''

''No more!'' he roared suddenly. ''No more, God damn
it!''

She sobbed, more in confusion now than anything else.
"But—"

"Do you need to see the proof that 'tis over before
you'll stop lying to me?" he cut her off to demand. "Do
you?"

Not waiting for an answer, fitzAlan flung open the door
and almost dragged Isabel into the street. Two passing
merchants stared at them in surprised disapproval. She
scarcely noticed. All she could think of was Edmund,
her young brother, her childhood playmate, her companion and strength during the endless months of darkness.
Would they tell him why he was going to die, or just run
him through? Would he know that she had failed him?

Her eyes blinded by scalding tears, Isabel stumbled after fitzAlan, the punishing pace he set almost causing her
to fall several times, only his vice-like grip on her arm
keeping her upright. She heard the thud of his boots on
wood and was distantly aware that she was once again
within the walls of a castle. Minutes later, Edmund's image was replaced by Simon de Villiers' startled face.

It was strange that she could see Simon so clearly,
thought Isabel, because everything else seemed lost in a
hazy mist. She had a vague impression of a small room,
of stone walls and light from a narrow window falling on
to a table. FitzAlan's brother-in-law sat there, sort-
ing through piles of official-looking documents. At their
abrupt entrance he rose to his feet, surprise and concern
crossing his face as he glanced from her to fitzAlan.

Without uttering a word, fitzAlan jerked Isabel roughly
forward, at the same time riffling through the parchments
scattered over the table.

"Guy? What in the name of—?"

For all the notice fitzAlan took of him, Simon might
not have spoken. "Look at that," he snarled at Isabel,

yanking a parchment from the pile and thrusting it under her nose. "Look at it well, my lady." Releasing her at last, he stepped back.

A blurred jumble of markings swam before Isabel's vision. Why couldn't she see properly? The fine mist at the edges of the room seemed to be drifting closer, enveloping her in its clinging tendrils. Isabel squeezed her eyes shut for a second. When her lashes lifted she found herself looking at a name. It was quite clear, quite distinct, quite unmistakable. *Edmund, Baron de Tracy.*

Fearful, utterly unaware now of the two men near by, she let her eyes move slowly up the document, seeing other names but only vaguely noting that she was scanning a list of some sort. Her gaze came to rest on the inscription at the top of the page. For an aeon of time the words meant nothing. Then Isabel read them one by one.

Killed at Lincoln, in this year of our Lord, one thousand, one hundred and forty-one, fighting on the side of God and King Stephen.

The words blurred again as the strange mist returned, thicker this time. Had fog suddenly permeated the room? She couldn't see anything at all now, and there was an odd buzzing sound in her ears. Isabel turned around slowly. Someone was with her, but she wasn't sure who it was.

She took an uncertain step forward, one trembling hand outstretched—then pitched headlong into infinite blackness.

"Jesu, Guy, what the hell have you done to her?"

FitzAlan glared at his brother-in-law over Isabel's unconscious body. He hadn't been able to prevent himself from catching her when she fell, and now the feel of her, cradled helplessly against his chest, sent shafts of agony through him. And rage. He'd never known such fury before. Rage at her, at himself for wanting her, at a war that had turned her into his enemy.

"I made her face the truth," he grated, laying Isabel down on a bench by the door.

Simon threw a puzzled glance at the disordered pile of documents on his table. "What truth?"

Guy's hands flexed as he stood looking down at Isabel. "She told me her brother held his castle for the Empress, that he had sent her to Gloucester, that she was estranged from him." The words were low and clipped, as though it hurt him to speak. "'Twas the truth, all right, but in reverse. De Tracy was loyal to Stephen; *she* served Matilda."

"De Tracy?" Simon strode over to the table and picked up the parchment on top of the pile. "Killed at Lincoln last February," he read aloud. "On our side." His eyes met fitzAlan's icy gaze. "I suppose this is what you meant when you told me there was something wrong, and rushed off. I don't remember anyone of that name, but you know what a shambles everything became after Stephen was captured. God alone knows who was there. Are you sure there's no doubt?"

Guy gave a mirthless laugh. "That innocent face took you in as well, did it? I'm not surprised. 'Tis her stock in trade. Matilda very kindly warned me herself." He whirled suddenly and struck the wall with his clenched fist. "*God*, why didn't I *listen*?"

"Does it matter?" asked Simon, looking surprised. "Obviously you've put a stop to her activities." When fitzAlan didn't reply, de Villiers glanced down at Isabel's unconscious face and muttered, "Hard to believe, isn't it? How did you find her out?"

"The man you've had watching Rainald the Tanner. I met him on his way back here to report..." Guy stopped, an abrupt movement of his head indicating Isabel. The bitter, humourless smile pulled at his mouth again. "The peasant disguise was good."

De Villiers nodded absently. "'Twas safer. What are you going to do? Let her hang with the rest?"

FitzAlan's quickly indrawn breath sounded shockingly harsh in the still room. Simon's brows drew together. He watched his friend watching Isabel and his hazel eyes slowly widened as he took in the tightly drawn stillness in the other man's body, the white-knuckled fist still clenched against the wall.

"By the Holy Rood," he said softly. "'Tis her, isn't it? The girl you told me about years ago. You wrote to her father when we were in Normandy with Stephen in '37, after he granted you the barony, and got a letter back saying she was already betrothed, about to be wed."

"Drop it, Simon."

"But—"

"*Drop it!*"

"You fool!" De Villiers refused to back down, even when fitzAlan turned a look of fury on him. "This might not be her fault. If her husband is one of Matilda's—"

"*She's never been married, damn you!*"

The explosion of sound pierced Isabel's unconsciousness. Shouting, she thought confusedly. We're under attack again.

Then the past vanished into the receding mists. The present returned—with brutal, stunning clarity. Edmund had been dead for months and she hadn't known it.

Grief tore through her, constricting her heart, but hard

on its heels raced anger, fierce and implacable. Matilda had known of Edmund's death and had deliberately kept that fact from her. It was so very simple. The look that had passed between the Empress and Brien fitzCount was all too plain now. He had been warning Matilda, reminding her that she could still threaten Edmund's safety to ensure Isabel's obedience. She had been used—cold-bloodedly, callously used.

And fitzAlan—so ready to believe her guilty. So ready to condemn her. He had not asked her one question, had not given her one chance to explain. Still half dazed by shock, lashed by rage and a deeper pain she told herself was grief for Edmund, Isabel forgot the fleeting moments when fitzAlan had shown her tenderness despite his suspicions, forgot that he *had* asked for the truth. She remembered only his accusations and her helplessness against them. He had scorned her honour, but she had more than all the rest, Isabel thought bitterly. Including fitzAlan. She had been right not to trust him, for he seduced with soft words, with heat and passion and false promises of safety. There *was* no honour in this world of fighting and hatred and betrayal, a world that had taken everything: her family, her home, her freedom.

Her anger flared higher, searing, blazing, white-hot. She opened her eyes.

FitzAlan and de Villiers were glaring at each other across her, but as she made a move to sit up Isabel saw the scowl fade from Simon's face and he reached down a hand to steady her. She didn't even acknowledge his presence. In that moment of bitterness and pain she despised everyone. Pulling her arm from Simon's grasp, disdaining any assistance, she stood up. They would not take her pride as well.

FitzAlan's eyes were like daggers, but Isabel faced him

unflinchingly. "I am your prisoner, my lord. You have already judged me and found me guilty. Will you be my executioner as well?"

"Don't tempt me," he grated through set teeth, reaching out to wrap powerful fingers around her wrist. His voice was as hard and controlled as her own, but the white line about his mouth betrayed the fury still lashing him.

Isabel saw it and didn't care. Let him hate her. Let him kill her. Nothing he did could hurt her now. She lifted her chin in a gesture that deliberately exposed the vulnerable line of her throat. Stormy grey eyes challenged him, proud and scornful.

De Villiers cleared his throat. "I think we should all sit down and—"

"Shut up, Simon." FitzAlan wrenched his gaze from hers, yanked the door open, and thrust Isabel outside with barely leashed violence. He glanced briefly at his brother-in-law. "Don't say anything about this to a soul. I'll speak to you later."

"Well, of course not, but…"

De Villiers was left talking to the air, a very thoughtful look on his face as he leaned against the doorway and watched fitzAlan stride across the bailey, towing Isabel behind him.

She wouldn't say anything, vowed Isabel, gritting her teeth against the agonising pain in her side. She would not beg fitzAlan to slow down.

The return journey through the town had been uphill most of the way; her legs were trembling and her breath was coming in short, uneven gasps as the castle gates came into view, but she would not protest. She would fall and make him drag her the rest of the way first. The thought had no sooner entered her mind when she tripped

over the first slat of the drawbridge and fell to her knees
before she could save herself.

FitzAlan stopped immediately, turning hard, relentless
eyes on her. He retained his hold on her wrist but made
no move to pull her to her feet. Isabel reached out and
grasped the heavy chain attached to the drawbridge, fighting for breath and the strength to drag herself upright. She
was acutely aware of fitzAlan standing over her, powerful
and dangerous, as though waiting to crush any sign of
defiance or rebellion. To her dismay, hot tears burned her
eyes in frustration at the physical weakness that kept her
kneeling in such a submissive attitude at his feet for several more seconds.

"Save your tears, my lady," he advised, the cold mockery in his voice bringing humiliated colour into Isabel's
face. "You have no more need of such tricks." His grip
tightened on her arm and Isabel found herself upright
again.

For some strange reason she couldn't seem to relinquish
her hold on the chain and braced herself for the wrench
she was sure would follow when fitzAlan started towards
the castle gates. It didn't come. Instead, the arm he held
captive fell back to her side as he loosed her, and he stood
staring into the distance, his face set in grim lines. The
silence seemed broken only by the sound of Isabel's laboured breathing.

"Why?" fitzAlan said at last. His voice was low and
controlled, but his hands were clenched at his sides and
his glittering eyes would have frozen hell-fire.

Isabel stared up at him, too distraught to answer immediately. Indeed, she was not even sure what he was
asking.

"Was your betrothed Matilda's man?" he went on, still
in that frigid tone. "Did he even exist or was he an in-

vention to put me off? Were you so enamoured of the woman that you remained with her after your father was killed?''

He turned blazing eyes on her and his voice suddenly roughened. ''Why, damn you? Was the Countess such a gentle mistress that you would risk your life for her? That you would continue to lie to me after everything—?'' He broke off abruptly, his mouth tightening into a thin, angry line.

Isabel shook her head in bewildered denial. Her chest still heaving, she drew in a gasping breath. ''Betrothed?'' she managed, and immediately fell into a helpless fit of coughing which sent another stab of pain through her stomach.

Holding her free arm against her cramped side, she struggled to regain control of herself. She could hear fitzAlan firing more questions at her, sensed his rage was slipping out of control again, but could only flinch from it. Her own anger had been vanquished, leaving her defenceless, by that gruelling uphill climb. It took energy to sustain that degree of emotion, she discovered, and what little she had left was directed at physical recovery.

''What a talent. That look of innocence. No wonder you were so useful to the Countess.''

That registered. Remembering past insults, Isabel finally looked up, into a steely-eyed glare that was like a sword-thrust to her heart.

''My God! You can even look stricken to order. But it won't work this time, my lady. You seem surprised. Remember when I ordered you to strip in that hut? I looked at your face that night and thought—Jesu! What does it matter? You must have lost count of the number of men who have seen your charms.''

Isabel went cold. Her trembling increased, but this time

the violent tremors were caused by the fresh wave of anger which surged through her. He was just like the rest. Believing what he wanted to believe. Seeing what he wanted to see. Never looking beneath the surface.

She released the chain and straightened, taking a quick step towards him. "You want the truth?" she cried shrilly. "Then have it! You're right. I *have* stripped before. In front of a whole company of soldiers! Right down to the skin! Is that what you wanted to hear? Is it, my lord?"

Half blinded with rage, hardly knowing what she was doing or where she was going, Isabel went to brush past him. FitzAlan's hand shot out, his long fingers clamping around her arm. He jerked her back to face him and Isabel couldn't repress a sharp cry of fear at the violence in his eyes. He looked as if he hated her.

When an incongruously cheerful voice spoke from somewhere behind her, she went absolutely rigid with shock.

"Saints be praised! Just the two people I wanted to meet."

Isabel saw the same shock replace the ferocity in fitz-Alan's face a second before his gaze flashed to a point beyond her. His hand slid downwards, holding hers in a grip that was suddenly unbreakable. And yet he wasn't hurting her, she realised shakily. Still feeling more than a little unbalanced, she glanced back over her shoulder.

Ralf the pedlar stood in the centre of the drawbridge, a pleased smile stretching from ear to ear. "I thought I'd have to comb the whole town for you," he began jovially, coming forward. Then, as his sharp eyes took in the unnatural stiffness of the other two and their frozen expressions, he groaned with mock-consternation. "Oh, no! Don't tell me I've interrupted a marital squabble. Well, never mind…'' He grinned even more broadly. ''I'm told 'tis a symptom suffered by all newly…''

The rest was abruptly swallowed on a nervous gulp, the grin vanishing, when fitzAlan's eyes turned glacial. ''You were looking for us?'' he demanded, his tone not encouraging Ralf to waste any more time in pleasantries.

''Aye, my lord,'' confirmed the pedlar with extreme sobriety. ''About an hour after you left us this morning a party of soldiers arrived. Nasty-looking lot. They had orders to search every village in the area, but they didn't take anything. Master Thomas said they must have been looking for people, not things, and thought you should be warned, so…'' A deprecating shrug completed the explanation.

''That was very good of you,'' whispered Isabel, rather surprised that she could speak at all. Her breathing had returned to normal and the terror that had seized her when fitzAlan had turned those savage ice-blue eyes on her had receded somewhat, but her limbs still felt shaky and she found it difficult to properly comprehend what Ralf had said. She felt fitzAlan glance down as she spoke and carefully kept her eyes lowered, not risking even a brief look at the pedlar.

''Was anyone hurt?''

Ralf shook his head. ''A few bruises, my lord. Nothing to speak of, and the mess can be cleaned up. Dame Sybil took her ladle to one of the soldiers when they started shoving their swords into the mattress, but they only laughed and pushed her outside until they'd finished.''

''She was fortunate,'' muttered fitzAlan grimly. He pulled a small leather bag out of his tunic and counted out several coins. ''This should help repair any damage those louts caused. Convey my thanks to Dame Sybil and Master Thomas and my apologies for bringing trouble upon them." He handed Ralf the money. "And take something for yourself; you must have lost a day's trading to chase after us."

Ralf ventured a tentative smile. "You are most generous, my lord. I'll guard this well."

"You'll need an escort," nodded fitzAlan. "I'll arrange it."

"'Tis not necessary, sir," interposed Ralf hurriedly. He gestured to the castle behind him. "While I was enquiring for you I fell in with a party of men who are heading in my direction shortly. 'Tis only the last mile or so I'll have to travel alone and 'twill be dark then. I'll be safe enough."

"Then I'll wish you Godspeed." Clearly fitzAlan considered the pedlar capable of looking after himself. And, equally clearly, Ralf was only too anxious to be on his way before the hostilities he had interrupted broke out again. He left without any further references to the pitfalls of early married life.

Isabel watched him vanish beneath the barbican and felt as though she had been abandoned to face the enemy without weapons or protection. The shield of cold indifference, the sword of anger, had both been snatched from her by Ralf's warning. Instead of worrying about what fitzAlan might do to her after her last defiant outburst, she could only think that he might be in danger.

"Will they come here, do you think?" The frightened question was out before she could stop it.

FitzAlan looked down at her. His face was shuttered now, stern and remote, his light eyes cool and expressionless. He still held her hand. "I'm taking you to Ashby Chase."

"What?" Isabel's brain reeled at the abrupt statement. Did he think *she* was endangered? Why should he care?

A cell awaited her, and certain death—unless she could throw herself on the Queen's mercy.

"Don't you understand what's happened?" he demanded. "Ralf thinks we're married."

Isabel was beginning to feel dizzy. "What does that matter?" she asked bewilderedly. "'Tis those men who—"

FitzAlan dismissed the soldiers with an impatient gesture. "Do you think Ralf deals only in ribbons and such trifles? He spreads gossip faster than a travelling minstrel, and too many people here know I don't possess a wife—yet."

There was an appalled silence. Isabel jerked her hand from his, holding it out as though to ward him off.

"Would you rather hang?" he queried harshly, correctly interpreting the horrified comprehension on her face.

She flinched, her head moving slowly from side to side, but more in denial of what was coming next than in answer to his question. "No," she got out, her lips barely parting to allow the words to escape. "I won't. I'll speak to the Queen. You can't deny me a proper trial. I'll—"

"You're not going anywhere near the Queen," he interrupted with brutal finality. "Removing you from her vicinity is the least I can do after bringing you here to betray her."

"I didn't..." But the protest was a hopeless sigh, almost inaudible. If fitzAlan heard it he gave no sign, just continued to watch her with narrowed, implacable eyes.

"Why are you doing this?" she cried out suddenly, completely unnerved under that ice-cold stare. "You don't...you can't wish to marry me."

"Wish?" His eyes went even harder. "You think I wish it to be known that I brought a traitor here?"

Isabel stared at him. "'Tis your own reputation you want to save, not mine...or my life," she accused, her voice trembling. "Do you think me a fool? You won't even have to marry me. Ralf won't talk—why should he? With that purse on him and those men after us, he'll keep silent. All you'll do is imprison me in your castle."

"If I have to," he agreed with a cool arrogance that utterly appalled her. "But we will be married, my lady. There's one thing you've forgotten. Your brother's death left you heiress to Tracy Castle, and I intend taking it for the King."

Isabel felt as if he'd slapped her. She actually staggered back a step. She went hot then cold, she couldn't seem to think, and something hurt deep inside her. The sheer unexpectedness of the pain stole her breath. Instinctively she tried to retreat, shrinking within herself, desperately seeking that distant place where she was beyond hurt, but fitzAlan spoke again, pulling her back to awareness with terrifying ease.

"Who holds it for the Empress?" When Isabel only continued to gaze up at him blankly, he added impatiently, "The castellan—who is he?"

"I...I don't know," she stammered, only now realising the implications in his question. She had been too numb, too bewildered, to think beyond the fact of her brother's death. Too much had happened in too short a time. She hadn't thought about the situation at Tracy, had not even wondered how Edmund had managed to escape his gaolers to join Stephen at Lincoln.

And then, as she looked into fitzAlan's eyes, she saw something else. Once again, her own words had damned her.

"Well, at least you don't deny 'tis the Empress's men who hold Tracy." His voice was quiet and held a world of bitterness. "How soon after the boy's death did you hand it back?"

Isabel couldn't answer. Tears welled in her throat, blocking the passage of either protest or plea, and only years of hard-won control prevented her from giving way to them in front of fitzAlan. That, and the last vestige of pride left to her, because somewhere in her mind grief for Edmund was being overshadowed by a silent warning.

She had to get away. She had to run from fitzAlan before he damaged her beyond recovery.

A sudden clatter of hoofs brought her back to an awareness of their public surroundings. FitzAlan, also, glanced around. As a solitary horseman went by, he stepped in front of her, partially shielding her from view, then grasped her arm and propelled her swiftly across the drawbridge and into the castle in total silence. Isabel followed helplessly.

Pausing only to send a page running to fetch her maid, fitzAlan marched her all the way to the ladies' solar, deliberately avoiding the crowded hall. "When Ellen gets here, tell her to pack your things," he ordered curtly, throwing the door open. "We leave as soon as I've spoken to the Queen."

Mercifully the room was empty. Isabel went past him without a word or look. She had no intention of obeying him, but she wasn't going to argue. Let fitzAlan believe her cowed and defeated, so he would leave her alone to think.

"And don't think of leaving," he added, echoing her thoughts in a way that sent an icy shiver down her spine. Again she wondered if he could read her mind. "I intend posting a guard outside this door."

One second later the latch clicked shut with ominous softness.

* * *

Guy took two steps away from the solar door and had to stop. His hand went out to the stone wall to brace himself. It was shaking, he noted distantly, dragging air into his lungs. Every breath was agony. His chest hurt and he felt sick, as if someone had just kicked him in the gut. Every muscle in his body was knotted with unbearable tension. A pulse throbbed painfully in his temples.

"Isabel," he whispered achingly. A tiny echo sighed back at him.

A full minute passed before he could move again.

Chapter Ten

"I will never marry him! *Never!*" Isabel hurled the pile of blue velvet across the bed and snatched her old grey dress from Ellen's slackened grasp.

"But my lady, Lord fitzAlan is with the Queen now. If she permits it—and why should she not?—then—"

"Ellen, I *can't* marry him." Isabel paused in the act of stepping into the worn garment and met her maid's worried brown eyes. "I can't marry a man who hates me—" her voice wobbled dangerously but she quickly brought it back under control "—who believes me to be a traitor, without a single question or…or…"

The last word refused to emerge as a little voice reminded her that fitzAlan *had* asked why, out there on the drawbridge. Would he have listened to her then, if she had not flung that furious retort at him before they were confronted by Ralf? She would never know now.

Biting hard on her lower lip, Isabel brushed away a traitorous tear. He'd deserved it, she told herself, deliberately fanning the flames of anger again as she tugged her gown over her shoulders. Hauling her all the way from the Bishop's castle at a pace he must have known was impossible for her to keep up with, until she'd had no breath left with which to explain. She would not cry over such an overbearing, ill-tempered brute. She would not shed one tear! And she would not meekly wait around to be married to him!

"I know he was very angry," ventured Ellen, shuddering at the memory. "But surely my lord fitzAlan would not wed you if he truly thought—"

"He doesn't wish to wed me. 'Tis his honourable reputation he's worried about. And he thinks to hold Tracy Castle for the King, now that my brother..." But Edmund's death was still too raw a wound, still too painful to discuss. Unable to continue, she gestured to Ellen to fasten the ties at the back of her gown.

The girl obeyed, sympathy in her eyes as she gazed at her mistress. "That woman should be imprisoned for life," she grumbled. "To let you find out in such a way... She must be every bit as cruel as they say, my lady."

"I hated her and made no secret of it," Isabel said softly. "It probably amused her to keep me there, unknowing, continuing to act as her lady-in-waiting, having to obey every order, every whim. And then my ignorance became useful. But I am not ignorant this time," she added, determination hardening her voice. "And I won't be used again."

Ellen looked doubtful. "What can you do, my lady? If the Queen orders the marriage, you must obey."

"Not if I can't hear the order," Isabel muttered grimly. "And I don't intend to be here to listen to it."

"Not be here? But what...how...where will you go? Is there someone in Winchester who might help you?"

Isabel thought briefly of Simon de Villiers and as instantly dismissed the notion. He owed loyalty to fitzAlan by ties of friendship as well as family, and would return her to his brother-in-law before she could blink. And there was no one else, except…

"Ellen, is Ralf still here? The man who was asking for us?"

Ellen's jaw dropped. "My lady, you aren't thinking of running off with a *pedlar*?"

"No," agreed Isabel, her sudden hope dying as the inevitable consequences of this course of action sprang to mind. "FitzAlan would think of him, too, and Ralf's life wouldn't be worth a straw." She took a couple of paces across the room, thinking hard. "Where did those women go? You know, the poor creatures in the wagon."

Ellen forgot herself so far as to sit down plump on the bed. "You wouldn't," she uttered in horrified accents. "My lady, you *couldn't*! 'Twould not be decent, 'twould not be safe!"

"But he'd never think to look for me in such company."

"I'll tell him," averred Ellen, bouncing to her feet in her agitation. "I swear I will. You don't know those women. They…" She hesitated, seeming to grope for words, then waved a hand wildly at Isabel's dress. "You think your gown old and shabby, but they would rip it from your body because 'tis better than the rags they wear. And then they'd throw you to whatever man happened to be passing for the money you'd earn for them."

Isabel knew her face had whitened; the pictures conjured up by Ellen's speech awakened all her most terrifying memories. But if she let fitzAlan carry her off and marry her she would be completely powerless against a man who despised her. She had to get away.

"I can't marry him," she repeated softly, despairingly. Why couldn't the other girl understand? Ellen had been so sympathetic earlier, had believed at once in her innocence when Isabel had told her what had happened.

"There is my father's alehouse," murmured Ellen hesitantly, unable to resist the desperation in Isabel's eyes.

"Oh, Ellen, the very place. Would your father object, do you think?" The words tumbled over each other in her eagerness. "'Twould only be for a day or so while I try to get a message to the Queen. Once I speak with her, tell her the truth, she will surely not force me to this marriage."

"My father needn't know who you are," said Ellen. "But, my lady, consider. 'Tis not the sort of place you are used to, and we still have to get there. 'Tis a mile or so outside the town, past the meaner suburbs to the east. There is only the one room and the customers are rough. They're as likely to—"

"Is it meaner than a dungeon so dark that you can't see your hand in front of your face?" The low question cut through Ellen's objections like a scythe through dry hay. "Is it meaner than a place so foul that you can't bear to touch your own skin except to brush off the things crawling over you?"

Ellen shook her head, her eyes enormous in her startled face.

"Then help me," begged Isabel, holding out an imploring hand.

"If my lord ever finds you here, scrubbing tables, *my* life won't be worth a straw," muttered Ellen two hours later, as she wielded a brush with more energy than accuracy. "I wish you would not do that, my lady. 'Tis not seemly."

Isabel pulled her hands out of a wooden bucket of sudsy water and dried them on her gown. "He won't harm you,

Ellen. I only said that about Ralf because he's a man, and for some strange reason fitzAlan seemed to think... But never mind that," she added hastily. "And you must remember to call me Isabel."

"It doesn't feel right, my lady," protested Ellen. "'Tis all very well putting on your old gown and pretending to be a serving-girl so we could pass that dolt at the solar door. You don't have to do the work as well. Look at your hands, pray."

"They've looked worse," retorted Isabel drily. "Truly, Ellen, I would rather do something to earn my keep. Your father has been so good allowing me to stay, and—"

"He doesn't know your true station, remember," interposed Ellen, lowering her voice and glancing over at one of the tables, where her parent was enjoying a tankard of his own home-brew. "He's too busy preening himself on acquiring the prettiest serving-maid for miles around. It worries me, my lady. Word spreads, and some of the clods who come in here would sell their own mothers for profit. Soon this place will not be safe for you."

"'Tis only until I can find someone to convey a message to the Queen, begging her to see me."

"If you would let me—" began Ellen.

But Isabel shook her head quickly. "No. I've told you. He knows you were with me and may have set someone to watch for you."

"Probably that impudent squire of his," agreed Ellen, a scowl marring her usually placid features. "You never saw anything like the way he marched me back to the castle earlier. You would have thought I was under arrest."

"Just like his lord and master," muttered Isabel, seizing a broom and attacking the mouldy rushes on the floor. "But I'll see you don't suffer for this, Ellen. I'll tell the

Queen I ordered you to accompany me." She hoped she could keep that promise.

Ellen took the broom from her. "If it comes to that I can always use the excuse that Father needed me," she answered calmly. "But what about you, my lady? You say I can't go, and Father—well, look at him; can you see him being taken to the Queen's presence?"

Isabel turned to contemplate her host. Ellen's father, Jack, had greeted his daughter with the testily expressed hope that she had not left the safe position at the royal castle that he had gone to considerable trouble to obtain for her. Having been reassured on this point, he had grudgingly accepted Ellen's explanation that she had been given leave to visit him to see how he was coping alone, and had promptly put his daughter and her companion to work. His own duties appeared to be limited to joining his patrons in a drink whenever he was thirsty, which seemed to be often. Long, unkempt hair, several missing teeth, and a nose that looked as if it had met more than one fist in its owner's lifetime did nothing for his general appearance.

Isabel had to admit he was not messenger material, but she was beginning to question the wisdom of her panicked flight from the castle. She hoped fitzAlan would begin his search for her on the road to Gloucester; he might even think she had sought shelter with Dame Sybil, but the hope was a weak one. He knew Ellen was with her and was perfectly capable of tracking down their whereabouts. And here she was, trapped outside the city without money or the means to get a message to Matilda.

"If I had some token to send with him…" she thought aloud.

"Father would still be questioned," Ellen reminded her. "With King Stephen imprisoned, the Queen is more closely guarded than ever. They'd want to know who sent him. If he says his serving-maid he'll be laughed at; if he tells the truth—''

"He'll be forced to lead fitzAlan straight back here,'' finished Isabel despairingly. "Oh, Ellen, what am I going to do? I thought perhaps one of the customers might take a message, but…'' Her voice died away as she glanced anxiously out of the unshuttered window.

Hearing the stamp of hoofs that had alerted Isabel, Ellen came to stand beside her. "Soldiers,'' she announced, peering out. "They'd be on foot if they were looking for you, I think, but perhaps 'twould be safer to get behind the counter. 'Tis darker in that corner.''

Isabel hurriedly took Ellen's advice, retreating to one side of the room, where a rough table near the fireplace served as a bar. Several barrels stood behind it, the shelf above them holding crude wooden tankards. She shrank into the furthest corner just as the door was pushed open, thankful that Jack had not yet seen fit to light the sconces against the shadows of late afternoon.

Three soldiers entered, calling loudly for Jack and seeming to fill the room. Two of the men flung themselves down on a bench, scabbards clattering, while the third strode forward, kicking Isabel's abandoned bucket out of his path. Water spread across the floor in a greasy stream, mingling with the pile of filthy rushes. The fetid odour of damp refuse filled the air and the soldier made a disgusted face.

"Faugh! This place stinks!'' He reached down and hauled Jack off his bench. "Come on, Jack, you lazy rogue. On your feet. 'Tis rent day and we want a drink as well.''

"Aye, 'tis thirsty work collecting rent,'' one of the

others called out. He seemed to find the remark hilarious, because he broke into raucous laughter.

The fellow still holding Jack by the scruff of the neck grinned and shook his victim with casual contempt. "The wench at the last place didn't want to pay up," he explained with a leer. "Said she didn't have the money, so we had to persuade her." He scratched obscenely at the front of his tunic. "Thirsty work, like Hal said."

"What do you say we let your girl do likewise, Jack?" queried the man named Hal. "About time she helped out like a dutiful daughter." He gave another coarse guffaw.

"I'll pay in coin like I always does," growled Jack, but his eyes flickered uncomfortably towards Isabel for a second.

His captor followed the direction of his gaze. "Well, well." He released Jack and took a step in Isabel's direction. "What have we here? A new wench, by the Rood."

Ellen darted past him to join Isabel behind the table. She snatched up three tankards and filled them with ale, her movements swift and practised. "Here." She slapped the drinks down. "Father, get the rent money."

Isabel, backing further into the shadows, dared to breathe again when the soldier went to pick up the ale-cups. His eyes were still fixed on her, but she knew he could see little in the dark corner. Perhaps they would down their drinks and leave. She saw Ellen's father reach behind one of the barrels and draw out a small sack.

"Not so fast."

The softly spoken command came from the third man, who had remained silent until now. He was slightly different from the others, Isabel saw, watching him with apprehensive eyes. His voice was more cultured and he was cleaner, his black hair close-cropped and his beard neatly trimmed. "Let the girl bring the drinks," he ordered, lounging on the bench at his ease.

The man near the table snickered and rejoined his companions, snatching the sack out of Jack's hand as he passed.

Isabel glanced uncertainly at Ellen.

"You'd better do it," her maid whispered. "They've never...hurt me, but try not to protest if they touch you. It'll only make them worse."

Isabel nodded and gritted her teeth. Picking up the drinks, she crossed the room and set them down on the trestle, careful to keep her face turned away from the window. The two men-at-arms leered but promptly buried their noses in their cups. The other picked up his drink and took a long swallow, watching her over the rim of the tankard. She started to turn away.

"I didn't say you could move, slut."

Isabel froze.

"What's your name?" he asked, casually tossing back the rest of the ale. He held the cup out to her.

Trying not to let her hand shake, Isabel reached out to take it. As quick as a striking adder, the soldier's fingers fastened around her arm. She was yanked off balance to land on her knees in front of him. "I said, what's your name?" he repeated menacingly.

"She's my cousin, Isabel," said Ellen quickly, moving from behind the table. But when Hal lowered his tankard and glared at her she halted, uncertain.

"Your cousin?" The quiet voice turned sardonic. "You hear that, Jack? We never knew you had a niece. Never knew you had brother or sister, in fact." The man shook his head in mock-reproach. "My lord likes to know everything about his tenants, Jack. He's not going to be pleased that you've kept this little morsel to yourself."

"She's no niece o'mine," grumbled Jack, shrugging helplessly when his daughter turned a horrified look on him. "Just a friend of me girl's. But 'ware how you treat her. She's from the castle. The royal castle," he added for emphasis.

"Interesting," mused the soldier. He narrowed his eyes at Isabel, who looked up at him, frightened but desperately trying to keep her wits about her. She had to hold on to her control. If she stayed quiet and calm he wouldn't hurt her.

"Lately come to Winchester, have you, girl?" Not waiting for an answer, he stood up and dragged Isabel closer to the window. She barely had time to struggle to her feet before cruel fingers tangled in her hair and her face was jerked up to the light. Frowning, he studied her for a moment, then, with an impatient curse, yanked the ribbon away and unwound her braid. Her eyes watered when her hair was pulled so roughly, but she refused to make a sound.

"Long, dark hair…young…beautiful," he murmured thoughtfully. Then, much louder, "How did you come to Winchester? From where? Were you with a man? Where is he now? Did he abandon you here?"

Calm! She had to stay calm. The rapid fire of questions was deliberate, she knew, designed to scare her into blurting out the truth. She had seen the technique used before—don't give the victim a chance to think of a convincing lie. It was almost working, too, but his insistence on a supposed escort kept her mind clear by sheer instinct alone. There was no time to question her motives; she just knew she would never mention fitzAlan to this man.

"Is he coming back?" The soldier gave her hair another painful jerk. "Answer!"

"I don't know what you mean," Isabel choked breathlessly. "There's no man."

His eyes bored into hers for another nerve-stretching minute, then he seemed to relax and accept her answer. He smiled and the hand in her hair turned caressing. "That's very sad. No man. We'll have to see if we can mend the situation."

"I don't want no trouble," put in Jack uneasily. "I've paid me rent; you've no right—"

"Then leave if you don't want to watch." The words were uttered with such chilling disinterest that Isabel's stomach turned over and her legs started to tremble. Already cringing under the hand in her hair, she suddenly felt terrifyingly weak. She watched the other two men get to their feet, matching expressions of anticipation on their coarse features.

"This one's mine," Isabel's captor drawled. He hadn't taken his eyes off her once. "But you can have the other if you didn't get enough at the last place."

The whole room seemed to explode in seconds. An enraged roar rent the air as Jack leapt forward. "I'm a free man," he bellowed. "You've no right—"

A resounding crack cut him off when one of the men-at-arms grabbed a bench and swung it. The rickety wood splintered under the impact and Jack crumpled, blood welling from a gash on his forehead. Ellen screamed and was instantly seized by the other man, who, laughing at her wild struggles, began to force her down to the floor.

Isabel didn't see anything else. Without any warning whatsoever, the man holding her swung his foot back and kicked her legs out from under her with a careless, emotionless violence that wrenched a panic-stricken scream from her throat. She sprawled flat on the hard wooden floor, her cry abruptly silenced as all the air rushed out of her body. Before she could recover he was upon her, his ale-scented breath almost making her retch when his mouth crushed down on hers. She felt the sharp edge of his teeth trying to force her lips apart and tasted blood.

Choking with revulsion, Isabel tried to fight him, but her own fear made her helpless. She couldn't see, couldn't breathe; her entire body was immobilised by the weight of her attacker. He shifted slightly, tugging at her skirts, and she got one arm free. She heard him grunt as her nails raked across his face and he pulled back, releasing her mouth. She gulped in a lungful of air and forced her eyelids open. Hard black eyes gleamed down at her. His fist clenched and drew back. He smiled, a smile that was neither gloating nor excited, but almost inhuman in its utter coldness. The fist began to descend.

Isabel screamed again, twisting her head from side to side, catapulted brutally into panic-stricken hysteria. Almost senseless with terror, she wasn't even aware that her screams went on and on. Nor did she see the sudden eruption into the alehouse of two more men.

Her assailant's fist was stopped in mid-air. Less than a second later he was jerked up and around to meet a devastating punch straight to the jaw. The nauseating sound of breaking bone was immediately followed by a crash as another blow to the side of the head dropped him like a stone.

Strong hands grasped Isabel's arms. Uncomprehending, she renewed her struggles, her screams weakening to rasping sobs. She was pulled to her feet and managed to aim a kick at her attacker that didn't have a chance of connecting. She sobbed harder.

"Isabel! Stop it!" Powerful hands shook her hard. "*Stop it!*" roared fitzAlan.

She stopped fighting, blinking up at him through a mass

of tangled hair, her eyes wild, her breath coming in convulsive gasps. "Guy," she whispered.

He didn't answer. Backing her up to a bench, he pressed her down on to it and left her. Not until she had been sitting there for several minutes did Isabel realise that no sound at all had come from her torn and bleeding lips. She put a shaking hand up to her mouth, her eyes falling on Ellen, who was kneeling by the fireplace, clutching the tattered edges of her dress together over her breasts and watching her father anxiously. FitzAlan bent over Jack as he began to stir.

Isabel's gaze skittered nervously past them to the two men-at-arms, now held at the end of a very businesslike sword attached to the hand of the young man she had seen with Guy at the church.

"We didn't know they'd run away before you'd finished with them," one of the soldiers was grumbling sullenly. He eyed the sword-point warily before peering past it to the body on the floor. "You've killed our Baron's knight over a couple of alehouse wenches. He isn't going to like that."

"I doubt he's dead," said fitzAlan coldly, getting to his feet. He glanced contemptuously at the unconscious man. "But he'll make sure the next wench he fancies isn't another man's property. As for your Baron, whoever he is, tell him…" He stopped short, his eyes moving swiftly to Isabel.

She had risen and now stood staring at him, trembling visibly and feeling as if a puff of wind would knock her down again. In frightening contrast fitzAlan looked tough and completely immovable, and bigger than ever in the confined space of the alehouse. His mouth was set hard and his eyes were filled with a cold rage that was all the more dangerous for its very restraint.

And he had spoken of her as though she were no more than a female to be used and then discarded.

"No," she whispered, her voice still painfully hoarse. "I'm not—"

"Be quiet!" he snarled at her.

But Isabel was too distressed to heed him. "I won't go with you!" she choked. "I won't ma—"

The distraught protest ended in a sharp cry as fitzAlan's open hand flashed out, striking her cheek with enough force to whip her head to the side. The silence that followed was finally broken by a nervous laugh from one of the men-at-arms.

FitzAlan turned on him immediately. "Get out of here, and take that filth with you."

Isabel stood as if turned to stone, her face still averted. He had actually hit her this time, she told herself dazedly. *Really* hit her. Strange, her cheek wasn't even stinging, just slightly warm. He hadn't hurt her, and yet pain overwhelmed her with battering force. She felt as though she was dying inside.

Why? Despite the threats, the insults, the accusations, had she thought he would never physically strike her? Had her dream hero been so deeply embedded in her heart that her mind had never stopped believing in him? She had thought he could do nothing more to her, but he had. Oh, dear God, *he had*! She had thought she knew suffering, but she had not. Loneliness and fear and grief had never been like this. The loss of her family, the futile years of servitude, even Edmund's death—none of it had hurt like this.

There was sound and movement in the room, but Isabel heard and saw nothing. Dreams and reality had collided in her shocked mind with stunning force, sending her hurtling over the edge of that invisible precipice, and the fall had broken her into a thousand agonising pieces, like brittle shards of glass that could never be whole again.

Moving very, very slowly, she wrapped her arms around her waist and sat down on the bench. It didn't matter what fitzAlan did to her now. It didn't matter what happened to her. Nothing mattered any more—except the truth that was breaking her heart.

She loved him.

"My lady?"

It was Ellen, looking a little pale but seemingly recovered. A homespun woollen mantle was fastened across her shoulders, hiding her torn dress.

"Come, my lady, 'tis time to go."

Isabel rose obediently, allowing her maid to drape a vaguely familiar red mantle over her own shoulders. She didn't know where they were going, nor did she care. She followed Ellen outside, not thinking, not feeling.

Horses whickered restlessly, held by a small urchin who watched Isabel emerge from the alehouse with round, inquisitive eyes. Quite a crowd had gathered, lured by the fight and the presence of gentry in such a squalid neighbourhood. The sibilant hiss of a sword being drawn sounded behind her and instantly the crowd dispersed, melting away into the shadowy alleys off the street.

"You'll ride with me, mistress," ordered a brusque voice. "The grey is for my lady."

"'Tis Will, my lord's squire," Ellen whispered in Isabel's ear. "He has enough sauce for a king's fool, but impudence I can stomach so long as I don't have to ride something that big on my own."

Reins were put into Isabel's hand. She felt a firm grasp on her arm and a second later she was on Chalon's back.

Will made sure she was secure, then lifted a nervously protesting Ellen on to his own horse.

"Hush your tongue, mistress," he ordered impatiently. "I'm not going to drop you."

Their voices faded into the background as Isabel's eyes came to rest on the third horse. A big black. Romulus. His head came around, brown eyes alert as fitzAlan strode out of the alehouse, ducking his head to negotiate the doorway. He made straight for the big warhorse, mounted, said something to Will, and started along the street.

He hadn't come near her, hadn't even glanced in her direction.

It was Will who leaned over and smacked Chalon's rump, sending the horse after fitzAlan. Tossing a coin to the ragged urchin, he brought his mount alongside Isabel, not speaking, but clearly ready to offer assistance should it be needed. She sensed the long look he directed at her, but continued to stare blindly ahead.

Time passed. Vague pictures swam before Isabel's eyes: a cobbled section of street where children ran heedlessly between the horses' hoofs, the high walls of the city on her left, then fields to either side of the rutted road. Somewhere along the way they were joined by Simon de Villiers and several men-at-arms, but Isabel scarcely noticed. Unable to hide physically, she had simply closed everything off, shrinking from further pain like any wounded creature.

The numbing stupor got her through the next few hours. Through the long ride, through the noise and confusion when they reached their destination, through the hurried ceremony that followed almost immediately, during which she moved and spoke when so directed like one in a trance. Until, finally, there was night and blessed silence, and she was alone with no one to witness her pain. She lay in a huge, curtained bed and felt the ice around her heart begin to melt, her mind begin to function again.

Very carefully, as though testing a raw wound, Isabel thought about her present situation. She was married to a man who believed her to be a traitor and a spy, a man who had stood beside her during a ceremony that bound them for life and had not once looked at her, nor touched her except to push a heavy, engraved ring on to her finger.

Isabel raised her left hand and peered at the ring in the dim light cast by the clock-candle burning near the bed. There were faint etchings in the gold, but she couldn't make them out. Her eyes lifted to the candle. Its flame had sunk well past the midnight mark. Would he come to her bed? He had desired her once, and now she was his wife. Did he still want her? Had his desire been completely destroyed by hatred?

Isabel whimpered softly. She curled up in a tight ball as though to stop herself from breaking apart. The solar. Look at the solar, she ordered herself. Tapestry-hung walls, flames dancing in a fireplace, a table and chair between the two window embrasures, an enormous studded chest and a smaller one near it, and sheepskin rugs. Warmth and comfort, even luxury. She felt so cold. Would he come?

Think of the other people she had seen. FitzAlan's sister, Joanna, serfs and soldiers, a wizened yet bright-eyed old man who had welcomed her profusely, a priest intoning Latin. But her mind's eye saw only one face, one man. He had married her. She was his wife. Would he come?

Isabel lay very still, her muscles so rigid with tension that she doubted she could have moved anyway. Her eyes watched the flame of the clock-candle sink ever lower. She watched until dawn, until utter weariness overtook her without her being aware of when she slept.

He never came.

* * *

"Now, my lady, you must eat something."

Isabel didn't respond. It was a foolish suggestion of Ellen's anyway, she reflected. She would be sick if she tried to eat.

"You've been sitting there the whole morning in nothing but that flimsy shift, just staring through the window at all that water. 'Tis not right. Lady Joanna will think you don't like her."

That got her attention. She even felt a twinge of amusement. Isabel turned her head. "You sound just like my old nurse, scolding me for not playing with my cousin whenever she stayed with us."

A look of relief replaced the frown on Ellen's face. "Thanks be to the Blessed Virgin. You're with us again," she muttered beneath her breath. Then, raising her voice, "I don't think Lady Joanna expects you to play with her, my lady, but she has been asking if you are feeling more rested. She knows you've been through...a difficult time."

A difficult time, mused Isabel. A small ironic smile curved her lips. "Is that what he told them?" she murmured, glancing out of the window again.

The prospect that met her eyes was strangely comforting. Beyond the placid waters of a small lake, a golden forest of trees stretched as far as the eye could see. Ashby Chase. Her new home. An island fortress surrounded on three sides by a deep moat which emptied into the lake situated on the eastern side of the keep. It was a pretty setting. The late morning sun was beginning to break through the clouds. It glinted on the water, reminding her of fitzAlan's eyes. Isabel's hands clenched in her lap.

"My lord said that he'd brought you from Gloucester,"

volunteered Ellen, setting a trencher of bread and fruit on the table, "where you'd been held since your father's death. But you heard all that yesterday, my lady."

She hadn't, but there was no need to tell Ellen that. Instead Isabel laughed shortly, a bitter little sound that held pain. "If he only knew. 'Twas near enough to the truth."

"Well, no need for you to fear captivity again," stated Ellen in bracing tones. "An entire army could drown trying to get into this place. For myself, I think the moat alone would have been quite enough, but I dare say one gets used to the feeling that we might all sink." She pulled up a chair and patted it invitingly. "At least swallow some milk, my lady. Lady Joanna mixed a little wine and honey with it, and she'll be disappointed if you don't try it."

"I don't suppose anyone would live here if there were any danger of sinking," replied Isabel, ignoring the rest of Ellen's speech. But she rose and walked over to the table, moving stiffly because of muscles chilled from sitting in the stone window embrasure for so long.

"My lord's sister seems a sweet lady," Ellen chattered on, pouring the warm milk into a goblet. "And my Lord de Villiers obviously adores her."

Pain slashed through Isabel again, clutching at her heart. It left her so weak that she had to put a hand out to the table before she could sit down. She tried to recall her impression of Joanna in an effort to distract herself, thinking back to their arrival. A lovely girl, not much older than herself, she thought, with fitzAlan's silvery-fair hair, her beautiful face gentle and anxious as she hurried from the keep to greet them. She had smiled uncertainly at Isabel and had started to say something, but then Simon had put his arm around her waist and had led her away, his head bent over her fair one, his expression tender. Joanna had looked up at him, open adoration in her glowing sapphire eyes.

The memory became too painful. With a shaking hand Isabel picked up the goblet. Maybe the milk would wash down the lump in her throat. Her gaze followed Ellen as the girl moved about the room, straightening the crimson velvet bed curtains, placing another log on the fire. Draped across the carved wooden lid of a nearby chest were the clothes given to her by the Queen. Isabel wondered when fitzAlan had found the time to pack up the garments. And he'd had Chalon ready saddled for her, also. Had he been so sure of finding her at the alehouse?

"Ellen, your father!" she exclaimed suddenly. "Is he all right?"

"Aye, my lady." Ellen grimaced wryly. "Father has a hard head. My lord offered him a place here in case those men cause any more trouble, but he refused." She shrugged philosophically. "'Tis the only life he's known—keeping an alehouse. He'd miss it."

"But what of yourself?" Isabel asked softly. "Your place with the Queen. I never thought... How selfish I was—"

"Never say so, my lady! The Queen knew I would accompany you here. She ordered it. Besides, you were not yourself and who could wonder at it? After so many shocks I was surprised you could stand up at your own wedding."

"My wedding." The whisper hung in the air. It still didn't seem quite real. She was a wife and yet not a wife. Even saying it aloud didn't help. "I'm married."

"Aye, my lady," agreed Ellen placidly. "Not an hour after we arrived. And what a stir it caused, too," she added, quite as though Isabel had not been present.

"There were tongues wagging a plenty, I can tell you, at such a hasty wedding, but they were soon stilled when my lord announced he was leaving immediately, and—"

"Immediately? He's *gone*?" Isabel shoved her chair back so quickly that it almost toppled over. FitzAlan wouldn't...*surely* he wouldn't...leave without seeing her? Did he intend everyone in the castle to know he did not want the wife he had married in such a hurry? Did he intend to ignore her completely?

Then Isabel saw Ellen's stunned face and realised that her maid, at least, did not know she had spent the night alone.

"I thought my lord must have told you," the girl said, still looking confused. "He's leaving today. The siege engines have gone already."

"Siege engines?" repeated Isabel slowly, sinking back on to the chair as understanding flooded her. "That's why Simon had so many men with him. The Bishop must have given him leave to help fitzAlan. They're going to capture Tracy Castle. No matter how long it takes." And a siege could take weeks, she knew. Weeks in which an attacking force could be rallied and sent against the besiegers.

Springing to her feet again, Isabel snatched up her gown. "Quickly, Ellen, help me dress. I have to see him."

Ellen hurried forward automatically. "But my lady," she almost wailed in obvious puzzlement. "My lord said you were to rest today. What do you mean to do that cannot wait—?"

"Help him," said Isabel, heading for the door before Ellen had her gown properly fastened.

She was through it before her maid could draw breath to protest.

Chapter Eleven

The tower stairs were lit only by narrow window slits cut into the ten-foot-thick walls at irregular intervals, but Isabel didn't hesitate. This was no time for doubt and despondency and moping in solars. The pain would return, she knew, cruel and cutting, but pride and hurt meant little compared to the fear that she might never see fitzAlan again. No matter what it cost her, she could not let him leave without trying to speak to him. She could no longer hide from the truth she had faced yesterday.

She loved him. She loved fitzAlan. And it was not the five-year-old image of a man that she loved, but the man he was now. Arrogant, strong, passionate, proud—she loved him. He might never know of her love, might never want it, but she was his wife. He would know that her loyalty was his.

Filled with equal parts dread and determination, Isabel careered down the staircase, trying to remember the way to the hall and bailey. Her soft leather shoes made little sound on the stone steps and she was so lost in her thoughts that she didn't hear other footsteps coming as rapidly towards her. The last arrow slit had just flashed past when a large shadow loomed on the wall in front of her. Unable to stop, she collided heavily with the man ascending the stairs, only his strength and quick reflexes preventing them both from tumbling the rest of the way.

When the tower walls swung back into focus Isabel found herself clutching a chainmail tunic, quite unaware of the metal links cutting into her palms as she gazed straight into the ice-blue eyes of her husband. His hands held her slender arms in a grip that hurt, and his mouth was only inches away from her own. For a mindless second, forgetting everything but the warmth and strength of him, Isabel swayed closer.

"What were you trying to do? Break your neck?"

Her head snapped back. The harsh question was like another slap in the face. Her teeth sank into her bottom lip, biting back a cry, and she winced. It was still tender from the soldier's abuse, but the pain helped her fight back incipient tears. What had she expected? she asked herself mercilessly. A concerned enquiry about her health? Just concentrate on what you have to say.

"I had to see you," she whispered, unable to speak any louder under a look that was as stern and forbidding as she had feared. "To tell you—"

A loud clatter of arms from below interrupted her. FitzAlan half glanced back over his shoulder. "We can't talk here," he said curtly. "Go up to the solar."

When Isabel hesitated his mouth crooked in a faint reflection of the wry half-smile she remembered. "Where did you think I was going?" he asked, turning her around and giving her a little push.

Now doubting that she would be able to speak at all, Isabel began to climb the stairs, acutely aware of fitzAlan behind her every step of the way. She tried to pull her scattered thoughts into some sort of order, but all she could do was wonder if the cold, level gaze he had given her betokened indifference or anger. What was she going to face when they reached the privacy of the solar? What was he going to do to her for running away?

Her imagination promptly sped through a catalogue of punishments which ranged from an hour in the stocks to a beating. She had just got to incarceration in a convent for the rest of her days when they arrived at the top of the stairs.

Ellen was hurrying out of the solar. Isabel stepped back so she wouldn't bump into the girl and instantly cannoned into fitzAlan instead. The heat of his body scorched the length of her back. He felt very solid and very big. She shot into the room as though pursued by demons, not even hearing Ellen's murmured, "I'll return later, my lady." Behind her the door closed with a decisive snap.

Isabel walked over to the window and stared out, not seeing a thing. Her mouth went dry, her heart raced, and her legs shook. The past few days seemed to hang like a heavy stormcloud over the room, seething with half-truths and suspicion, misunderstandings and mistakes. She wanted to explain, but didn't know if fitzAlan would listen; longed for gentleness, but was braced for anger.

When fitzAlan spoke right at her shoulder she nearly leapt a foot into the air.

"Your gown isn't fastened," he murmured, his voice soft and deep. "And..."

Isabel didn't have to look around to know he had caught sight of her over-tunic, still reposing on the chest. A tide of red flooded her cheeks. Now he would know that she had rushed out of the solar, half dressed, to find him.

Wheeling about, she parted her lips to say something—anything—to distract him, and not a word came out. He was standing less than one pace away, so close that her swift movement caused her gown to brush across his hauberk, catching on a metal link. He glanced down at it.

How could a man dressed in chainmail move so quickly and silently? she asked mutely, watching as he took the soft linen in one big hand and carefully freed the material. She had a sudden unnerving vision of those long fingers moving as gently over her flesh, and bit her lip again on a shiver of awareness.

FitzAlan's gaze immediately flashed to her mouth, his eyes darkening so abruptly that Isabel's knees went weak. This time heat suffused her entire body. She had to sit down, she thought, looking dazedly around for a chair. Before she fell down.

"Don't…" he began, then bit off the rest, his hand clenching on the fabric he still held. Isabel prayed he couldn't feel the trembling in her limbs.

Then, with a rough exclamation that made her heart jump, fitzAlan jerked his hand away and strode over to the chest. "Put that on," he ordered, picking up her overtunic and throwing it at her.

This didn't seem the time to remind him that he had seen her wearing considerably less. Isabel obeyed, watching in trepidation as he paced over to the door, then back to the fireplace. There he halted, staring down into the flames, but his stillness had a taut, barely restrained quality that kept her heart beating much too fast, and though he seemed totally absorbed in the glowing fire Isabel sensed he was aware of her every movement. Clutching the velvet bliaut to her, she waited, nervous chills replacing the heat of a moment ago.

FitzAlan looked up, his gaze locking with hers. "You wanted to see me?"

"Aye," she managed. "But…don't you want…? Aren't you angry…?" She stopped. What was the matter with her? Since when had fitzAlan needed encouragement to show anger? That fleeting, intense look had addled her brain as well as scrambled her insides.

His face never changed expression. "You wanted to see me?" he repeated evenly.

Isabel gulped on a mouthful of air. It suddenly occurred to her that total disregard of her escapade was a very subtle punishment indeed. And effective. She felt as guilty about running away as if she had just robbed a lame beggar of his last groat.

"You're leaving for Tracy," she stammered at last.

It wasn't a question, but he nodded, his eyes narrowing slightly.

"There's a way into the castle. You won't need your siege engines."

FitzAlan was silent for so long that Isabel wondered if he thought she was lying. She was just about to speak again when he said, "If you mean undermining, it takes too long. I presume serfs are still living there and I'd rather break in than see innocent people die of hunger while—"

"I didn't mean undermining."

He frowned. "What, then?"

"Against the south wall of the bailey there's an empty dovecote. Some of the stones in the wall are loose. If you can pull them out you can make a hole big enough for a man to get inside. He could open the postern and—"

"While we're being fired upon from above? I think not."

The interruption was sardonic, but Isabel merely shook her head, intent on finishing before he cut her off again. "One or two men wouldn't be seen. 'Tis where—" her breath caught and she glanced away, flushing slightly "—where the pleasance used to be. 'Twas a wilderness years ago and will be more so now. If you created a diversion, drawing their attention elsewhere…''

She fell silent again, unable to tell if the mention of the garden had aroused similar memories in fitzAlan's mind.

''Quite the little strategist,'' he murmured. Then, before Isabel could decide how to take *that*, his gaze sharpened. ''You said *if* we can pull the stones out. Don't you know if they'll move?''

''They did once. Edmund and I loosened them enough, but…'twas a long time ago.''

FitzAlan took a step towards her. ''After your father was killed?''

''Aye.'' Her voice dropped and went toneless. Just for a moment the solar slid away and she was back at Tracy Castle. ''We couldn't lift them. Edmund was too young, and I wasn't strong enough. And then…'twas much too late.''

''You and Edmund?'' Guy asked very quietly.

But Isabel blinked, pushing the past and the question aside. Her hand made a tiny movement of finality. ''That's all.''

''Is it?''

She looked up, almost fearfully. Now he was going to yell at her.

''There's a lot I don't know, isn't there, Isabel.'' He made it a statement.

''I…'' She didn't know what to say. Hope flared within her so strongly, so quickly, that the force of it frightened her. She could only nod mutely, her hands gripping each other so tightly that her fingers went numb.

''And I don't have time to hear it,'' he muttered, more to himself than to her.

She was so tense now that her muscles were beginning to quiver. ''Must you go today?'' she breathed.

Guy moved suddenly, taking another swift step towards her, his blue eyes glittering, and Isabel promptly lost her nerve, jumping back out of reach. He must not touch her. If he did she would break down completely and beg him to hold her, beg him not to leave her. "I...I mean, your arm is scarce healed, and—"

He had stopped the instant she retreated, halting in the middle of the room. The fierce glitter vanished, leaving his eyes cold and distant. "'Tis best that I go now."

The clipped remark choked off the rest of her sentence and her hopes. Despair engulfed Isabel in a swamping wave. Her shoulders drooped and she turned her face away, staring at the floor, hardly able to listen when fitzAlan continued speaking.

"After Stephen was captured I swore to serve the Queen until his release, to obey her commands as I would the King's. She wants me to take Tracy immediately, before the Empress realises no word has reached her from Winchester and enlarges the garrison."

"The Queen," repeated Isabel dully, only hearing the words "obey" and "command". "Of course. She ordered you to marry me."

For the first time a note of impatience sharpened his voice. "Damn it, stop looking as if I've just hit you again! I know you didn't want to marry me, but 'tis not as though I'm forcing myself on you!"

And we both know that force wouldn't be necessary.

For a minute Isabel thought she'd said the words aloud, or that fitzAlan had. They seemed to whisper through the room, mocking her.

"'Twas you who didn't want to marry me," she cried, trying to drown out the tormenting echo. She met his eyes defiantly, but she was shaking. Perhaps he was right to go, she thought despairingly. Perhaps the time spent away from him would help her regain some control over the wild emotions roiling inside her.

She was lying to herself. She would be only half alive without him.

"I have to leave," he said in a surprisingly gentle voice. "While I'm gone, Isabel, think on this. I could have told the Queen about your meeting with Rainald. You would have forfeited Tracy Castle immediately, and 'twould have been granted to me to hold for the King. I didn't have to marry you to get it."

Isabel had gone very still, almost forgetting to breathe. She couldn't worry about breathing when she had to understand what fitzAlan was saying. And what he was saying seemed to be in direct conflict to the hurtful reasons for their marriage he had given her on the drawbridge yesterday. Had she misunderstood him? But if that was so...

"What *did* you tell the Queen?" she asked in a suspenseful whisper, her eyes clinging to his.

He shrugged, watching her as closely. "Little enough. She's too busy making arrangements to leave for Bristol to worry about us. She and Prince William will be hostages in place of the King. When Stephen reaches Winchester safely, the Earl of Gloucester will be released and his son detained. When the Earl arrives in Bristol, Matilda and the prince will be allowed to go free and Gloucester's son likewise."

"It sounds complicated."

"Exchanges of such important prisoners usually are. Runaway ladies are soon overlooked by comparison."

Her eyes fell. He had dashed her down again. Just when she thought they were starting to talk more naturally. What was she supposed to think? If he truly believed there was more to her actions, if he had married her to protect her life or reputation, why couldn't he spare a few insignificant minutes to listen to her now? It would take him three days to reach Tracy with a small army and cumbersome siege machines slowing him down—what did one hour more or less matter?

"Well...well, then—" her only recourse seemed to be in stiff formality "—I wish you Godspeed, my lord, and...and success in your...that is..." Her lip quivered and she stopped dead, willing herself not to cry.

Guy appeared to hesitate for a second, those intense, light eyes burning into hers. His jaw clenched. Then he turned abruptly and strode to the door.

"My lord!"

He stopped, his hand on the latch. "What?"

The tone wasn't encouraging, but desperation spurred her on. If she did nothing else, she had to explain the one half-truth that, to her distraught mind, was the most damaging. "What I said to you...on the drawbridge...about stripping for...for a whole..."

FitzAlan released the latch and turned slowly to face her. Quite suddenly he looked extremely dangerous.

Isabel hurried on while she could still speak, almost slurring the words in her nervousness. "'Twas the truth... but 'tis not what you think. 'Twas not done willingly... We were all forced...all of us...men and women alike...old and young...exposed to mockery...but that was all. They didn't...didn't... I was still very small... They thought I was a child like Edmund...but the older girls..."

She stopped and tears came into her eyes. "I'm still a maid. Please believe that, at least," she finished brokenly, not caring now if he saw the naked pleading in her eyes.

"'Tis a lie that is easily disproven," he said coolly, but the ferocity was gone from his expression.

"I know."

Very slowly, fitzAlan came back to her, gazing down at her face for a long moment. His ice-blue eyes seemed to touch her every feature, one by one. Isabel held her breath as his hand lifted. Gently, so very gently, his fingers wrapped around the back of her neck, warm beneath her hair. Holding her still, he bent down and brushed his mouth against the cheek he had struck. For an infinitesimal second his lips parted slightly and lingered.

"We'll talk when I get back," he murmured against her skin. "God keep you, lady." Then he was gone.

Isabel stood alone in the solar. "Guy, I love you," she whispered after him. And in her heart she allowed hope to blossom into fragile life again. He had not said that he believed her, had only touched her for that fleeting moment, but she knew what she had felt. The powerful hand, holding her so carefully, had been shaking.

"Two days," sighed Isabel, sealing a small jar of dried herbs and laying it aside.

An answering sigh came from the fair-haired girl standing next to her. "I know. Already it feels more like the two weeks Guy promised. But remember, we swore not to count the days, Isabel. Why, I won't even mention Simon more than ten times today."

"Well, that's once," murmured Isabel sceptically, and grinned at her new sister-in-law. The light-hearted expression still felt strange to her, but she was getting used to it.

Joanna grinned back, her serene beauty sparkling into the quick, unexpected mischief that Isabel had seen in fitzAlan.

In the two days since the men had been gone the girls had become close friends, beginning from the moment

Joanna had knocked timidly on the solar door soon after Guy had left. Isabel had opened it, taken one look at Joanne's over-bright eyes and trembling mouth, and had promptly burst into tears herself.

The next several minutes had been spent, as Joanna put it, enjoying a good weep on each other's shoulders. They had finally calmed down, smiled sheepishly—albeit damply—at one another, and Joanna had demanded the whole story, from Isabel's meeting with Guy right down to their arrival at Ashby Chase.

Isabel had told her, unable to deny herself the relief of letting the truth out at last. To her considerable surprise Joanna had been entirely on her side.

"Don't tell me what that brother of mine is like," she had said fervently. "One look from those eyes when someone had displeased him and we'd all be walking around on eggshells. I don't wonder you couldn't bring yourself to tell him what was happening. But he's not always like that," she had assured Isabel hastily. "Guy can be very gentle. Amazingly so for such a big man. I remember the time I found a wounded falcon…"

And Joanna had launched into the tale, thereafter regaling her fascinated listener with other stories of fitz-Alan's past. Isabel had consumed the tales the way a starving person consumed food and drink, and had demanded more.

"'Tis only fair to my poor Simon," protested Joanna now, laughing. "I swear my tongue is worn out with stories of Guy's exploits. And now this latest one. Two weeks to march over a hundred miles, capture a castle and march back? He must be going to take your advice, Isabel. A normal siege can take forever. Look at this place. Impregnable."

"'Tis not Tracy," Isabel agreed. "My maid is still

wondering whether she ought to learn to swim. With the drawbridge raised 'tis the only way out of here.''

"Or in. Guy told me not to lower the bridge for anyone except the villagers until he gets back. Although, these days, no one with any sense leaves their drawbridge down.''

Isabel tried to stifle a pang at the thought that Guy had left instructions for their safety with his sister and not his wife. She was being too sensitive, she told herself. Joanna had been living at Ashby Chase for many months and the serfs knew her well. She could see one now, hurrying through the herb garden to the little hut where they worked.

It was the elderly reeve, Fulk. As he drew nearer Isabel tensed suddenly. He looked pale and alarmed, even frightened. She touched Joanna's arm in warning, feeling the other girl stiffen as she, too, glanced through the open door.

"Nothing can have happened to them this soon," Joanna whispered, crossing herself. "Fulk, what is it? 'Tis not…?''

"No, my lady…ladies,'' he corrected himself breathlessly, skidding to a stop just inside the door. "Your husband and my lord are safe, I presume. Not but what 'tis trouble enough that they must needs be gone, leaving us with this madman on the other side of the moat. But it might be nought. Perhaps he's got the wrong place.''

"Got the wrong place?'' Joanna looked at Isabel as if hoping for enlightenment. "Madman?''

"Aye, madman,'' asserted Fulk, nodding vigorously. "He accuses my lord of injuring one of his knights who was trying to recapture a runaway slave, and says he won't budge until he receives compensation. I said I would fetch an answer and he smiled as though he knew my lord is not here, and replied that my lady would do as well, in fact better.''

"He *must* be mad!" exclaimed Joanna. "Do you mean to say the fellow is going to besiege us because Guy hit one of his men who was about to…? That is to say… Good heavens! You don't think he means Ellen, do you, Isabel?" she amended hurriedly, remembering that no one at Ashby Chase knew of Isabel's sojourn in the alehouse.

"Jack is a free tenant," Isabel managed to reply, a shivery premonition of danger beginning to creep along her nerves. Something was very, very wrong here, and the feeling that, somehow, she knew the cause was overwhelmingly strong.

"Then he can sit there until Guy comes back," Joanna pronounced. "When he'll regret ever leaving his castle. You may tell him so, Fulk. And then ignore him."

"And so I would, my lady. Let him shout himself hoarse out there, I'd say, but there's more."

"What?" asked Isabel. The inner tremors grew stronger.

"His men have rounded up the children from Ashbrook—'tis one of my lord's villages a mile or so from here," he explained when Isabel made a small querying sound. "I don't know why, but I don't like it. Why all of them if he's searching for one slave?"

"That doesn't make sense," Joanna agreed. She turned puzzled eyes on Isabel again. "If his quarrel is a personal one he might try to starve us out before Guy comes home, but…does he mean to take village children hostage? Their ransom would hardly make it worth while."

"Did he give a name?" Isabel whispered, holding Joanna's sapphire gaze as though the guileless, open sincerity within would ward off the evil moving closer. But she knew. She knew before Fulk spoke. She knew the rebel baron who had been ravaging the countryside, the man whose name Ralf had been unable to recall. She knew and fought against knowing.

"Eudo de Raimes."

Joanna's startled face jolted Isabel into the realisation that it was she who had spoken, not the reeve.

"Fulk?"

"Lady Isabel is right, my lady. 'Tis the name he gave."

"Isabel? Do you know him, then?"

"I know him." A chill calm enveloped her, a sense of inescapable fate. "He is the man who murdered my father and sister when he attacked Tracy Castle, who made my other sister's life such a hell that she killed herself rather than endure it any longer, and who then would have forced me to wed him in her place."

"Mother of God," breathed Joanna. "What happened?"

"Our priest managed to get a message out to the King, who sent Miles, Sheriff of Gloucester, to rescue us. He took us to Gloucester since Edmund was too young to hold Tracy alone, and then the Empress landed in England, the Sheriff went over to her almost immediately, and we were prisoners once again."

"And Guy knows nothing of this? No, of course he doesn't. We'll have to send someone after him. Thank the saints a messenger will travel faster…" She paused when Isabel shook her head. "Don't worry, Isabel. I know we've only a small garrison left, but he can't get in and you're hardly a runaway slave, no matter what de Raimes intended in the past. Besides, he may not know about you; his purpose may be nothing more than he says."

"He knows. I don't know how he guessed 'twas me with Ellen the other day, but he swore vengeance three years ago when he was banished to his smaller estate and forced to hand Tracy to the Sheriff of Gloucester, and he doesn't forget.''

''Well, if he thinks we're just going to hand *you* over, he can think again,'' stated Joanna fiercely. ''And so I shall tell him.''

She marched out of the hut, eyes sparkling with unaccustomed wrath. Isabel and Fulk hurried after her.

But even Joanna's courage was shaken at the sight and sounds that confronted them when they mounted to the walkway at the top of the curtain wall.

Across the broad, still water of the moat stood at least a dozen mounted soldiers, more than enough to overcome the serfs, since most of them would have been at work in the fields. The sound of high-pitched wailing from the woods indicated that the village women were being held there, out of sight but close enough to hear what was going on. But the most blood-chilling sight of all was the man who sat his horse a little apart from the others. Before him, almost under his horse's hoofs, knelt four or five small children, bound together and obviously terrified.

''Holy Saint Peter save them,'' cried Joanna. ''They'll be trampled.''

Her clear voice carried easily to the waiting horseman.

''An interesting alternative to hanging, my lady,'' he called back. ''But my business is not with you. Ah, I thought so.'' He nodded once in satisfaction as Isabel stepped away from Joanna and stood apart. ''Lady Isabel de Tracy. I am rarely mistaken.''

''In this instance you are sadly at fault, my lord,'' retorted Joanna. ''This is my sister, Lady Isabel fitzAlan.''

''I can get a clear shot from here, my lady,'' murmured

a young soldier near them. "While he's stewing over that information."

"No!" protested Isabel quickly. She turned to Joanna. "De Raimes's men are…are…" She couldn't think of words bad enough to describe them. "He deliberately picks the most brutal, the most savage… The children would be killed immediately. The women, too."

Joanna nodded. "Do nothing," she instructed the man. He lowered his bow reluctantly. The other men stationed along the wall returned grim faces to the tableau below.

"'Tis me he wants," Isabel continued. "And he knows we're helpless."

As though he had heard the low-voiced conversation on the wall, de Raimes cupped his hands around his mouth and shouted again. "One name or another matters not. Your surrender for the life of these brats, Isabel. I'll even withdraw my men to assure your so-called sister that I don't want her brother's castle. She can lower the drawbridge for you, then raise it again without hindrance. You have until that cloud above you moves past the sun, then I string this peasants' spawn from the nearest tree. One by one."

"Dear God," whispered Joanna, glancing at the sky. They only had minutes. "How does he expect to get away with this? 'Tis against every code of honourable warfare. Doesn't he care for his soul, or his own life? If he kills those poor children, Guy will kill *him*."

"Guy is at least three days away," said Isabel with dreadful calm. She hadn't bothered to look up. There was no alternative to surrender, and she knew it. "Plenty of time for de Raimes to lock himself into his keep. He'll do it, Joanna. I know him. He won't stand back and negotiate a time to allow us to summon help. The man is evil. Vice is his pastime. He'll hang those innocents in front of us all unless I go to him.''

''You can't! There must be something we can do. Our archers are top marksmen. If—''

''What of the men we can't see, my lady?'' broke in Fulk grimly. ''Those in the woods. If we attack, they would have their instructions.''

An angry murmur of frustrated agreement sounded along the wall. Isabel knew that some of the men had wives in those woods.

''Oh, dear God, why didn't I call the villagers into the castle?'' Joanna wrung her hands in despair, beginning to weep.

Isabel flung her arms around her sister-in-law. ''You weren't to know this would happen,'' she cried. ''No one could have foreseen this.''

''Aye,'' nodded Fulk. ''We're in country loyal to the King and my lord didn't expect trouble. Least of all from a creature like that, lost to all decency and proper codes of conduct. Evil, indeed. Don't blame yourself, lady.''

''Fulk is right, Joanna.''

''But that doesn't help you,'' sniffed Joanna. She glanced skyward again, where a brighter haze was appearing at the edge of the cloud, and made a sound of mingled anger and helplessness, clutching Isabel tighter.

Isabel gently disengaged herself. ''Tell them to lower the drawbridge, Joanna.'' She turned to look out over the battlements again and raised her voice just as the sun broke through. ''We accept your terms. Tell your men to stand back. I will come out.''

And so this is how it ends, she thought minutes later as she walked with steady steps across the wooden planks. There would be no chance to tell fitzAlan the truth, no chance to discover how he felt about her, no chance at life and happiness. Joanna had vowed to send a message to Guy as soon as they were out of sight. She had agreed, had even reassured her sister-in-law that de Raimes was unlikely to kill her immediately. But in her heart Isabel had known it was too late. She would die by her own hand before the man she was approaching so unflinchingly had the chance to dishonour fitzAlan's name by using her for his amusement.

And if there was any justice remaining in this world, she would take de Raimes with her when she left it.

Chapter Twelve

The most frightening thing about Baron Eudo de Raimes, Isabel decided several hours later, was that he didn't *look* vicious, or even particularly dangerous. He wasn't a tall man, nor strongly built. Rather he was not much taller than herself and almost comically rotund. In fact, she thought, tonsure his greying hair and put him into a plain robe and he would have passed for a tubby, somewhat benign-looking monk.

Until you looked into his strangely colourless eyes. Then you saw evil—soulless, malevolent evil.

But Isabel would not permit herself to do that. Instead she glanced about the small chamber off the hall into which she had been ushered, thanking whatever saint had been responsible that de Raimes was apparently going to keep her to himself. It wouldn't last, of course. She knew his methods. Sooner or later his men would take their turn with her. If she was lucky, she would be dead before they had their chance.

The room was dim, lit only by rushlights high up on the walls, and furnished sparsely with a trestle, some chairs and a bed. She would not permit herself to look at that either.

"A cup of wine, my dear Isabel? Meat will be on the table shortly, but perhaps a refreshing draught beforehand. We'll drink a toast."

"To your early death," returned Isabel coldly. She might be light-headed with fear, but she would not give this vile creature the pleasure of seeing it.

De Raimes laughed, but the sound had a nasty ring to it. "Dear me, I can see a lesson in manners will be called for. Just a small one, not too painful. I enjoy spirit in a woman until I'm ready to crush it. Your sister Alice was sadly lacking in that respect. She became quite boring, indeed."

Rage erupted inside Isabel. She felt hot blood shoot straight to her head, making her temples throb. "She had spirit enough to fling herself from the tower to be free of you. That took more courage than you'll ever possess. And don't think I'll hesitate to do the same."

The falsely affable mask slipped for a second, then de Raimes was smiling again. She remembered that avid, anticipatory smile. It sickened her.

"A fitting end, perhaps, to go like her," he responded blandly. "After all, Alice did sacrifice her virtue for you and that grubby brat of a brother—Edward, was it?"

"Edmund," enunciated Isabel through gritted teeth.

"Aye, Edmund. Well, I will surely keep your desires in mind, Isabel. I might even throw you over the battlements myself when I've finished with you. Or mayhap 'twould be more pleasurable to watch it done by another. An interesting question. And there is a knight here who would be happy to accept the task. A small reward for having to live the rest of his days with a deformed jaw, thanks to your husband."

"The rest of his days will be counted on the fingers of one hand when Guy hears of this," Isabel spat. "As will yours." But her voice quivered on the last word as she remembered the cold, dispassionate violence of the man in the alehouse. She had not one, but two enemies to face, and didn't know which was more terrifying.

De Raimes' smile broadened. "Oh, I think not. You haven't looked around, Isabel. Did you not notice the gatehouse?"

She had. Isabel repressed another shudder. The entrance to de Raimes' castle was a death trap, no less. A long, narrow corridor of stone with a portcullis at each end, it was designed to render an invading force helpless once they had entered its confines, when both grilles would be dropped. The men within would then be fired upon through holes in the roof, picked off like pigeons in a cote, Isabel had thought when she had ridden through it earlier.

"Only a fool would risk that gatehouse," she said, turning a haughty shoulder on de Raimes. "And my husband is no fool." She took a few steps about the room, hoping the movement successfully concealed her dread.

Her captor chuckled. "Perhaps not, but he's a man of unusual strength and courage. Such men are inclined to be reckless."

Isabel stopped her pacing about the room and looked at de Raimes in surprise.

He laughed. "I've seen your husband before, my dear. So has Boisson, the man he struck the other day. At Lincoln, to be precise. Aye, I was there. Really, your surprise is most unflattering. I swung my sword a time or two before retiring from such a dismal cause."

"Ran away, you mean."

"Hmm. You appear to be as reckless as fitzAlan." De Raimes' voice lost some of its smooth mockery. "We'll see how far it takes you when you watch him try to clear the gatehouse the way he charged through a whole company of men that day, sword flashing right and left, trying to get to the King. He was fortunate to get away with his life, but sooner or later his luck will run out.''

Isabel smiled. ''A man of strength and courage, indeed,'' she said softly. ''Thank you. I will treasure the memory you've just given me.''

De Raimes' eyes narrowed as her meaning sank in. ''Why, you little bitch!'' he said softly. ''You—''

The door opened. A serf hesitated apprehensively in the entrance. ''Your supper, my lord.''

''Well,'' barked de Raimes, turning on the man, ''come in, fool! Do we have to starve while you hover there?'' He glared back at Isabel. ''Very clever, my lady, but overhasty. You give yourself away.''

''How so?'' Isabel heard herself ask the question but her attention was suddenly drawn to the servant setting food and trenchers on the table. A loaf of bread was plunked down not far from her. And a knife. Its blade gleamed dully in the shadows.

''You love him.'' De Raimes nodded as her head jerked back to him. ''And you can't have been married long. The last I heard you were still in Gloucester with the Empress Matilda, so, whether fitzAlan loves you also or has yet to lose interest in your pretty face and form, he will come for you. I shall enjoy watching you observe his futile efforts to save you.''

''You're mad,'' she whispered in horror. ''Revenge I can understand. You swore to destroy my father and take his castle when he refused your offer for Alice—'twas evil, but no worse than many another who coveted another man's property. But why the rest of us? Why fitzAlan?''

De Raimes shrugged carelessly and picked up the lid of a warming dish, inspecting the food beneath it. He waved the servant away. "Get you gone. And don't come back until I call for you.

"Why the rest of you?" he repeated as the man departed. "I swore to destroy the house of de Tracy, Isabel, not merely your father. Revenge is never sweet unless 'tis thorough. Hugh de Tracy refused me his daughter as if I had less worth than the slave who cleans out the garderobe tunnel. As for fitzAlan...did you think killing three of my men would go unnoticed? He was recognised."

"So they were your soldiers at the ford," Isabel realised.

"Of course. And the description of fitzAlan's lady I found most interesting." He replaced the lid of the dish and came to stand beside her, staring at her with malicious eyes. "Did you think I had forgotten how you smuggled that message out of Tracy, forcing me to lose almost everything? I've been waiting a long time, watching the roads, asking about new arrivals in the large towns. There was a slight chance the girl at the ford was you, and Boisson had orders to keep his eyes open while he was collecting rents. The fool was careless, of course, but then he didn't expect to find Lady Isabel de Tracy in a flea-ridden alehouse. However, when he recovered his senses your name was all I needed. After that a visit to Jack proved most enlightening."

"What did you do to him?" she whispered. She couldn't meet that cold, unblinking stare.

"Not a lot, unfortunately. His bluster turned to co-operation quite soon. 'Tis how I learned that you'd been at the castle. Some discreet enquiries there yielded the information that fitzAlan was about to take Tracy, leaving his new wife at home. Amazing how far a little coin will go. The only thing I couldn't discover was how he managed to get you out of Gloucester and marry you after all.

The man must be extraordinarily persistent. I thought I had put him off rather neatly four years ago. The tale will make very interesting hearing."

"I don't know what you're talking about, but even if I did I wouldn't tell you anything."

"Ah, I can see you will prove much more rewarding than your sister. But remember, Isabel, if you dislike your present position, that once I offered you honourable marriage. A brief moment of madness, I admit. I must have been drunk."

"Honourable marriage? To you?" She looked at him at last, with such obvious disgust that de Raimes' face darkened. "The very state of holy wedlock would have been defiled."

"Keep going, madam," he grated through set lips. "You will only make things more painful for yourself later, and more pleasurable for me." Suddenly his hand moved, fastening around one slender wrist so tightly that Isabel's bones cracked. Her eyelids flickered, but she made no other sign. He laughed softly. "Aye, very pleasurable, but first we'll eat, while I describe some of the activities you can look forward to. You shall learn the delights of anticipation, my dear."

With surprising strength he jerked Isabel forward, releasing her just as abruptly. She hit the edge of the table with bruising force, her upper body sprawling over its surface. Her splayed arms sent the dishes clattering.

De Raimes made an annoyed sound with his tongue. "How very clumsy of you, Isabel. I think you should serve my meal first as penance. On your knees. That may begin to teach you your proper place."

Isabel hadn't moved. A fierce, terrified elation raced through her veins as her eyes fell on the knife only an inch away from her hand. Her fingers closed over the handle, the half-raised posture of her body shielding the movement from de Raimes. It had to be now. This might be the only chance she would have. She would stab de Raimes and then turn the blade on herself. A quick end, rather than torture and rape at the hands of those barbarians in the hall.

It was true, she thought distantly as her muscles tensed. One's whole life did flash before one's eyes at the moment of death. Oh, Guy...*Guy*...

"This is all you'll get from me," she cried, coming up and around with a swiftness born of wild desperation.

He was closer than she had expected. Her hand was still at table height. There was no time to raise it and draw back for a stabbing blow. With the swing of her arm, the knife flashed through the air, light dancing off its footlong blade. It caught de Raimes low in the body, slicing across and downwards.

Apart from the soldier at the riverbank, which had been accidental, Isabel had never attacked anyone in her life. Her reaction paralysed her. She hadn't expected her stomach to churn, her throat to close up, at the sound of ripping fabric and flesh. Sickened, she staggered back, her trembling hand almost dropping the weapon. For a moment she couldn't believe she had actually struck, then she stared in horrified fascination at the dark red stain spreading diagonally across de Raimes' belly and down to his thigh.

He looked down also, appearing as horrified as she. His hand clutched at his groin. "You've cut me," he said, as if not quite believing it. Blood welled between his fingers. "You vicious little bitch," he roared suddenly. "You've damned near castrated me. Guards! *Guards,* damn it!"

The door burst open. Men rushed into the room. Belatedly Isabel remembered what else she was supposed to do. She tried to lift her hand, but the knife now seemed as heavy as a sword. For some reason she could only move with nightmarish sluggishness, while everyone around her tore past with dizzying speed.

Someone knocked the knife from her hand. Another man flung his arm around her throat and held her, pulling her slightly off balance so she couldn't struggle. His free hand wrenched her arm around, cruelly forcing it up against her back. The rest crowded around de Raimes, who had staggered to a chair. Isabel watched it all in a daze, barely conscious of the pain of the soldier's grip.

"'Tis not deep," said a nervous voice. A man in the long robe of a clerk or scribe bent over the injured baron. "A glancing blow, but will take time to heal. 'Tis a sensitive spot, my lord."

"I know that, damn you," snarled de Raimes, his face pale and sweating. "Just bind it somehow so I can get on my feet and deal with that slut."

"Leave her to us, my lord," growled a voice in Isabel's ear. "We'll take a slice out of her own sweet flesh." He jerked her arm higher.

A gargled sound came from the doorway and every eye turned that way. The man who stood there was dark with coal-black eyes. One side of his jaw was swollen and bruised, his mouth almost invisible. The swelling made it impossible to discern his expression, but it was easy to see that the lower half of his face would always be grotesquely twisted.

Isabel felt her blood freeze. She almost passed out with terror. There would be no mercy for her now. When de Raimes had exacted his revenge he would hand her over to his knight, who would complete her destruction. She didn't need to listen to the words when she could read her future in their eyes.

''No. You'll have your turn, but Boisson and I have a score to settle with the bitch first.'' De Raimes' breath hissed out and he cuffed the man working over him. ''Clumsy fool! Watch what you're doing.''

''Your pardon, my lord, 'tis awkwardly—''

''Get on with it!''

'''Tis done, my lord.'' The man shuffled back a few paces, bent almost double. ''But I must beg of you, my lord, not to move impulsively. You should be laid on your bed for several days at least.''

''Several days? Aye, 'twill serve.'' Deadly eyes went to Isabel's ashen face. ''You'll learn the pleasures of anticipation, my lady, where you can do no damage. We'll see how much fight is left in you after some time in the dungeon. Mayhap you'll prefer the company down there.'' He gestured to the man behind Isabel. ''Let her go.''

She staggered and almost fell when the man obeyed. Her left arm hung uselessly at her side, agony tearing through it from shoulder to wrist as the circulation returned. Someone grabbed her elbow, thrusting her out of the room, and she cried out with the pain, then clamped her teeth into her lip. She tried to think, but waves of agony kept washing over her, dulling her mind. Dimly she was aware that de Raimes was being carried by two men, that she was being prodded and pushed down a flight of stairs.

It could have been hours or minutes later that Isabel found herself staring into a dark pit. More stairs led downwards. Hadn't she seen something like this once before? she thought vaguely. She had been with fitzAlan and—

''Your quarters, my lady,'' purred an evil voice at her side. ''You'll find they are an improvement on the last place I provided for you. This time you will have light, the better to see your company.''

A soldier went ahead of her, holding a rushlight. It flickered over stone walls, glinting on darker, shinier patches here and there. At the foot of the stairs he shoved the torch into a wall sconce, pushed Isabel further into the gloom, and retraced his steps. The air was bitterly cold and still, with the peculiar lifelessness that pervaded closed-off places. It smelled of rotten straw, damp and an overpowering stench that caught in her throat, almost choking her.

''When I've recovered you'll be released, Isabel,'' de Raimes called down to her. ''Think about what will happen to you when that times comes. Remember how your sister Constance died.''

Just before the trapdoor slammed shut, cutting off de Raimes' harsh laughter and the additional light from above, Isabel saw an indistinct lump in one corner.

The lump didn't move. How long she stood there, just as immobile, staring at the bundle of rags, Isabel never knew. As her eyes adjusted to the darkness she saw that the dungeon was a fairly large open area, the light from the sconce barely reaching the furthest walls. A row of darker rectangles indicated smaller cells along one side. Water dripped somewhere. In several places it ran down the walls. Panic licked at the corners of her mind. Blackness, the dank chill, the faint rustle of tiny creatures in the darkest corners—it was terrifyingly familiar, threatening her very sanity.

''This isn't the same as before,'' she whispered to herself, still frozen to the floor. ''You have light. If anything moves you can see it coming.'' Her gaze shifted to her fellow prisoner. ''And 'tis not Edmund, but 'tis human company.''

She took a tentative step forward and then another. The stench grew worse, making her gag, but it was not until Isabel was standing over the motionless form that she realised why. She was alone in this dreadful place after all. Death had long since claimed her companion.

Thunder woke her out of a fitful sleep. Isabel started up, bewildered, as the low rumble faded away. Had she been dreaming? Thunder could not penetrate the layers of stone above and around her.

Rubbing a weary hand over her face, she tried to estimate how long she had slept. Beyond the small cell the light from the sconce was barely discernible. Soon she would have to use the last of the rushes. That meant three nights, she thought. Three nights she had been imprisoned here—the last one without food or water, since the guard had not come at his usual time.

At first she had been surprised when a flask and a chunk of bread had been tossed down to her that first night, until she had remembered that de Raimes did not want her dead just yet. For a while she had considered starving herself, but one thought made her force down the bread and drink the water. She had been given a chance of survival. Every day she spent in the dungeon meant that fitzAlan came closer.

The knowledge had steadied her. With a strength Isabel had not known she possessed she had beaten back panic and calmly taken down the rushlight, dividing the rushes into smaller bundles to conserve the light. She could do nothing about the cold or the slick damp that covered the walls, but she had gathered as much straw as she could and had made a bed in the driest of the cells. By sheer force of will she ignored the sounds of pattering and gnawing near the body in the corner. And she looked for a way out, though she knew there was none. It passed the time.

Today, however, de Raimes had obviously stopped the food and drink. Fear coiled inside her. Perhaps he was planning to weaken her before she was released from the dungeon. He must be very sure that his fortress was safe from fitzAlan.

"But it isn't," Isabel whispered, getting stiffly to her feet. "He'll find a way in. You have to believe that. You *have* to."

Her voice echoed eerily in the cold air and she shivered, chafing some feeling into her frozen hands. She had to be strong. Joanna's messenger would have reached Tracy by now. She could survive another day or two—even in the darkness. She would not think of her dry mouth or her empty stomach, or the clammy chill of the dungeon that had seeped into every bone in her body. She would not think of the pitiful remains in the corner. She would keep busy. While she still had light she would continue to search for a way out; she would—

A distant explosion of sound scattered her thoughts like leaves in the wind. It was followed by another, much nearer, and then a third, the echoes becoming one continuous thundering roar that seemed to go on forever. Isabel stood as though chained to the floor, her heart galloping out of control like a runaway steed as she tried to make sense of the unholy din.

It was too soon to be fitzAlan, she told herself, reason overwhelming her first impulsive hope. And no storm made that much noise. Unless de Raimes' castle was falling down by itself, he was under attack from someone, and if no one came for her she could be buried alive, forgotten, trapped in the darkness until death overcame her.

Shaking with terror, Isabel put a hand to the wall in an attempt to hold on to something solid, only to have it scoot across the slimy surface, almost throwing her to the ground. Her frightened cry was smothered by yet another explosion that shook the stones next to her and sent a dozen small creatures streaming out of the dark corners and across the floor, their high-pitched squeaks audible even above the shattering reverberations assaulting her ears. Beyond the doorway the dim light flared suddenly, illuminating the fleeing rats with an unearthly orange glow. Tiny red eyes gleamed at her for a moment before disappearing.

She cried out again and thought another voice answered. Holy saints, was she losing her mind? Isabel froze, straining to hear.

"Isabel!" This time the yell reached her over the crash of falling masonry.

"Guy!" she screamed, starting forward. She trod on something soft and screamed again.

"*Isabel!*"

He sounded closer. Isabel stumbled out of the dark cell into a scene that made the priests' descriptions of hell seem tame.

Where part of the roof and the top of one wall had been there was a jagged, gaping hole. Dust still swirled above the pile of stone and rubble on the floor below it, creating a hazy curtain behind which red and orange flames danced and writhed like living things. The staircase had all but been buried under the collapsing wall.

"Guy," she called out again, looking wildly about her. Then she saw fitzAlan, halfway down the steps, almost unrecognisable with sweat-darkened hair, his face streaked with dirt and dust. Isabel started to run towards him just as another block of stone came away from the wall, hurtling downwards. It tore the sconce from its bracket before crashing to the floor, sending debris flying in all directions.

Isabel fell back, flinging her hands up to protect her head. She felt a sharp blow to her arm and gasped, retreating further. Through the cloud of dust she saw fitzAlan sheath his sword and crouch at the edge of the stairway. Putting his hand to a crumbling step, he vaulted down to the ground and landed running.

His hand reached for her as the whole building seemed to shudder under another assault. "Come on," he shouted, urging Isabel towards the stairs. "This place is about to fall apart."

She followed blindly, stumbling over the shifting piles of stone blocking the stairway. Her foot caught and she wrenched it free of its shoe, clinging to fitzAlan's hand all the while as he half led, half pulled her upwards. Through eyes watering from smoke and dust Isabel saw daylight and the castle entrance and knew they had reached the guard-room. They were halfway across it when an enraged, strangled shout came from behind them.

"*FitzAlan!*"

She knew that distorted voice. Boisson had been waiting for them.

Guy whirled. Isabel saw his face go taut an instant before he whipped an arm around her and dived for the floor, taking her down with him. As soon as they hit the ground he rolled, shoving Isabel beneath him.

"Stay down," he rasped.

The clang of a sword blade ringing on the stones where she had just been standing made the order unnecessary. Isabel flattened herself, only risking a glance over her shoulder when she felt Guy's weight lift off her.

He came up off the floor in one swift, powerful lunge,

slamming the full force of his body into Boisson and driving him back towards the dungeon before the man could gather himself for another swing. The heavy two-handed sword fell with them, sliding along the floor as the two men wrestled each other in a deadly silence broken only by the sound of fists meeting flesh and their hoarse breathing.

Isabel watched in horror. She had seen Guy fight before at the river crossing, but then he had been quick and efficient. In this encounter there was no time for swordplay or skill. It was bloody, primitive, brutal. Both men were fighting for their lives. She saw Guy jerk back to avoid a slashing blow to the throat, then they closed again, rolling right to the edge of the treacherous stairway.

Isabel cried out. She couldn't see who was on top. The smoke was too thick. She was too far away. Sobbing, gasping for breath, she began to crawl across the floor. She had not moved more than a few inches when one of the men broke free, his fist smashing downwards. His opponent's head snapped back over the edge of the drop and was still. And at last Isabel saw who it was.

She collapsed on the floor again, not moving as fitzAlan got to his feet. Her eyes studied Boisson. He didn't look dangerous at all now, she thought, lying there like a mummer's puppet flung down with its limbs every which way and the head at an odd angle. Her gaze lifted to fitzAlan's face. Now *he* looked savage, his eyes still glittering with deadly ferocity. There was a raw graze across one cheekbone. Blood ran from a cut on his jaw.

He hunkered down beside her just as a flaming beam from the ceiling crashed to the ground only inches away. Isabel didn't even flinch.

"He recognised you," she whispered. "At the alehouse."

"Did he?" FitzAlan slid one arm around her shoulders and the other beneath her knees. Very carefully he lifted her into his arms. "We have to get out of here, darling. 'Tis quicker if I carry you. Trust me."

She wondered why he was speaking to her in such a quiet, gentling tone, then realised how stiffly she was holding herself. Her hands were splayed across his broad shoulders as if she would push him away, and for some reason she couldn't seem to relax them.

"I'm sorry," she managed. Even her teeth were clenched tight; she could barely speak. "I don't know what's wrong with me."

He held her closer. "It doesn't matter."

Then suddenly there was cool air on her face and light that hurt her eyes. And a familiar voice speaking to fitzAlan.

"Guy! Thank the lord you found her."

Isabel looked around. As abruptly as it had become paralysed, her tongue was loosened. "Hello, Simon. You've got a black eye."

De Villiers' hazel eyes shot from her face to fitzAlan at the bright greeting. One brow went up.

"Shock," said Guy tersely. He handed her over to Simon. "Get her away from all this smoke. I'll be with you in a minute."

"Place is about to collapse," agreed Simon. "Come on, little sister."

"That wasn't very nice of him," protested Isabel as Simon strode off with her. She cringed at the too cheerful sound of her voice. What was wrong with her? First her unnatural stiffness with fitzAlan, and now this. She couldn't seem to stop talking. "He's always leaving me with you. Not that I don't like you, Simon, but you would think if the man goes to all this trouble to rescue me he could at least stay around afterwards.''

"He'll be back. Guy swore to bury de Raimes under his own keep and he's going to see it done."

"Very thorough," she approved with an abrupt about-face. "I want to watch. I'm the last of my family and I have to watch. He killed my father, you know. And my sisters. And who's to say that Edmund wouldn't be alive today if…?'' The dreadful spate of words at last dried up. It was followed by a strange feeling of detachment, as if she'd suddenly gone somewhere else.

De Villiers' shrewd eyes scanned her face. "Then we'll watch," he said. A few yards further on he stopped at the edge of a grove of trees. Several horses were tethered there. "It shouldn't be long now," Simon continued, setting her down on the grass. "We've been bombarding the place since dawn."

Isabel looked back up the slight incline to the castle. Sounds of fighting could still be heard from the far side of the bailey, but it was easily apparent that de Raimes' men were outnumbered and outclassed. And the castle itself no longer provided any defence at all. Flames shot through a window high up in the keep. Half the gatehouse was missing.

The cause of the wreckage was not hard to find. A hundred yards away two great mangonels had been set up. Even as she watched, the arm of one was released, propelling a huge boulder through the air with terrific force. It soared over the wall and hurtled into the side of the keep, enlarging the hole already there. A second rock followed immediately and a wide, jagged crack appeared in the wall.

"Great shot!" exclaimed Simon. "Right into his foundations."

"There's so much damage," murmured Isabel, sinking to the ground.

"'Twas built on marshy land, fortunately for us," Simon told her. "Not like Ashby Chase, which is built on rock, with the lake and moat put in later. A few years of storms with plenty of rain would probably have undermined this place anyway. Once the foundations go, the rest follows."

"That's why the dungeon was so damp." The words were a soft murmur, almost to herself, but Simon heard them.

"De Raimes kept you in a dungeon?"

Isabel nodded.

"God's teeth! A good thing Guy didn't know that before he st... I mean, before he killed the bastard."

Isabel looked at him. "How?" she asked serenely.

De Villiers hesitated.

"Do you think I'll grieve over the manner of that monster's death, Simon? How did Guy kill him?"

"No, you're too damned calm," he muttered. "Well, I'll tell you, but remember that we didn't know what we were going to find when we finally broke in. Hell, getting here was bad enough. We practically grew wings and flew. One look at the gatehouse told us that way would be suicide, so we launched a full-scale attack to distract them from you and get Guy over the wall. It worked, but I thought he was going to lose his mind when we found de Raimes locked in his solar and you were nowhere to be seen. The coward choked out that you were still alive and hadn't been harmed, but it didn't save his neck. Guy strangled him."

Isabel's gaze went back to the crumbling keep. "And now he's going to bury him." She wasn't shocked at fitzAlan's actions.

"Aye." Simon actually shuddered. "He didn't even give de Raimes time to grab a weapon. 'Twas vengeance, pure and simple. I've never seen Guy like that. In battle he's unstoppable, but I've never seen him kill a man in cold blood before."

"Not vengeance. Justice."

Simon nodded, looking uncommonly solemn. Then he stiffened. "Look! There it goes."

There was a shattering roar. Before Isabel's awed eyes one entire side of the keep plummeted to the earth, leaving the interior exposed. Burning timbers crashed to the ground, to be extinguished in the billowing cloud of dust.

"Guy," she cried, starting up.

"Don't worry. He'll be here."

Isabel sank back to the grass, beginning to shake. The crash had jolted her out of her odd tranquillity. Somewhere deep inside her a tightly coiled tension was unravelling with frightening speed. She was starting to feel her bruises. One of her feet throbbed rather painfully. She seemed to have lost a shoe, and her dress was not only dirty but torn in several places.

She wasn't the only one. There was a girl sitting next to her who was barely recognisable as female. Her dark hair was a wild, half-damp tangle, her face and hands begrimed with a black substance that had the most awful smell. It reminded Isabel of the dungeon.

It was a full minute before she realised that she was looking at a reflection of herself in the polished metal shield that Simon had propped against a tree to protect her from any stray arrows.

"Oh, Mother of God, look at me!"

The sharp, high-pitched cry brought Simon's head around. "What's wrong?"

"*What's wrong*?" Isabel's voice soared. She stumbled

to her feet, wiping her hands uselessly on her tattered dress before holding them out. Her nails were torn and rimmed with black, as filthy as the rest of her. "Look at me!"

For the first time de Villiers seemed to notice the state she was in. He grinned. "Don't worry about it. Look at any one of us. We're not dressed for a Court feast-day. What's Joanna going to say about my eye?"

"Oh, Simon." Isabel smiled back waveringly through suddenly brimming eyes. "You know Joanna will be overjoyed to see you in any condition." She burst into tears.

"For God's sake, Simon! I thought you were looking after her. What the hell…?"

At the sound of his brother-in-law's furious voice Simon looked vastly relieved. "She was all right until a minute ago," he protested. "Cool as a nun's kiss. Then all of a sudden—"

"Never mind. I shouldn't have left her, but I thought she didn't want…" FitzAlan broke off, reaching out to grasp Isabel by the shoulders.

She shrank away from him, covering her face. "*No!* Don't touch me!"

"Oh, God. Isabel…" Ignoring her frantic protests, Guy took her wrists and pulled her hands away from her face. "Sweetheart, don't be afraid of me, *please*. No one is ever going to hurt you again, I swear it."

With one glance from the weeping girl to fitzAlan, Simon turned and strode back up the hill towards the castle. Neither of them saw him go.

"I'm not," Isabel sobbed, trying to pull away from fitzAlan. "'Tis de Raimes…what he did…"

Guy's face went white. He looked as if she'd hit him.

"Christ Jesu! Did he rape you? Did any of them?" His fingers tightened on her wrists. "Isabel, tell me!"

"No!" she cried, momentarily ceasing her struggles. "Do you think I wouldn't have died before they could dishonour you so?"

"Never mind my bloody honour!" he exploded, pulling her closer. "I'm concerned about you! What did that bastard do to you?"

"He threw me in a dungeon." Isabel started to cry again, shuddering sobs racking her body. "There was a corpse in there and rats, and the rushes were almost used up. It was going to get dark and I'm so filthy and cold and—"

"Dear God. Come here, darling. Stop fighting me. Hush now. Hush, sweetheart." Taking no notice of her feeble attempts to bat his hands away, Guy pulled Isabel into his arms, holding her tight, murmuring to her, soothing her.

After a long time the tears stopped. Isabel remained very still for a minute, thinking about how much worse she must look with red-rimmed eyes and tears mingling with the dirt on her face. "You can let me go now," she sniffed into his mail-clad chest. "I've probably got fleas all over me, or worse, and I'm not crying any more."

"No, but you're... Stop shaking, damn it! It's tearing me apart."

"'Tis...'tis the cold," she stammered. Had her mind gone, or had she really heard that tormented note in his voice?

"I know. I know, sweetheart." He folded her closer, his voice a deep, gentle murmur again.

She must be imagining things, Isabel decided. His kindness must have gone to her head, but she would not read too much into it. Now that the nightmare of her captivity had receded somewhat in the safety of his arms, she suddenly remembered, with painful clarity, the way they had parted, the truth still unspoken between them. He still thought her a traitor. He still thought her his enemy.

"I really am all right now," Isabel insisted quietly, keeping her face lowered. She tried a tentative push against his chest. A mountain wouldn't have felt more solid and immovable. "I'm sorry I made such a spectacle of myself."

FitzAlan simply shifted his hold and lifted her off her feet. The beginnings of a smile lurked deep in his eyes, setting Isabel's heart racing when she ventured a glance up at him.

"Little idiot," he said very softly. "I'm never going to let you go again."

Chapter Thirteen

Isabel had clung to those words all the way home, wrapped snugly in fitzAlan's cloak, held fast in his arms. Every time she had protested that she could ride alone and was not fit to be near anyone until she'd had several baths he had laid his hand over her mouth and told her to hush.

Isabel had eventually hushed. It was so sweet to be held thus, to feel so cherished and protected. For a few precious hours she had savoured the sensation, and had determinedly closed her mind to the thought that only the most hard-hearted man would not have offered comfort in her present condition.

Torches were already flaring on the castle walls when the first wagons carrying the dismantled mangonels rumbled across the drawbridge. Men surrounded them, asking questions, full of their own tale to be told. And Joanna had sped down the outer stairway, crying and joyous at once. She had embraced Simon, patting his face and exclaiming over his bruised eye, and had then flown to Isabel, taking her in her arms and weeping over her enough, so her husband had said, to raise the level of the lake.

Joanna would have drawn Isabel indoors then, but

fitzAlan would not permit her to walk. Her carried her up to the solar and delivered her over to the care of his sister and Ellen, leaving her with a look in his blue eyes that clearly said *later*.

And now later had come. Isabel was sitting on a stool by the fire, dressed in a filmy shift borrowed from Joanna, a mantle over her shoulders for extra warmth, when the door opened and he was there, tall and strong, the sconce lights gleaming on his fair hair. He had obviously cleaned up also, and shaved. The heavy chainmail was gone; he wore a long dark blue tunic, embroidered with silver thread and loosely belted at the waist. Soft knee-high boots, fashioned of calf-hide for light indoor use, were laced about his leggings. His white linen undershirt was open at the throat, drawing Isabel's gaze upward.

Vivid blue eyes glittered in his tanned face. Shadows cast by the open door slanted across the strong lines of nose and jaw, softening the hard line of his mouth. The graze along his cheekbone somehow managed to emphasise the tough, assured air he wore so easily.

Realising how she was staring at him, Isabel quickly looked back at the fire, leaning sideways a little so that her still-damp hair fell forward, partially shielding her face. She saw Joanna glance up when fitzAlan remained standing in the doorway.

"Guy? Is something wrong?"

There was a long pause, then he came into the room. "No, nothing's wrong."

There was an oddly arrested note in his voice. Isabel wondered what he was thinking, then Guy spoke again and the question was driven out of her mind.

"I'll care for her now. Go put a poultice or something on Simon's eye before he uses up all the raw meat in the kitchen."

Joanna laughed, apparently sensing nothing amiss, and kissed Isabel's cheek. "She's been through a terrible ordeal," she told her brother severely, drawing Ellen out of the solar with her.

Guy shut the door after them. "Does she think I need reminding?" he muttered.

Isabel didn't answer. She heard the key turn in the lock and a fear that was just short of primitive assailed her. She was suddenly far too aware that they were alone and wouldn't be disturbed until morning, too aware that the man whose overpowering masculine strength filled the room was her husband and had certain rights, too aware that the last frail layer of her protective façade had been shattered forever when she had wept in his arms and let him comfort her.

The utter vulnerability in loving a man who seemed to retain his formidable control no matter what the situation, while she fell apart, was terrifying. She felt exposed, raw. As if she stood naked before him, her very soul bared. Nowhere to hide. Defenceless.

"Isabel."

The softly murmured name was like a hand stroking over her flesh. She started to tremble deep inside, a nervous quivering that was beyond her control. The tremors increased when fitzAlan crossed the room and hunkered down beside her stool.

He reached out a hand and brushed her hair back over her shoulder. "You're hiding from me," he accused gently, watching the cool silky strands cling to his long fingers. "I asked you not to."

"That…" Her voice sounded rusty, as if she hadn't used it for a long time. "That was before…"

The caressing hand stilled and withdrew, but not very far. His forearm rested across one thigh, his fingers only inches from her own. "Before I frightened you into running away from me."

Isabel shook her head. She stared at their hands, hers slender, small-boned and delicate, his so tanned and strong. She remembered how he had killed de Raimes. He could break her.

"Why deny it? 'Tis the truth." He was looking down, too, Isabel saw, risking a fleeting glance through her lashes. Without warning, his hand lifted to cover both of hers. "You're afraid now. I can feel you trembling."

Trembling and weak, she thought. Weak with a love that I can't speak of until you know the truth. Trembling with the fear that you might not believe in the truth or my love.

When she didn't respond, Guy removed his hand and reached into his tunic. "I have something for you," he said casually, producing a small wooden box. It was fashioned of sandalwood, beautifully carved, and no larger than was needed to hold a psalter. In fact, as Isabel knew well, that was exactly why the box had been made.

Guy placed it on her lap and stood up. "I believe you gave that to the priest at Tracy for safekeeping when you were sent to Gloucester. He said you treasured it beyond any other possession."

Her fingers touched the carved lid, trembled, and withdrew. Then all at once understanding dawned. Her eyes flew upward, looking at him for the first time. "The priest... You know... I didn't think you'd had time to take Tracy...you came back so soon—"

"I should never have left you," he burst out, startling her. "God, Isabel, if anything had happened to you, if he had..." Biting off the rest, fitzAlan reached down and pulled Isabel up and into his arms. "Forgive me," he groaned hoarsely. "Forgive me, my darling. I can't stand here and not hold you. Let me do that, at least. I swear I won't hurt you, I won't do anything to frighten you; I just need to hold you, to know you're alive and safe. *Isabel...*'' His arms tightened convulsively and he buried his face in her hair. A violent shudder racked his powerful body.

The box and her mantle fell unheeded to the floor. Shock held Isabel utterly still. FitzAlan was holding her as if he would make her part of himself, as if he could not bear to be separate from her. This man who had strangled another with his bare hands to avenge her, who had faced danger and death without flinching, was trembling with the need to have her as close to him as possible.

Hope broke over her in tumultuous waves. Unaware that she was holding her breath, Isabel slowly slid her arms around his waist. Very gradually she leaned into his strength, letting him take her weight. He was so warm. Sensation after sensation assailed her. The heat of his body, the strength of his arms, the fierce rhythm of his heart against her cheek. Swept by an overwhelming longing to touch him, she let her hands relax, absorbing the feel of the hard muscles of his back against her palms.

Guy tensed the instant she moved, as though bracing himself for resistance. Then, as he felt her soften against him, his hold changed. It was no less intense, but suddenly Isabel felt a gentling in him, as if he held a tiny helpless creature in his hands and was afraid of bruising it.

''Isabel?''

She felt the whispered question rather than heard it.

''I'm not afraid.'' How could she fear this man who cradled her so tenderly, whose much greater strength would only be used to protect her? Who, in one swift, unexpected movement, had let her see that he was as vulnerable as she? "Can't you feel?" she murmured. "I'm not shaking any more."

Guy's mouth moved against her. "I hope not," he breathed. "God, Isabel, I hope not." He was silent for a moment, then said, very low, "Can you forgive me? I hope for that, too, because I don't think I'll ever forgive myself."

"Because of de Raimes? You weren't to know."

She tried to raise her head, wanting to see in his eyes what she was feeling in his embrace, but Guy cupped her cheek, holding her still against his chest. "For de Raimes, for believing that bitch at Gloucester even for a minute, for losing my damnable temper and not giving you a chance to tell me the truth."

Isabel's heart jolted. The truth. No wonder he was so conscience-stricken and gentle. He knew what had happened years ago.

Guy gave her a little shake, rocking her against him. "I know what you're thinking," he murmured. "There's no need to tense up on me. Your priest only knew about the past. I knew you were innocent of any willing betrayal before I left here."

"I don't… You believed in my innocence before you left?" she repeated incredulously, not sure she had got it right.

"Absolutely."

"But…but…I hadn't told you anything."

"You didn't have to. Once I knew you were still… untouched…only one explanation made sense: that the Countess had some hold over you."

"Aye," she confirmed dazedly, unaware of clinging closer. "'Twas Edmund. I didn't know he had been killed. Matilda never told me. 'Twas why I fainted that day. I don't even know how he escaped from Tracy." She couldn't get the words out fast enough, terrified that Guy couldn't possibly believe her, no matter what he said. It sounded so unlikely.

His mouth brushed across her hair. "Edmund knew that some of the garrison had been called to Lincoln to fight for Matilda. 'Twould have been easy enough for a determined boy to climb the wall and follow them. He wasn't confined indoors. He told your priest he was old enough to fight to regain de Tracy honour."

Tears sprang into Isabel's eyes. "Old enough to fight?" she choked. "He was barely fifteen."

"Old enough," Guy said gently. "But I wish I had known, at Lincoln."

"Could you have kept him safe?"

"Maybe." He shrugged slightly. "That's what you were trying to do, wasn't it?"

"Aye." Her lip quivered again, but she pressed her cheek to fitzAlan's tunic and held on to her control. "*I* was going to sacrifice our honour. After de Raimes sacked Tracy he kept us in a dungeon for three months until Alice was forced to become his mistress, and had it not been for Edmund I would have lost my mind."

"'Tis all right, sweetheart, you don't have to—"

"But I couldn't do it," she continued, as if he had not spoken. "I met Rainald to gain some time, not because of Edmund. I couldn't—"

"Betray the Queen," he finished for her.

But Isabel shook her head against him. "No," she whispered vehemently. "I told myself that, but the truth was I couldn't betray *you*." She felt his mouth lower to her cheek and hurried on. "I wanted to tell you the morning you left, but you were in such a hurry to be gone and—"

"I had to leave!" Releasing her abruptly, fitzAlan

pulled Isabel's arms away from him and held them, gazing down at her face as if the sight of her tormented him beyond bearing and yet he still could not bring himself to look away. A ragged laugh escaped him at the startled look in her eyes. "You don't know why, do you, little innocent? God damn it, we were married! I couldn't stay here and not throw you on that bed and take you, again and again and again, until you couldn't hide from me any longer!"

Isabel's eyes widened even further and he groaned. "Oh, hell, now I've frightened you again."

"No," she said faintly. "I thought... You left me alone...after the alehouse... You didn't speak, you didn't even *look* at me."

"Don't you know why?" he demanded, his hands tightening on her arms. "Mother of God, I'd just struck you. 'Twas to stop you becoming completely distraught, but I was afraid to look at you, afraid to come to you that night in case I saw fear or revulsion in your eyes."

"Afraid?" she squeaked. "*You*?"

"You think I'm immune to fear?" FitzAlan gave another short laugh. "Believe me, I could have written a book on the subject when Joanna's messenger found us."

Isabel shook her head in wonderment, then, quite unexpectedly, a tentative, almost teasing little smile flickered across her face. "You hide your feelings rather well, also, my lord."

Guy went completely still. "I've never seen you smile," he said huskily. "Until now."

His hands slid down to hers and an expression of such intense emotion burned in his eyes that Isabel glanced away, suddenly shy and uncertain. She felt him lace their fingers together and trembled with a strange mixture of excitement and trepidation. He must feel something for her. He must, to look at her like that.

"You didn't hurt me that day," she said softly, her voice breathless with the pounding of her heart. "It sounded bad, but—"

"*Sounded* bad? My God, I've heard that slap in my head ever since. Do you know what it did to me to strike you like that? To see you go so pale and still? Do you know what it did to me to see that animal on top of you, about to…?" He broke off, closing his eyes as though in pain.

"I thought you were angry because I'd run away."

There was a loaded silence. When fitzAlan opened his eyes again they were a brilliant, glittering blue. His hands gripped hers almost painfully. "I was," he said on a raggedly indrawn breath. "Angry with you, aching for you—" his voice dropped and went wholly intense "—in love with you."

Isabel felt as though one of the mangonels had just rolled over her. She couldn't seem to catch her breath. If Guy hadn't been holding her, she was sure she would have dropped to the floor. She had dared to hope he felt more than desire, but that he loved her… She was afraid to believe in so much happiness all at once.

"You hated me," she whispered. "When we met again at Gloucester you hated me."

"*No!*" He pulled her closer. "I was angry, but I've never hated you, Isabel. And even the anger was mainly at myself because I couldn't stop wanting you, even after Matilda warned me of your…usefulness."

Isabel glanced away, flushing. "She lied."

His voice gentled. "I know." When she didn't move, he freed her hands to capture her face, tilting it gently up to his. "Darling, I swear I started questioning her story

as early as the next day. There were so many things that
didn't add up. I began to see the nervousness in your eyes
whenever I got too close to you, and when I kissed you
at the inn I knew that Matilda had lied about one point at
least. Then, just as I was convinced of your innocence, I
discovered you'd lied about your brother and I caught you
with Rainald. Everything just seemed to go red. I was
nearly crazy with pain and rage. I kept throwing those
accusations at you, hoping desperately that you'd deny
them, explain them somehow…''

He dragged in another uneven breath, his eyes moving
from her brow to her mouth as though engraving every
detail on his mind. '''Twas as though I'd lost something
beyond price. That day in the garden…you were so innocent, so gentle, so untouched by war and betrayal. I
couldn't have you, but I carried the memory of that day
into every battle, into every stupid, meaningless coun-
cil, to every siege. It gave me something to fight for,
the knowledge that there was still one uncorrupted heart
somewhere, one thing pure and unchanged. You were
with me everywhere.'' He looked into her eyes, his own
anguished. ''Can you understand that, Isabel? Losing that
memory felt like losing part of myself, but I never hated
you. I couldn't hate you. I love you!''

She was starting to believe him. She had to, Isabel
thought. No man could speak with such passionate urgency, look at her with such naked yearning, and not
mean what he was saying.

'''Tis all right, sweet,'' he said quickly when she didn't
answer him. ''I won't rush you. I know you need time,
but I had to tell you. I can't bear you to be frightened of
me.''

''I'm not,'' she whispered brokenly. ''Oh, Guy, how

could I be frightened of you? I love you. I've always loved you."

"Oh, God, Isabel..." With the swiftness of movement that always surprised her, Guy swept her into an embrace that almost crushed her. "I love you," he vowed fiercely, as though she might still doubt him. "I love you! You're my life, my heart."

For a few moments he was content to hold her, then the solar spun before Isabel's vision as she was lifted into fitzAlan's arms.

"What are you—?"

"Hush," he commanded. "We've talked enough. You need to sleep, and if I hold you any more..."

A small smile curving her mouth, Isabel nestled trustingly against him as Guy carried her to the bed. Throwing back its bearskin cover, he lowered her carefully to the mattress and stood looking down at her. She lay perfectly still, knowing that when the light, filmy shift settled over her body it revealed more than it hid. When his eyes returned to her face they were almost black with desire. A spasm of nervous excitement tightened her insides.

"I'm not very sleepy," she whispered.

"Sweetheart..." Guy sat down on the end of the bed. There were lines of tension about his mouth, but his hand was gentle as he cradled her lacerated foot. "You've been hurt," he said gruffly. "Abused and frightened and hurt. You need gentleness tonight, not a man on the knife-edge of control."

"I'm not afraid."

FitzAlan's eyes flashed to her face, then very carefully he bent and pressed his lips to the cut across her instep. It was the most tender of caresses and yet Isabel felt a tingling sensation shoot straight up her leg to the most secret part of her.

The tiny sound she made brought Guy's head up. A muscle clenched in his jaw. "Aren't you? I frightened you once before, that first night in the hut, and I want you a hell of a lot more now."

"Ohhh." A fiery tide of colour rushed to Isabel's cheeks. She put her hands over her face. "You knew…all this time… You remembered…"

"No," he said, a soft laugh escaping him at her obvious embarrassment. "I wish I had; 'twould have given me some hope that you might come to care for me."

When Isabel peeped at him through her fingers, Guy laughed again. "I only remembered tonight when I came in and saw you drying your hair," he assured her, his blue eyes gleaming with tender amusement.

Isabel lowered her hands and held them out to him in an invitation that was as ancient as womanhood. "I wasn't afraid of *you*," she murmured, her face still flushed but glowing with love. "Only that you would hate me."

His eyes shut for one second, then he moved, coming down on the bed beside her. "No, never," he breathed, taking Isabel into his arms. "Never, my darling girl."

Isabel went into Guy's embrace without an instant's hesitation or fear or memory of the past. Here there was no brutality, no force. There was only fitzAlan, leaning over her, his eyes brilliant with love and desire, his strong arms drawing her closer. And his mouth. That beautiful, hard mouth descending on hers in a kiss that held passion and tenderness, excitement and safety.

Her shift vanished in one swift movement, but in her husband's arms she felt no embarrassment. Even when Guy left her for the few seconds it took him to remove his own clothes, his murmured words of love and praise still warmed and reassured her.

Isabel lay looking up at him, her lips softly parted and

moist from his kisses, eyes heavy-lidded with love and longing. He came back to her in a barely controlled rush, gently parting her legs, his mouth and hands caressing her body in a way that made her move sinuously against him, and which wrenched a low moan of need from his throat.

The heat and strength of him that had alarmed her that first night now enthralled her. She couldn't touch him enough in return. Her fingers widened, sliding over the bunched muscles of his shoulders, down through the golden hair feathering his chest, across the ridged hardness of his stomach. But when she would have moved lower in her innocent foray Guy captured her hands with one of his and pinned them gently above her head.

"Not this time, sweet," he said raggedly, moving over her, slowly letting her feel some of his weight and the first seeking touch of his body. "Relax, darling," he whispered against her mouth. "I'll be so gentle with you…so careful…"

Isabel gasped and clung to him. She felt her body stretching, a slight resistance, but there was no pain. And then she gazed up at him, her hands gripping his shoulders and absorbed the incredible feeling of having him inside her.

FitzAlan's eyes blazed down into hers. "At last," he growled, his face taut with control, his breathing harsh. "Mine…at last!" He slid one arm beneath her hips to lift her against him. "Hold me, sweetheart. Hold me *tight*!"

Isabel was already clinging to him. A strange insistent pressure was beginning to build within her. She wanted… wanted… Then, just as the pressure became almost unbearable, Guy's mouth came down on hers and he began to move.

When Isabel at last returned to an awareness of her surroundings it was to feel the gentle touch of Guy's mouth, moving over her throat in a series of feather-light kisses. Her arms were clasped loosely around his back and she lay completed relaxed beneath him. The kisses moved to her face and she opened her eyes.

Guy was gazing down at her, an expression of such tenderness in his face that Isabel felt her heart shake.

"Did I hurt you, little one?"

"Never." Her grey eyes were luminous with emotion. The closeness she felt was more than the joining of their bodies; it was all-encompassing, and shared, for in taking her he had also given himself. "I didn't know," she whispered, touching his face wonderingly. "'Twas like nothing...'twas so...oh, Guy..."

"I know, sweetheart." He moved to the side, kissing away her soft protest and holding her close to the warmth of his body. "'Twas like nothing I've ever felt before either. I love you, Isabel."

"Even though I'm no longer that innocent child?" she asked suddenly, not quite teasingly.

Guy's arms tightened about her. "I don't want that child," he assured her. "She was a dream I held dear, but 'tis the woman you are now that I love—sweet and true and courageous." He held her close for a moment, then drew back so he could see her face. "And 'twas not for the hand of a child that I wrote to your father a year later."

"Four years ago? You wanted to marry me four years ago?"

Guy smiled briefly at her astonishment. "Aye. Stephen had just granted me the barony, and I decided 'twas time I had a wife. I know now that my letter fell into de Raimes' hands. I was in Normandy with the army, otherwise I would have gone to Tracy to claim you. It must have amused that bastard greatly to write back saying you were betrothed. And I never questioned it.'' His mouth tightened with remembered pain and anger. ''Twas stamped with your father's seal, and I just accepted it—and then flung myself into battle after battle, trying to forget you, never knowing why you continued to haunt me, until I thought you had betrayed me.''

''So that's what de Raimes meant about putting you off years ago,'' Isabel exclaimed. ''Oh, Guy, if you only knew how I longed for you, how I dreamed that one day you would rescue me.''

''And instead I let you be captured and pitchforked into the same nightmare again.''

The bitter statement made her cry out in protest. ''Even if I'd told you everything, you wouldn't have known 'twas de Raimes' men at the ford. They recognised you, and described me well enough for him to start making enquiries. *I* didn't suspect anything until it was too late. And besides,'' she added softly, lifting a hand to stroke the tension from his face, '''twas not the same as before. This time I knew you would come.''

''If I'd had to storm hell itself,'' he confirmed huskily, turning his head to kiss her palm.

Isabel made a small sound of contentment and snuggled her head into his shoulder. She had never felt so loved, she decided sleepily, so cherished, so secure. Guy had given her so much... Her eyes snapped open.

''Oh, my psalter!'' she exclaimed, coming up on one elbow.

FitzAlan quirked an eyebrow in lazy enquiry. ''What?''

''My psalter. 'Tis in the casket you brought me. I have to show you...'' She glanced over her shoulder, spying the box on the floor near the fireplace.

''Wouldn't you rather wait until tomorrow? You must

be exhausted.'' He started playing with the dark hair spilling over his chest.

''Are you?''

Guy smiled up at her, a smile that held male triumph, utter possessiveness and love. Before Isabel had taken another breath she found herself on her back, gazing up at him bemusedly. ''I could go out and conquer an entire army,'' he told her, bending to kiss her on the mouth.

''Just bringing my psalter will do for now,'' Isabel murmured when she could speak again, revelling in the teasing intimacy of lovers that was still so new to her.

The smile turned indulgent. ''Well, if that is all your ladyship desires…''

Swinging himself off the bed, Guy strode across the room. Firelight danced over the powerful musculature of his body as he bent to retrieve the box. He grinned when he turned back towards the bed and saw Isabel watching him with a mixture of shyness and feminine appreciation that brought a blush to her face. ''You'll get used to it, sweetheart.''

Isabel sat up and concentrated on the small casket he placed beside her. She was trying to open it with one hand, while the other held the bearskin to her breasts, when Guy reached down and retrieved her shift. Very gently he drew the bed covering away. His eyes caressed her, then he lowered the shift over Isabel's head, tucking her arms into the full sleeves.

''You'll get used to me looking at you, too, my beautiful little wife,'' he murmured, kissing the warm cheek nearest him.

Her eyes smiled shy appreciation of his understanding as she opened the box. She lifted out the illuminated psalter within and handed it to him.

Guy gave her a questioning, half-quizzical glance, but

accepted the book, its leaves parting easily at his touch. Isabel, watching closely, saw him go very still as he saw what lay between the pages.

The fragile, preserved petals of a peach-coloured rose glowed softly in the sconce light.

"I should have taken you with me years ago and damn the consequences." His deep voice held an intensity of feeling that Isabel had never imagined even in her most private dreams.

She placed her hand lightly over the rose, her eyes meeting his with an answering depth of emotion. "I'm with you now," she murmured. "I'll be with you forever."

FitzAlan covered her hand with his. "Forever," he echoed.

It was a vow Isabel knew would be kept for the rest of their lives.

* * * * *

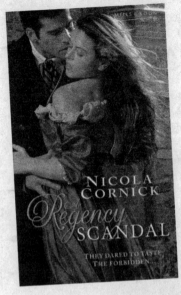